"Exceptional culinary detail and page-singeing sexual chemistry combine with a fascinating group of characters to produce a sophisticated modern romance that ties into the current foodie craze. This debut—first in a projected 'Recipe for Love' series—will win over most contemporary romance fans." —*Library Journal*

"In her wickedly entertaining debut, Edwards dishes up a captivating contemporary romance expertly seasoned with plenty of sizzling sexual chemistry and deliciously tart humor." —*Booklist*

"The simmering chemistry comes to a boil in this deliciously sensual and delightfully amusing debut." —*Orlando Sentinel*

"This playful culinary confection is a lighthearted and entertaining romance that will delight readers. With all the behind-the-scenes revelations, you'll never look at cooking and meal preparation in the same way again. Steamy and satisfying fare, indeed." —*Fresh Fiction*

"I LOVED *Can't Stand the Heat*. Louisa Edwards has written a great debut novel, and I look forward to reading more of the Recipe fo... the seco..." —*Beautiful Reads*

"A deliciously f... aracters are well writte... ssion." ...ws Today

"Snappy, exciting, adventurous, ... expected. *Can't Stand the Heat* . . . is one of the best light-hearted culi-

PAPERBACK

On the
Steamy Side

LOUISA EDWARDS

St. Martin's Paperbacks

This is a work of fiction. All of the characters, organizations and events portrayed in this novel are either products of the author's imagination or are used fictitiously.

ON THE STEAMY SIDE

For information address St. Martin's Press, 175 Fifth Avenue, New York, NY 10010.

EAN: 978-0-312-35646-0

Printed in the United States of America

St. Martin's Paperbacks edition / March 2010

St. Martin's Paperbacks are published by St. Martin's Press, 175 Fifth Avenue, New York, NY 10010.

10 9 8 7 6 5 4 3 2 1

For my parents, Jan and George,
who gave me my adventurous palate and always
encouraged my vivid imagination and passion
for the written word.

ACKNOWLEDGMENTS

Thanks to my stellar agent, Deidre Knight, and the smart, savvy ladies of the Knight Agency, whose advice and support are indispensable. To my incomparable editor, Rose Hilliard, for her championship through the launch of this series. Also to Jeanne Devlin, my tireless and energetic publicist, for her incredible work and help. These women all routinely go so far above and beyond the call of duty that it's hard to imagine what my career would look like without them. I suspect it would be pretty bleak. So thanks!!

The first draft of this book would never have been finished without the cheerleading (and butt-kicking, when I needed it) from a very special group of women: the Queens of Peen. You know who you are, and you know I appreciated every second of it. Extra thanks go to my duo of muses, Kristen Painter and Roxanne St. Claire—you make every day of sitting alone in front of my computer feel like a party! I adore you guys.

My family gets special mention for this book because many of the dishes mentioned come straight from my childhood. My mother even helped perfect the already-perfect recipe for Delmonico Pudding, which appears in the back of the book! Other recipe-testing thanks go to the lovely Megan

Blocker, home cook par excellence and food blogger extraordinaire.

And, as always, the biggest thank you of all to my husband, Nick, who never flags, never wavers, and never complains when I serve him frozen pizza for the fifth night in a row while I'm on deadline. Beta reader, sounding board, best friend, and love of my life all wrapped up in one tall, delicious package. I'm truly the luckiest woman in the world!

It's wonderful to have so much support and help as I write—if this book is any good at all, it's thanks to all of you. Any mistakes are mine alone.

PROLOGUE

Trenton, NJ

May 1995

Black caps launched into the air, gold tassels flying, and everyone around him broke into ecstatic cheers.

High school was over, life and its myriad possibilities stretched out in front of them like a wide, open highway—and all Devon felt was dread.

Time up. No more excuses. He had to tell his dad today.

Pushing past his jubilant classmates, Devon kept to his tried-and-true method of avoiding unwanted attention. He kept his head up and looked neither right nor left, and moved with unwavering purpose, as if on a mission of life-or-death importance.

He ignored the occasional glances he caught from the corners of his vision, as well as the familiar catcalls and kissy noises.

After a dozen years in the Trenton public school system with these knuckle-headed losers, Devon was immune to moronic comments about his looks. Nicknames like "Pretty Boy" and "Baby Face" had long ago lost all power to faze him. He never flinched, never blushed, never showed weakness.

But was that enough for his old man?

Devon spotted his family clustered stiffly under one of the gymnasium's raised basketball hoops. Angela Sparks smiled when she saw Devon, and raised one hand to wave at him. She looked older than the other moms, even though she wasn't. Still, underneath the worry lines and graying hair was the source of Devon's overblown, inconvenient looks.

Devon's younger brother, Connor, shot him two thumbs up, then made the code signal for "Mom and Dad are driving me nuts, so I'm sneaking off." Devon jerked his head once in agreement. He didn't need any more of an audience for this, anyway.

Connor grinned and said something to their dad, who grunted and waved him away. Phil Sparks was never anything but gruff, although Devon easily read the quiet pride and satisfaction in the man's eyes as he followed Connor's exuberant jog across the gym floor to join his buddies.

That look, accompanied by a complacent "boys will be boys" shrug, was never aimed in Devon's direction. Never had been, never would be. It was one of the main ways Devon knew there was something about him that was just . . . wrong.

As a rising junior, Connor would be the starting quarterback next year. He played football in the fall and baseball in the spring, and excelled at both. At sixteen, he was already as tall as Devon, and the accident of genetics that cursed Devon with perfectly symmetrical features, vivid blue eyes, and the much-loathed long lashes had bypassed Connor entirely. Not that he was ugly or anything, just normal. Average.

In short, Connor was everything Devon wasn't. For instance, Connor was a nice person; too annoyingly nice for even Devon to despise.

Devon, on the other hand, was the opposite of nice.

He was also the opposite of average. Who the fuck *wanted* to be mediocre? Most of his graduating class did, as far as Devon could tell. They wanted nothing more than to go to Rutgers, get a boring desk job, get married, and die.

Devon already knew. That kind of life wasn't going to be enough for him.

"Hi, guys," Devon said, projecting his best nonchalant, devil-may-care attitude. "You caught the show, huh?"

Angela's eyes brightened, the deep, electric blue of them sparkling with rare happiness. "Wouldn't have missed it for the world," she said and clasped him close in a quick, hard hug.

Phil frowned. Big surprise there. "For God's sake, Devon. You couldn't comb your hair before you went up on stage? You look like somebody dragged you through a bush backwards."

Yeah, Devon wanted to say. *But if I'd slicked my hair down you'd have complained I looked like a brown-nosing nerd, so what's the point?*

He managed to hold his tongue, though, because he had bigger issues than his hair to tackle, and he wanted to get it over and done with in the middle of this crowd where there was a slight chance his dad would be too embarrassed to go all out and explode.

"We are so proud of you," his mother jumped in, ever the peacemaker, and Devon smiled at her. He was grateful for the lie, or at least for the affection that prompted it.

"Thanks, Mom."

Phil snorted like a startled racehorse. "Speak for yourself. For me, I can't see being proud of a kid too lazy to take advantage of the work and sacrifices his parents made so he could go to a good school and get into a good college."

And there it was. The opening Devon had been waiting for and dreading in equal measures ever since he got his letter from the Academy.

"I know there wasn't anything listed in the program," Devon said, swallowing down the nerves that wanted to make his voice shake and fade. "But I actually do have some plans for next year."

"What? You get a football scholarship when I wasn't looking? Oh, wait. That's right. You wouldn't even try out for the team."

Unwilling to be sidetracked into the old, old argument, Devon persevered.

"I did get a scholarship, but not for football." He set his

jaw and lifted his chin until he gave the illusion of staring down his nose at his father, even though Phil Sparks was a good three inches taller.

It was an effective expression. Devon knew because he practiced it in the mirror. Phil's glower deepened.

Deep breath in. "Dad. Mom. I got accepted to the Academy of Culinary Arts with a full scholarship."

And then he braced himself for impact.

"Oh, honey," Angela said, darting a glance at Phil. Whose face suddenly appeared to be carved from stone.

"My son," he said thickly, pushing the words past his clenched teeth. "Going to school to learn how to cook."

"Now, Phil," Angela said, hands fluttering. But Devon didn't want her getting in the middle. For once, for once and fucking all, he wanted to have it out with his father.

He got right into Phil's face, tension shooting down his back and vibrating his bones. "Yeah, Dad. I want to be a chef. What about it?"

"It would be a fine career if you were my daughter. But come on, Devon, what am I supposed to tell people? That my son is going to school to learn how to bake pies with a bunch of fairies? Why don't you just get a job styling ladies' hair at the beauty parlor, then you can really make your old man a laughingstock."

"Right. Because that's what matters, Dad—what the neighbors think, or the guys down at the union hall. I'm sure you'd like it better if I stuck around the neighborhood and started working for you, snaking toilets and grouting showers. Real appealing."

Phil's face went red. "It was good enough to put food on the table and clothes on your ungrateful back."

Direct hit. Score one for Devon.

Part of him wanted to take it back, knew he was crossing the line, but he couldn't. If he faltered for even a second, he was done for.

Brazening it out the only way he knew how, Devon said, "I want more than that, Dad. I want to be somebody."

"Sure," Phil scoffed. "And you're gonna get famous slinging hash in some diner? Or better yet, gonna make somebody a nice little wife someday. Shit. You got no clue how to be a man."

A hideous combination of rage and tears surged into Devon's throat and threatened to choke him. He wanted to scream at his dad, tell him how hard he'd fought to be admitted to the Academy, the most prestigious culinary school in the country. Tell him what an honor it was and how many graduates of the Academy went on to open their own restaurants to critical acclaim and enormous success.

But it wouldn't make any difference. Cooking wasn't ever going to impress Phil Sparks. The fact that his son loved it, and was actually gifted at it, was nothing more than an embarrassment.

With a superhuman effort, Devon stomped down on the emotion and locked it away, deep inside. All he allowed onto his face was a twisted half-smile.

Rocking back on his heels, he said, "What I know is that ten years from now, I'm going to look back on this conversation from the Jacuzzi in my Park Avenue apartment and laugh my ass off. I'll be rich and famous and successful, and I will have done it all on my own."

Phil ground his teeth, the sound audible even over the chatter and squeaking shoes of four hundred recent graduates and their families.

"Damn straight you'll do it all on your own. I'm not supporting this foolishness. You want to throw your life away in some kitchen, throw away all the hard work your mother and I have done to give you better options than that, go right ahead. But don't expect any help from me."

Devon laughed, shocking himself with the bitterness of it. "I gave up expecting anything from you a long time ago, Dad."

And then he kissed his mom on the cheek, waved to his brother, and walked out of the school without a backward glance.

He was finally on his own for real.

Devon told himself it was nothing new, he'd been alone in every way that mattered for years—but it felt different, somehow.

Well. He'd get used to it.

CHAPTER ONE

Lower East Side, Manhattan

September 2010

"I've got fantastic news! Prepare to congratulate yourself, yet again, on having the intelligence, and the money, to hire me."

Devon Sparks squinted through the dark miasma of illegal cigarette smoke and the humid press of sweaty, raucous bar patrons to see his publicist, Simon Woolf, wrinkle his nose and give the stool beside Devon's a swipe with a cocktail napkin before perching on it.

"You look uncomfortable, Si," Devon drawled, amused. "You disapprove of my taste in dive bars?"

Devon caught Simon's derisive sneer as he looked around Chapel and the dingy, smoke-filled underground room they were in. Propping his elbows on the scarred oak bar, Devon cocked his head and watched his personal publicity shark move his ever-present PDA fussily out of the way of a few crumbs scattered around the bowls of bar mix, popcorn, and wasabi peas.

Simon ought to see the place when the real after-hours crowd came out—kitchen crews coming off service, off-duty cops, and ER docs mixed with punk musicians and the avant-garde theater crowd.

Holding himself rigid to keep from brushing elbows with any of his fellow bar patrons, many of them pierced and tattooed and leathered up, Simon didn't appear to appreciate the democratic nature of the scene.

"I don't see why we couldn't have met at your place." Simon's aggrieved tone had Devon rolling his eyes and holding up a hand to the bartender. Christian was an old friend; ex-employee, actually. He'd know what to fix Simon.

"Order something," Devon told him. "You look like you could use it. And you know exactly why we're meeting here." Devon had just finished a grueling season of the show, culminating in a week-long shoot at a chain fondue restaurant where no fewer than seven idiot servers had spilled molten cheese or chocolate on him. "I'm fucking exhausted, and I wanted a drink."

A silky note of malicious amusement threaded through Devon's tone as he continued, "And you agreed because it's your job to do whatever the hell I say."

After the week he'd had, it was a balm to Devon's soul to be back in the position of dealing with underlings who could be relied upon to twist themselves into pretzels to avoid pissing him off.

The premise of Devon's show was that he went into unfamiliar professional kitchens for a single night and cooked any type of food, for any size restaurant, with tools and a staff he'd never worked with before. The tag line of the show was *Anything you can do, I can do better.*

The producers had sent him all over the place, from banquet halls serving shrimp cocktail to hundreds of guests, to tiny, hole-in-the-wall corner joints. It was the Cooking Channel's top-rated program, watched by millions across the country. It was big enough to have spawned a series of spoof sketches on *Saturday Night Live.*

The fact that Devon was sick to death of it was his dirty little secret.

"No, it's my job to keep you in the superstar stratosphere to which you've become accustomed," Simon corrected, peering suspiciously at the martini glass Christian set before him. "What is this?" he asked, taking a tiny sip. Which turned into a longer guzzle. "Hey, it's actually not bad."

"Not bad," Devon snorted. "Hey, Chris, you hear that?"

The bartender cut his dark gaze to Devon, straight, hippie-length brown hair swinging against his shoulders.

"I sure did, and boy, do I ever thank him for the kind words," Christian drawled, tipping an imaginary cowboy hat to Simon. Devon wasn't sure his publicist caught the sardonic edge Chris gave to the gesture.

Simon took another sip, brows drawn in concentration. "It's clear like a martini, but it has a more complicated flavor, something I can't place."

Devon sat back on his barstool. This ought to be good.

"White peppercorn-infused vodka, junipero gin, dry vermouth, ouzo, and a dash of white crème de menthe. I call it a Fuck Off & Die." Christian smiled, wide and insincere, before moving off down the bar to take another order.

Simon gaped after him for a moment, then shrugged and took another drink. Devon sniggered into his glass of straight Kentucky bourbon—yeah, it was that kind of night—and Simon gave him a cross look. "What? It tastes better than it sounds."

"It would have to," Devon said. "Come on, spill. What's so important you braved the perils of the Lower East Side to come and meet me? I know you're not here for Adam's going-away party."

If there were anyone Devon considered a friend, it was his former executive chef, Adam Temple. The other reason Devon had chosen Chapel for his post-shoot decompression was that Adam and his one true love were about to leave the country for an extended vacation. Tonight was Adam's big sendoff. There was an outside chance it would be amusing.

Simon shook his head. "Right, my news. Are you ready?"

Devon raised a sardonic brow. "This better be the fabulous news you think it is, Si."

In the past, they hadn't always been in complete agreement on what constituted a wonderful career move for Devon. But then, Simon's single-minded intensity of purpose was his biggest recommendation as a PR guy, so Devon supposed he shouldn't complain.

Looking a little apprehensive—and why wouldn't he?
Devon had more than earned his reputation for intolerance
of incompetence both in and out of the kitchen—Simon
cleared his throat. "Well. We should've asked that rude bartender if he stocks champagne behind the bar. Although,
really, what are the odds? We'll have to celebrate without the
champers. You'll love this! Here, take a look." With a flourish, he produced a copy of *Restaurant USA*, a magazine that
reported on news and trends in the food industry.

Devon took it and flipped idly through the first few pages.
"What? Looks like the standard stats and stories to me.
Fewer Families Dining Out. Spain is the New France. What
do I care about that?"

Simon grabbed the magazine back and turned to a dog-
eared page Devon hadn't noticed.

"There," he said, pointing a triumphant finger at the head-
line.

Devon squinted at the page and felt his blood congeal to
the consistency and temperature of gelato.

*Cooking Channel Superstar Named #1 Chain Restaurant
Operator.*

"No."

Was that weak bleat Devon's voice?

"You bet," Simon beamed. "The Sparks brand beat out
every fast-food chain in the country. They graded on profit-
ability and name recognition, and you won!"

"Oh, God, there's art with it," Devon moaned, snatching
the magazine out of Simon's hand. There beside the article
was one of Devon's publicity stills. Devon stared at his intense blue eyes, his artfully tousled dark brown hair, the seductive expression on the face that had landed him at #23 on
that big list of Top Fifty Hottest Men.

Then his gaze drifted to the right and fell on the mania-
cally grinning white-painted face of the beloved red-haired,
yellow-jumpsuit-clad icon.

"You don't look happy, Dev."

Was that a hint of nerves Devon detected in his publicist's voice?

It sure as shit better be.

"Not happy? I'm sharing the limelight with a fucking clown. I beat out the king, the colonel, and the little girl with the red braids. Wait till everyone I know sees this. They're going to laugh their asses off! Simon. Christ. You're supposed to be the best publicist in the city—that's why I hired you. How could you let this happen?"

"This is a good thing," Simon, ever the Spin Master, protested. He snatched the magazine back and snapped it shut, as if by covering up the evidence he'd dissipate the head of steam Devon was building up. "When people visit New York, or Miami, or Vegas, they want to eat at a Devon Sparks restaurant! You're the go-to guy. This survey proves your effectiveness as a brand."

"What if I don't want to be a goddamn brand?" Devon shouted, uncaring of the heads that turned or the voices that began whispering.

Shouting felt good. He hadn't let loose in a while. "I'm a serious chef, or at least I used to be. A real chef would be humiliated by this so-called honor. My restaurants serve haute cuisine, for Christ's sake, not burgers and chicken nuggets! I'm going to be a laughingstock."

"Now, Dev," Simon said in the soothing tones reserved for lunatics and hysterical children. "You're making too much of this. It's not like this story is going to get picked up by the news media or anything. *Restaurant USA* is a trade pub; no one even reads it. Do you read it? I never read it."

Devon gritted his teeth against the urge to reach across the bar for a bottle to bean Simon with.

Just then the bar door opened, distracting Devon from his homicidal thoughts and admitting a swirl of laughing, shouting people. Giving them a quick glance, Devon stiffened. He knew them. Christ, he'd employed half of them at one point or another. The New York culinary world was not unlike major league baseball—there was a finite number of talented players, and the biggest managers traded them back and forth.

"Hey, Sparks," one of them called out. "Congratulations

on the chain, man. Should we start calling you Ronald?" And the crowd erupted in laughter.

"You know who reads trade publications, Simon? People *in the fucking trade*. That's who. My peers. My friends. My goddamn employees." Devon gestured at the crowd and lowered his voice. "This so-called 'honor' will be proof to them that I've sold out, lost myself, ransomed my soul to the capitalist gods."

That I'm not a real chef, and never will be again.

The worst part? Devon was starting to think they might be right.

"Whoa, enough with the drama," Simon protested, nerves pitching his voice high and grating. "That *Restaurant USA* piece isn't worth all this, Dev, come on."

Devon stared at his PR manager. "Shit. You pitched the magazine, didn't you? The whole thing was your idea."

As soon as he said it, Devon knew he was right. It was exactly Simon's style, aggressive and bold, heedless of the cost.

"Who, me?" Something in Devon's face must have registered how much he wasn't buying what Simon was selling, because the guy held up his hands in surrender. "Okay, okay! Maybe I did pitch them the chain thing. I thought it would be cool, show how successful you are! Success breeds success, Dev, you know that. I definitely never thought you'd get this bent out of shape about it."

"You *never* think," Devon said, his throat so full of hot anger he could hardly force the words out. "You just push and push, and you don't fucking think about what kind of shit you're pushing me into. Because I'm the one that has to swim in it, not you. Well, no more. I'm done eating what you shovel, Simon. You're fired."

Horror flashed in Simon's eyes, and the denials and cajoling started at once, but Devon had zero trouble tuning them out. All he felt was a bone-deep sense of relief.

It wouldn't fix everything, but it was a start.

"You can't do that," Simon protested, aghast.

Devon bared his teeth in a parody of a smile. "Haven't you heard the hype? I can do anything."

"I wrote that hype!" Now Simon was shouting, too, his purple cheeks clashing with the deep brown of his Zegna suit and the artful highlights in his dirty-blond hair.

"What are you going to do," Devon asked, grinning, "sue me for copyright infringement? Give it up, Si, it's over."

"We'll see about that," Simon said, clambering down from the barstool. "I've worked hard for you, Dev, you know I have. And now that things are finally coming together, now that you're finally living the life you said you wanted, you're going to throw it all away? And for what? No, I refuse to accept it. I'm leaving now. I'm going to give you some time to think about this before one of us says something he'll regret."

"Don't hold your breath expecting me to change my mind."

Spittle flew from Simon's mouth. "I'm Simon Woolf. I don't sit around hoping for things to happen, I *make* them happen. I made you!"

Simon threw his arms wide, forgetting about the cocktail still sitting on the bar. The drama of his exit was heightened considerably by the shattering martini glass and spray of Fuck Off & Die all over the woman standing behind him.

The woman, unsurprisingly, squawked in unhappy surprise as several ounces of chilled liquor cascaded over the back of her head.

"What on God's green earth?" the woman sputtered, the words thick and smoky with the cadence of the South. Her brown ringlets dripped with Simon's cocktail.

Devon got a brief glimpse of bright green eyes and round, pink cheeks before she turned on Simon, hands on curvy hips, sneaker-clad toe tapping.

"Do you mind?" Simon snarled. "We were in the middle of a private discussion."

Even viewing her face in partial profile, Devon was impressed by the expression of affronted shock that came over it. *Holy shit,* Devon thought, *Simon better run.*

A fizzy feeling of intoxication better than anything he'd

ever found at the bottom of a bottle was still coursing through Devon's veins. He was riding high on life, grooving on the idea of having his life *back*, not being indentured to the producers and DPs and makeup artists, and oh, yes, *publicists* required by the show, for three months of glorious hiatus while the producers set the next season. He was nearly perfectly happy right now to sit back and watch the bonus surprise floor show.

"I most certainly do mind," the woman informed Simon with icy civility. "Maybe you didn't notice, sir, but you just doused me with your drink."

Vibrating with anger, Simon looked around and pointed to a stack of cocktail napkins halfway down the bar. "There. You're closer to them than I am. Now, Dev, as I was saying . . ."

The woman interrupted Simon once more by tapping him on the shoulder.

"Excuse me," she said to Devon. "I hate to interrupt, but I need to speak with your friend here."

Simon glared at him in an angry appeal for help, but Devon spread his hands wide and said, "How can I deny such a polite request?"

The woman turned those glowing green eyes on Devon for the first time. One white, long-fingered hand swept the dark brown curls off her forehead and revealed a fresh-scrubbed, pink-cheeked face. The face wasn't so much beautiful as it was interesting. Her chin was too pointed, her dark brows a touch too heavy for her face, and her skin was too pale, making her brilliant green eyes appear almost startling. This woman spent zero time at the spa getting buffed, plucked, and tanned. She looked nothing like the perfect, sophisticated women he usually dated, models and socialites and actresses. But there was something compelling about her, some mysterious allure in her sweet, wide-eyed gaze that kept Devon's attention.

Even when he knew, instinctively and immediately, that she was way too nice for him.

"Thank you," she said in that husky voice that somehow

carried over all the combined chatter and hubbub of the crowded bar. "You've restored my faith in Yankee mothers— I was starting to think none of you boys up here had any home training whatsoever."

Too nice, maybe, Devon amended silently, *but she's no fragile flower.*

An opinion confirmed when she poked one stiff finger into Simon's chest and faced him down like a scrappy terrier. "You, however, ought to be ashamed. What would your momma think if she saw you treating a woman this way? Hmm? Throwing a tantrum like a little baby and soaking my shirt, which is probably ruined now, and all you can do is point out some napkins? Which is about as useful as a pogo stick in quicksand."

Simon smoothed back his sandy hair, tightened his tie, and tried for a charming smile. He fished out one of his embossed ecru business cards.

"Please feel free to send the dry cleaning bill to my secretary."

"No, thank you, that won't be necessary," she said with a disdainful sniff.

"Then what *do* you want?"

The woman gave Simon a look that bordered on pitying. "Merciful heavens, you really don't know, do you? An apology."

Devon leaned one elbow on the bar, getting a certain amount of perverse pleasure out of watching the slippery bastard wriggle.

Finally, through white lips and gritted teeth, Simon gathered enough of his customary sangfroid to choke out an unconvincing, "I'm terribly sorry for the inconvenience. I'd just received a shock," here Devon got another glower, "and wasn't as careful as I might have been.

"Apology accepted," the woman said graciously.

Simon managed a smile, then rescued his PDA from the bar, dusting it off compulsively. Waggling it at Devon, Simon said, "I'll call you tomorrow."

He vanished into the throng standing three-deep by the

bar before Devon could assure him he wouldn't be changing his mind.

"Your friend could use a refresher course in manners."

Devon looked back at the brunette. The shirt she'd been so incensed about was fit only for a consignment shop, as far as Devon could tell—brown and purple stripes in some dull fabric that looked scratchy. But when she plucked at the back of it, screwing her face up in distress at the cold cling of wet cloth, the front molded to high, generous breasts and a gently curved waist.

She glanced up and caught him looking, and the spark that struck when their eyes met was hot enough to ignite the alcohol she was drenched in.

Not at all his usual type, Devon thought. Then again, he'd just told the guy who'd made him famous to go take a flying leap.

Clearly, today was a day for embracing the unusual.

CHAPTER TWO

All of Lilah's sass and bravado dried up under the scorching heat of this man's eyes.

She swallowed, the clicking sound of her throat loud in her ears, and tried to remember what she'd been saying.

A trickle of moisture down her spine brought her back to herself.

Right. Rude friend, itsy-bitsy altercation where timid, spineless Lolly let new, improved Lilah out to play, and the whole while, this one lounging back on his barstool, watching with a lazy smirk and the most intense ice-blue eyes she'd ever seen.

Now Mr. Rude was gone, and evidently he took Lilah's gumption with him, because she was blinking at the vision of masculine perfection before her like he was the first bunny ever to hop into her briar patch.

And was he ever a hot one. Like, movie-star hot, with the sardonic charm and sexy smile to match. Artfully tousled brown hair, knife-blade cheekbones, and a pair of eyes the same color blue as a blazing summer sky. And those eyes were trained on her like a bird dog with a duck in its sights.

Lilah wasn't too used to being the focus of anyone's attention. For most of her life, she'd tended to fade into the background, especially around extra-beautiful people like this man.

Even her decidedly unglamorous and average-in-every-way ex-boyfriend took years to notice Lilah existed. Humiliating, considering they'd both taught at the same high school.

The man before her lifted his drink and gestured at the clammy shirt sticking to her skin. "That looks uncomfortable."

Why are you still talking to me?

"Yeah," Lilah said, fanning the fabric and trying to encourage air movement. "I don't know about dry cleaning, but it could sure use a run through the wash. Me, too, I guess! I don't know what the heck was in that drink, but I'm all sticky."

Those intense blue eyes flashed darker, and he arched a brow. "What you need is a long, hot shower."

Breathing fast and not really sure why, Lilah took momentary refuge in glancing around the bar for Grant. Her longtime best friend and brand-new roomie had abandoned her upon arrival at Chapel. His best bud, and boss at the restaurant, was about to leave for two weeks, so they were having some kind of good-bye boys' pow-wow. Lilah hadn't really felt comfortable crashing it.

"I don't know where my friend has got to," she said. "Or I'd head on home and hop straight in the bath."

"You don't want to go home alone?" His voice was like rough silk.

Lilah shivered, then laughed at herself. "I just moved here; I wouldn't bet two nickels on my ability to navigate my way back to the apartment on my own."

He smirked a little. Lilah had never much cared for smirking, but this guy had it down pat.

"In fact, I had divined that you are not from these parts," he said. "You don't hear a lot of pretty Southern drawls like yours up here in the heart of Yankee territory."

Lilah hoped it was too dim inside the bar for him to see

her blush. "Well. When they were handing out the charm, you must've gotten all yours plus your friend's portion, too."

He smiled at her, sparkly even white teeth bright against his tanned skin.

Lilah grinned back. She felt a little like Rosalind Russell trading barbs with Cary Grant. Was this bantering? She'd always wanted to banter! It was every bit as stimulating as she'd imagined.

He seemed to like it, too, because he was unfolding himself from his barstool and sauntering over to her, every move imbued with lithe grace. He came close enough to whisper in her ear. His breath was warm where it fanned through the curls at her temple.

"If you're ready to get out of here, you want to come home with me? I'll let you use my shower. I promise it'll be good and hot."

Holy cats, was this really happening?

Five days ago, Lilah had been stuck in a boring town with her boring ex, teaching Shakespeare to a bunch of bored teenagers.

Now?

Lilah blinked hard to clear her eyes. Yep, still standing in a dingy, underground Lower East Side dive with the handsomest man she'd ever seen live and in person cooing unmistakably indecent—and undeniably enticing—proposals in her ear.

Moving to Manhattan might have been the smartest thing she ever did.

The woman blinked at him, a visible tremor rushing through her.

Devon knew he was coming on strong, probably stronger than a woman like this, who clearly bathed in eau d'innocence every morning, was used to. But he couldn't quite bring himself to back off—she was too enticing. Her open, unguarded face was like a shaft of pure sunlight burning through the dim underground bar.

Though clearly taken aback, she wasn't speechless for more than a second, which only made Devon want her more.

"Well, shoot, sugar. I guess it's true what they say about New Yorkers."

"What's that?"

"That all y'all are in a boot-scootin' hurry every minute of every day."

Devon shrugged and finished his drink, enjoying the blaze of bourbon in the back of his throat. "I don't see the point of wasting time. We're both adults. I want you. You want me. Why shouldn't we have what we want?"

She drew in a sharp breath, her gaze heating. "Lots of reasons," she said. Then, with a self-deprecating laugh, "None of which I can seem to recall right at this very second."

Devon grinned. "So what are we waiting for?"

Not wanting to give her time to remember the many logical and reasonable arguments against going home with a total stranger, Devon grabbed her by the hand and started for the door. Paolo would be waiting on the street with the Bentley, no doubt relieved that Devon was calling it a night this early.

"Wait!" She dug in her heels and pulled against Devon, laughing. He really liked the sound of it, he decided, kind of husky and low, but full of happiness.

"No, you said it, babe—I'm a New Yorker, and time is money to me. I've got places to be, showers to run . . . women to kiss."

"But I don't even know your name or anything about you," she protested, and Devon felt the world screech to a halt.

She didn't recognize him. She wasn't just playing it cool, doing a good job of pretending to treat him like a regular guy—she actually thought he was one.

Devon got hard so fast, the southward rush of blood actually made him dizzy.

Weird.

Devon couldn't remember the last time he had any interaction that didn't somehow involve or reference his celebrity status. His chef friends ribbed him mercilessly for selling out and becoming successful, all the while wishing they could find some sucker to sell *their* shtick to. Women mostly tended to fawn and gush, all with an eye toward getting into his Ferrari, bed, and wallet. Not necessarily in that order.

"I don't know your name, either," he hedged, wanting badly to prolong the moment. "Does it matter?"

"What's in a name?" she said, as if to herself. Her gaze dropped slightly; Devon wanted to kiss the adorable furrow between her brows.

"Is that really all that's stopping you?" Devon wanted to know.

"Well. Not your name, as such, but the fact that we've only just met . . ."

Devon studied her, the way consternation drew those straight, too-heavy brows together. The way she nibbled at her lower lip, making him wonder what it would be like to suck that plump, pink morsel into his own mouth.

She was clearly nervous, out of her depth, and Devon found himself strangely moved.

Nope, not his usual type, not by any stretch.

Knowing his dick was going to hate him for it, Devon sighed and said, "Look. If you want, we can have another drink and hang out for a while, maybe wait for your friend to show up. I don't want you to be uncomfortable."

When she met his eyes again, Devon saw a flame of desire hot enough to match his own, plus a new, steely determination.

"Uncomfortable," she said. "Lord. I've been doing the comfortable thing my whole life, it seems like. And what did it get me? I think it's about time I did something a little uncomfortable."

He needed to buy a minute or two to calm down or risk shocking a bar full of people. Giving his intrepid companion his best seductive smile, he said, "How about a kiss to seal the deal, then?"

Oh, now there was a brilliant plan. Sharing a kiss with the most compelling woman he'd met in weeks—months— maybe years? That was a surefire way to calm things down.

Then she slid one tentative hand around the nape of his neck, stood on tiptoe, and laid her rosebud mouth gingerly against Devon's—and he knew it was absolutely the best plan he could possibly have come up with.

CHAPTER THREE

In the instant before her lips touched his, Lilah was equal parts terrified and intensely proud of herself.

Terrified, because what in the name of heaven was she thinking of to be fooling around with this man who, whoever he was, was obviously good-looking enough to get any woman in this bar, much less a transplanted ex-high school teacher from Appalachia.

And proud of herself, because she was, to all outward appearances, confidently ignoring the ludicrous gulf between their relative levels of suavity and sophistication and going for what she wanted.

Right then and there, Lilah came up with a new mantra: *What would "Lolly" do? Okay, now do the opposite!*

So far, following the mantra was a huge success. How huge a success she didn't even comprehend until the moment their lips met and Lilah was forced to redefine everything she thought she knew about kissing.

The gentle brush of his mouth on hers sent electricity arcing down her spine, shivering out to her fingers and toes, heating and coiling things low in her body. The deepest, most-involved soul kiss she'd ever shared with Preston, back home, couldn't compare to this—and the man hadn't even slipped her any tongue!

Lilah's mouth buzzed and tingled and she thought dazedly that the fact that this guy could send shivers racing up and down her spine with a peck on the mouth in the middle of a crowded nightclub spoke volumes about . . . something.

She gave up trying to puzzle it out and surrendered to the moment.

The man gave her one last nuzzle and lifted his head. Lilah blinked hard to clear the clouds from her vision.

"Wow," she said, then immediately wanted to kick herself.

"I know exactly what you mean. So what do you think? Want to embrace discomfort and see where the night takes us?"

Lilah studied him as well as she could in the muddy light.

Maybe she was naïve—okay, no maybe about it, she was definitely naïve—but she knew in her heart that this guy was no ax murderer. And the way he'd pulled back and offered her a graceful out made her feel, perversely, a hundred times more willing to follow him home like a lost puppy.

And then there was that kiss. Not only the way it curled her toes, but the delicacy of it, as if he'd read her hesitancy over getting down and dirty in such a public place and had responded with the sweetest kiss imaginable.

He was almost certainly a Romeo type, but what man who looked like him wouldn't be? And in the end, it didn't matter. This wasn't about finding the love of her life, Lilah reminded herself. It was about stretching and risking, stepping out of the shell she'd imprisoned herself in for so long and finding a new way to be in the world.

Taking her courage in both hands, Lilah nodded.

The smile that spread over his handsome face was filled with dark, seductive triumph.

Oh, Lordy. What had she gotten herself into? Lilah shivered, but even she couldn't have said whether it was trepidation or straight-up anticipation.

"Wait," she cried, suddenly realizing how empty her hands were. "I left my pocketbook on the bar!"

"Want me to get it for you?" he offered, but Lilah shook her head.

"No! No, it's fine. I'll just run quick and grab it. You stay put."

Without pausing to see if he followed her instructions, Lilah whirled and pushed back into the crowd surrounding the bar, her cheeks stinging with heat.

Second thoughts immediately filled her mind. He could be anyone, do anything . . .

Oh, my stars and stripes, what am I doing?

She finally managed to thrust her way to the scarred wooden bar, but her purse was nowhere to be seen. Before her heart could plummet through the floor, however, the bartender, a smallish man with straight brown hair to his shoulders and a smile in his eyes, leaned over the bar.

He held one hand out, the strap of Lilah's pocketbook dangling from one finger.

"You found it," she said. "Thank you so much."

"Not a problem," he drawled, but when she moved to take her bag, he lifted it out of reach.

"If I give this back to you," he said, eyes intent on her face, "are you gonna leave with that fella over there?"

Lilah bit her lip, then forced herself to stop. She wasn't Lolly anymore, she didn't have to be so embarrassed and worried about what people thought all the time.

"I'm thinking about it," she told him. "Why, do you know some reason why I shouldn't?"

The bartender cocked his head. "No," he said after a moment. "I don't believe I do. We go back a ways, me and him. He's a good guy, deep down, even if he doesn't always act like it. I was actually thinking about warning *you* to be nice to *him*. He's had a rough couple of months; he could stand something nice for a change."

Lilah paused, struck by the sincerity in the man's face.

"Don't worry," she said. "I'm not a psycho or something. Your friend is safe."

"Then you kids have a fine old time," he replied, lowering his arm so she could snag her purse.

"Hey, um . . . do you know Grant Holloway? The guy I came in with?"

"We're acquainted."

"Could you let him know I left? And that I'm okay?"

The bartender nodded, and Lilah gave him a little wave of thanks.

Slipping back into the press of people, Lilah couldn't help craning her neck to see if her mystery man still stood waiting for her by the door.

And if her heart fluttered with joy when she saw that he was, if she couldn't restrain her answering grin when he smiled down at her . . . well. Even without the bartender vouching for him, the sense of rightness that settled over her shoulders like a warm quilt would've been enough to propel her out of the bar at this man's side.

The air outside Chapel was crisp and refreshing after the stale bar full of moving bodies. Lilah followed her . . . shoot, what should she call him? Lover? Ugh, that didn't sound right . . . to a sleek black car.

A short, compactly muscled man moved from his position leaning against the hood to open the back passenger door.

"This is Paolo, my driver."

Was this normal? Did everyone in New York have a driver?

Resolving not to gawk and stare at every little thing like a tourist, Lilah gave the impassive, black-clad Paolo a regal nod and climbed into the spacious backseat. The leather was smooth and warm against her skin. She was immediately concerned about the nasty stain her damp shirt was probably leaving.

Lilah twisted on the seat in an effort to spare the leather and look graceful at the same time, which was met with an odd look from her handsome new friend when he slid in beside her.

Conversation was stilted as the car pulled out into traffic. Lilah wasn't sure what the protocol was for making small talk with one's soon-to-be sexual partners.

Somehow, she didn't think Emily Post had an entry covering that little dilemma.

He asked where she was staying—an apartment in Chelsea—and she asked where he lived—on Park Avenue.

That shut Lilah up for a second; even with her spotty under-standing of Manhattan geography, she knew that was a pretty swanky neighborhood.

Every snippet of information only added to his mysteri-ous allure and the surreal feel of the entire situation.

When the car pulled smoothly up to a gorgeous white-marble corner building, with windows two stories tall and a gold-trimmed awning out front, Lilah wasn't even surprised.

Sure, she thought. *Where else would Prince Charming live?*

This modern-day castle was staffed with quietly polite doormen and a concierge—there was even a guy who offered to run the elevator for them, but her companion declined. They stepped into the large, sumptuous box and the doors whispered shut.

Lilah blinked at her reflection in the antique brass of the doors. It was polished to such a high gloss, she could see the whites of her own wide eyes.

She glanced at the man beside her, and he seemed to take that as an invitation. He stepped in closer and trailed his fingertips down the bare skin of her arm below her puffed shirtsleeve, leaving a trail of goose bumps in his wake.

A bell-like chime made Lilah jump, and then the elevator door shooshed open to reveal a single white-paneled door, which her companion unlocked and opened.

He ushered Lilah into a spread straight out of *Architec-tural Digest*. It looked like some avant-garde director's inter-pretation of Hamlet's castle, all Danish modern and slick.

A low-slung black leather couch faced one of those out-sized flatscreen televisions all men seemed to want more than life. The coffee table in front of it was low, too, a glass and chrome contraption that appeared to be using some sort of gravity-defying magic to stay standing. Everything in the room was sleek, clean, spotless, and utterly unwelcoming.

She was kind of glad she didn't have to live here; she'd be afraid to sit on that flat-cushioned couch, and if she so much as looked at the white paper-globe lamp in the corner, she was certain it'd topple right on over.

Before Lilah could work herself into a tizzy over the

multitude of ways her natural klutziness could be a bad, bad thing, the apartment's owner saved her from thinking by touching her hand and turning her brain into pudding.

"Where were we?" he asked with a sly smile.

Not to be outdone, Lilah took a bold step forward and plastered herself to his front. "Right about here, I think."

His chest expanded against hers like he was drawing a deep breath and Lilah reveled in the sudden, heady sense of power.

The gorgeous man ran his hands up her arms and around to cup the wings of her shoulder blades. He made an "ick" face and stepped back at once—not exactly the reaction Lilah was hoping for. Then she remembered her unfortunate accident with his friend's drink.

Laughing, she said, "Hey, didn't you promise me a shower?"

When Devon bought the penthouse four years ago, he knew it was going to take a crapload of work to make it the showroom residence a rising star needed.

To create the master bathroom, he had to knock out a wall to expand the space into the large, gracious room they now entered. His curly-haired companion took one look at the gold-flecked green tiles forming an abstract mosaic that filled the back wall of his glassed-in shower and whistled through her teeth.

Devon smiled and jammed his hands in his front pockets to keep from pointing features out to her like an excited realtor.

But the rest of the bathroom wasn't too shabby, either, if he did say so himself. He watched her run a hand over the frosted glass of the counter holding the freestanding oval Waterworks sink.

The floor and walls were tiled in large squares of warm, naturally tumbled stone; the lighting was soft and yellow.

"Well, golly," she said. "If I had a bathroom like this, I'd never want to leave it."

Satisfaction filled Devon. He rocked on his heels. "It was the first thing I redid when I bought this place."

He'd had very definite ideas about what he wanted the master bath to look like; he was a plumber's kid, after all. And yeah, it may have occurred to him that coming up with the most decadent, luxurious bathroom possible could be interpreted as a "fuck you" to the old man.

"You designed this?" The woman's voice dragged Devon out of his musing. She gestured to the mosaic tiles in the shower stall. "It's beautiful."

For some reason, her frank admiration suddenly made Devon want to squirm. "It's nothing. Just a doodle I had in my head."

"I know a little bit about design," she told him, "and I'd say you have a knack for it. If I had to guess . . ." She tilted her head to one side and considered him. "Yes. I think you must be an artist. No! You own an art gallery—being in charge would suit you, I bet."

"Very astute," Devon laughed. "Being in charge suits me completely, balls to bones."

"Graphic," she said, wrinkling her nose. "And don't think I didn't notice; you didn't deny the gallery thing. I pegged you right! I know it."

Enjoying himself immensely, Devon sketched a courtly bow. "What can I say? Give the lady a cigar."

"I have a knack for sizing people up," she said. "When you've conducted as many auditions as I have, it's a necessary skill."

"You're in theater," Devon said.

"Used to be," she said. "Until very recently."

"You said you conducted the auditions. I take it you're not an actress, then."

"Gracious, no. I directed and taught."

"What kinds of plays?" Devon was mildly amazed at himself, making light conversation with this incredibly enticing woman in the intimate, sexually charged atmosphere of his personal bathroom. But he was actually kind of digging it. And it was more than the novelty of conversing with someone who wasn't after anything from him.

It was her.

"Shakespeare is the obvious one," she said. "But he's only obvious because he wears so well. Many of his plays are shockingly relevant to our modern world. I've also done Brecht, Ibsen, Chekhov . . . we mostly stuck to the classics."

"Reinterpretations of the classics can be transcendent," Devon replied, thinking of the signature dish on the menu at his flagship restaurant, Appetite. It was steak frites, the quintessential bistro dish, re-imagined as a layered torte of sliced, seared filet, parsley butter and seasonal vegetables fried in duck fat. It was one of the dishes mentioned in the *New York Times* review that got him his four stars; it was on the menu to stay.

Realizing he'd been standing there silently for a moment too long, Devon said, "Well, I'll let you get to it, then. I'm going to go find something clean for you to change into."

She hesitated as if she had something to say, but then smiled and thanked him again.

Devon left the bathroom quickly, before images of her stripping down and getting wet made it impossible.

CHAPTER FOUR

He waited as long as he could, but it had been a few years since Devon had been forced to wait for anything he truly wanted, and he was out of practice.

So when he tapped on the bathroom door and she called "Come in," Devon wasn't surprised to be sucked into a humid fog. The shower was still running, everything in the bathroom steamed up and misted over. He knew he was probably supposed to turn his head away or squeeze his eyes shut or something, but he'd never been very good at doing what he was supposed to do. He zeroed in on the glass shower door as if his eyes were high-beam xenon headlights that could penetrate steam.

No such luck.

"I've got a shirt here you can put on," Devon said. "When you're done."

"I'll never be done," she moaned. "Seriously. You're going to have to cook my meals and serve them to me in here, because I am never leaving this shower."

Devon laughed despite the frisson of nerves accompanying her blithe demand that he cook. "Can't blame you. That shower is one of my favorite places in the entire world. And I've been all over."

"I've never been anywhere but Spotswood County,

Virginia, and New York City," she said. "But I don't need to travel the world to know there's not much out there that could compare with this."

It was almost unbearable to stand in the moist heat of the bathroom knowing she was barely five feet away from him, completely bare and wet as a seal. The tension was terrible. Devon savored it for another minute, then said, "Okay, I'll be in the living room when you're done."

"Wait," she said when his hand was on the slippery doorknob. "I can think of one thing that would make this shower even better."

From the tremor in her voice, Devon thought he could guess what that one thing was, but he wanted her to say it. "What's that?"

He could almost hear her swallow. His pulse jumped.

"If you were in here with me."

The pleasurable tension Devon had been enjoying instantly morphed into a need so voracious it made his hands shake. Getting his clothes off took longer than he wanted, and then there was the delay of locating a couple of condoms in his medicine cabinet. It felt like an eternity, but it was mere seconds before he was opening the shower door and sliding in behind her. He tucked the condoms into one of the recessed openings in the tiled wall, easily accessible.

That done, Devon allowed his brain to short out under the pinprick sting of hot water on his shoulders and the melting heat of the skin of her back against his chest.

She squeaked when he touched her, as if, despite her invitation, she was startled to find herself sharing space with him.

He probably lost hero points for taking her up on her offer when she was clearly still nervous. So be it. Devon had never aspired to be anyone's hero.

And the next instant she was reaching back with both hands and grasping his hips to bring their bodies into even closer contact.

Devon bent his head to her warm, wet neck to hide his

gasp at the aching perfection of being pressed so tightly to her. He palmed her shoulders then crossed his arms over her breastbone, mouth exploring the delicate skin of her neck.

He hadn't gone completely soft since that kiss in the bar, and now he was as hard as he'd ever been in his life. When she made a purring noise—a goddamn purr!—and nestled back against him so that his cock rode the sweet dip at the small of her back, Devon was the one who trembled.

He didn't know it was possible to be that hard and not go off.

But apparently so, because she shimmied against him, wet skin and silky hair sliding deliciously, and Devon groaned. The weight of the water pulled at her curls, drawing them straight down until the inky strands reached to the small of her back.

He could feel his heartbeat in his cock, heavy and fast.

Blinking away the water droplets, Devon hung his head over her shoulder and watched his own hands smooth over the gentle slope of her chest to cup her full, round breasts. He loved her body, all womanly and welcoming, curvy and soft where he'd grown used to the angles and jutting bones of his fashionably thin dates.

And the way she arched against him when his thumbs skated over her nipples! The unconscious sensuality of her response melted Devon's mind.

He plucked her nipples to make her moan, fascinated by the way her every reaction registered throughout her entire body.

Sudden, desperate curiosity seized him. He caressed down her sides, making her shiver, and tested the fit of her hips to his palms. Perfect. His fingers wandered to her belly button, stroked the taut skin of her abdomen, then dipped lower to play in the nest of curls between her thighs.

Even in the warmth of the shower, with mist all around them, the heat of that secret spot sent excitement raging through Devon's bloodstream.

She shuddered in his arms, twisting, although if she was

trying to escape from his touch she was doing a piss-poor job of it. When Devon probed deeper and found her clit, her lips parted on a silent moan.

Devon sank two fingers into the hot, wet depths of her, thrilling with dark satisfaction when her hips jerked into his hand.

Her head fell back against his shoulder, eyes closed, mouth open. When he flexed his fingers, the ones buried inside her, she turned her face to his neck and the groan she gave vibrated against his skin.

Calling on all his skill—which ought to be considerable after the last few years; a hit TV show made a guy very popular with the ladies—Devon gently stretched his fingers apart, rubbing his knuckles against the nerve-rich skin of her opening. His thumb found her clit again, pressing and circling in a rhythm that faltered when he felt her mouth open against his neck.

The first hesitant touch of her tongue to the place where his neck joined his shoulder went to Devon's head like a shot of bourbon.

Skill be damned, one open-mouthed kiss from this chick and Devon was the one getting weak in the knees.

He had to have her. Now.

Pulling his fingers from her body elicited another heartfelt groan. Devon panted and clasped her hips, struggling not to clamp down tight enough to leave bruises.

"Last chance to back out," he rasped.

The sudden stillness of her body gave Devon a wicked pang of fear, but she loosened again almost at once. A deep breath expanded her ribs against his arms, then she leaned away from his chest and deliberately planted her palms on the tiled wall in front of them.

The move pushed her delectable ass so firmly into Devon's groin that lights went off behind his eyes. He almost missed the look she sent over her shoulder.

Hair black and sleek with water, cheeks flushed, eyes fever-bright with desire. She opened lips swollen from rubbing against him and said, "No regrets."

Devon almost came right then and there. Throttling himself down, he bent over her back and laid his mouth to the beautiful curve of her spine.

It was hard to pry his locked fingers from her hips even for so essential a task as reaching blindly behind them for a condom, but Devon managed it. He ripped the packet open with his teeth and rolled the latex down, cursing the seconds it took, precious seconds when he wasn't touching her.

But it was all worth it when she stretched her back and languidly parted her thighs, allowing him to catch a hint of her pink folds beneath the sweet cleft of her dimpled buttocks.

The shower beat down on his back and shoulders, a steady drum of water that numbed his skin and filled his ears with white noise. As Devon took himself in hand, gingerly so as not to over-stimulate, and guided himself to her core, he felt all the sensation in his body focus on that one spot, where his throbbing cock was notched against her.

With a muffled moan, Devon surged forward and into her. There was no resistance, only softness and slick heat opening before him and enclosing him in a tight fist of pleasure.

"Ah," she said, her voice high and gasping. "Ah, ah."

He thrust once, then again, and each movement of his hips against her brought another sweet, shocked exclamation from her throat.

Her legs trembled against his; her hands scrabbled at the wet tile. Devon could feel the thunder of her heartbeat where his mouth was pressed, open and panting, against her heaving back.

Feeling none too steady on his feet himself as pleasure coiled tighter in his belly, Devon was suddenly seized by the very real fear that their knees would falter at the exact same moment and they'd go crashing to the shower floor.

With a muttered curse, he pulled out, mourning the loss of her snug, velvety heat the instant he stepped back.

"Why'd you stop?" Her plaintive voice forced him to scoop her up for a kiss.

"I don't want to break my dick when we take a dive on these slippery tiles," he said when he could tear himself away from her mouth.

There was something undeniably amazing about the fact that she blushed at that, when they were standing naked in his shower, in the middle of some of the hottest sex of his life.

"Oh," she said, uncertainty hitching in her voice. "So you want to stop?"

Devon laughed. He couldn't help it.

"Oh, Christ," he wheezed. "You kill me."

"It's not that funny," she said tartly. "What am I supposed to think?"

"That's the problem," Devon said. "You're not supposed to be thinking at all. Let's get back to that, shall we? Here."

He swept an arm across the low bench jutting from the side wall of the shower, knocking Bumble and bumble shampoo and Aveda body wash to the floor.

She jumped at the clatter of plastic bottles, but her eyes got really big when Devon settled himself on the ledge, long legs stretched out, erection spearing up fiercely from its nest of dark hair.

Devon patted his thighs and gave her a cheerful leer, hoping to jump over the fit of nerves this little interruption had brought on.

"Want to come sit on my lap?" he asked, waggling his eyebrows. "I promise I'll give you a lollipop after."

"My Aunt Bertie taught me never to take candy from strange men," she said, putting her hands on her hips. God, what a picture she was, water coursing over her naked form, beading and dripping from the tight buds of her nipples and pooling in the shallow divot of her navel.

Devon licked his lips.

Her eyes followed the movement of his tongue. She mimicked him, maybe unconsciously, and her voice was strained when she said, "And boy, let me tell you, you are about as strange a man as any I've ever encountered."

Devon let his gaze heat with his desire for her. He moved one lazy hand to cup his balls, rolling them gently in their sheath of flesh. Pangs of arousal shot up his spine and he arched his back slightly, never taking his eyes off hers.

She licked her lips again and said, "But since I'm on a new campaign to do the opposite of what Aunt Bertie always told me . . ."

With that, she stepped into the open vee of his thighs, ran her fingers into his wet hair, and bent to take his mouth with hers.

It was heatstroke, Lilah thought to herself. She was delirious from the heat of the water. Or the thickness of the sodden air meant she couldn't get enough oxygen for a decent breath and her brain was slowly suffocating.

Something had to account for her trampy behavior. Lilah could hardly believe herself. First, okay, the decision to have a one-night stand. Definitely a little on the loose-woman side, but in her defense, the provocation was enormous.

He was, quite simply, the most beautiful man she'd ever seen. Far more appealing than his sheer masculine perfection, however, was the raw desire he didn't bother to hide whenever he looked at her. The way it made her feel to be wanted like that—well. Was it any wonder she was being so forward?

Inviting him into the shower, shamelessly bending over for him, displaying herself to his gaze. Even now, she knew she should be shocked at herself, but if she were honest, all she really felt were sharp prickles of heat racing up and down her limbs, prompting her to go even further.

Lilah stared down at temptation incarnate, sprawled on the shower ledge like a decadent Roman awaiting the start of an orgy.

And he was hers for the taking.

The glass doors of the shower were completely fogged, enclosing them in a private world of heat and moisture that felt very far away from normal, everyday life, making it easier to let go.

His thighs were hard and strong where they rubbed against the outsides of her legs, the coarse hair there sensitizing her skin. She kissed him again, shivering despite the heat and luxuriating in the slick press of his tongue. When she had to either breathe or pass out, Lilah lifted her head and let her hands slide from his hair, petting the wet locks that clung to her fingers.

Lilah wanted to climb him, like honeysuckle up the side of a wall. The ledge he sat on wasn't wide enough for her knees, though, and as she surveyed the situation, she wondered what he could possibly intend her to do.

Sit in my lap, he'd said, and with a flash of heat that made her lightheaded, Lilah thought she dimly saw what he meant.

Oh, Lord love a duck, this was going to end badly. She'd slip for sure, or her not-inconsiderable weight would be too much for him, or, or . . .

Lilah set her jaw and deliberately blanked out her over-stimulated brain's nervous babble.

Buck up, girl.

Without giving herself a chance to chicken out, she straightened and turned her back on him, lowering herself to his lap and taking in his hard, hot erection all in one swift move.

Too swift almost, as the width of him opened her up and surged deep. Her gasp was drowned out by his shout, though, and his hands flew to steady her hips as Lilah wobbled and would've tumped right over at the overwhelming sensation of being impaled.

"Oh, like that, yes," he moaned, his mouth hot and sharp against the nape of her neck, and Lilah shivered and relaxed around him.

Not sure where to rest her hands, she let them fall to the tops of his hairy thighs on either side of her. He didn't seem to have any such trouble; his hands roamed freely up her quivering sides and around her heaving ribcage, weighing her breasts and testing the resilience of her sensitive nipples with gentle tweaks. Lilah couldn't make her hips be still. Her inner muscles clenched and released, and when he pinched her nipples again, the tide of pleasure snatched her up and wrung her out, climax breaking over her like a wave.

When her body went limp, he petted his way down her arms, lifting the useless noodles to link behind his neck. Lilah drowsed, content as a cat, and let him arrange her like a doll.

His . . . *cock*—she forced herself to think the word, getting a little thrill of naughtiness from it—was still as hard as ever, an iron rod deep inside her that teased and tormented with short, pulsing thrusts that wouldn't let her arousal die.

He smoothed his hands down her body again, almost like he was sculpting her, until his hard palms wrapped around her trembling flanks.

"Ready?" he asked.

Before Lilah could summon the brainpower to ask what she was supposed to be ready for, he lifted and spread her thighs wide, settling them again on either side of his legs. Her toes left the floor and all her weight pressed into his lap, sending his cock harder and higher into her body. Lilah gasped, her nerve endings sparking and firing, desire mounting again.

In this position, every minute shift of his hips made her sob out a breath, the sensation so intense she was hardly aware of it as pleasure. His hands returned to her breasts, warm and smooth and sure, and the counterpoint made Lilah feel utterly taken and surrounded by him.

Every feeling his long, deft fingers, wicked mouth, and steadily pumping hips gave her swirled together into a maelstrom of light and color. Lilah lost track of time. She lost track of herself. She knew nothing but the way he played her body.

When she came the second time, it was slower, more excruciating, pulses and tremors that felt endless and overpowering. His hoarse cries echoed off the shower walls, his hands went rigid and still—and then they both hung there, gasping in the cooling fall of water.

CHAPTER FIVE

When Devon walked into Market, he didn't necessarily expect to be greeted with a red carpet and a phalanx of trumpeting heralds.

Sure, he'd become used to a certain level of fawning admiration over the years of his meteoric rise to fame and fortune as the darling of the gourmet food world and the Cooking Channel's biggest star. That, plus his undeniably perfect face, was usually enough to get him the best seats/floor tickets/ ungettable reservation. Special attention to his needs and desires was a fact of life.

Well, most of his life. There were still a few places left in Manhattan he could go to remind himself of what the real world felt like. A certain dive bar on the Lower East Side, for example. And here—at Market, the all-organic hit restaurant owned and run by his former executive chef, Adam Temple.

Adam was a friend. Or as close to a friend as Devon got these days. And he'd never admit it, but part of why he valued Adam was for exactly that lack of interest in *Devon Sparks: Star!* When Adam talked to his former boss, Devon felt like . . . *Devon Sparks: Talented Chef and Ordinary Guy.* Considering he hadn't been either of those things in a long time, and had worked hard to reach that state of affairs, talking to Adam was usually sort of restful.

Damned if Devon couldn't use the rest after yesterday's hellacious shoot.

The last shoot before a three-month hiatus, he thought to himself with satisfaction. He didn't know how he would've coped with the five seasons of the show if the shooting schedule hadn't included these breaks. This one felt long overdue.

The original plan had been to enjoy himself during his time off; charter a jet to St. Maarten, go out for tapas in San Sebastian, do a London pub crawl, or visit friends in Paris. The world should be his fresh, harvested-that-morning-off-the-coast-of-Prince-Edward-Island oyster, with a bonus surprise pearl inside.

Instead, here he was at Market, inwardly marveling at his own heretofore-unsuspected mushy marshmallow center.

Devon frowned, mentally prodding the sore spot.

He couldn't quite believe it, but he was actually sweating the fact that after last night's amazing, no-holds-barred, extremely satisfying sex, his anonymous hookup flew the coop under cover of darkness, leaving Devon to wake up in an empty bed, in an empty apartment.

Not that this was a new state of affairs, he reminded himself. He didn't particularly enjoy sleeping with women when there was actual sleep involved. Not that he threw them out when he was done with them; even he wasn't quite that big a shit. But if they hopped out of bed the moment the afterglow dimmed and started tossing their Dolce & Gabbana dresses back on, Devon didn't exactly scramble to stop them.

And nine times out of ten, that was the end of it. He didn't do reruns, and he had an assistant whose whole job was essentially to block calls from Devon's legion of one-time bedmates.

He didn't even know the woman's name. When both parties were unwilling to divulge the most basic personal information, that was a pretty good sign it wasn't a relationship that was going somewhere.

Which was, of course, exactly what Devon had in mind when he seduced her into coming home with him.

So why was he still thinking about curly dark hair and laughing green eyes?

Shaking his head to rid it of useless, unproductive thoughts, Devon concentrated on the reason he was here at Market at ass o'clock in the morning.

Adam Temple, whose fucking career Devon had fucking well launched by hiring him on at Appetite all those years ago, had called in a favor. And what did Devon do? Come running like a little lapdog.

Adam wanted a real vacation—the kind a chef with a hit Manhattan restaurant almost never got. A quick jaunt down to Atlantic City? Maybe. Enough time to go someplace anyone with half a brain would actually want to visit? No way.

Except Adam, being Adam, had found a way. Instead of leaving his precious baby in merely capable hands while he jaunted off to Europe to spend time with the woman of his dreams, Adam had hit on a sweet jackpot of an idea. He'd convinced Devon to step in as executive chef.

For two whole weeks.

Devon remembered how his chest had tightened up when Adam first asked him; how disappointed he'd been. Of course Adam wanted something from him. Eventually, everyone wanted something. The notion that any of his so-called friends weren't simply biding their time for the perfect opportunity to suck Devon dry was laughable. It was always a bad idea to forget.

Devon glared around the empty dining room. So no one had bothered to roll out the red carpet for his first day at Market. Fine. But was it too much to ask that there at least be a peon or two polishing glassware and setting tables? Granted, Devon hated waiters of every size and stripe, but they had their occasional uses. For instance, greeting a visiting chef during off hours and telling him where the hell everybody was.

Instead of the busy, bustling front of house Devon had expected, however, he got an abandoned dining room, tumbleweeds all but blowing between the tables.

Between the emptiness of his apartment this morning and now this, it was like he was cursed. If Paolo hadn't turned up right on time to drive Devon across town, he would've started to wonder if something apocalyptic had happened, leaving him the last man alive in the city.

He put his hands on his hips and waited, impatience, annoyance, and an ugly stew of anxiety about the coming dinner service turning an already black mood into a real thunderstorm.

It was such a different experience, standing in an empty restaurant without the distraction of customers. After designing and opening five fine dining establishments in the last ten years, Devon was a veteran of the décor wars. He could pick out fabrics and choose between leather seat coverings with the best of them. He scanned the still, dim Market dining room with its soft moss-green walls and hammered bronze light fixtures with their swirls of vines and leaves with a critical eye. The tables were blond wood, bright and glossy with clean, minimalist lines. Devon liked the banquettes, too, straight-backed and private, in some sort of velvety material that looked very inviting. He strode toward the horseshoe-shaped antique zinc bar that connected the smaller back dining room to the larger front room.

This was ridiculous. He didn't have time to stand around here all day.

Hoping to find a sous chef barking orders, a pastry chef kneading dough, a freaking dishwasher, for shit's sake, Devon pushed through the swinging doors that led into the kitchen.

There were signs of life back there; Devon heard the familiar, comforting clang of a stainless-steel pan hitting a cast-iron cooking range, followed by a breathy rasp of sound, almost like a moan.

Devon quirked a brow. The restaurant wasn't as abandoned as it seemed. He paused, suddenly struck by the very real possibility that he was about to come upon Adam in a state of nature with the woman Devon had played Cupid to set him up with.

Well, sort of. Invading his friend's kitchen with an uninvited camera crew and filming the very private confessions of Adam's lady love, Miranda Wake, might not go down in history as the all-time most romantic matchmaking scheme. In fact, Adam had been beyond ticked about it, as Devon recalled. Still, Devon stood by the results. Adam and Miranda were disgustingly happy together; every time Devon saw them, he expected to hear the faint twittering of cartoon lovebirds swirling overhead.

Really, when he thought about it, maybe Adam owed *Devon* a favor, not the other way around.

Another clatter from the kitchen. Familiar with the aphrodisiacal effects of an empty restaurant on a newly-in-lust couple, Devon cracked open the kitchen door with a measure of caution. He could stand to go his whole life without viewing Adam's unmentionables doing the naked mambo with Miranda's.

Not that he'd be opposed to seeing Miranda's unmentionables—he was willing to bet she stripped down pretty well for an obnoxious, snarky, red-headed firecracker.

But the sight that greeted Devon sent images of Miranda's potential hotness flying out of his head.

A woman stood on the gleaming work counter running down the center of the kitchen, balanced precariously on the tips of her white canvas sneakers to reach the top shelf of stacked pots and pans. She was taller than Miranda, he registered instantly, and sported a halo of untamed dark curls obscuring her profile from view. His heartbeat quickened.

A breathy moan he'd heard before echoed through the room. Unbelievable.

He had a mere five seconds to admire the delectable roundness of the backside presented very conveniently near eye level before the woman's ankle wobbled dangerously, causing a lightning-fast chain reaction of shriek, flail, slip, and hey, presto! Devon's arms were full of warm, wriggling womanhood.

CHAPTER SIX

"Well, hello," Devon said, his mood brightening like day breaking over the Brooklyn Bridge.

The woman stopped squirming and peeked out from behind her mass of sable curls. Her silvery green eyes went wide and round as saucers, and Devon savored the startled "meep" that squeaked from her strawberry mouth.

Oh, yes, today was looking up.

He wanted that mouth, so he took it in a deep kiss that exploded over his tongue with her already familiar honey-thyme flavor.

And when her tongue slipped into his mouth to explore and curl against his, Devon had to stiffen his suddenly shaky arms to keep from dumping her on her ass.

The tickle of her tongue tracing his lips combined with the memory of that pretty, heart-shaped ass brought Devon to aching hardness. The swift rush of arousal shocked him to his core. What was he, a teenager? He'd already had her once; he shouldn't be this stirred up.

He couldn't remember the last time he'd been so hungry after a simple kiss.

Except it didn't feel all that simple, and when it ended, the woman pulling away slowly and with many lingering nips and bites to his sensitive mouth, Devon had to swallow down his own moan of disappointment.

"That was a heck of a hello," she said, the molasses-slow words drawled out low and husky, making him think of tobacco and bourbon.

"It could've been good morning," he told her, "if you'd stuck around long enough."

Shit, why did he say that? Made it sound like her running out had hurt his feelings or something.

"I had to get to work," she protested, a pretty blush mantling her cheeks. "Besides, I wasn't, you know, too sure of the morning-after etiquette. And my Aunt Bertie always says, if you don't know the right thing to do, err on the side of politeness."

Devon blinked. "How is it polite to leave without saying good-bye to your host?"

"Ah!" She lifted a finger in triumph. "Exactly! Because I'm the anti-Aunt Bertie now, I did the opposite of what she would've done. Not that she would ever have been in that situation in the first place."

Devon felt his mouth pull into a reluctant smile. "You don't think I could seduce your Aunt Bertie?"

"Doubtful. She's a Baptist—the kind who's referred to regularly as a 'pillar of the church'—and also, my Uncle Roy is a peach. She'd never stray. Plus, you're not her type. Too sexy and charming for your own good."

"Poor Uncle Roy," Devon murmured. His mind was finally starting to process some of the barrage of information her nervous babble produced.

"Oh, Uncle Roy's all right," she said, flush still high on her cheekbones. "A real good ol' boy, but a heart of solid gold, I swear. That's Aunt Bertie's type; the kind of guy I always thought I'd end up with. Only that didn't work out, so here I am, and here you are, the polar opposite of anything I ever thought I'd want!"

"Christ." Devon stared down at her, working hard for his customary cool. "You sure know how to make a guy feel good about himself. Where the hell did you come from, anyway?"

Her eyes narrowed at his tone. "From where gentlemen don't swear in front of ladies they've just met," she countered with a toss of that messy head. Her chest was still rising and falling too quickly, a sign that he was not the only one affected by the world's hottest kiss of greeting.

"Oh, but ladies do go home with gentlemen they've just met?" Devon asked silkily. "Get naked? Take showers together? Spend all night making each other crazy?"

"All right, all right! I give," she said, laughing. "I'm afraid you're right; I can no longer lay claim to the title of 'lady.' But you, sir, are no gentleman for pointing it out." She gave him a stern look, but her eyes were dancing, inviting him to share the joke.

"So what does Aunt Bertie think about you moving to New York City?"

"You mean Gomorrah? Babylon? Sin City? She wasn't any too thrilled, I'll admit. But a girl's gotta do what a girl's gotta do."

"Tell the truth." Devon curled her higher in his arms, close enough to whisper against her soft, fragrant cheek. "After last night, you're afraid she might be right. You're worried Sin City might already be corrupting you."

She smiled, a slow, sweet curl of her lips. "Sugar, I'm counting on it."

Devon stared into her eyes and counted his heartbeats in the throb of blood through his groin.

"I'd say you're well on your way," he told her in a voice that sounded like he'd been gargling rocks.

"Hey, not that I don't appreciate the White Knight routine, but do you think you might be willing to let a girl stand on her own two feet?"

"I don't know," Devon said. "You didn't seem to be doing such a good job of that up on the counter."

She shrugged cheerfully, not a hint of blush or embarrassment darkening her cheeks. "I'm better on good ol' terra firma. Well, not tons better, I'm still pretty much the Queen of the Klutzes, but at least there's not as far to fall and therefore less chance of a broken ankle." She twisted in his arms, eyeing the distance from her perch to the ground. "Speaking of broken ankles . . . Be careful when you put me down. I just got this job; I can't afford to be limping around the restaurant."

"Adam hired you?" Crap. Devon had a strict policy against fraternizing with restaurant employees.

"Yup," she said. Then added, "Sort of. It's complicated."

She was starting to squirm again, which felt outrageously good, so Devon put her down before he got distracted and dropped her, thereby fulfilling her broken-ankle fear.

"Seems like a yes or no situation to me," Devon probed.

She wobbled slightly when her feet hit the gleaming hardwood, but she righted herself quickly and ran a careless hand over her shirt. It was another unflattering rag, pink with embroidered blue flowers on the collar, and it hung on her, as if she'd bought the wrong size. The cut of her baggy brown pants did very little to showcase the assets he'd admired last night. If he'd seen her across a crowded gallery opening or at an opera gala, he might not have given her a second glance. And he would've been missing out.

She turned back to the counter for a moment, swiping her palm across the shiny metal surface as if checking for incriminating evidence. Devon eyed the way the curve of her waist flowed into her hips.

Maybe he would have given her that second glance, regardless.

"You'd think so, wouldn't you? Unfortunately, my life doesn't really seem to work like that. I exist in a constant state of *maybe*, *almost*, and *who knows*. Hey, what are you doing here, anyway? Are you a customer? It's pretty crazy you'd choose this place to come and eat, after last night and all. What are the chances? Only we're closed. I think. You'd have to ask someone who's been working here longer than five minutes, and they're all downstairs, having a meeting about something top secret."

Apparently satisfied with the state of the countertop, she turned back and looked at Devon expectantly.

"No, I'm not a customer."

"Oh." She got that adorable frown line between her brows. "Are you . . . did you come here for me?"

Devon wasn't sure how to answer. He didn't want to hurt her feelings with the truth—that he'd had no idea she was working at Market and if he had, he probably wouldn't have slept with her in the first place. Nor did he want to lie and say he'd searched high and low for her, or had Paolo track her down, or something equally stalkeriffic that might raise false hopes.

He stood there, trying to come up with a response, and for the first time, Devon noticed the distinctive slightly acrid scent of hot oil—was she frying something? Ugh. He wrinkled his nose and tried not to cough.

"Oh, shoot!" she said, grabbing a large spoon from the counter and whirling to check a large pot of something bubbling away on the stove.

There was a smudge of flour along one high, pretty cheekbone. She didn't move like any line cook Devon had ever worked with. There was no economy of motion to her, no swift moves at all. She was all elbows and leaning, taking her sweet time, as casual about whatever she was cooking as Devon was about choosing a tie.

It was disconcerting; nothing about cooking had ever been casual for Devon.

"What the hell are you doing with all that oil?"

She looked down as if surprised to see her hand circling the slotted spoon through the frothing, spitting oil. "Cooking lunch," she replied with a touch of uncertainty. "What's it look like?"

"It looks like you're performing some sort of science experiment," Devon told her bluntly. "What are you frying? It smells . . . odd."

"I found some chicken livers way at the back of that fridge over there; didn't look like anyone was gonna use 'em for any fancy dish anytime soon, so I appropriated them."

"Good God," Devon said, revolted, as she began lifting golden brown nuggets of fried liver from the oil and setting them on folded paper towels to drain. "You're not actually planning to serve that to anyone."

"Hey, now," she bristled. "This is my Aunt Bertie's recipe. It won first prize at the county fair four years running."

"I don't care if it won an Emmy, it looks sickening and it smells worse."

Devon had nothing against organ meats, in general; they'd been en vogue among New York chefs for years now. But these humble balls of artery-clogging noxiousness were a far cry from sautéed sweetbreads with butter and sage, or seared foie gras with quince jelly. There was something so . . . peasant about chicken liver. It seemed trashy, in the sense of being destined for the garbage bin. Or possibly a dog biscuit.

"Don't yuck my yum," the woman said, narrowing her eyes at him. "It's rude. Anyway, you don't have to eat it. Grant asked me to fix up a quick lunch while he talked to his boss, so that's what I'm doing. It wasn't easy to find anything to make in that larder, either, let me tell you."

"I find that supremely difficult to believe." Market had one of the most varied, interesting menus in the city—Adam stocked his pantry and walk-in with the freshest, most beautiful produce the local farmers' markets had to offer, and now that it was high summer, the markets were offering quite a bit. All simple stuff that any monkey could cook.

Devon hesitated. "Grant," he said. "That wouldn't be Grant Holloway, would it?"

"That's right." Pique had pinched her rosebud mouth tight. "I'm staying with him."

Holy fucking shit. Devon had spent the hottest night in recent memory with Grant Holloway's . . . what, girlfriend? Why else would she be staying with him?

Okay, they could be just friends . . . but as Devon looked at the woman standing beside him, the inherent, unconscious sensuality of her, he knew, in his gut—no red-blooded, heterosexual man would ever be able to be "just friends" with her.

If she wasn't Grant's girlfriend, Devon thought grimly, it wasn't because Grant didn't want her.

CHAPTER SEVEN

"Devon Sparks!"

Devon winced and shot Grant's maybe-girlfriend a swift sidelong glance, but her eyes were wide with something that looked a lot closer to panic than recognition of his famous name.

Clutching his elbow, she only had time for a quick whispered, "Please don't mention anything about last night!" before Adam was upon them, his entire crew clomping up the stairs like a herd of rhinos behind him.

Being relegated to dirty secret status was a novel experience for Devon. He couldn't say he liked it much, especially since it added fuel to his suspicions about a possible romantic entanglement between the woman at his side and Grant.

Although why Devon should care was a whole other story.

"Temple," he said, acknowledging his friend, who was currently doing a great impression of an overgrown Labrador.

Adam bounced over, flush with happiness, excitement radiating from every pore. Normal, mundane day-to-day life tended to get Adam flying like a kite; the guy had the gift of passion, for sure. Still, this was something extra.

"Thanks for doing this, man. Miranda and I, we appreciate it so much! See, Frankie, what'd I tell you?"

52   LOUISA EDWARDS

"Told me the man would be here. Didn't venture to say much about whether he'd be staying. Hello there, Lolly."

The laconic Cockney voice drifted over from the kitchen doors where Frankie Boyd was leaning, fingers of one skinny hand rummaging in the pocket of his painted-on black jeans. Presumably for smokes. Frankie was famously addicted to silk-filtered Dunhill's; he'd once told Devon he plunked down his hard-earned cash for the outrageously expensive British imports because he took his vices seriously.

Devon sneered a little, more out of habit than real animosity. He and Frankie had butted heads when Frankie was one of his line cooks back at Appetite, but that was years ago. Frankie was Adam's sous chef now, and by all accounts, an integral part of the kitchen.

"Wait a second." Devon turned to the woman at his side with an incredulous eyebrow lift. "Your name is 'Lolly'? Like, short for lollipop?"

She stiffened visibly, her thick, straight brows drawing down like thunder. "Lilah Jane Tunkle," she said. "Do not call me Lolly. Ever."

Oookay.

Devon cleared his throat and turned back to Adam. "Two weeks, that's what we agreed on."

"Yup. You man the helm here for fourteen wonderful days while Miranda and I check out the farmhouse cooking in the German countryside."

A sound exploded from the woman next to him. That sound could most accurately be described as "Eep!"

Lilah Jane Tunkle. Christ, what a name. Devon sent her a questioning look only to find that she was gazing back at him with a shell-shocked expression that suggested she was beginning to understand the scope of her faux pas.

Devon was grimly pleased. *That's right, doll face,* he wanted to say. *You thought it was an anonymous screw with a guy you'd never have to see again? Not so much.*

They glared at each other for a moment, Lilah looking more appalled by the minute.

"That was quick," Frankie put in. "What did you do to take the piss out of our Miss Lolly within ten minutes of meeting her, then? Grant's not going to be happy."

Devon gritted his teeth at the mention of the restaurant manager's name. Shit, why was he so ticked? "Grant can kiss my ass," Devon growled.

"Grant," Lilah replied, recovering her dignity, "who, I believe I've told you, Frankie, is the only person allowed to call me by that loathsome nickname, is my friend. He got me the job, bussing tables. I start tonight—"

"What a coincidence," Frankie cackled. "So does Dev, here."

Friend. Ha. Wonder if that's how Grant sees it?

Then the rest of her statement penetrated. "Wait," Devon said. "Do you mean to tell me you're fouling up this kitchen with your disgusting jumped-up dog food and you're not a chef or a line cook? Not even a fucking dishwasher?"

Lilah pinched her lips together in a disapproving way. "No, I'm not a chef, Mr. Potty Mouth," she said with flagrant disregard for Devon's authority. "But I had permission to use the stove."

Devon, who had strong feelings about civilians, superlative kissers or not, infiltrating professional kitchens, was about to respond forcefully when he caught the impatience rolling off of Adam in waves. The guy was all but dancing in place, like a kid in line for the bathroom. He was clearly ready to get his show on the road.

Evidently Lilah recognized the signs as well. "I think I'll just take my 'dog food,'" she enunciated with offended gravity, "and find Grant. I'm supposed to get him to start showing me the ropes."

"Good idea," Adam said heartily. "He's still down in my office, probably moaning over the sad state of the menus. Miranda always writes the descriptions of each week's dishes, but she's been too busy researching her book and packing our bags to take a look at them."

"Right," Lilah nodded. "And thank you again, Adam, for

the opportunity. I promise, I won't let you down." Carefully folding the corners of the oil-soaked paper towels over the still-steaming chicken livers, Lilah scooped up the nasty bundle and said, "Well, I'll just leave y'all to your little conversation."

Devon watched her go, torn between annoyance and relief. He didn't like the feeling of uncertainty about Grant's prior claim on her, even if Lilah clearly thought of herself as free. Devon controlled his breathing carefully. He detested this type of drama.

Although why he should be so worked up, he couldn't explain. It wasn't like it was ever going to be more than a one-time thing with Lilah.

Right?

Lilah seethed with a mixture of sparking nerves, jumpy stomach, and righteous indignation. Along with a healthy dose of dread.

Holy cats, what a mess. Everything was all catawampus. Lilah closed her eyes in distress.

She could just about picture Aunt Bertie laying down the law while deftly rolling out a piecrust. "Lolly," she'd say, up to her elbows in flour, "Lolly-girl, you've gotten yourself in a real pickle this time."

The I-told-you-so would be heavily implied.

Well, there was no use having a conniption over it now. What was done was done. Last night, Lilah had the wildest sex of her admittedly somewhat staid life—and this morning, it turned out that her perfect, mysterious, anonymous lover turned out to be her new boss.

Peachy.

And not only that, but he was a jerk! The things he'd said about her food made Lilah's fists clench even now, minutes later. And she wasn't the type to hold a grudge.

Oh, mercy, what if he told everyone about last night? Her cheeks burned at the thought of it. Or what if he wanted a repeat performance, and threatened to fire her if she didn't comply?

Lilah paused. She couldn't quite believe he was *so* bad, but then, what did she really know? Yankees were capable of anything, as her Uncle Roy liked to say.

And everything had been going so well up until now! Lilah loved New York, from Grant's tiny, cramped studio to the crowded 1 train she rode to get from his place in Chelsea to the restaurant on the Upper West Side, to the amazing liberation of following her heart (and her body) and having (supposedly) anonymous sex last night.

Getting dumped by her boyfriend just might be one of the best things that ever happened to her. It had prompted her to move to New York, which was a good choice, she remembered thinking this morning as the subway swayed around a curve and a businessman jostled her arm, spilling coffee on her hand. New York was exactly what she needed. Everything was going to work out perfectly. Lilah Jane Tunkle's life had finally begun! She was a sophisticated woman now, hip with the times and comfortable with her own sexuality!

And then Devon Sparks had to go and ruin it all by turning up at Market and being a big horse's ass. And by looking unconscionably attractive while doing it.

Lilah sighed, loud and gusty, as she clattered down the kitchen stairs toward the narrow hallway that led to the prep kitchen, storage pantries, staff locker room, and the chef's office. She went over the layout of the restaurant once again in her head, determined not to get lost.

Of course, it still took her several false starts and one detour into a dark, dank room where curing meats wrapped in linen hung from the rafters before she found the office.

Where her oldest friend in the world, Grant Holloway, was sitting at an ancient green metal desk, banging his head with a hollow sound of despair.

"Why me, God?" he moaned. "Have I displeased You in some way? Mercy, please, I beg you."

Lilah rolled her eyes. "Drama queen! Up and at 'em. Tell Lolly what's the problem."

Grant raised moist cornflower blue eyes to hers, his mussed

blond hair making him look like a cherub recently awak-
ened from his afternoon nap on a passing cloud.

"Lolly! Where on earth have you been?" He rushed to
her and threw his arms around her, cracking her ribs with
the force of his hug. "I couldn't find you anywhere last
night, and then I had to hear it from Chris . . . from the bartender, that you'd left with Devon Sparks! I didn't believe
him at first, but when you weren't anywhere in the bar and
you didn't come home . . ."

Lilah drank in the familiar cool-water smell of her best
friend.

"The bartender had it right," she said, affecting as much
airy unconcern as she could.

"No," Grant said, pulling back and searching her face as
if for signs of demon possession.

"Oh, yes." Lilah waggled her brows to make her point
clear. "I got me some sugar last night."

He went a little green. "Sweet fancy Moses on buttered
toast. You had sex with Devon Sparks."

"Why so dismayed?" Lilah wanted to know. "You've been
after me to find someone new since I turned up on your doorstep with a suitcase and a broken heart."

"Your heart wasn't broken, just a little bruised. And I
wanted you to find someone wonderful." Grant scowled.

Lilah started to feel a little protective of Devon, all of a
sudden. It was okay for her to find him annoying and arrogant, but for some reason, she didn't like hearing Grant bad-
mouth him.

"Are we talking about the same person?" she asked. "Tall,
dark, and hot like burning?"

"That's him," Grant agreed, lip poking out like a petulant
child. He'd always been so damn cute, Lilah thought fondly.
He'd grown up all controlled and organized, but when he
looked like this, she could still see the little neighbor boy
who'd tromped down the lane separating their families'
farms, all skinned knees and sun freckles, to ask her aunt
could Lolly come out to play.

"Lilah, I hate to be the one to break it to you," Grant continued, "but Devon Sparks is an asshat."

"Grant!" Lilah was scandalized. "Language. And anyway, don't worry. It was strictly a one-time deal; I'm sure he's as eager to forget all about it as I am."

Grant gave her a look that clearly stated he knew what she was full of, and it wasn't rainbows or sunshine, but he didn't contradict her.

Full of gratitude for the reprieve, Lilah said, "So what were you moaning about when I first came in?"

Reminding him of his earlier grievance proved the perfect distraction. "The menus aren't done!" Grant cried. "Adam's leaving for two whole weeks and taking Miranda with him, and the menus will never be done right again!"

Lilah held out a hand. "Give me the menus, let me see what I can do."

Clutching them to his chest, Grant gave her a suspicious look. "You've never worked in a restaurant in your life. There's nothing fancier than a fried chicken shack in Spotswood County. How will you know what to write?"

"I taught *Hamlet* to teenagers, Grant. I think I can handle one stupid menu. Gimme. And eat some of these fried chicken livers before they get cold."

Grant exchanged the menu for the paper towel full of tender, crunchy morsels with a happy sigh.

"Oh, Lolly. Your aunt's recipe? I have died and gone to heaven."

Lilah preened a little. Here was a man who knew what was good. Stupid Devon Sparks. What did he know about anything? Nothing, that's what.

The menu was printed in pretty script on a legal-sized piece of what looked like recycled paper. The heaviness of the paper felt good in her hand, and she liked the nubby texture of it.

Grabbing a red pencil off the corner of the desk, Lilah perched on the sagging couch set against the back wall and started marking it up.

"Your boss? Might need remedial kindergarten," she commented, changing *apetiser* to *appetizer* with raised eyebrows.

"He's gotten lazy," Grant slurred, mouth full. "Ever since Miranda came along he's been unloading this job on her. He had to do it himself today and he rushed it, because he wanted to have it done before Devon got here. To take over our restaurant and turn all our lives into a living hell."

"Gracious." Lilah was taken aback by Grant's vehemence. "Is it really that bad?"

"Bad doesn't begin to describe it! We're about to be under the thumb of one of the most famously dictatorial chefs in the industry! I used to work for him, back when he opened his first restaurant, Appetite, and I tried to quit about once a month before I finally managed to make it stick. It's not going to be good, Lolls. You might want to rethink this whole brand-new beginning you're trying on for size. Let me find you a job bussing tables someplace else."

"No! I want to be at Market. I like it here, all the folks I've met have been so kind and welcoming. And you said yourself, no other good restaurant is going to hire someone like me, with no experience at all, and pay a decent wage. I'm willing to impose myself on my oldest, dearest childhood chum like that, but my aunt didn't raise me to be a charity case."

Not entirely true—Lilah had felt like a charity case most of her life, living with her aunt and uncle. They hadn't tried to make her aware of her status in their household, never reminded her that she wasn't theirs, but she'd felt different from her cousins, all the same.

With Grant, though, Lilah knew herself to be on solid ground. Grant had always just liked her; no duty, obligation, or charity about it.

He smiled at her now. "I've loved having you in Manhattan with me. Even if my apartment's not really set up for two people."

"It's cozy," Lilah said. "Think how nice it'll be when winter comes." She was looking forward to the snow. Virginia didn't see a lot of it.

"Sure, except now it's summer and we're baking like two little cinnamon buns in a pan. Seriously, Lols, are you glad you came? I know it's only been a few days, but it was a big change for you."

"It was time and past. I needed to experience life outside of the county."

Grant's mouth twisted. "You never did fit in with those white-gloves-and-pearls Virginia debutantes, did you?"

"No more than you. It was destiny that we became friends."

"Right, destiny. Or the fact that our family's farms butted up on the same crick."

Lilah laughed, because Grant wanted her to. He didn't like to think about his past as a misfit, she'd noticed. When he'd moved to New York right out of high school, Aunt Bertie had shaken her head and made dour predictions about the fate of a country mouse in the big city, but Grant had never looked back. Lilah knew for a fact that she was the only person he still kept in touch with from their high school class—not that many of those bubble-brained jocks and twittering debs had the sense to know what they were missing out on.

They didn't like Grant because he was different in some way they sensed, but couldn't define.

And they didn't like Lilah because she wore clothes that used to belong to her older (male) cousins and refused to follow their lead when it came to Grant. Or, well, anything.

"Have I thanked you for taking me in and letting me stay with you?" Lilah asked.

"At least twice a day since you moved up here," Grant said. "And from now on, there's a moratorium on calling your new life 'an imposition.' I love having you here. Even if my apartment is tiny enough that even with you over on the pull-out couch, I woke up when you got the hiccups that first night."

"Missed me last night, didn't you? Admit it." Lilah crossed the last T with a flourish and stood to hand the finished product over the desk.

"Gladly," he told her, taking the menus and casting his eyes over them quickly. "Actually, I missed you more this morning when I had to get my own breakfast for the first

time since you arrived. You turned into a damn fine cook
while I wasn't looking. And Jesus, Adam really can't spell for
shit, can he?"

"Your vocabulary has gone down the toilet." Lilah laughed,
a tiny bit shocked. Her sweet little friend was all grown up.

"Yeah, sorry." Was he blushing? Cutie. "But you'd better
get used to it, I'm afraid. My potty mouth is nothing compared to the sewage most of those cooks upstairs spew during an average dinner service."

"I can't wait. You gonna share those livers, or what?"

They shared a companionable moment munching happily
on the crispy, salty treats with their surprisingly rich, velvety centers. There was a hint of cayenne in the batter, which
fired the roof of her mouth and made her throat tingle pleas-
antly.

She couldn't believe she'd allowed that condescending
man upstairs to knock her off balance.

"So." Lilah swallowed, unsure of what she was even feeling. She knew it was better to sweep it under the rug and let
it stay there, but she wasn't quite able to let it go. "Devon
Sparks. He's some kind of big shot, huh?"

Grant paused, eyes wide and intent on her face. "You really don't know? Lolly, he's a huge deal. He's got his own
show on the Cooking Channel, restaurants from Miami to
Las Vegas. Christ, I think Target sells his own special line
of spatulas or something."

Lilah blinked. Well. She already knew Devon was rich,
but she hadn't realized he was a celebrity. Although it made
a certain amount of sense, now that she thought about it—
his air of superiority when he talked about food, his chauffeur, his gorgeous apartment.

It was interesting, though, that he hadn't clued her in on
his fame. Lilah remembered how squirrely he got when the
subject of names came up, and looking back, she could see
he was the one who'd pushed for anonymity. She hadn't noticed at the time, since it suited her perfectly, but now that
she thought on it, she felt it must mean something. Surely a

man as arrogant as Grant was making out would've been trumpeting his status up and down the bar, expecting groupies to fall all over him.

Instead, he'd coaxed and seduced nervous, clueless Lilah into his bed without mentioning one thing about being famous.

The incongruity of it poked and prodded at her. If her life were a play, this would be highly significant character information about the new leading man. *But it's not a play,* she reminded herself. *Even if Devon Sparks is more than a perfect face and a towering ego, so what? It was one night of meaningless, albeit enjoyable, sex. And now it's over.*

She couldn't afford the distraction of trying to be nice to Devon Sparks, the man no one seemed to like. She had a new life to start, a new job to learn, and new friends to make.

And if the surface of her skin from her toes to her fingertips tingled at the thought of being that close to Devon again? She'd just have to ignore it.

As she and Grant headed for the staff locker room to don their server uniforms, she asked, "What's the name of Devon's show, anyway?"

Idle curiosity, she thought defensively. *It didn't mean she was interested in him as a person or anything.*

Grant snorted. The arch look he sent her was clear even in the dim light of the back hallway.

"You know what he does on his show?"

Lilah shook her head.

"He goes to a different restaurant in every episode and does one dinner service there; supposed to prove he can cook any kind of food perfectly, under any conditions."

"Sounds entertaining enough."

Tongue firmly in cheek, Grant said, "It's called *One-Night Stand with Devon Sparks.*"

Lilah's jaw dropped. Grant grinned, and pretty soon, Lilah cracked a smile, then he snickered and she chuckled, and before she knew it, they were bent double, cackling fit to bust something.

What the heck, Lilah thought, wiping her streaming eyes. *It's laugh or cry.*

CHAPTER EIGHT

Devon felt a smile tugging at his mouth. Damn, that Lilah Jane was a sassy little piece.

"Oi, she had you sussed with one glance, didn't she? Clever as a cat. Honestly, if it weren't for Jess, I'd be right tempted. Adam? Have a ball in Deutschland, mate. Don't do anything I wouldn't do." Frankie palmed his cigarettes and tapped one out of the pack, grinning cheekily over his shoulder as he headed for the back alley.

Devon gave the departing Brit an irritable glance. The punked-out chef had recently gotten involved with a young photography student/waiter who also happened to be Miranda's brother.

The staff at Market evidently conducted business as if they were running a soap opera rather than a restaurant. It made his head pound to think about navigating the swamp of high emotion and illicit love affairs.

He deliberately avoided thinking about the fact that he was personally responsible for the latest daytime drama at Market. That was over and done with; they'd both expected never to see one another again. The fact that they were working together changed nothing.

There was no reason to refer to what happened last night, and lots of reasons to pretend it never happened at all.

"What just happened?" Adam looked bewildered for a second, then brightened. "Oh, hey! Never mind. You know where everything is, right? Or Frankie and Grant can show you. But you'll be okay?"

And there went Devon's palms again, clammy and cold. In the heat of every moment in Lilah's presence, he'd forgotten his nauseating stress over tonight.

It had been a while—okay, years—since he ran the same kitchen night after night.

Summoning the bravado that had gotten him through countless disastrous filming sessions, Devon said, "We'll manage to muddle through while you're busy on your phoneymoon. Why the hell is it just a vacation again?"

"Please, like I haven't asked Miranda to marry me a dozen times. But she says until it's legal for Jess to marry the man he loves, she's boycotting the whole institution." He shrugged, one corner of his mouth curled down. "It's freaking impossible to argue with sisterly devotion, man. I've stopped trying."

"And after all my fine work getting you two paired up, too," Devon said. When that failed to brighten Adam's expression, Devon gritted his teeth and made an awkward stab at being reassuring. "It'll work itself out, I'm sure. Go on, get out of here. Don't worry about a thing. Market will still be standing when you get back."

Adam nodded, eyes downcast. "I'm looking forward to the trip. To some time alone with Miranda, seeing new places and trying new foods, getting new ideas for the menu—but . . ."

"But it's hard to leave your baby," Devon finished. "Look. Nothing will change. You built this place from the ground up; it's your philosophy, your ridiculous idealism, your staff, your food. I'm only here for a short stint, like a *stage* in reverse."

In restaurant terms, a *stage* was like an apprenticeship. A young, up-and-coming cook would work in the kitchen of an established chef, soaking up knowledge and techniques, gaining valuable experience, padding his resume, and generally working like a dog doing all the kitchen's scut work.

Adam's lips quirked into a smile. "I suppose I can live with that. Man." He shook his head. "What I wouldn't give for a good PR guy right about now. Devon Sparks, the Cooking Channel's brightest star, doing a *stage* in *my* kitchen."

"Don't look at me," Devon said. "I fired Simon Woolf last night. I'm going to have to take care of spinning my own life for a while."

"Dude." Adam sounded impressed. "Out of the blue? And he didn't keel over with some kind of cardiac episode?"

"Simon's still alive and kicking, as far as I know." Devon smirked. "Although he might be feeling a bit bruised this morning—your new busgirl went for him like a pigeon after a half-eaten bagel."

"Sweet little Lilah?" Adam blinked in shock.

"Well. To be fair, he doused her in about five different kinds of liquor."

"Christ, Devon, only you," Adam said, slinging a casual arm around Devon's shoulders. Adam was the one person who touched Devon casually, like a buddy, anymore. Celebrity status came with its own bubble of personal space—or maybe it was just Devon and his general vibe of smug superiority. Devon had no illusions about his personal appeal. Luckily, the camera cared more about the shallow exterior than deep internal goodness—and Devon's exterior happened to be extremely marketable.

"Come on, Adam, you ridiculous puppy. Show me around your kitchen and give me your last-minute instructions. I know you want to."

Adam laughed. "Yeah, the same way I know you won't listen to me. But whatever, man, let's do the dance anyway."

Devon let himself be tugged away from the stainless-steel counter he'd been leaning on, and as his hand trailed the smooth, cold surface, the image of a curvy brunette balanced above him flashed through his head.

A tremor went through Devon, shocking him down to his bones. He tried to pinpoint what he was feeling, the clarity of every sense, the heavy beat of his blood through his veins. Everything seemed sharp and real, time speeding along at a breakneck pace, and that's when it hit him.

He felt alive. For the first time in years. And he could date the start of the feeling to a specific moment—when Lilah Jane Tunkle tumbled off a countertop and landed in his arms.

Frankie propped his shoulders against the dirty alley wall, bricks hot from the late summer sun, and blew out a careful smoke ring.

He fucking well loved to smoke. The nonsmokers' rise to power had relegated smoking to a sort of cultural taboo, a naughty, thrill-seeking behavior that cranked Frankie up just right. They'd gather in alleys and doorways, the smokers, like a cult of danger-loving desperadoes, shivering and sharing a light in the winter, sweating together in the summer. He'd met more interesting people while sharing a fag than on tour with his punk band.

And then there were the times like this. When no one else was feeling the itch just at the moment, and he ended up alone in some out-of-the-way corner, with a lungful of precious, fragrant nicotine and enough space to think.

At the moment, most of Frankie's thoughts revolved around his new boss, that tosser, Devon Sparks. Sparks was, in Frankie's unabashedly biased opinion, pretty much the King of the Tossers. An arrogant little pisser playing cock of the walk, with his fancy cars and screaming hordes of women throwing themselves at him like he was John fucking Lennon. It was beyond ridiculous, but then, Frankie supposed he wasn't exactly the Cooking Channel's demographic. He didn't even own a bleeding telly.

Frankie exhaled and watched the blue smoke dissipate into wisps above his head. The *clickety-click* of a bicycle slowing to a stop a few meters away made him smile.

Jess Wake.

"Hi," was Jess's breathless greeting as he squatted to chain his bike to a drainpipe.

"That the best you can do?" Frankie said, extending a lazy hand. "C'mere and give me a proper hello."

Jess's cheeks were flushed, either from the exertion of the bike ride, the heat of the day, or from seeing Frankie. Impossible to tell, and it didn't matter, anyhow. His perfect milky redhead's complexion showed even the most minor change in Jess's body chemistry. Frankie adored it.

Eager as ever, Jess came to Frankie's hand at once and allowed himself to be folded into the shelter of Frankie's much-taller frame. The trust implicit in the melting line of his body against Frankie's made things low and deep in Frankie's gut go wobbly.

"You took off so early this morning," Jess said into Frankie's shoulder. "You should've woken me."

Frankie's chest tightened at the memory of Jess at dawn, sprawled out over the tasseled sultan's pillows piled around their apartment like an artist's garret from the twenties, his sweet mouth slack with sleep.

"Made too pretty a picture to disturb, Bit," Frankie told him. "Besides, wasn't a thing you could do to get me ready for this morning."

"Nothing? You sure about that?" Jess pulled back far enough to arch a brow up at Frankie. The bright, mischievous expression on Jess's puckish face made Frankie's breath catch hard in his throat. Fucking hell, he was gone over this one. He felt the knob of Jess's shoulder under his palm, loved the curve of his own elbow round the back of Jess's neck. Frankie savored the way they fit together. These things were his. For now.

While Frankie was woolgathering, Jess's cheerful leer smoothed into a more serious look. "So Devon's here? He's really running the kitchen tonight?"

Frankie leaned back against the wall once more, giving himself a little distance. He brought his neglected cigarette to his lips with jerky fingers.

"Looks that way."

Jess scowled. "I still don't understand why Adam doesn't leave you in charge while he and Miranda bum around the

German countryside. You're the sous chef! It's your job to run things when he's not around."

Frankie covered the sudden tension in his limbs by propping one combat-booted foot on the wall behind him. "It's Adam's choice, innit? He's the boss."

"Well, I don't think it's right," Jess said, obstinate as a mule. "He's not only your boss, he's your best friend. You'd think he'd have a little more faith in you."

Closing his eyes briefly, Frankie bought time with another drag on the cigarette. He could feel the frustration pouring off of Jess in waves, the righteous anger on Frankie's behalf. It was beautiful and humbling and scary as fuck—because Frankie had no idea how to tell Jess the truth.

Adam had offered to make Frankie chef de cuisine. He'd earned it, Adam said, those steady brown eyes watchful on Frankie's bloodless face. He'd do a good job leading the crew while Adam was away. Adam was proud of him.

And Frankie had turned him down.

Now, looking into the brilliant blue eyes of this young man beside him, so full of life and ambition and potential he was near to bursting at the seams with it, Frankie's gut churned with a mixture of shame and determination. Jess wouldn't understand. How could he? Frankie barely understood it himself.

"No snarling at Adam for this," he cautioned Jess. "It's his place, his crew. And Devon Sparks is a fine chef." Frankie was proud of being able to choke that out without a hint of sneer. "And like your sis said when she came up with the scheme, it's great publicity, yeah?"

"I guess," Jess grumbled. "But I bet he's only doing it to prove once again that he's *the best chef in the world.*" That last part was said in a faux shock announcer's voice, ripped verbatim from the intro to Sparks's blockbuster show.

Forcing a laugh, Frankie ruffled Jess's dark auburn hair and sucked the last millimeter of goodness out of his cig.

"C'mon, Bit. Give us another kiss before we have to head into the trenches."

That cleared the stormy look right off Jess's wonderful

face, clouds blowing away in the summer breeze until only sunshine was left.

But autumn is coming soon, Frankie couldn't help but think. *All good things come to an end sooner or later.*

CHAPTER NINE

Where did the day go? Lilah wondered dazedly. Hours spent staring at table settings and practicing clearing dishes quietly and efficiently. Now it was time for supper, even though it was only four-thirty. They had to eat early, before the restaurant opened. Lilah didn't mind; those chicken livers were a distant memory and her stomach was talking.

"We all eat together?" Lilah questioned, nerves making her voice flutter high. She cleared her throat, hoping Grant didn't notice.

Which was nuts, because not only was Grant a very observing sort of person, he also happened to know Lilah better than anybody in the world. He gave her a sympathetic look, but he was all chin-up-and-shoulders-back when he spoke.

"It's called family meal," he explained firmly, leading the way back up the dim, poky employee staircase that led from the basement offices and locker room to the kitchens and dining room. "One of the prep cooks usually makes it from whatever's leftover. At some restaurants it can be pretty grim, but Adam believes serving good food to the employees leads directly to good food for the paying customers."

Barely paying any attention to Grant's lecture, Lilah twitched her shoulders uncomfortably in her spanking-new forest-green shirt. All the front-of-the-house staff, from Grant as maitre d' to Lilah as the lowly new busgirl, wore the same uniform of black pants and green button-up top. When Grant had handed her the shirt, she'd been sure it was too small, that when it buttoned she'd have what her Aunt Bertie called "gap-osis" pulling across her chest and exposing her serviceable cotton bra, but she should've trusted her friend. Grant would never deliberately set out to make a laughing-stock of her, if for no other reason than that they shared the mutually assured destruction of knowing each other's deepest, darkest secrets.

Anyway, the shirt fit fine, no unsightly tugging or pucker-ing, but it still felt oddly tight, more tailored than she was used to.

"Relax, hon," Grant said, giving her shoulder a squeeze. "Why so tense?"

"It's like stage fright," Lilah said. "Opening-night jitters. Don't worry about me, I'll do what I always told the kids before a show."

"What, imagine everyone in their underwear?"

"No! Gross. And ineffectual. Stage fright actually comes from a feeling of being unprepared. Spend a few minutes before you go on stage running through what you're about to do in your head, and you'll be fine."

"So you're standing there thinking to yourself over and over: 'I'm about to go eat a yummy meal with some very friendly people who are all going to love me'?"

"Pretty much. And see? Feeling better already."

"Then let's hit it."

Not giving her any more time to wring her hands, Grant pushed open the door to the big, gleaming kitchen. Lilah rushed past the counter she'd tumbled off of earlier that af-ternoon without looking at it, sure that if she did, a hot red blush would give her away.

It took a lot to embarrass Lilah Jane Tunkle; a childhood living on hand-me-down affection got a person used to all manner of little humiliations. But taking a tumble off a coun-tertop straight into the arms of the God's-truth handsomest—and, as it turned out, most unpleasant—man she'd ever had the misfortune to meet? Well, Lilah wasn't superhuman, after all. Just the memory of his warm, steely arms and the surprise in his shockingly blue eyes was enough to make her squirm.

She and Grant stepped up to the long U-shaped bar where the staff was gathered. A strange and wild-looking assembly assessed her with varying degrees of interest. If she were a more fanciful person, she might think of Oberon's court in *A Midsummer Night's Dream*—this crew was that foreign and strange to Lilah's admittedly unsophisticated eyes.

Oh, sure, none of them had horns—although tall, lanky Frankie's black hair stuck up every which way, giving him a decidedly demonic appearance. And the boy next to him, all big blue eyes, fair skin, and dark red hair, had something elfin and spritely about him. Frankie, who'd already made a strong impression with his loud welcome and brash manner, was the sous chef, sort of like the second-in-command. Frankie, Grant, and Adam were the triumvirate of power behind Market.

The boy sitting so close to Frankie was called Jess, she thought, or something similar. Lilah was pretty sure she'd met him briefly at Chapel. He was wearing green and black, like Lilah, so he must be a server.

A diminutive woman with round cheeks and short cropped hair bounced over and threw an arm over Lilah's shoulders.

"What's up, bitches?"

Lilah could feel her mouth primming up. She'd never heard so much cussing in her life! Not without being able to send someone to the principal's office for it, anyhow.

The woman at her side gave her a casual squeeze and bumped hips with her. Lilah remembered her from the round of meet and greets the day before. A flower name, something incongruously demure—Lily? Rose?

"Yo, Vi, baby!" A slim Mediterranean-looking fellow hailed the newcomer. "Don't bogart the new girl. Some of us want to get to know her better."

He accompanied this greeting with a grin and an overblown eyebrow waggle that made Lilah laugh.

"Shut it, Milo. We're doing girl talk," the woman shot back. Milo had called her "Vi," which jogged Lilah's memory. Violet Porter, the pastry chef, Lilah remembered.

"Shee-it. Mean to say you're a girl, Vi?"

Lilah felt the sudden stiffness in the arm across her shoulder, but Violet's breezy reply gave nothing away. "What. Just 'cause I got bigger swinging balls than any of you . . ."

The chorus of hoots and hollers gave Lilah cover to surreptitiously glance at her new friend. There was a strain around Violet's pretty mouth that hadn't been there before.

"It must be hard," Lilah said sympathetically. "Being the only woman in the kitchen, I mean."

Violet started, wide eyes going wider with surprise, as if she'd forgotten all about Lilah.

"Aw, it's easy. Easy-peezy lemon squeezie," Violet said, shedding the momentary hints of stress with a laugh. "Yeah, it's a bit of a sausage fest, but the guys here are all right. The Market kitchen is awesome to work in. Other places? Not so much with the equal opportunity and way, way more with the ass-gropage."

At which point Violet demonstrated said ass-gropage with a sharp pinch and a demonic grin. Lilah yelped and danced backward out of Violet's grasp, tripping over her own feet and landing full in the lap of the man behind her.

Twice in one day! That had to be some kind of record.

"Sorry! Oh, I *am* sorry, please excuse my clumsiness," she said, mortified. Getting her feet under her, Lilah looked up into the face of one of the cutest guys she'd ever seen. Seriously, if she hadn't already met and been swept off her feet by Devon Sparks, this one would've caught her eye in a big way, with his wide mouth, sparkling hazel eyes, and messy chestnut hair.

"Hello there, lovely," the cute guy said, giving her a friendly smile and big, callused hand to shake. "Guess I wasn't around yesterday when Grant introduced you to the crew. I'm Wes Murphy."

"And what do you do here at Market?" Lilah inquired politely. She'd already learned that every cook was assigned to a particular station, from grilled meats to fish to the cold appetizers like salads.

Wes rolled his eyes good-naturedly at the general laugh that went up at Lilah's question.

"Did I ask something wrong?" she said, bewildered.

"Not a thing," Wes assured her. "They're just being assholes about the fact that I don't have a station of my own because I'm a lowly ACA extern. Otherwise known as galley slave."

"Or kitchen bitch," Frankie, the devil-horned sous chef, put in. Violet shrieked with laughter.

"Shut the fuck up, Vi," Wes protested, red staining the tips of his ears.

"What's the ACA?" Lilah asked, more to defuse the rising tension than anything else, although she was definitely curious.

"Academy of Culinary Arts," Grant explained. "ACA students are required to spend time in a professional kitchen as part of their graduation requirements."

"That sounds interesting," Lilah said, struggling not to look around for a bar of soap to clean all their mouths out with.

Wes made a face. "Sure. If you enjoy spending your days dicing onions, shucking oysters, making stock—all the kitchen shit work."

"Surely once you put in your time learning the basics, the chef will promote you and let you learn the different stations," Lilah said. It was only reasonable. "After all, you're here for your education."

"Hear that, everybody?" Wes crowed. "That's what I've been trying to tell you! This woman is my goddess." He pulled Lilah up onto the stool next to his.

Grant shook his head. "I don't know why you ever worry about a thing, Lilah, when you have the gift of making people fall in love with you at first sight."

"Hush your mouth," Lilah said, feeling heat surge back up her neck and into her face. "Now you're trying to embarrass me so I'll forget to be nervous."

"Right," drawled a voice from directly behind Lilah. "From what I saw before, it would take an act of God to embarrass you."

Lilah stiffened, recognizing the lazy tones of Devon Sparks. She could practically hear his smug smile in the way he drew out the word "Right."

Spinning on the stool, Lilah titled her chin up and looked him square in the eye. "A true gentleman would gloss over . . . the way we met and allow us to start fresh."

She'd been right about the smile, although as she stared into his TV-perfect face—cheekbones like knife blades, and that barely-there cleft in his chin, Lord have mercy—the smile slipped from smug into something darker. Hotter. Lilah shivered without meaning to, and Devon's eyes sharpened at the visible tremor.

He leaned in, too close for propriety, too close for comfort, too close for Lilah to draw a deep breath without smelling the faint traces of his no-doubt pricey cologne—and under that, something else, something real and tantalizing. Lilah struggled to breathe normally, minutely aware that every person in the room was watching, but it was impossible to remain completely unaffected.

This man was inside me last night, she thought, and felt her heart kick over the traces and head into a full gallop.

And then his warm breath caressed her cheek and she couldn't help it. Her eyelashes fluttered closed.

"You've never seen my show, have you?" Devon asked, his voice soft and almost gloating. "If you had, you'd know better than to expect gentlemanly behavior from me."

Lilah's eyes popped open. She sat up straight, craning her neck back to catch Devon's eye.

"Is that supposed to be a come-on? That *Oh, watch out for me, 'cause I'm so bad* thing? Because I have to tell you, you're barking up the wrong busgirl. I used to teach high school, sugar, I know all about bad boys. And I've had enough of them to last me a lifetime."

Frankie whistled under his breath, the loud sound in the sudden silence reminding Lilah of their avid audience.

Devon stepped back smoothly. He did everything smoothly, Lilah noticed. As if he were perpetually aware of being watched. She couldn't help but contrast today's slick act with last night's more genuine-seeming responses. Which one was the real Devon Sparks?

She caught something, a tension around his mouth that told her she'd surprised him. The thought warmed her all the way through.

"It wasn't a come-on," Devon clarified. "It was more of a . . . friendly warning. I don't date employees—which you'll be, if Adam ever actually leaves and lets me get to work!"

"Family meal first, Dev," Adam said, sauntering over. "My last supper with the crew before Miranda and I hit the road."

Lilah smiled at the obvious satisfaction in Adam's voice when he referred to his girlfriend. Devon, she noticed, rolled his eyes.

Before Devon could make the snotty comment she was sure was on the tip of his tongue, a young man hurried from the kitchen with a tray full of food.

"You need help, hon?" Lilah asked, ready to jump up.

"No, thank you," the guy said. He was handsome in that brooding Latino way, Lilah noticed, although his bright gray eyes spoke of a varied heritage. His quiet voice as he asked the other cooks to clear space on the bar was only lightly accented.

Adam clapped his hands together and tugged Devon up to the bar. "Billy! My man. What have you got for us today? Billy Perez," he said to Devon. "He started as a dishwasher, moved up to line cook a few months ago."

Devon nodded, saying nothing, but Lilah noted the curl of his lip as he stared down at the plates heaped with colorful vegetables and spicy-looking chicken.

"The protein is a shredded adobo chicken; there's corn tortillas and sliced avocado to go with it."

"And this other mess?" Devon asked, pointing at a smaller bowl.

Billy's cheeks reddened, but he drew himself straight and said, calmly enough, "I wanted to try a play on one of my favorite things to eat from when I was a kid in Mexico. Grilled corn with crema and spices is a common street food. I pulled the cornsilk out and flash-grilled the ears in their wrappers, cut the kernels off the cob and mixed them with some homemade chile-lime mayonnaise. The topping is grated parmesan, because it's what we had in the walk-in, and a little fresh cilantro."

"And the flecks of red?" Devon demanded.

"Diced sweet pepper."

The ex-dishwasher was stoic under Devon's interrogation, but Lilah still didn't like to watch it. Where did Devon get off being so dismissive?

Unable, or unwilling, to keep her mouth shut, Lilah said, "Well! Are we gonna talk about it all night or are we gonna eat it?"

Billy shot her a quick, grateful look out of the corner of his eyes and Lilah winked.

"Right! Dig in, guys!" Billy produced a couple of serving spoons and they all passed the plates around.

Wow.

"I've never had Mexican street corn, Billy, but this is pretty darned delicious," she told him. It was an effort to stop eating long enough to talk without her mouth full.

The corn had a caramelized flavor from the grill, and the tender, firm kernels popped in her mouth. Swathed in tangy, spicy mayo with a good citrus kick, one of Lilah's most familiar flavors of summer, sweet corn, turned into her newest addiction.

Murmurs of appreciation followed by complete silence as everyone got down to the serious business of eating attested to the fact that Lilah wasn't alone in feeling transported by Billy's simple family meal.

Lilah watched the others, then inexpertly rolled her first soft taco. It was messy but scrumptious.

She closed her eyes, the better to savor the way the cool,

buttery avocado cut the smoky spice of the moist chicken, and when she opened them, Devon was gazing directly at her, a heat that had nothing to do with the spicy food in his stare.

Swallowing was hard when her mind was suddenly filled with images of the night before, but she managed it.

Lilah fell into the deep blue of his intent gaze, breath quickening, blood pounding in her ears.

Adam startled them out of the moment with a heartfelt, "Hot damn, Billy. Best fucking thing I ever did, putting you in charge of family meal."

Billy flushed again, this time from obvious pleasure in the compliment.

An infinitesimal sneer tugged at Devon's mouth. "When you're finished enjoying your street food, Adam, there are a few things I'd like to go over with you."

His voice was silky smooth, but Lilah heard the derision in it. Devon, she saw, hadn't taken a plate. He wasn't even going to try the food?

Evidently not. Without a glance in Lilah's direction, not that she cared, Devon turned on his heel and stalked back to the kitchen.

Lilah caught the frown Adam sent after him, but she couldn't tell if it was anger or concern. For herself, Lilah felt zero ambiguity.

Devon Sparks might be the sexiest man this side of the Mississippi, and he sure enough had a line of charm on him, but all that pretty packaging couldn't hide the arrogance inside.

Lilah told herself it was a darn good thing he wasn't interested in pursuing their attraction . . . thing . . . whatever. She couldn't afford to be seen as getting special treatment or attention from the man who was evidently going to be calling the shots around here. It was her first night doing this job, and everyone at the family meal table knew she was only there because she was friends with Grant. Lilah had to focus on proving herself, prove that she could make it on her own—

she couldn't be fretting over Devon Sparks, analyzing his every move for flirtatious intent.

Last night was an aberration, never to be repeated. He'd all but said so.

Now all she had to do was forget it ever happened.

CHAPTER TEN

Devon stood in the Market kitchen and surveyed his new domain. Like an annoying song on endless mental repeat, the shock announcer voice that ended every episode of *One-Night Stand* popped into his head.

One-Night Stand with Devon Sparks—the best chef in the world. Join us next week as Devon proves his prowess once again, taking a kitchen by storm to cook a menu he's never seen, with tools he's never touched, and a staff of chefs he's never worked with. From four-star French cuisine to humble Indian takeout . . .

And Devon's image would flash on the screen, cocky half-smile in place. And he'd say, "Anything they can do, I can do better. Watch and see."

Spoken with utter confidence. Devon had learned how to do that; he could give every outer indication of total and complete self-assurance in any situation. The trouble was that when the cameras were switched off, he didn't always *feel* it.

Which occasionally got him into trouble.

Today, for instance. Market's doors would open to the public in exactly one hour, and Devon would be expected to competently and calmly execute dinner service. Which shouldn't be a big deal, right? He'd done it, and done it well, at his own restaurant across town for years before he built an international reputation as a chef able to whip any kitchen, however dysfunctional, into shape in the space of an hour-long show.

Sure, the show was staged. But that was the deal with so-called "reality" TV. In general, it bore very little resemblance to reality. Not that *One-Night Stand* was scripted, exactly, but were the situations manipulated to get good pacing and action, the results the producers wanted? Devon knew they were.

Maybe that's why this felt so different, Devon mused. There were no cameras here, no production crew to step in and call "Cut!" if things went sour. It was just Devon. On his own. And despite the fact that nothing that happened in the Market kitchen would be televised, Devon felt more exposed and alone than he had in years.

He buttoned his signature white chef's jacket with the rolled short sleeves, imagining it as armor. His name was embroidered in royal blue silk on the breast, but there was no restaurant logo beneath it. In spite of the fact that it was his name, money, and star power that kept a small empire of restaurants afloat, he was no longer the acting executive chef at any of them. For the past four years he'd been a wanderer, a tramp, bumming from restaurant to diner to banquet hall for that damned show.

Market was just another stop on the railroad for Devon— this kitchen, as vibrant and warm as it felt when Adam showed him around this afternoon, would never be Devon's home. It was Adam's show, from opening credits to final shot, and as Devon watched the choreographed hustle the line cooks performed as they finished prep, it ticked him right off that yet again, he was leasing, not buying.

Confident that none of that showed in his expression or body language, Devon was startled out of his reverie by Frankie's annoying Cockney accent.

"Feeling a mite nervous, are we, mate?" Frankie asked, showing that unsettling ability to read people that Devon remembered from Appetite, back when Devon ran his own kitchen and Frankie was a lowly line cook. Thinking about it now, Devon wasn't surprised the man had risen to sous chef—that pinpoint accuracy in judging situations made him a huge asset to any busy kitchen.

Devon didn't bother to resist rising to the bait. "Of course. Of all the kinds of food I've tried my hand at over the years, Adam's particular brand of crunchy-munchy eco-friendly emo-cuisine might be the toughest to master."

Devon awarded himself a point when he saw Frankie stiffen. Honing in on the weakness, Devon continued, "Sure, it's not poaching perfect duck breast *en sous vide* or working with exotic ingredients like tamarind or pacu fish ribs—but with that ridiculous restriction of his, no food from further away than a one-hundred-mile radius around the restaurant?" Devon shook his head in mock awe. "Well, the winter months must be a bitch. How many ways are there to cook a turnip, anyway?"

"Plenty, if you've got half the talent Adam has."

"Hmm." Devon let his lips twist in a way that he knew projected cool amusement. "And who was it that discovered Adam and gave him his start, I wonder?"

Frankie opened his mouth but before he could say anything, Devon waved it away with a languid hand.

"Doesn't matter. That was then, this is now. And thank the kitchen gods it's not winter, so we have no root vegetables to contend with. It's summer, that season of glorious fresh fruit and vegetable bounty. And in the spirit of Market's mission, I went to the Union Square greenmarket and picked up a few things to add to tonight's dishes." Allowing himself another curled lip, Devon stared straight into Frankie's black eyes and said, "The menu needed a bit more curb appeal before I'd be willing to have my name associated with this restaurant."

"You jumped-up piece of shit," Frankie exploded, tossing his knife to the counter. He made an abortive move as if to hurdle the huge wooden kitchen block separating him from Devon, but the *garde manger* guy, a scrappy little Italian— Milo?—rounded the corner of the salad and cold apps station to grab Frankie's arm.

"Quit it, man," the smaller man said, shooting Devon a

disgusted look. "Chill. Adam's only gone for a coupla weeks. We just gotta get through it. Don't go making trouble."

"Bugger off," Frankie sneered. "What's this ponce going to do, fire me? He knows damn well Adam didn't leave him with that kind of authority. Did he, Hollywood?"

Devon tilted his head, studying the pugnacious thrust of Frankie's rough-shaven chin. All activity in the kitchen had ceased; every line cook was watching to see who would come out on top of this dog pile. Devon smiled. It wasn't a nice expression, he knew.

"You're right. I can't get rid of you, no matter how obnoxious you are. But don't fool yourself; if your plan is to make the next two weeks a living hell for me, I'll give as good as I get. This is my kitchen for fourteen days; you'll cook whatever the fuck I say you'll cook. If I want to add a nice pavé of dog shit and horse testicles as a special, you'll cook it, and perfectly."

Calmly, with deliberate steps, Devon rounded the butcher block and moved into Frankie's personal space. When they were nose to nose, Devon said, "And if you think I'm going to allow a snot-nosed punk like you to throw me attitude, then you've taken one too many stage dives, *mate*. Now get back on the line and get ready for service."

Without waiting to see if he'd be obeyed, Devon turned, hands on his hips, to shout to the rest of the cooks, "That goes for the rest of you monkeys! Keep your head down, do your job, and we won't have any problems. Give me static, and I'll make you wish you'd decided to become an accountant like Mommy and Daddy wanted. Now get to fucking work. You've got prep to finish. The new menu items are taped to the inside of your low boys."

Amid a flurry of disgruntled grumbling and sullen stares, the cooks bent to the squat miniature refrigerators below each station. The lowboys held all the prep items necessary for every dish that came out of that station—plus a few extras, courtesy of Devon's sneak afternoon delivery. For instance, along with the containers of softened butter, minced shallots, chopped parsley, and squirt bottles of dry vermouth for the pan sauce that normally accompanied the roast chicken, Devon had added large tubs of brown sugar, handfuls of ripe, unpeeled lychee, and bottles of rice wine vinegar for a tart, citrusy gastrique to spoon over the finished chicken.

He'd gone down the menu and augmented every too-simple recipe with more expensive specialty ingredients, things that looked great on a menu. That should take this place to the next level—not that the cooks appeared grateful in any way.

Devon crossed his arms over his chest and watched the frowns and shrugs, the low-voiced conferences. They didn't seem to know what to make of his additions—the lychee, in particular, was raising eyebrows. Milo, the skinny line cook who reminded Devon of kids he grew up with in the North Ward of Trenton, fingered the spiny magenta orbs dubiously.

Peeling back the thin skin with his thumbnail, Milo made a face at the slimy texture of the white flesh beneath. Devon rolled his eyes.

"Peel them. Pit them. Chop them. Boil them with the vinegar and sugar until the liquid is reduced by a third. Strain it. Bring it up to the pass with the chicken; I'll plate it," he said.

Milo started peeling, his movements slow and halting. The rest of the cooks got to work, too, and Devon turned away. They'd figure it out. He didn't intend to coddle the Market crew. This was his chance to dictate a menu again, to have the kitchen make something he came up with, rather than slavishly cooking someone else's idea of good food. It was a relief to take back some measure of control.

Lilah wished fervently for a moment to pause, breathe, and possibly pay someone a million dollars to rub her feet. Who knew feet could hurt this badly! And she'd been a drama teacher, for sobbing out loud.

Maybe it was the frantic pace, the sense of always being a beat behind as she raced from table to table, clearing plates, filling water glasses, replacing dropped knives/forks/napkins.

"You're doing great," Jess, the poor unfortunate waiter to whose tables Lilah was assigned, assured her in passing. He couldn't stop for a pep talk because he was carrying a fully loaded tray out to the front of the house. Lilah flashed him a quick smile anyway, thankful for the encouragement. Even if it was a big fat lie.

She wasn't doing great. Unless it was considered "great" to drop not one, but *two* separate trays of dirty dishes in the middle of the dining room, creating such a loud crash her eyes had snapped to the older gentleman at table seventeen to make sure the noise hadn't shocked him into cardiac arrest.

The guest, who looked like Colonel Sanders wearing a conservative navy suit, was fine. The other customers, however? No fewer than four people had commented on her twang, in grating, isn't-she-cute tones that ought to be reserved for little girls attempting to play the piano for their parents' friends.

And everyone wanted something! Busboys (and girls) were dressed just like the servers, so inattentive diners had a hard time telling them apart. Lilah would've thought the people in her section would at least be able to distinguish her plump, curly-haired self from slender, redheaded *male* Jess, but no such luck. One table had insisted on giving their order to her, and in her panic, Lilah had whipped out a pen and written their menu choices on her palm. She didn't have a notepad! The highly trained professional servers might be able to remember four different appetizers and dinners with different temperatures for the meat entrees, all in their heads, but Lilah wasn't too proud to admit she couldn't.

Jess had laughed long and hard when she'd showed him the scrawled order, her sweaty palms already smudging so that it was hard to tell if Mr. Pushy wanted steak tartare or salmon terrine. Grant shook his head but gave no lectures; he was too busy dealing with the bartender crisis. Which, thank the good sweet Lord for pregnant bartenders who quit without notice, because Lilah was strung tight enough without Grant raking her over the coals.

Nerves jangling, she jostled past the knot of servers clustered around the computer where they entered their orders and pushed open the kitchen doors. A lady at table fourteen needed a new bread plate—the one she had showed a visible finger smudge that looked innocent to Lilah, but apparently was entirely unacceptable.

The swinging kitchen door opened onto the pit of hell. Lilah shrank back from the immediate blast of heat, ovens pumping, flames leaping from the grill and illuminating the intense set of Frankie's usually sardonic face. The sous chef was working in a silent rush while everyone around him shouted and swore, hurrying up and down the line, slipping on wet spots on the floor.

Gone was the serene, happy kitchen of this afternoon. Gone was the cheerful crew of lovable, quirky cooks Lilah had gotten to know over corn salad and tacos at the family meal.

These people were angry, red-faced demons who looked like nothing so much as the tormented souls in the illustration of the fifth circle of hell in her ancient copy of Dante's *Inferno*. And presiding over these lost souls was the devil himself.

"We're in the shit, you fucking monkeys," Devon Sparks shouted, kicking a trash can so hard that it fell over. "Get your heads out of your asses and back in the game!"

Beyond some extra hunching of the shoulders, not a single person acknowledged Devon's rant. Not that Lilah blamed them. If anyone ever spoke to her like that, she didn't know what she'd do. It was appalling, truly, and she couldn't help clucking her tongue a little, even though she knew it made her sound like an old biddy. Luckily for her, the clatter of pots and pans and curses of struggling chefs drowned it out nicely.

Now how in the world was she supposed to get to the dish-washing station where the clean plates were stacked? There were a whole lot of fast-moving, knife-wielding objects between here and there. Lilah did her best to suck in her belly and attempt to become invisible, squeezing past flailing arms and shuffling feet.

"You!"

The enraged voice of the head chef froze the blood in Lilah's veins and turned her feet to immovable blocks of ice.

Oh, Lord. Here we go.

Pasting on a pleasant expression, Lilah faced him with a light, "Yes? Can I help you?"

Sparks lowered his head like a bull about to charge. "You can get the hell out of my cooks' way, is what you can do."

Lilah's eyes darted to the dishwashing station, so close and yet so far. "I just need one little, teensy plate and I'll be out of your hair," she said.

Oh, no, please don't tell me there aren't any clean bread plates . . .

"Christ!" he snarled, accepting a full dinner plate distractedly and wiping spattered sauce from the rim with the white cloth tucked in the apron tied at his waist. "If there's anything you don't need, it's more plates you can smash on the dining room floor."

Lilah winced. She should've known he'd heard that.

Devon turned away to send the waiting server out with a heavily-laden tray, then turned back to Lilah, eyes snapping. He pointed directly at her.

"One more fuck-up like that . . ." He raked her with a scathing, dismissive glance, mouth pulling into a sneer. "And I don't care how pissed Grant gets, I'll kick your ass out of here in a heartbeat."

CHAPTER ELEVEN

The kitchen gods Devon had thanked earlier were evidently intent on reminding him that control was an illusion. From the instant the first order for the first four-top came in, Devon's first dinner service as Market's head chef was an unmitigated disaster.

Nausea swirled in his stomach, sending hot flushes of blood straight to his head. He probably looked like a maniac, the way he'd been running his fingers through the carefully ordered spikes of his hair. He was at the pass executing orders, calling out tickets and plating the food that came up as quickly as he could, but everything was out of sync. The cooks were struggling with the last-minute menu additions, and to make matters worse, plates were starting to come *back*.

It was bad enough to have a customer send a steak back to the kitchen to be refired because it wasn't done to the right temperature—but to have a whole table send back all four entrees because they flat-out hated the food? Devon wanted to throw up.

Instead, he yelled. And yelled some more. At Lilah Jane, no less, who was so completely out of her depth here, it made his lungs hurt just to look at her. And to top it off, he'd shown some of his jealousy over Grant and just what exactly the handsome restaurant manager wanted from Lilah.

Anyway, what was he thinking, wasting time on front-of-house stuff in the first place?

He refused to acknowledge that if it were anyone else, he'd have fired her instantly, dinner rush or no dinner rush.

"I'm sorry, what did you just say?" Lilah pulled herself up, as regal as a queen, and gave Devon the kind of stare he hadn't seen since Principal Dryden threw him out of assembly for clowning around.

"You heard me. No more plates on the floor," he told her, already softening his voice. Christ, he was such a sucker. Those big green eyes, though, *damn*. But she didn't look as if she took this quite seriously enough. Raising his brows, Devon delivered his final shot: "And I don't care if you have to leave your shirt as collateral, the next time a table tries to give you their order, you promise them you'll be right back and *go get Jess*."

That got her. Lilah's cheeks blazed and her mouth opened but no sound came out.

"That's the thing about an open kitchen," Devon said, tilting his chin toward the open pass through to the dining room. "Not only can they see in, I can see out."

As if on cue, Grant appeared on the other side of the window.

Every muscle in Devon's body clenched. Here was Lilah's knight in shining armor, come to rescue her from the evil bastard executive chef. The thought burned going down like a gulp of straight chili juice.

Devon pointed at the manager and ground out, "If you're here to tell me to keep it down because the customers are complaining, then I'm here to tell you what the goddamn customers can do with their bitching. They tune in to see me scream at cooks every week, they can damn well sit through one evening of it at Market."

"Lord, how I wish the only problem were the nastiness of your mouth combined with your startling lung capacity," Grant moaned. The blond man was actually wringing his hands in distress, Devon noted with a sinking sensation.

"It better not be about your gal pal, either, because she

had it coming and I still went easy on her," he said, ignoring the gasp of outrage from behind him and wiping a spill of sauce from the edge of a white bowl holding a quivering morel custard on a bed of lemon-scented asparagus. He spun the bowl onto the server's tray and barked over his shoulder, "Where's the goddamn endive salad? The custard is ready to go."

"Coming up behind you, Chef," panted the Italian kid who'd held Frankie back before.

"Nowhere near good enough," Devon spat at him, snatching the plate from his hands. "It's a salad, you idiot, not open-heart surgery. Be faster." Turning back to the server, Devon shouted, "What are you waiting for? Go!"

"Chef." Grant was practically vibrating with the urgency of his message. "Please."

The front of the house was as big a mess as the kitchen, Devon knew. Five minutes into service, Grant had appeared at the pass to let Devon know that Samara, the lovely and exotic bartender who delighted guests waiting for their tables with her blend of charm and expertly made cocktails, had called in sick. And it was the kind of sickness she'd diagnosed with a little white plastic stick and was going to take nine months to recover from.

Devon cursed like a drunken frat boy when Frankie couldn't rustle up a last-minute replacement, and told Grant to have the servers mix the drinks for their tables. He sure as shit couldn't spare anyone from the kitchen. They'd figure out how to replace Samara later.

"Is this about the bar?" Devon demanded. "If your precious waitstaff can't manage to shake a few martinis . . ."

"No, no." Grant shook his head. "I mean, yes, that's been a . . . challenge tonight, and if we could think of anyone to call in for the second half of service, we should do it, but this is actually personal."

"Christ, Holloway, I don't give a shit about your personal life," Devon said. *Not entirely true,* a voice in his head whispered. *Wouldn't you like to know exactly what Lilah is to him?* Whirling, he held up the same ticket he'd been staring at for thirty minutes. Way too long. "How long on table six? One book trout, one roast chicken, two rib-eye, one rare, one normal?"

Nothing but panicked glances.

Devon wanted to tear his hair out. "How long?" he bellowed. "Answer me."

"I need five more minutes, Chef," Frankie called after a peek at the fish station. The tall sous chef was a blur at the grill station, flipping and checking meat, turning and cross-hatching the marks on the steaks.

"Christ on a cracker," Devon muttered. "You're ready to go with the rib-eyes, aren't you, you fucker. It's the goddamn fish holding everything up."

The guy on fish was young. Holy God, Devon thought, watching him. There was raw talent there, for sure, but not a lot of experience. "I'm sorry, Chef," the kid gasped out now. "I've never done celery foam before, and it keeps separating on me."

"His name's Wes. He's an extern from the Academy of Culinary Arts," Grant said, making Devon jump. He hadn't noticed the other man coming into the kitchen, but he was here now, standing at Devon's side and looking extremely unhappy about something.

"I don't care if he's the Pope on loan from the fucking Vatican," Devon gritted between clenched teeth. "Somebody get on fish and help him with that sauce!"

Quentin spun away from sauté and wordlessly grabbed the whisk out of Wes's hand. Satisfied that the situation was dealt with, Devon turned his attention to Grant.

"You'd better be back here because the dining room is out of clean forks, and not because you're about to plead some bullshit personal issue that's going to take you out of commission."

"There's someone here . . . maybe we should go down to the office."

"You're insane. I can't leave the line in the middle of

service. Oh, for the love of— Spit it out, Grant! What, are you having a kid, too?"

The restaurant manager winced. "Funny you should ask . . ."

Even through the chaos of the worst case of weeds Frankie'd ever battled, he caught the sound of Grant's flat, unhappy voice. It made Frankie look up and take notice in time to see, at the other end of the kitchen, the back door leading to the alley open to admit a tall woman holding a small boy by the hand. The woman wore the navy blue uniform of a police officer.

The little boy was skinny, all dark hair and big blue eyes. His solemn mouth was pulled into a thin line, as if he was afraid but unwilling to show it with so much as a tremble.

Frankie stared down the line, through the smoke and leaping flames from the grill and the scuttling bodies of hustling cooks, and wondered what else could possibly go wrong tonight.

"What the hell is going on?" Devon asked, motionless at the pass. Frankie's attention was caught by the intense stare Devon had leveled on the child wearing a ratty *Justice League* T-shirt and a wary expression. A faded green backpack dragged on the floor beside the boy, strap clutched tight in one white-knuckled fist.

Grant stepped close to Devon the Tosser. "Your assistant told them you were here. Apparently they tried to call from the station house but couldn't reach you. I guess in all the, um, excitement tonight, no one was bothering to answer the kitchen phone?" Grant tried to keep his voice down, but Frankie was close enough to hear.

He vaguely recalled an annoying ringing at intervals throughout the evening, but on some level he'd thought it was a ringing in his ears caused by extreme stress and volcanic rage, so he'd ignored it. Frankie couldn't remember ever being buried as deep in the shit as they were tonight, and the blame for it lay squarely at the feet of their fearless temporary leader.

Who started weaving through the running cooks, ducking hot trays and steaming pots. "Where's his mother?" Devon asked.

That made Frankie drop a steak back onto the grill. Checking his going concerns, Frankie determined the meat could all be let go for a minute or two. This was too good to pass up. He followed the Tosser to the back of the kitchen, noticing that Grant's sweet piece, Lolly, appeared to agree—she was drifting toward the incipient drama like she was magnetized.

The cop regarded the Tosser coolly, unimpressed with his bluster. She was evidently a woman of great perception and insight. "Heather Sorensen was arrested earlier this evening; she's being brought up on charges of driving while intoxicated and reckless endangerment."

"Your son was in the backseat," Grant supplied softly from Devon's right.

Instant meltdown. Frankie could've sworn he heard the sound a vinyl album makes when the needle scritches over it. Or maybe that was only in his head.

Bloody hell. The Tosser had a kid. Frankie stared at the boy's still, pale face. Poor little bugger, with a dad like that.

Falling back on aggression, which Frankie knew to be his default setting, the Tosser rounded on the cop. "And let me guess, Heather needs my help. After spending the last ten years as her personal ATM, I guess I shouldn't be surprised. Well, Officer, my checkbook is in the office downstairs, I'll go get it and we'll clear this whole mess up."

"I'm afraid that won't be necessary, sir." The calm voice of the cop stopped Devon's move toward the stairs.

"Why is that?" he ground out, sounding like he was speaking around a mouthful of broken glass.

"Because Ms. Sorensen isn't asking for bail money. She has voluntarily agreed to enter a rehabilitation center and is asking that you assume temporary custody of one Tucker Sorensen for one month."

The boy, Tucker, squirmed his hand out of the cop's grasp and folded his arms across his chest.

Devon stared down at his son, and the expression on his

face hit Frankie hard. There was something there, as the man watched his child make the same defensive gesture he himself made on a regular basis. Something torn and bleeding that made Frankie want to stand shoulder to shoulder with Devon and maybe help prop him up.

"I can't," Devon rasped into the awkward silence. "I'm not the kind of . . . I don't have time for a child. What would I do with him?"

A high, distressed noise came from Frankie's right. So soft nobody else probably heard it, but it made Frankie turn to look at Lilah. Tears stood in her pretty green eyes, her throat working visibly.

The policewoman—Officer Santiago, her badge said—gave Devon a long, appraising look. Then she glanced down at Tucker, who was staring at his scuffed sneakers. Angling her body away from the boy, Santiago tilted her head to indicate she wanted a private word with Devon.

Stepping forward, Devon leaned in to hear what she had to say. Without thinking twice about it, Frankie followed suit.

"Sir. If I were to understand you to be declining custody at this time, my next move would be to contact Child Protective Services and get Tucker started on the foster-care process. Ms. Sorensen indicated to me that there was no one else, no other family to turn to. Is that your understanding as well?"

Devon's eyes closed. "Yes. Heather was a runaway. I'm not even sure where she was from originally."

"And what about your family?" the officer probed. "Do you have anyone who could come stay with you for a few weeks, help out?"

Devon laughed, the sound as harsh as a gunshot. "I haven't spoken to my family in years."

"That's too bad," Santiago said. "In situations like these, it's best if the child can stay with a close family member. But if that's not possible, or if the family members aren't willing to accept that responsibility, then perhaps foster care is best."

With that chilling pronouncement, she turned back to Tucker and wrested his hand back into hers. The boy didn't

even look up. Of everyone here, he seemed the least interested in how the evening was progressing.

Until Lilah spoke up, her sweet voice cutting through the
hushed tension.

"Wait," she said. "Wait, don't leave. Devon wants him.
He'll take custody."

CHAPTER TWELVE

Lilah clapped a hand over her mouth, but it was too late to call the impulsive words back. And really, when she looked into Tucker Sorensen's suddenly blazing blue eyes, she wouldn't if she could.

That child needed someone to speak for him.

From the look on Devon's face when she dared to raise her gaze to it, Lilah realized with a shock that maybe the father needed someone to speak for him just as badly.

Devon looked like someone had just heaved a sack of rocks off his back. A glimmer of relief strong enough to make Lilah's eyes water crossed his face for a split second before the customary hardness settled over his features again.

His eyes narrowed to slivers of frozen steel as he looked at Lilah. Snared by the intensity of that look, Lilah did her best to stand tall and hold onto the moment when she knew she'd done the right thing for the father as well as the son.

The police officer cleared her throat. "Sir? Can I leave him with you?"

Without sparing the officer a glance, Devon prowled over to where Lilah stood. Her knees went to jelly, but she managed to stiffen her spine.

In a low, vicious voice that sent shivers down her back, Devon said, "Lilah Jane Tunkle."

She gulped. "Yes?"

"You're fired."

No. Not possible. She'd only just started! An angry protest welled up in her chest, but Devon forestalled it with a single raised finger. "If you can keep the kid quiet and out of the way until closing, you've got a new job. Nanny."

Boy, when they talked about life in the fast lane in New York City, they weren't kidding. Lilah gaped at Devon, feeling like she was spinning out in a racecar doing 160.

Devon crossed his arms over his chest and stared her down. "Take it or leave it."

Okay. She'd messed up quite a bit as a busgirl. And hadn't enjoyed it that much. And this situation here, with little Tucker staring up at her like she could make or break his world with a single word—okay, she'd pretty much brought that on herself. Lilah looked into those blue eyes, the same shade as his daddy's and well on their way to being just as shuttered and shadowed, and knew she couldn't walk away.

"Done."

Satisfaction gleamed in Devon's eyes an instant before Lilah held up her own forestalling finger and added, "On one condition."

He rocked back on his heels. "You're not in any position to make demands."

"Bull pucky," Lilah said bluntly. "You don't want Tucker getting lost in the system any more than I do. And I understand, with the restaurant and everything"—*"everything" being a euphemism for "your incredible self-involvement,"* she thought but didn't say—"you could use some help looking after him. I'm agreeing to be that help. Out of the goodness of my heart, and for the same salary I was promised for bussing tables."

Devon's fine mouth quirked. It wasn't fair he should look so handsome when making such a derisive face. "I haven't the first clue what a busgirl makes these days, but I'm sure that's doable. Was that your condition?"

"No," Lilah said, ticked at Devon's casual dismissal of the money issue. Her salary might be pocket change to him, but it was all that was keeping the wolf from her door. Shoving it from her mind, she continued firmly, "No, my condition is that you stop referring to Tucker as 'the kid.' He's got a name; use it."

Devon blinked, obviously taken aback. She braced herself for questions as to why she was making an issue out of this when there were so many other details to discuss, but instead Devon's gaze flickered toward his son. For a strange, suspended instant Lilah wondered if Devon was going to refuse, but then he shrugged and said in a bored voice, "Fine. Are we through here? We've still got an hour of dinner service to go."

In fact, the kitchen had ground to a complete standstill while the Sparks family drama played out in the back. Lilah saw line cooks hop to at Devon's words, though, and soon enough the bustle of a working kitchen covered the cop's transfer of Tucker's clammy little hand to Lilah's. Officer Santiago looked well satisfied with the way things had turned out, albeit in a cool, phlegmatic way. Lilah supposed she'd seen lots worse in the course of her career than a self-centered rich guy hesitating to take responsibility for his illegitimate child.

Without a backward glance or a word to Tucker, Devon strode back up the line and started barking out orders, chivvying the cooks along like a hound amongst the hares. He shouted for Frankie, who rolled his eyes and clapped a long-fingered hand on Lilah's shoulder. She looked up at him, expecting some joke. The serious expression in his black eyes surprised her, but not as much as his quiet voice saying, "You did a good thing, luv."

With that pronouncement, he loped back up the line to his station and spun easily into whirling dervish mode, flipping steaks and chops, bending and sliding to a beat only he seemed to hear.

Grant gave Lilah a brief hug and studied her with concern. "You going to be okay?"

Lilah paused, catching her breath and her balance. The world had just tilted sharply to the left and back again, but the cold hand clutched in hers reminded her that this was no time to space out.

"I'm fine," she said firmly. "We both are. Right, Tucker?"

Devon's son nodded mutely. Lilah eyed him, wondering if he was too nervous to speak or what.

Grant shifted from one foot to the other. "Lolly. Hon, I hate to do this to you, but I've got to get back out front. Lord only knows what the servers have gotten up to, and with the bartender situation, I've gotta . . ."

"Go on," she said, forcing a laugh. "Shoo. We'll talk later, okay?"

"Great," he said with relief, and gave Tucker a quick smile before hurrying off.

Leaving Lilah alone with her charge. She looked down at him, and he looked cautiously up at her.

Stalemate.

"Okay," she said. "You're gonna have to help me out here. I used to teach kids a few years older than you, and I've got lots of younger cousins, but I've never nannied before, so if I do something wrong, you hafta let me know."

Big eyes tracking her every move was her only response.

"My name's Lilah Jane Tunkle and I'm from a tiny town in the foothills of the Blue Ridge Mountains. Do you know where that is?"

Tucker shook his head, dark curls trembling against his round cheeks. He was really an uncommonly adorable boy. Not surprising, considering he owed at least half of his genetic material to Devon Sparks.

Lilah glanced toward the front of the kitchen where the chef was plating food with single-minded determination, his broad shoulders set in lines so tense they looked about ready to snap.

She didn't understand the gulf that existed between Devon and Tucker. Why could Devon barely look at his own son? Why didn't he have joint custody already? And what was with this mute kid? Her cousins never seemed to quiet down.

"Virginia," she told him now. "The Blue Ridge is part of

the Appalachian Mountains, one of the oldest mountain ranges in America."

Tucker didn't appear to be listening to her; instead, his gaze had followed hers to the pass. He was staring at his father like Devon was a stranger, or a puzzle he couldn't work out. It made Lilah's heart squeeze like a wrung-out wash-cloth.

"We'll see your dad later," she said, steering the boy gently toward the stairs leading down to the locker room and office. She figured they'd be better off to get out of the way.

But Tucker showed his first sign of life, twisting his hand free of hers and planting his feet like a baby mule.

Lilah raised her brows. "What? You want to stay up here?"

Tucker cast her a sidelong glance and, quick as that, the scared kid melted away, buried under a sullen expression.

At a loss, Lilah gestured around them. "Tucker. Come on, this can't be fun for you. Come on downstairs with me and we'll . . ." Damnation. Lilah had no idea how to finish that sentence. What on earth were they supposed to do for the next hour?

Panicking, she said the first thing that popped into her head. "We'll play hangman!" Her cousins liked to play the word game on long car trips, Lilah knew.

The kid snorted, a look of deep scorn arching his brows. Lilah stared. If she'd had any doubt about his paternity before, those doubts were now assuaged.

"Look, kiddo. Everything I know about nannying comes from movies like *Mary Poppins* and *The Sound of Music*—I realize it's your job to start out surly and untrusting and I'm supposed to win you over with my charm and warm heart and incomparable singing voice, but unfortunately for both of us, Tuck, I am so not Julie Andrews. So what do you say we skip that part and head straight for being buds?"

Tucker looked at her blankly. Dear sweet Lord in heaven, was it possible the child didn't know what she was talking about?

While she was still struggling with the horror of a kid

who didn't know who Mary Poppins was, Tucker opened his mouth and dispelled any worries she'd had about his ability to speak.

"You talk weird, Lolly."

His ability to speak politely, however, was still in question.

"I'm from the South," Lilah said. "As I think I already mentioned." She struggled for a moment against the hated nickname, then reluctantly added, "And that's 'Miss Lolly' to you."

Tucker stared at her challengingly. "Does everyone down there take so long to say stuff? You sound like the big chicken in the cartoons."

Oh, he did *not* just compare her to Foghorn Leghorn.

Trying to be glad that the child was familiar with Warner Bros. cartoons—at least he had *some* grounding in the classics—Lilah pursed her mouth and said, "Maybe no one ever explained this to you before, but making fun of the way someone talks is not a great way to make a friend."

Tucker shrugged. "Whatever. I don't care about making friends. And I don't want to play hangman, either."

"Well, what do you want to play?" Lilah felt like she was at sea in this conversation. Who would've thought one ten-year-old would be more challenging than a roomful of hormonal teens?

"Hide-and-seek," Tucker said, smiling for the first time. The grin transformed his pointed face, bringing a sparkle to his eyes and revealing a previously hidden dimple in his left cheek.

Hoping to encourage this kinder, cuter Tucker, Lilah smiled back. "Okay, that sounds like fun. But there are rules, right? Every game has rules."

Tucker cocked his head, giving every appearance of listening carefully. Gratified, Lilah went on. "The first one is the big one: No getting underfoot."

He squinted. "No kidding. I don't want to be stepped on."

"Not literally under someone's foot," Lilah said, chuckling. "I mean don't get in anyone's way."

"Oh," Tucker said, his mouth curving down into an expression far too bitter and adult for his age. "No problem. I'm good at that."

Hating the way his mouth curved into an unhappy bow, Lilah hurried to clarify. "I mean the dining room and the kitchen are both off-limits. Got it?"

Tucker shrugged again. Evidently, he liked to shrug. If Lilah had shrugged at her Aunt Bertie, she'd have been snatched bald-headed. Lilah reminded herself that it had been a traumatic evening for Tucker, and that maybe Yankee children were raised differently than she had been. Allowances could be made.

When he took off running, though, with no warning other than a toothy grin that seemed to say "Sucka!" Lilah pressed her lips together and considered that, Yankee or not, a rude kid was a rude kid.

When she caught that Tucker, he was getting a lesson in manners he wouldn't soon forget.

CHAPTER THIRTEEN

Devon blinked sweat out of his stinging eyes and panted, hands planted on the stainless-steel counter. His right palm edged up against something sticky the color of plums, which part of his weary brain recognized as the port wine demi-glace for the grilled rib-eye entrée. He hung his head and watched the reduced sauce stain his hand purple and just could not be bothered to move.

Every muscle ached, in that trembling sort of exhaustion he hadn't experienced outside of the weight room at Clay, the ungodly expensive gym he trekked downtown to use religiously five days a week.

The worst service of his entire life was over, and all Devon could feel was a numb dread that it was only the first night of a full two weeks of torture.

All around him, cooks were cleaning up their stations in morose silence. Devon watched them mopping up spills and shuffling leftovers into the walk-in coolers and knew he ought to say something. Anything. About how tonight sucked ass, but tomorrow was a brand-new day. Blah blah blah.

Instead, he forced his hands up to the buttons on his soiled, stained chef's jacket and started working toward freeing himself from the thing. He imagined once he got it off his shoulders it would feel like being released from a straitjacket.

He wanted, desperately, to go to Chapel and get obliterated. Shrugging out of the jacket, he happened to look up and catch Frankie's baleful eye. Yeah, the Chapel plan wasn't going to happen. Frankie's punk band was playing on the bar's dingy stage later that night; with a single glance, the sous chef made it clear Devon wasn't wanted.

A perverse desire to thrust himself into unwelcoming company almost sparked Devon's natural defiance, but he shrugged it off. Devon didn't like to admit mistakes; he hadn't gotten where he was today by being liberal with apologies. But he was honest with himself, always, and he knew the lion's share of the blame for tonight's debacle rested squarely on his shoulders.

Not only had he introduced new menu items at the last second, as if he were running a challenge on a reality TV show rather than a restaurant kitchen, but he'd let his personal life throw him into the biggest tailspin imaginable.

The image he'd been trying, with varying degrees of success, to suppress all night came shooting back to the forefront of his mind.

Tucker. His son. Standing right in front of him, looking up at Devon like he was some guy off the street.

Devon barely recalled a word of his exchange with the police officer who'd brought Tucker in. He counted it as a minor victory that he seemed to have carried on a coherent conversation when his mind was filled with nothing but static. From the moment it became clear that Heather was asking him to take Tucker—Jesus, what the hell kind of trouble was she in, anyway? She swore she'd never do this—Devon's feet had felt nailed to the floor, his mouth coated in superglue, his brain stuffed with buzzing cotton.

And it had taken the worst busgirl in the history of the restaurant business to break him out of the trance.

Remembering the stricken look on Lilah Jane's face when she realized she'd just inserted herself into Devon's fucked-up family politics, he had to smile. Fuck it all, he hoped no one ever knew how close he'd come to bending her over his arm and kissing her senseless for that little bit of meddling.

The woman was a breath of sweet, fresh, uncomplicated air in the restrictive, claustrophobic prison that was Devon's life.

And if that was dramatic, so the fuck what? He was a celebrity, damn it, he was supposed to diva it up whenever possible.

The kitchen had emptied while he'd been ruminating, and Devon frowned. Where the hell was Lilah, anyway? He thought she'd bring the kid—Tucker, he reminded himself with a reluctant smile—into the kitchen once service was over. Maybe she didn't know what time it was.

Thinking perhaps she'd gotten Tucker to sleep on the couch in the office downstairs, Devon balled up his dirty jacket and threw it on the pile of crusty brown kitchen towels for the night porter to deal with, and headed for the door that hid the stairs to the lower level.

Thoughts of Lilah and sleep in the same brain space reminded Devon to congratulate himself on how handily he'd removed Lilah Jane Tunkle from the roster of restaurant employees, making her fair game for seduction.

Fine, if you wanted to be a stickler about it, she'd still be working for Devon when she became Tucker's nanny, but that was a short-term gig, and besides, Devon had never made any hard and fast rules to govern the sexual practices of domestic help, so he was more than willing to give himself leeway on this one.

Now what to do about Tucker. Devon pitied the kid—it sucked ass to be stuck with a father who had no idea how to be a parent. His own dad spent the first eighteen years of Devon's life screwing him up royally; the last thing Devon wanted was to inflict the same fate on someone else. It would probably be better for everyone if Devon just stayed out of Tucker's way, kept the contact to a minimum. And it was only for a month, he reminded himself. That was good. Talented as he was, there had to be a limit to the amount of damage Devon could inflict in four weeks.

He stepped into the cramped, poorly lit stairwell and paused. Now that service was over and the constant clang

and clatter of pans and dishes had ceased, Devon could
savor the silence. Not to mention the all-too-rare moment
spent unobserved, skulking on the stairs. He let his shoulders slump, only for a second, but the instant's release from
the tension of keeping up his super-chef façade was nearly
orgasmic.

Pure, thick, blessed quiet enveloped him for all of ten
seconds before he registered a faint but frantic voice calling,
"Tucker? Tucker!"

Any peace Devon had achieved in the wake of service
shattered like an etched crystal goblet.

He hurried down the stairs toward Lilah's increasingly
panicked voice.

"Tucker, so help me, this isn't funny anymore. Quit hiding this instant and come here!"

Fear gripped Devon's stomach in an iron fist. He broke
into a run and nearly collided with Lilah. He held her plastered against him for a beat, trying to find his equilibrium.
Her eyes were wide and silvery green in the darkness, her
breath coming in short pants that pushed her chest against
his. Devon endeavored not to notice the softness of her
breasts or the way her hair had escaped from its severe bun
and spiraled in corkscrew curls around her pale face.

"What the fuck have you done with my son?" he asked
with what he considered to be admirable calm.

Lilah scowled and wrenched out of his arms. "*Tucker* is
perfectly fine," she stated. "We've been playing hide-and-
seek and he doesn't seem to know when to quit, that's all."
Shoving her hair distractedly behind her ears, Lilah raised
her voice to a shout. "Tucker, come on! Your dad's here now,
and he's ready to take you home!"

Somewhat mollified by Lilah's assurance that Tucker was
merely hiding, not kidnapped or something as Devon's paranoid brain had instantly assumed, Devon stuck his hands in
the pockets of his jeans and wandered after Lilah as she
combed the locker room, office, and staff bathroom.

No Tucker.

"I have to say, Lilah Jane, you certainly know how to

impress a prospective employer. Has he been hiding this whole time?"

He could practically see the steam shooting from her ears as she held in a snappy response. Devon wished she'd just let it fly.

Huh. It had been years since he'd tolerated backtalk of any kind. But there was something invigorating about sparring verbally with Lilah.

Not to mention distracting. Devon was self-aware enough to recognize that on some level, he was trying to provoke a fight with Lilah to keep from having to confront the rising tide of nauseating fear that his son was missing not two hours after being given into Devon's care for the first time.

"Of course not. I don't have much nannying experience, Mr. Sparks," Lilah said through gritted teeth. "But I've been around a lot of kids and I've never lost one yet. I'm sure he's gone upstairs and we'll find him in the dining room."

But Tucker wasn't in the dining room, nor was he in the kitchen, the pantry, the walk-in cooler, or behind the bar.

"Son of a bitch," Devon swore, knocking a barstool sideways. It skidded across the polished wood floor with an ugly noise, and Lilah flinched.

"Stop it," she hissed at him. "You think he's going to come out with you cussing and knocking the furniture to pieces?"

"Come out of where?" Devon demanded, pulling his iPhone from his back pocket. "The kid's gone. We have to call the cops."

"He's not gone," Lilah insisted, starting to look tearful. "He's just scared. And you're not helping." *You big brute* was how she wanted to end that sentence, Devon could tell.

Hanging onto his precarious patience, Devon flipped through his wallet for the card Officer What's-Her-Name had given him earlier. He punched in the number and held his phone to his ear, glaring at Lilah the whole time.

"Officer . . ." He glanced back at the card. "Santiago?"

Out of nowhere, a small body hurtled through the restaurant like a Lilah-seeking missile and attached itself to her legs.

Surprise rounding her mouth to a perfect O, Lilah reached a hand down to Tucker's messy hair.

"I don't wanna go with the cops," Tucker wailed, face scrunched, eyes and nose streaming. Jesus, Devon thought through the crashing adrenaline in his bloodstream. At least the kid comes by his dramatic streak honestly.

"Hello? Hello?" came the tinny, cold voice of Officer Santiago in Devon's ear.

"Wrong number," he said hastily, hitting the "end" button on the touch screen.

Tucker, not seeming to realize that he was in no imminent danger of being led off in handcuffs, continued to cling to Lilah's legs and cry.

Devon watched, feeling helpless. He didn't much enjoy the sensation.

"Oh, sugar," Lilah crooned, curling her body over Tucker's protectively. Devon marked it down for future reference—Lilah Jane was a sucker for tears.

"Where were you?" she continued, her voice soft and low. "We looked and looked; it was as if you vanished."

Tucker pulled himself together enough to point to the corner banquette. It was a round booth with an oval six-top at the end of a wall lined with regular four-top booths. Devon looked more closely and saw a narrow crevice where the square and round booths didn't match up perfectly. Holy shit. He wouldn't have given good odds on a rat's chance of wedging itself in there, much less a ten-year-old boy.

"Why didn't you come out when we called?" Lilah wanted to know.

"I thought . . ." Tucker got off his knees and wiped his face with the side of his fist. It didn't escape Devon's notice that he stayed pinned to Lilah's side, though. Like he was looking to her for comfort because he was afraid.

Afraid of Devon.

Smacked between the eyes by that little revelation, Devon almost missed Tucker's explanation.

"I wanted to wait till everyone left. I wanted to go to the train station."

"For what?" Lilah asked, bewilderment clear in her tone.

Tucker shifted uncomfortably and crossed his arms over his chest.

The confusion cleared from Lilah's pretty face. Sympathy warmed her eyes to the color of summer leaves in Central Park.

"You wanted to find your mom, huh?" she said quietly.

Devon locked eyes with his son for a brief moment. That one look told him everything he needed to know.

Without waiting for Tucker's confirming nod, Devon turned on his heel and walked a few paces away. He pulled out his phone to complete the image of a polite man trying not to allow his cell phone conversation to disturb others.

If he waited through several long, deep breaths before he dialed his driver's familiar number, well, that was no one's concern but Devon's.

Dimly, he was aware of Lilah behind him lecturing Tucker on safety and consideration for others, and reassuring him that he didn't need to run away. This was only for a few weeks and then his mom would be back.

Devon closed his eyes and blocked out everything but the sound of his own clipped voice giving Paolo the order to come pick them up.

CHAPTER FOURTEEN

Well, if that didn't just rip your heart right out. Lilah ran her fingers through Tucker's tangled waves and tried to get her pulse to stop leaping around like a frightened doe.

Tucker had cried himself out. He sat slumped in the barstool next to hers, lashes forming dark crescents on his cheeks. His head rested on the bar, his breathing deep and even.

Lilah watched him sleep and felt a fury she'd never before experienced welling in her throat like a scream waiting to come out.

The good Lord alone knew what could've happened to him out there. Such a little boy, for all that he acted so tough. Only a baby, really—he'd wanted to get to his mother. That was all he knew.

Because his father could barely even call him by name, much less take an active role in his life.

Lilah still didn't know all the specifics—although she'd be darned sure she got the scoop from Grant—but she knew enough from her own personal observations to hope like heck that Tucker's mother was a steady, loving presence in Tucker's life. That DWI and rehab business didn't give Lilah tons of hope, but she was prepared to reserve judgment on Heather Sorensen.

On Devon? Not so much.

The man was pacing by the front door, watching out for his car and driver to arrive. He hadn't so much as spoken to Tucker when they found him.

"So what's going to happen when your big, fancy car gets here?"

Devon turned and fixed her with an emotionless stare. "What do you mean?"

"I mean," she hissed, jabbing a finger in Tucker's direction, "are you ready to take him on all by yourself? Since you haven't even looked at him in the last fifteen minutes, I thought I should check."

"Why should I look at him? I've hired you to do that for me. Which answers your other question. When the car gets here, we're all getting in it, going to my apartment, and going to bed."

Lilah felt flames leaping up the sides of her face. "Oh, no. You hired me to take care of Tucker—my fee does not include taking care of you, too."

She resolutely ignored the memory of his skin against hers, wet and hot from that sinful shower.

Devon's eyes shuttered, making them at once mysterious and seductive. "I assume you're objecting to the notion that I expect you to 'take care' of me in the sack. I assure you, that's not the case. You'll have your pick of guest bedrooms for the duration of your stay."

Lilah struggled with that for a moment. On the surface, there was nothing wrong with what Devon was proposing. A live-in nanny, that was a thing, right? And it made sense for their situation, because of the late hours Devon would be putting in at Market. Lilah didn't really want to be trekking all the way down to Grant's Chelsea apartment after midnight every night, anyway.

But some innate, feminine sense of caution warned Lilah against putting herself in close proximity to Devon Sparks for any length of time.

That innate sense was proved right when Devon left his post by the door. Perched on her stool, Lilah fought down the tremor that wanted to take her limbs when Devon prowled closer and closer.

He stalked her down until his broad-shouldered, lean-hipped body warmed the air that touched Lilah's skin. Staring up into his unbelievably gorgeous face, Lilah tried hard to hold onto the anger she still felt over Devon's handling of his son.

"I don't know if I want to live with a man who can't manage to teach his son basic manners like not running off and worrying people sick," Lilah said breathlessly.

Devon's eyes flashed with need. "I haven't had much of a chance to teach the kid anything," he said, his voice heated and raspy in the silent restaurant. "And I'm not sure I'd be very good at giving lessons in manners. I could probably use a refresher course myself."

"That's true enough," Lilah said, sucking in air when Devon's hand came up to rest lightly, delicately, on her shoulder. The one point of contact burned like a lightning strike.

"If you come to stay with us," Devon said, sliding the hand down her arm to circle her elbow briefly before continuing its path to clasp her hand, "you can boss us both around to your heart's content."

Their fingers interlaced, palm to palm, and for some reason, the simple hold made tears spring to Lilah's eyes. It had to be the lingering effects of an emotional day, she reasoned, trying to get her mental engine to turn over.

Clearing her throat, Lilah disentangled her fingers. "That, Mr. Sparks, is an offer I can't refuse. But just so we're clear. I am not Jane Eyre. And you're for darn sure not Mr. Rochester."

His lips quirked. "I'm not sure I follow."

"I'm not going to fall in love with you," Lilah said baldly. "And there's not going to be any hanky panky, either. I'm there for Tucker's sake, not yours."

"Fair enough."

Lilah breathed out a sigh of relief, oddly tinged with disappointment she didn't want to analyze. "So you'll respect my wishes?"

"Oh, I respect you," Devon said, one corner of his mouth kicking up in a way that sent shivers cascading down Lilah's spine.

He leaned closer. His voice was pure, unadulterated wickedness breathed into her ear. "But just so we're clear? I have every intention of doing my damnedest to seduce you, charm you, and woo you until all you want is to be under me again. In the shower, in my bed, on my kitchen floor—I'm not through with you yet, Lilah Jane. And I don't think you're through with me, either. Not by a long shot."

They stared at each other for a long moment until a discreet knock at the restaurant's locked door startled Devon out of it.

"The car's here," he told her. "Can you get Tucker?"

Paolo opened the rear passenger door and came forward to help Lilah negotiate the sleeping child into the car while Devon locked the restaurant behind them.

Jingling the keys in his pocket, Devon stood on the restaurant steps, reluctant to turn around. What if he'd scared her off? What if he'd pushed too hard and she was even now handing Tucker over to Paolo and walking away?

Man up, Devon.

The surge of happiness and relief he felt when he turned to find her already situated in the car, his sleeping son's head in her lap, compelled Devon to confront the fact that he was already counting on Lilah's presence too much. And for too many reasons.

Yes, he wanted her, and while the scope of that desire was unexpected, the physical desire itself was familiar and unthreatening. Devon had wanted—and gotten—many women before Lilah, and he was sure there'd be many after her.

What troubled him as he approached the sleek, black car was the extent to which his heart warmed and swelled at the sight of Lilah Jane cradling Tucker's small body against hers.

They looked safe and happy together, a pretty picture by anyone's standards, and Devon almost couldn't bear to get in the car with them and spoil it.

His presence, he felt obscurely, would taint the picture somehow.

And that's when he realized that as much as Tucker might hate and fear his father, Devon was just as scared of his own kid.

CHAPTER FIFTEEN

The interior of the car smelled just as she remembered it from the night before, like leather and money. The backseat was roomier than it seemed like it should be for anything other than a minivan; there was room for Tucker to curl up next to Lilah and snuffle back into sleep.

Beside her, Devon radiated heat. Lilah tried not to squirm. His thigh wasn't actually touching hers, she knew. The bench seat was wide enough that there was ample room for everyone. Still, every hair on her body seemed to stand at attention.

Devon wanted her. For more than a single night. He wanted her enough to risk having her walk out on him and leave him alone with his son—an eventuality Devon was clearly keen to avoid.

Too keen.

Keeping her voice low and even, Lilah broke the silence gripping the car. "Not that I mind carrying Tucker, technically it's probably in the job description, but is there a reason you didn't want to? Because the way you keep him at arm's length is starting to make me feel like a wet hen. As in 'madder than a.'"

A muscle ticced in Devon's chiseled jaw. It was the only

sign he gave that he'd even heard her, and if she hadn't been watching for it she'd have missed it.

Lilah wondered if she were truly prepared to be fired twice in one night. A soft sigh from Tucker as the dead weight of his head put her leg to sleep helped make up her mind.

"I swear. If it weren't for the fact that I know deep down you want your son to stay with you, I'd have headed for the subway and taken Tucker to Grant's apartment, boss man."

Devon snorted at that. "Sure. My deep-down, carefully masked goodness—and the fact that you have no desire to be arrested for kidnapping."

There was that.

"Besides," Devon said, all scrumptious heat and temptation beside her, "I thought we agreed you were going to be the boss."

Lilah tossed her head, trying to get her curls to wisp some direction other than directly into her eyes. "Deflect all you want; I don't hear you denying you wanted Tucker with you. And if you were so desperate to avoid custody, you could've let the officer take him away. Or give him to your parents."

Devon lounged back in his seat, every muscle in his long, lean body apparently relaxed. But when he shot her a glance, it was full of shadows.

"My parents," he scoffed. "Shit. My loving parents have never even come to eat at one of my restaurants. They—well, my dad. He never wanted me to be a chef. The fact that I made a bigger success of my life than he ever did? That's just salt in the wound. And anyway, think of the scandal. Heather and I were never married. Trust me, my parents aren't going to be rushing to introduce their bastard grandson to the whole neighborhood."

"Keep your voice down," Lilah hissed, covering Tucker's ear with her hand. "That's an ugly thing to say. And he doesn't need to hear any more about how no one wants him."

Devon's jaw went to granite. "He's sleeping like a rock. If moving from the restaurant to the car didn't wake him up, nothing will."

"That's not the point and you know it." Lilah was having

a hard time expressing her outrage in a whisper. "What is wrong with you? He's a little boy, not an inconvenience."

"You think the reason I haven't been part of his life is that it's not convenient? Of course you do. What else would you think?"

The bitterness in Devon's voice took her aback. She studied him for a moment as the fog of her own emotions lifted slightly and allowed her to see how wrung out he looked. And beneath the exhaustion was a lurking pain she couldn't give a name to, quite, but its presence reminded her of the momentary flash she'd seen in his eyes when the officer gave Tucker into his keeping.

Making her voice soft was easier this time. "If that's not the reason, Devon, then why?"

He looked away from her, staring out the window. "It doesn't matter. Because I'm a heartless prick."

"That's not an answer."

"Well, it's all you're getting."

And with that, they lapsed into a tense silence.

She must've dozed off, because she was barely aware of the car pulling smoothly into the garage, or Paolo coming around to unbuckle and lift Tucker free of the vehicle. Yawning, cold without that warm weight snuggling against her, Lilah struggled with her own seat belt until a pair of large, fine-boned hands brushed her fumbling fingers aside and deftly released the catch.

Blinking blearily up, Lilah saw Devon's hand held out, palm up, to help her from the car. She placed her hand in his, shivering minutely at the feel of his hard, callused palm, and let him draw her to her feet.

It was surreal to be back in this fairy-tale apartment building. Their odd procession of child-laden chauffeur, yawning nanny, and grimly reluctant father didn't turn any heads, but Lilah couldn't help comparing it to her first trip through the marble lobby and up to Devon's penthouse.

He unlocked the door while Lilah suppressed another yawn, this one strong enough to bring tears to her eyes. The driver preceded them into the apartment and carried the still-sleeping Tucker away without a word to Devon. Lilah stepped inside just in time to see them disappearing down a side hallway.

"He knows where to put Tucker?" she asked.

To her surprise, a dull red flagged Devon's high cheek-bones. "There's only one guest room that's suitable for a child," he said gruffly.

Heart warming strangely, Lilah laid a hand on Devon's tense arm. "You kept a room in your home for Tucker, even though you didn't have custody or get to see him."

Devon scowled. "It was smart business. Sometimes my producer or my agent likes to fly in from L.A. for a visit. They might bring their kids. It made sense to have someplace to put them."

"Sure," Lilah said, letting him get away with it. For now. But she smiled to herself, relieved to have another indication that her instincts had been right. She was willing to bet no producer's kid had ever stayed in the room Tucker was now sleeping in.

As if aware that she was humoring him, Devon set his mouth in a firm line and made a curt after-you gesture down the hall. Trying not to smirk and managing to yawn instead, Lilah went.

They passed several closed doors—the place was even more enormous than she'd realized the night before, distracted as she'd been—before Devon pushed one open and ushered Lilah into a pretty wood-paneled room filled with sleek modern furniture. The bed against the left wall was low and wide, set under a creamy tufted suede headboard.

"The bathroom is fully stocked; anything you need should be in there."

Lilah went where Devon pointed and found a white mar-bled bathroom with gorgeous antique mirrors on the walls and a deep tub with jets.

It wasn't quite as breathtaking as the master bath with Devon's beautiful mosaic shower, but it was still more luxu-rious than anyplace Lilah'd ever lived. And it was hers for the next four weeks.

She blinked at herself in the mirror. Yep, still plain Lilah Jane staring back at her, kinky curls, freaky green eyes, too-small mouth and all.

"Did you find the toothbrushes?"

Lilah looked blankly at the smooth mirror. It didn't appear to be a medicine cabinet, but there were no obvious cabinets or drawers, only a freestanding pedestal sink with a gracefully curved bowl.

A tanned, corded forearm dusted with mahogany hair moved past her face. Devon tapped his closed fist against the corner of the mirror and it swung forward on silent hinges revealing five shelves stocked with assorted jars and bottles.

Lilah reached in and snagged a toothbrush still wrapped in plastic.

"My, my. What a well prepared host you are."

Devon arched a brow and she met his eyes in their reflection in the mirror. "I want my guests to feel comfortable," he said.

"I guess I should be glad you're such a popular guy," Lilah said, trying to smile. It was only hard because she was so tired. "Did any of your guests leave a nightie, by chance?"

Devon's mouth quirked. "I might be able to rustle something up," he drawled.

"Thanks," Lilah said, and started working at picking apart the plastic encasing her toothbrush. After a moment, Devon left her, presumably to rifle through a pile of discarded thongs and teddies left here by his multitude of lady friends to find something Lilah could wear to bed. Maybe she should've been more specific about what she looked for in a nightgown.

Lilah went through the motions of her normal evening routine, getting jarred out of it from time to time by the extraordinarily shmancy soap, or *facial cleanser*, as it said on the box, and by the tiny tub of lotion—*crème luxe moisturizer*—which felt like pure silk on her skin.

She stared at herself in the mirror. What in the world was she doing here?

A soft knock at the bathroom door startled her. She

cracked it open to find Devon with some blue cloth draped over his outstretched hand.

"This should fit you," he said.

Lilah took it, almost surprised that the material felt like plain cotton rather than the racy satin or lace she'd half expected.

"Thank you," she said. There was an awkward pause where Devon didn't leave and Lilah didn't start changing into the nightie and neither one of them said anything.

The moment had a very odd feel, as if Lilah hadn't ever woken up from her nap in the car. As if she were caught in a dream.

Which must have been why, when Devon took a step toward her and bent his head to hers, Lilah didn't push him away but wrapped her hands around his strong shoulders and dragged him closer.

The heat that had been simmering in her belly since—well, practically since the night before—exploded into a fiery maelstrom that swept Lilah up and into Devon's arms.

His chest was solid and hard against hers, a wall of shifting muscle that made her want to rub herself against him like a cat. Devon's hands speared into her hair, fingers molding to her head and holding her for his mouth. Lilah couldn't help it.

She absolutely melted.

Never would've thought I was this kind of girl, she thought dazedly. The thought brought her up short.

Oh, wait. I'm not.

Lilah pressed her palms to Devon's chest and pushed until she could reclaim her mouth. Dragging in air like she'd been underwater for three minutes, Lilah gasped out, "Hold your horses, there."

Devon flexed his hands in her hair, sending prickles of sensation racing down her spine. "What's the matter, Lilah Jane?"

Ignoring the warmth that spread through her at the soft way he said her name, Lilah shuddered and pulled away. Her smile felt shaky, but it was there. "Come on now. You didn't think it was going to be that easy, did you?"

Huffing out a laugh, Devon said, "Looking back at today, I guess I should've known better. It's not like anything has turned out the way I thought it would since I met you."

Lilah leaned on the sink to hide the fact that she felt like a newborn colt trying to stand for the first time. "Unpredictable. I can live with that."

"More like 'harbinger of chaos,'" Devon corrected her. "Jesus."

"A little bit of chaos would do you good. And don't take the Lord's name in vain."

Devon pressed his hands together as if he were praying, but the look in his deep blue eyes was all sin. He grinned and bowed once, quickly.

"Yes, boss."

CHAPTER SIXTEEN

Devon wandered out to his living room. He didn't bother turning on any lights; the darkness suited his mood.

Everyone else in his odd new household was still in bed, tucked up and cozy, but despite the exhaustion weighting his bones, Devon's sleep had been restive at best. And now here he was, up at the ass crack of dawn, wondering if there was anything on TV at this godforsaken hour.

He was slouched into the buttery leather comfort of his ultra-modern couch, flipping through channels, when an unsettling feeling of not-aloneness crawled up the back of his neck.

Whipping to the side, Devon threw out the arm holding the remote and accidentally lost his grip on the thing. The all-in-one contraption that controlled every piece of state-of-the-art electronics in his apartment, from lighting to stereo to the enormous flat-panel television, flew from his hand and smacked against the opposite wall. Plastic snapped, batteries bounced in all directions, and Devon squeezed his eyes shut and said, "Well, shit."

And then he grinned, wondering if his pretty little nanny was about to scold him for naughty language again. Why that was such a turn-on, Devon would never understand.

Except when he squinted one eye open, it wasn't Lilah standing behind the couch, but Tucker.

The kid was sleepy-eyed and rumpled, hair smashed flat against his skull in a way that made one tuft poke straight out of the middle of his head. One small hand curled in a death grip around the ratty straps of the backpack he'd brought with him.

He didn't look fazed by Devon's language.

"What are you doing up?" Devon asked, working embarrassingly hard to keep his voice normal.

Tucker shrugged.

"You want to go back to bed?"

Tucker shook his head.

"Lilah's still asleep," Devon said, feeling helpless and hating it. Inspiration struck. "Do you want to go wake her up?"

Tucker shook his head again.

Devon was running out of options. Stalling for time, he hauled himself off the couch and went to gather the pieces of the remote control. Luckily for him, the thing seemed to be basically fine.

Snapping the batteries back into place, Devon scrolled through a few channels to make sure everything was working properly. All the while, he was hyper-conscious of the boy standing behind him.

Why was this so fucking awkward? Tucker was only a kid, but Devon was as nervous under his silent regard as he'd been when the *New York Times* critic was at Appetite.

All that comforted Devon was that Tucker seemed at least as jumpy, if not more, judging by the way the kid startled when Devon moved to sit back down on the couch. Maybe they were both feeling their way a little bit.

Casting a surreptitious sideways glance at Tucker, Devon said, "You want to watch TV with me? I could maybe find some cartoons. They still run on Saturday mornings, right?"

Tucker didn't answer in words; instead, he shuffled forward and perched on the other end of the couch from Devon. Who tried not to move too much or too quickly, as if Tucker were a deer at a watering hole, easily startled into bounding away.

It was only because Devon was so attuned to his son's every movement and expression that he noticed the flicker of interest when the screen scrolled past the Cooking Channel. Focusing back on the television, Devon winced. It was his show.

He paused in his channel surfing and glanced over at Tucker, who had settled deeper into the sofa cushions and appeared rapt.

"Do you really want to watch this?" Devon asked, incredulous.

Tucker didn't glance away from the opening credits. "Yeah, I like it."

Devon ground his molars and forced himself to look back at the screen. He despised watching himself. His idea of hell was to be strapped into a chair with his eyes taped open, à la *Clockwork Orange*, with *One-Night Stand* playing on an endless, soul-crushing loop.

They watched in silence for several minutes. Devon remembered this episode. It was from a few seasons back. His challenge had been to take charge of the kitchen at the Waldorf-Astoria Hotel during a wedding reception. Two hundred and fifty drunken guests in the Starlight Roof ballroom, half wanting steak tournedos, half wanting grilled salmon, all demanding perfection. They'd gotten a great promo for it, as Devon recalled, using teasers playing up the bride going toe-to-toe with Devon over the prosciutto and melon canapés.

Four million viewers had tuned in to see a tiny woman in a huge white confection of a dress begin her married life by exchanging curses with Devon Sparks. The actual screaming argument had been real; Bridezilla had stamped her little foot and tried to ram through the plebian, unimaginative ham-wrapped melon balls, but she'd thanked Devon later when the smoked duck breast and cherry chutney on chèvre wafers he sent up instead were a huge hit.

What the cameras didn't catch was the even uglier bout of tears and recriminations near the end of the reception, when the bride, after too many champagne toasts, had cornered Devon in the kitchen and attempted to seduce him. It was astonishing how many of his shoots for the show ended that way. That, plus the evidence of his own childhood observations, was almost enough to make Devon think that all women were turned on by being publicly berated.

All women except for Lilah, he amended with a private smile. His new nanny was more turned on by promises of obedience and gifts of plain pajamas than on-air shouting matches. Not enough to succumb on the very first night of their new arrangement—but he admitted to himself he would've been a little surprised if she had.

Devon didn't know when he'd ever found himself quite so fascinated by a woman. A glance at Tucker reminded him of the last time, and he sobered. Heather Sorensen was Devon's personal cautionary tale—*How Not to Get Your Heart Butterflied and Roasted*. Heather had taught him the dangers of getting in deep without really knowing each other.

Thinking of the soft slide of Lilah's mouth under his, the clean, lemon-thyme scent of her skin, Devon decided that the situation with Lilah was entirely different. He already knew they were compatible in bed. Well, in the shower. He grinned to himself.

She worked for him, sure, but it was only temporary. In a month, she'd be out of his life and things could go back to normal.

He wondered why the prospect turned his smile upside down.

"Take your troubles to bed with you and when you wake up they'll seem lighter." Lilah could hear Aunt Bertie singsonging it as clearly as if she were perched on the slick cream damask bedspread.

The phrase had always seemed like cold comfort at night when Lilah was fretting too hard over some teenage drama to get to sleep, but invariably the morning brought renewed proof that Aunt Bertie was one wise lady. This morning was no exception; Lilah had gone to sleep the night before with her mouth still tingling and swollen from Devon's lethal kisses, her blood still thick and warm in her veins, throbbing with frustrated desire and nervous excitement. That pulse-pounding thrill was balanced against the nightwear Devon had brought her last night. Tossing back the covers, Lilah looked down at herself.

Far from the tacky ribbon-and-lace confection she'd been dreading, her body was swathed in a pair of blue cotton pj's straight out of Devon's own closet. The cotton had the thin softness that only came from repeated wear. The drawstring pants were tight around her hips and too big everywhere else, making her picture them draping Devon's lean waist and long legs. There was something warm and comforting about wearing clothes that belonged to him.

The issue was clear: Devon Sparks was entirely too dangerous to Lilah's peace of mind.

Which wasn't necessarily a bad thing. She'd had oodles of peace and quiet back home, and she'd gotten good and sick of it.

She swung her legs out of bed and made her way to the sumptuous bathroom to brush her teeth. Even the toothbrush Devon provided for his guests was fancier than the plain one Lilah used, which her dentist had given her for free after her last visit.

As she scrubbed away, Lilah thought about Devon. And Tucker. And the fact that for the next month, her life was inextricably intertwined with theirs.

It wasn't exactly what she'd come to New York City looking for, she reflected. Trading her own family obligations for duties with a new family. And yet, something about this dysfunctional pair called to her.

The next month wouldn't have an excess of peace and quiet, that was for sure.

Lilah debated for all of ten seconds over whether or not to put her clothes from last night back on again. The forest-green shirt and black pants hadn't been her favorite thing when she first got them, and after wiping up multiple spills, picking up countless dirty dishes, and dropping several trays,

Lilah figured the outfit might ought to be thrown out back on the burn pile.

Satisfied with her rationale for wearing the pajamas a little longer, Lilah combed her fingers carelessly through her hair, snagging on the riotous curls, and twisted it into a knot on top of her head. She retrieved her bra from the tangle of clothes and shrugged into it. Comfort was one thing, decency was quite another. Lilah didn't have the kind of breasts that could go discreetly unsupported. The girls needed hoisting.

Lilah found her new employer and her new charge ensconced on the black leather Bachelor Special in the spacious living room. Their similar features, one face a miniature of the other, were bathed in the flickering blue glow from the television. Devon's voice, unmistakable, if tinny, drew Lilah's attention to the screen.

They were watching Devon's show, she noticed with amusement. At the moment, Onscreen Devon was shouting, red-faced and angry, at a cringing subordinate. Through the bleeped-out curse words, Lilah caught something about the salmon being raw in the middle.

"Morning, boys," Lilah said, making them both jump.

Tucker gifted her with a quick smile before turning back to the show, but Devon stood up and rounded the back of the couch to greet her.

"Good morning, beautiful," he said easily, his eyes drifting down her body. "There's something unbearably sexy about a woman in men's pajamas."

Lilah plucked at the fabric where it pulled taut at her hips and tried not to color up. "Thanks. I'm going to head down to Grant's apartment today and get the rest of my things, so you can have these back tonight."

"I've got at least twenty pairs of pajamas," Devon said, waving a dismissive hand. "Those look better on you than they ever did on me. Keep them."

"So that's the show?" Lilah said, gesturing at the television where Onscreen Devon was in a towering rage, throwing his dish towel at the wall, every third word covered by a high-pitched beep.

"That's the show that made me famous," Devon agreed, his tone sardonic. "For what it's worth."

"Lordy," Lilah said, drawn in despite herself. "It's too early in the morning for that much hollering and carrying on. Unless you made coffee?"

She clasped her hands and turned pleading eyes on Devon, who laughed.

"I did. I couldn't find all the parts to the espresso machine, but I scavenged a French press from one of my cabinets."

Lilah laughed. "A French press? Sounds like a medieval torture device. And what do you mean you can't find all of your coffee maker?"

Devon arched a brow at her. "I'm far too busy and important to make my own coffee on a daily basis. On weekdays, my assistant takes care of it. And on the weekends . . ." His voice trailed off and to Lilah's surprise, Devon's cheeks went a dull brick red. He flicked a glance at Tucker, who had dragged a tattered spiral-bound notebook from his backpack and started drawing during a commercial break.

And Lilah got it. The fully stocked guest suite was a clue. Women. Every weekend. And if his behavior with Lilah that first night was any indicator of his MO, it was a different woman every week.

She was just one of many.

Stomach twisting and dropping to her knees, she said, "On the weekends you usually have company." The kind of company who never got familiar enough with the kitchen to know where things were put away.

"Right," Devon said, sounding relieved. "Company."

Lilah was so completely out of her league here.

"I'll go pour myself a cup," she said brightly. "Can I get you anything while I'm in the kitchen?"

"Lilah," Devon said, his voice urgent.

"Nothing? Okay, then, back in a sec. Is the kitchen through there? Right, no problem, I'm sure I can find everything just fine. No need to trouble yourself." She was babbling. She needed to get a minute alone before she made a complete and utter fool of herself.

Lilah hurried through the doorway Devon had indicated and found herself in the most beautiful kitchen she'd ever seen outside of a magazine.

The countertops gleamed with polished black stone flecked with glints of copper and antique gold, providing high contrast to the beautiful red wood of the cabinets. Lilah had to do a double take to pick out the fridge; it was also covered in that same red wood, seamlessly integrated into the expanse of cabinetry.

The counter on the far side of the large room butted up on a small corner nook set up like a restaurant booth with benches on either side of a rectangular table. Immediately, Lilah flashed on an image of the three of them sitting companionably around the breakfast table, laughing and sharing the paper. Devon would take the Style section, Lilah would pore over the theater reviews, and Tucker would be giggling over the funnies.

She blinked to clear her vision. *Quit it,* she ordered herself. *You're acting like a love-struck idiot, painting pretty pictures of domestic bliss with a man who can barely even speak to his own son, and who has more lovers in a month than you've had your whole adult life.*

Beyond ridiculous, to imagine one month as a nanny with a crush could turn into a real family. Especially when Devon was clearly more comfortable with relationships that lasted no longer than a few days. Or hours.

All the same, it was a beguiling image, and Lilah had a hard time eradicating it completely even after she turned her back on the breakfast nook to find the coffee. She located it in a glass container that looked like a tall, slender pitcher on silver legs. Devon had left out a ceramic mug, Lilah saw. She could only assume it was for her, and the gesture warmed her. The mug was gray and green, with graceful abstract lines etched into the sides and a sweetly round belly. Lilah poured a cup and wrapped her cold hands around it, stealing as much warmth for herself as she could.

It was stupid to be upset. Stupid to feel blindsided. Devon was an almost unbearably attractive man with enough charisma to charm the spots off a leopard, as Lilah knew from delicious firsthand experience.

As if that weren't enough, he also had piles of money and a big hit television show. And Lilah knew he wasn't the kind of man to nobly and chastely refuse to take advantage of his fame.

Which, perversely, was something she liked about him. Lilah appreciated the fact that Devon was honest about his vices and habits. Back home in Spotswood County, there were a couple of men with their own small-potatoes version of local power and influence who threw their weight around all over the place, meanwhile pretending to a pious humility that set Lilah's teeth on edge. She much preferred Devon's unabashed sensuality and the glee he seemed to take in the trappings of his decadent lifestyle.

Forcefully suppressing memories of her own brief revelry in Devon's sensuality and decadence, Lilah carried her coffee back into the living room where Devon had resumed his seat on the couch. Her two boys were as far apart as they could be and still be on the same piece of furniture, Lilah saw with a stab of sorrow.

She noted the way Tucker dropped his drawing the instant *One-Night Stand* came back on. The way he stared at his father on the television screen, his eyes wide and unblinking, attention caught and held by a show no other ten-year-old on the planet would probably care about. And she caught the frequent glances Devon sent his son's way, full of confused yearning.

Lilah shook her head. They wanted to connect, she was sure of it. They just didn't seem to know how.

And in a flash, Lilah understood why she'd been so uncontrollably called to inject herself into the discussion about Tucker's custody. Beyond the fact that she couldn't bear to see the child shuffled off into the system when he had a father, alive and well and able to care for him standing right there, Lilah saw now that Fate had put her in the kitchen at Market that night for a very specific purpose—to help heal the broken relationship between father and son.

Everything in her longed to see a happy smile on Tucker's face when he looked at his dad; to be a part of the moment when Devon finally began to embrace fatherhood and his place in Tucker's life.

Lilah took a bracing sip of coffee and started hatching plans.

CHAPTER SEVENTEEN

Tucker slumped over his empty plate at the breakfast nook, kicking one heel aggravatingly against the table leg.

Lilah fought the urge to tell him to be still. He was such a quiet boy, any way he opted to make himself heard probably ought to be encouraged. And the noise was only getting to her because she was unreasonably and stupidly nervous.

She and Devon and Tucker were about to have breakfast together.

A small, insignificant thing, by anyone's standards, and yet Lilah hoped it would have far-reaching consequences. It was the first step toward making that vision she'd had earlier a reality.

Well, at least the part of it where Devon and Tucker were happy together, she amended hastily. Lilah wasn't sure she was ready to contemplate her role in that picture just yet, beyond being the wise fairy godmother–type who made it all happen.

Devon moved confidently around the kitchen, pulling ingredients and setting up his workspace. There was plenty of room for two to cook; it was nothing like the cramped little galley in Grant's Chelsea apartment. In Grant's kitchen, you couldn't stand side by side with another person and whip cream without knocking elbows.

But even with the extra space and scope of Devon's kitchen, Lilah was still having trouble concentrating on anything other than Devon's proximity. And surely he could walk past her without brushing against her! Every glancing touch made her suck in a breath, her skin thrilling to it like his fingers were charged with static electricity.

Devon was watching her, eyes hotter than a summer sky, as if he knew exactly what she was contemplating.

Giving her shoulders a quick shake, Lilah pinched her lips at Devon in what her students referred to as her "Mean Librarian" expression. Amusement crinkled the corners of his eyes and gave a sardonic tilt to his perfect mouth.

Lilah ignored him in favor of addressing Tucker. "What does your mom usually make you for breakfast, Tuck?"

Tucker stopped kicking the table. "She doesn't really make breakfast that often."

There was something off about the way he said it. Lilah frowned over at Devon, who shrugged. "Heather's not much of a cook," he said coolly.

"What about cereal? What's your favorite cereal, Tuck?" Lilah said.

Tucker made a face. "I *hate* cereal."

"All kinds?" Lilah questioned, surprised. "Even those sugary ones full of marshmallows?"

Tucker looked uncomfortable, as if he wished he could rewind the conversation and keep his cereal woes to himself.

"I guess those are okay," he said. "I get tired of them, though."

"Shoot," Lilah laughed. "My cousins used to love that stuff so much, my Aunt Bertie once wrapped up boxes of Lucky Charms and put them under the Christmas tree! I didn't know any kids got tired of eating candy for breakfast."

"I don't mind it for breakfast, but I get sick of it when we have it for lunch and dinner, too."

Now Devon was frowning, his hands slowing in their prep work.

"What other things does your mom cook for you?" he asked, his voice rough.

Tucker went back to kicking the table leg. "I don't know. Stuff. Bagels. I like the ones with sesame seeds. And I'm not a baby, I know how to order delivery. We get Chinese a lot. The guy, when I call? Mr. Han? He knows what I want just from the sound of my voice. He can tell, like magic, or like he's psychic or something."

It was the most Tucker had said at one time since he arrived in the kitchen at Market, which Lilah wanted to be happy about. But what he was saying was breaking her heart.

She exchanged another glance with Devon, whose hands were white-knuckled around the handle of the skillet he was putting on the stovetop. He was reading between the lines, too, Lilah knew, putting together Heather Sorensen's DWI with Tucker's tale of subsisting on no-cook meals and delivery while she was no doubt too intoxicated to take care of dinner herself.

Lilah wanted to cry. She wanted to march down to Heather's rehab center and read the woman the riot act. Most of all, Lilah wanted to demand how Devon could allow his son to stay in a situation like that—but it wasn't her place, she reminded herself. She didn't know the whole story.

And judging by Devon's teeth-gritting silence, there was definitely part of the story she was missing.

Trying to smooth over the rough moment, Lilah said, "Well, now that you're with your dad, the famous chef, you can bet you're gonna get some yummy meals. Are you hungry?"

Tucker nodded, which seemed to release Devon from his paralysis, because he started cracking eggs into the cold pan. The eggs were much smaller than Lilah was used to back on the farm.

"Go ahead and sit down," Devon told her. "I've got this."

Lilah took a last look at the weirdly tiny eggs and joined Tucker in the breakfast nook. Within minutes, Devon was setting full plates in front of them.

Lilah and Tucker stared down at the food, then looked at each other. It looked like loose yellow curds with sour cream and some kind of orange relish.

"What is it?" Lilah dared to ask.

"Scrambled quail eggs with crème fraîche and salmon roe," Devon said. Rather than sitting down with them, he tossed his dirty pans and utensils into the sink and started washing up.

"Aren't you going to eat with us? I promise to help clean up after," Lilah said.

"A good cook cleans his own station," Devon said with a quick smile. "Anyway, I don't eat breakfast. You two dig in, though."

Tucker dipped a wary spoon into the eggs and lifted it to his mouth. His eyes bulged a little, and he appeared to swallow with difficulty. They both snuck guilty peeks at Devon over by the sink, who hadn't noticed the byplay.

Tucker cut his eyes up at Lilah. There was a plea in them that let her know she didn't need to taste it.

"Sounds delish," she said brightly. "But maybe a little too rich for my tummy this early in the morning."

Devon frowned and wiped his hands. "I could make you something else. I've been on a Japanese kick lately; I think my assistant stocked me up with some umeboshi plums and nori to experiment with."

Tucker and Lilah exchanged a bemused look. Apparently picking up on the extreme lack of reaction, Devon explained, "Small pickled plums and seasoned dried seaweed. Part of a traditional Japanese breakfast."

There was a pause while Lilah and Tucker considered this. Lilah broke it by asking, "You know what? Do you have any flour?"

Devon blinked. "I think so."

"Baking powder? Salt? Buttermilk? Never mind, don't worry, I can find it. Why don't you have a seat and visit with Tucker?"

She started bustling purposefully around the kitchen, keeping a weather eye on Devon's face. Lilah hadn't had a lot of truck with professional chefs, but she knew all about the politics and potential drama involved with cooking in someone else's kitchen. Hopefully Devon wasn't too territorial.

Evidently not, because he watched her in silence for a minute before saying, "Help yourself. But I've got to go shower before I head over to the restaurant."

"This early?" Lilah asked, sniffing a gleaming, stainless-steel canister of white powder. Did all-purpose flour smell different from self-rising? Why was nothing labeled?

"There's always work to be done," Devon replied. "The prep cooks are probably arriving at the restaurant now, starting work on the stocks for the sauces. Deliveries come in from vendors all morning, from fresh fish to specialty items like foie gras. Adam," he snorted, "likes to pretend he's saving the world, one menu special at a time. He only orders from within a hundred-mile radius of Manhattan. Reducing his carbon footprint or some similar nonsense."

"Yeah, I think Grant mentioned something about that. Market's all about promoting local, sustainable food and cooking with seasonal ingredients. I grew up on a farm, so all that sounds kind of 'duh' to me. You don't think it makes sense?"

Devon leaned one hip indolently against the counter. "I don't think it's a smart way to run a restaurant," he clarified. "This is New York, not California. The growing season here is fairly limited. From October to April, the Union Square greenmarket Adam is so fond of doesn't offer much in the way of fresh produce beyond root vegetables."

He shrugged, drawing Lilah's eye to his lean chest and broad shoulders under the fitted black T-shirt he was wearing. "Call me crazy, but if I want to do a passion fruit dessert in January, I'm going to fly a shipment in from Brazil and not think twice about it."

To Lilah, it sounded like a well-worn debate, an argument Devon had trotted out for his friend, Adam, many times. She wondered how much of it Devon really believed in and how much was a put-on part of his famous bastard persona.

Then again, maybe it was naïve to continue on in this dogged assumption that there was more to Devon Sparks than the jaded, arrogant mask he presented to the world.

"Back home in Spotswood County, we cooked with seasonal, local ingredients because that's all we had," she said.

"And I won't say there was never a day when I wished for a big supermarket in town that would carry exotic fruits and cheeses and things I've probably never even heard of, but there was something wonderful about following the rhythm of the seasons. You could tell the date by what was on my Aunt Bertie's table: collards and kale braised with a ham hock in the winter, sweet baby turnips roasted with molasses in the spring. And nothing says summer like Silver Queen corn, barely boiled, dripping with butter and salt. You could look at any meal and know your place in the world, where you came from and where you were going." Even Lilah was surprised at the depth of longing that colored her voice.

"But that wasn't enough for you," Devon said.

"What?" Lilah said, startled.

"You left the idyllic pastoral paradise and made your way to the big, bad city. There must've been a reason." He smiled, challenge clear in his eyes. "Love affair gone wrong?"

Lilah laughed. "That sounds awfully soap opera, as if I had a grand passion that blew up, leaving me nursing a broken heart."

Devon gave her a searing look, as if he'd noticed her distinct lack of actual denial, but all he said was, "Well, I already know you didn't come to New York because you had a fantastic new career lined up."

"My childhood dreams didn't center around clearing dirty dishes and filling water glasses," she agreed. "I was happy enough teaching drama at the local high school, while it lasted. If budget cuts hadn't gutted the arts program in our school system, I might still be there."

"That's probably my cue to tell you how sorry I am, but I haven't had enough coffee to be able to lie effectively," Devon said. "I'm glad you got canned. Worked out great for me."

He gave her a lazy smile that made Lilah grin back. "Don't be sorry for me. It's not like teaching was my childhood dream, either. I fell into it, because it was easy and seemed stable and secure. Which turned out to be a giant illusion." Just like every other so-called "safe" choice she'd ever made.

"Anyway," Lilah continued, "I don't think I've done so badly in the career department. I get to hang out with my new pal, Tucker, for the next month. That sounds like a pretty great job anyone would love to have!"

Tucker didn't say anything, but she thought he wanted to. Something perilously close to hope flickered across his sulky young face, and it made Lilah's throat tighten.

Lilah went to the hidden fridge to search for buttermilk. There wasn't any, but the fancy Greek yogurt would work as a substitute.

"What are you making, anyway?" Devon asked carelessly.

"Biscuits," Lilah said, starting to mix them up on autopilot. She'd made them so many times, she didn't need a recipe.

Devon smiled a smug sort of smile, as if his expectations had been fulfilled. Lilah didn't mind. He'd change his tune once he tasted them.

"I thought you were going to get in the shower," she said.

"Right." He pushed off the counter and gave her a cocky eyebrow arch. "I'll be back in a few to see how the biscuits turn out."

Fifteen minutes later, Devon wasn't back yet, but a quick peek in the oven revealed a cast-iron skillet—enameled, Lilah'd sniffed in disapproval, but that was the closest thing she could find to the ancient, well-seasoned skillet she'd learned to make biscuits in as a child younger than Tucker—full of small rounds of dough puffing and crisping to a pretty golden brown on top. They were about done, she decided, and hunted up a pair of oven mitts.

"These biscuits were my favorite when I was your age," she told Tucker, who maintained his stoic silence. She was hoping if she kept up a sort of running commentary, eventually something she said would engage him enough to get him to talk back.

"My Aunt Bertie used to make a batch every morning. With as many kids as we had in the house, they were always gone before lunch."

Tucker made a little motion, a jerk of his chin that made

Lilah wonder if he was about to jump in. She paused for a second, but when he stayed quiet, she went on.

"My cousin Trudy likes biscuits with homemade strawberry jam, and her oldest brother, Walt, likes them with peanut butter. I know! Walt's bonkers, he'd eat peanut butter on anything, he's plum crazy for it. My favorite way to have biscuits is with red-eye gravy, this really thin, salty sauce you make by boiling country ham with strong coffee. Sounds funny to you, I bet, that a kid would like something with coffee—yuck! But it's good, I promise you."

Tucker rolled his eyes and made a puking face. The retching noises were rendered with the authenticity only a ten-year-old boy could produce. Lilah grinned.

Lilah found a cupboard stacked with meticulously matched sage-green china. Piling a couple of steaming hot biscuits on the plate, she set it in front of Tucker, saying, "But if we don't have red-eye gravy—and I'm not sure there's such a thing as a good hunk of country ham anywhere in Manhattan—the best way to eat fresh, hot biscuits is with butter and a little dab of something sweet."

Praying the enormous walk-in pantry held something simple like molasses or maple syrup, Lilah crowed when she found a squat little jar of honey. It didn't look like any honey she'd ever seen before; rather than being tawny gold in color and syrupy in texture, this honey was a pale, pale yellow and looked thick enough to spread with a knife. It was labeled "Acacia Honey" from Hawaii, but Lilah was willing to bet it would top her biscuits like a dream.

She was right. Across from each other in the cozy breakfast nook, Lilah and Tucker slathered the warm, tender biscuits with creamery butter and the strange, thick honey. It had an almost grainy texture that was a delicious contrast to the crumbly biscuits and melting butter. Tucker hesitated before taking his first bite, possibly a little gun-shy after his first breakfast, but once he tried it, his eyes lit up. After a few moments of silent, dedicated eating, Tucker looked up at her, honey smearing his mouth and crumbs dotting his chin, and said, "This is good."

Lilah tried to contain her joy at his initiation of conversation in a single smile. "I'm glad you like it."

He nodded and went back to eating. Lilah attempted not to worry that it had been an aberration and that Tucker had already resumed his self-imposed vow of silence. Just when she was about to start gabbing again to fill the quiet air, he slid her a glance. She smiled encouragingly, and with a tentative voice, Tucker said, "You had a lot of cousins, huh?"

Lilah was in the middle of one of her best Walt stories, the one where he convinced the twins, Hannah and Keith, to climb to the very top of the magnolia tree behind the house, when Devon came back in.

Fresh from the shower, Devon was devastating. A close shave emphasized the sharp angles of his jaw, the slight cleft in his chin. His hair was wet and spiky, a casually tousled look that Lilah was sure took several minutes and a couple hundred dollars' worth of product to achieve. He was wearing casual clothes, suitable for a day sweating in a hot professional kitchen, but even swathed in loose black pants and a plain white T-shirt, there was no denying his masculine beauty.

Still, Lilah thought she might prefer him as he'd been early that morning—sleep-mussed hair and a pillow crease running down his stubbled cheek.

Even from a few feet away, he smelled like soap and the spice of his cologne. Lilah inhaled as deeply as she could without being obvious. She smiled up at him.

"I was just telling Tuck about my family back home," she said.

Devon smiled back, but the happy expression faded as he took in the plates in front of Tucker. The one he'd prepared was nearly untouched and had turned into a cold, congealed mess of runny yellow mush and neon-orange fish eggs. The other plate was nothing but crumbs, and Tucker was in the middle of dotting his fingertip around the plate and picking those crumbs up with his sticky, honey-covered digit. He froze guiltily when he realized Devon was watching him.

Devon, bless his heart, tried to laugh it off. "Slow down, kid, I bet Lilah will make you more biscuits if you ask nicely."

He picked up Tucker's other plate and took it to the sink. Lilah watched him scrape the food off it into the garbage disposal, feeling awful. Some father-son bonding experience this was turning out to be! Tucker wouldn't eat Devon's food, but scarfed down her biscuits like he'd been on starvation rations for weeks.

His thin shoulders were hunched again, and he was curled in on himself the way he'd been before she started drawing him out with stories about her cousins' wilder days.

"I think the salmon roe was maybe a bit adventurous for someone his age," Lilah said apologetically.

Devon added the scraped plate to the dishwasher with a clatter. "Doesn't matter," he said with that wide, fake smile she'd last seen on the television screen. "No big shocker, I suck at figuring out what would sound good to a kid. I'm just glad you were here to fix him something he'd eat."

"Do you want a biscuit?" Lilah asked, her heart squeezing tight.

He shook his head without looking at them. "I've got to get to the restaurant. See you later. Or not, if you're asleep when I get home. Let Paolo know if you want to go out, he'll drive you anywhere you need to go."

With that, Devon was out the door. Lilah didn't want to read defeat in the slope of his departing shoulders, but she couldn't help but wonder if the first step of Operation Fatherhood had done more harm than good.

Luckily, family breakfast was only the beginning.

CHAPTER EIGHTEEN

The Tosser was on a right tear this morning. Frankie watched as Devon hissed a few choice words to Milo that nearly had the tough young buck in tears.

Their absent and much-lamented boss, Adam Temple, knew how to skin a man with the sharp side of his tongue, no question, but there was an underlying sweetness of temper to the man that Devon Sparks absolutely lacked.

Frankie knew they were in the shit from the moment he arrived at Market, yawning and cursing the breaking dawn, to find Devon already there, hassling the jolly old geezer who delivered the whole ducklings from up the Hudson River Valley. It weren't the executive chef's bailiwick to check in produce deliveries—that was one of Frankie's despised sous-chef jobs—but there the Tosser was, waving a clipboard around and looking incensed.

Maybe the arse didn't think forty pound of duck breast would see them through the night's service; maybe he didn't like the cut of the poor delivery knob's trousers. Either way, he was making a right git of himself.

Frankie shook his head and went inside. After all, if the visiting exec chef wanted to check in deliveries, that was his lookout. Frankie was happy enough to ditch the chore.

He hung up his battered black denim jacket in the employee locker room and took the stairs to the kitchen two at a time.

Nodding to Violet, who was rolling out what looked like a nice pâte brisée at the pastry station, Frankie bounded over to his beloved wood-fired grill and ducked his head into the lowboy to check his prep. He had plenty of the hand-mixed spice rub for the rib-eye, but he needed to chop and blanch buckets of watercress to be tempuraed later and then plated beside. He also seemed to be low on chopped rosemary and mint.

Ticking off tasks in his mind, Frankie nearly didn't notice Grant doing his stress dance on the other side of the open pass into the dining room. Grant had been on a hair-trigger ever since Devon Sparks showed up. Not that Frankie was elated to be back under the Tosser's thumb, but Grant looked close to nervous collapse.

Frankie suppressed an eye roll. Grant was a good mate, and a better manager, but the man could whip himself into a strop faster than anyone Frankie knew. As it usually all came to nothing, Frankie debated whether or not to put his oar in, but a particularly vigorous hand-wring from Grant decided the issue.

"Oi there, Grant. What's the crack?"

Turning an aggrieved face on Frankie, Grant ground out, "That . . . that . . . overbearing, arrogant, unfeeling bastard of an executive chef hired a new bartender."

Frankie blinked. "Well. How sodding dare he? That's just not on."

"Oh, shut it," Grant said disgustedly. "I know I'm being ridiculous. It's more about who he hired." Grant blew out a sigh that ruffled the wheat-colored hair lying across his forehead. With his cornflower-blue eyes and clear-skinned good looks, Grant was the poster boy for clean living and personal responsibility. It was amazing he and Frankie were such good mates, when you came to think about it.

"Who'd he hire, then?" Frankie asked soothingly.

Everything about Grant's expression and tone conveyed deepest tragedy. "Christian Colby."

"Chris?" Frankie was surprised. "From Chapel?" The Lower East Side pub was a favored late-night hangout with their crew, partly due to the grotty appeal of its hardcore punk music scene, and partly due to Christian Colby's undeniably fantastic cocktails.

"Yes," cried Grant. "And the worst part is, I know he's going to be brilliant, and when Adam gets back he'll want him to stay on, and then . . ."

"What?" Bloody hell, but this was fascinating.

"Then," Grant intoned solemnly, "he'll always be around. Where I work. *Every day.*"

Frankie started to point out that Grant saw Chris nearly every day after work, when the whole crew staked out the bar at Chapel until the wee hours of the morning, but then he paused. More often than not, he realized, Grant went home instead of out, pleading exhaustion.

It was believable; after a hectic dinner service with a fully booked restaurant, they were all knackered. For Frankie and his fellow line cooks, that often manifested as being wired, too high on the adrenaline rush of finishing tickets and banging out a complete service to go straight home to bed.

Especially when that bed was empty.

Frankie sighed. Jess had started cutting back on his hours at Market and getting involved with summer classes and photography clubs and other school-related things. NYU started in a little over a month, and the closer it got, the more Frankie was uncomfortably aware of the incongruity between the way he lived his life, and the life unfolding in front of Jess.

This was only a problem when they were apart. When they were together, Frankie was generally too happy to bother much about the future. But when Jess was off with his college friends, being an upstanding young member of society somewhere out of Frankie's sight, well, that was when Frankie started to think.

Thinking was a pisser. He tried to avoid it as much as possible, but in the early morning hours before daylight filtered through the grime-coated skylight in his tiny one-room attic loft, jokingly called the Garret, Frankie couldn't help but wonder how much longer he'd have with Jess before the younger man sussed out that there were legions upon legions of better men than Frankie with whom to dally.

For instance, Wes Murphy, the kitchen's new extern who was about Jess's age, single, and charming. Wes and Jess had struck up an aggravatingly fast friendship.

When their schedules meshed and both Jess and Frankie worked the same night, more often than not, they hit Chapel afterward. Those nights, Jess spent half his time with Wes. Granted, Frankie was usually on stage with his punk band, Dreck, and Jess was in the audience being a right fanboy, but still. Wes was there beside him, close enough to touch.

"You're not even listening to me, are you?" Grant demanded, shocking Frankie back into the here and now.

"I am," Frankie lied. "You're on about Christian and why it's a bad thing to have a bloody fantastic bartender coming to work here."

Grant threw up his hands. "Never mind. I know you think I'm being stupid. Just . . . whatever. Forget about it, Frankie."

With that, he stalked off, still shaking his head. Frankie watched him go with that squirmy feeling in his gut that told him he could've handled that better. Ah, well, you can't win them all, as Frankie's da used to say.

Shrugging it off, Frankie pointed himself toward the kitchen, intending to take care of the rest of his *mise en place*. A happy voice calling his name stopped him.

"Frankie! Hey!"

Joy bloomed in his heart. "Jess! Didn't know you were on today," Frankie said, turning in time to catch the bundle of slender, long-limbed young man that barreled into his arms.

"I wasn't," Jess mumbled into Frankie's neck. "I switched with Kristen. Just felt like I hadn't seen you in forever. You're out when I get home, or I'm asleep already when you come in."

"It's been a bad run," Frankie agreed, letting his arms relearn the wondrous heft and weight of Jess's warm, wriggling body.

"I'm thinking about quitting the photography club," Jess admitted. "It takes up so much time."

Time I could be spending with you. Jess didn't say it, but Frankie heard it on the air as clear as a bell.

Pulling back gently, he said, "Might want to think twice about that, Bit. Making friends in your club, aren't you?"

Jess refused to be pushed away, nudging back into Frankie's arms with a contented sigh. "Sure, but they won't stop being my friends if I quit the club. We'll have classes together once the semester starts, probably have to do projects and stuff."

In other words, they'd only be postponing the inevitable.

"You're here now," Frankie said, taking the coward's way out and avoiding the conversation. "Want to come out back and keep me company while I have a smoke?"

Jess gave him a stern look. It was ridiculously adorable on his gorgeous young face, all narrowed blue eyes, sweet mouth, and floppy auburn hair.

"That depends. On what number cigarette this is for you."

Frankie groaned. "It's not gone ten in the morning. Can't the mothering wait till I've at least had a nice cuppa?"

"No. You promised you'd cut back. So how many are you up to?"

"Three," Frankie confessed grudgingly. "That's not so bad, is it?"

"At ten o'clock?" Jess looked highly skeptical.

"Fine, don't come," Frankie said. "Best go check in with Grant, anyroad. See if anything wants doing."

Unworthy of him, perhaps, but Jess was after him all the time about the smoking. Maybe dealing with a stroppy Grant would remind him that there were worse fates to befall a young server than standing by the loading dock watching a sous chef smoke a fag.

"Fine," Jess echoed, sticking out his tongue. "Hey, is Wes here? I want to say hi before I find Grant."

Frankie couldn't help the torrent of jealousy that sluiced through his veins at the mention of the younger, closer-to-Jess's-age chef, but he could damn well keep it from show-ing on his face.

"Don't know, Bit, may as well see. I'm off to worship the nicotine goddess."

Without waiting to see if Jess found his new best friend, Frankie headed for the great outdoors. Devon was still loitering in the alley, Frankie was surprised to see, though the duck deliveryman had long since scarpered.

"All right, there, boss?" he asked, feeling his way.

The man startled out of a deep reverie, seeming to come back to himself from far away. "Oh! Yes. Fine. I'm fine."

"You look it."

"Shut your cake-hole."

"Erudite. Is that the sort of talk that goes over well at your big la-di-dah parties and red carpet soirées?"

"If I didn't need you on the line today, you piece of shit, I'd . . ."

"What? Toss a few swear words at me? Get in line, Sonny Jim, you wouldn't be the first nor the last nor the best."

Without meaning to, Frankie had moved into Devon's personal space so they were standing toe-to-toe, breathing hard, neither one wanting to back down.

Devon eyed him with loathing, but when his shoulders slumped minutely, Frankie took it as his signal to relax against the brick wall and light up. Confrontation over. Winner? Unclear.

"Heard about Christian Colby," Frankie offered, pulling in a drag of sweet, dark smoke.

"And I suppose you want to give me shit about it," Devon said, tensing. "If you think you can do so much better with the hiring, you should've told Adam to leave you in charge."

"No shit here, mate," Frankie denied, alarmed. "Chris is the best. Adam's been trying to get him back into a restaurant for years, but he'd never leave Chapel. How'd you convince him?"

"Called in a favor," Devon said. "After the disaster that was yesterday's service, I figured we'd need every advantage we could muster going into tonight."

"So you brought in a ringer. I like it," Frankie said, flicking ash into a puddle at his feet.

"This is the way we came in last night," piped a voice from the entrance to the alleyway, near the street.

Frankie looked up to find Devon's attention riveted on the woman and child outlined against the brightening daylight at the alley's end.

Squinting, he could just make out a cloud of curly dark hair on the woman, who was clutching the hand of a small-ish boy. Bugger, must be Nanny Lilah with Devon's son.

"Are you sure?" came the sweet voice of Grant's child-hood friend. "Hello?" she called. "Is this the back entrance to Market?"

A swift glance at Devon confirmed that the man was still paralyzed from the hair down, so Frankie called back, "It is! Welcome back, Lolly!"

"Don't call me that!" she yelled, but she was laughing and pulling the boy by the hand toward them. "I've told you and told you, Frankie, I . . ." Lilah broke off when she realized Devon was standing there, staring at them.

An awkward silence fell. Frankie broke it by stubbing out his cigarette and folding himself down to the kid's level. It wasn't easy; Frankie was built like a giraffe, all awkward-ness and height, but he managed. "Have you come to mess about in a real restaurant kitchen, then? Good on you. If you want, I'll show you around, introduce you to the gang."

Frankie was asking the kid, but he shifted his eyes up to Devon and Lilah, who looked like they could use some seri-ous alone time.

Devon, interestingly, appeared to pass the question on to Lilah, who flushed and said, "We don't want to get in the way, but well, yes, okay, thanks, Frankie, if you don't mind."

"Not at all." Frankie pulled out his best gallantry before offering his hand to the kid. "My name's Frankie."

"Tucker," the kid said, almost too quiet to hear. Nothing much like his da, as far as Frankie could tell. Less of a shouter, anyway. They shook on it.

Frankie stood up and prepared to lead the way into the restaurant, but a small hand on his arm stopped him. He looked down into Lilah's serious green eyes.

"No knives," she said firmly. "No cussing, no fire, and no letting him out of your sight. I learned that one the hard way, right, Tuck?"

Surprisingly, the kid grinned. It was shy and a little gap-toothed, but there was a spark of mischief there just waiting to be fanned into flame. Frankie put on the most responsible, upstanding expression he could manage and nodded. "No worries. There'll be no cocking about, I promise."

Her eyes grew big as Frankie smirked and whisked the kid into the kitchen.

CHAPTER NINETEEN

Operation Fatherhood wasn't proceeding exactly according to plan. Lilah had hoped Devon would drop everything the moment he saw Tucker and, well, do what Frankie had done—offer to show him around the kitchen, interact with him, and generally bond and get to know each other.

Instead, Tucker was inside being corrupted in the good-Lord-only-knew what horrible ways by the crazy sous chef while Lilah was stuck out here in a dank, smelly alley, about to have to justify herself to her new employer.

"We picked up my clothes and things from Grant's apartment, but the stores aren't open yet to go shopping for Tuck's things, so I brought him by here to, you know, say hi."

"Hi," Devon said, staring down at her.

"Hi." Lilah waved back weakly.

"So. You thought you'd come hang out at the restaurant until the shops are open?"

Seizing on the excuse, Lilah said, "Yes! Only for a little while. I hope that's okay."

Devon looked at the door into the kitchen. "It's fine. Here, take this credit card for the shopping trip."

"Really? I was just going to keep receipts and have you pay me back later," Lilah said, uncomfortable with the shiny silver of the platinum card.

"I insist. This will make it easier for everyone. Buy him whatever he needs." Devon appeared to struggle for a moment, then added, "And if there's anything he seems to *want*, like a toy or a game or something . . ."

Lilah's heart swelled. Maybe Operation Fatherhood was on the right track after all. "I'll let him pick one toy, as a gift from you," she promised.

Rather than looking pleased, however, Devon scrubbed a weary hand across his face. "A gift. Well, at least it'll be familiar territory," he muttered.

"What?"

His jaw tightened convulsively as if he were surprised she'd heard. Still, he answered her. "Tucker's used to getting gifts from me. It's been our main form of communication since he was born."

Lilah was conscious of an immediate need to pry. "Oh?" she probed delicately.

"Haven't missed a birthday yet," Devon said with a derisive lip curl. "Think that qualifies me as a candidate for Father of the Year?"

"I think it's always a good thing to let those we love know we remember them on the anniversary of their birth."

Devon snorted. "Right. And dropping a couple of C-notes every March eighteenth makes up for never seeing or talking to the kid the rest of the year."

The bitterness in his tone stung like a shot of cayenne pepper in the eye. "I didn't say that."

"Christ, Lilah." He sounded angry, but she couldn't tell if his rage was directed at her, or himself, or someone else altogether. "What do you want from me?"

Lilah set her mouth in a stubborn line. "For you not to swear so much. That would be an excellent start. Beyond that . . . I guess I'd like to understand your situation a little better."

Devon appraised her coolly, arms crossed over his chest, making his biceps bulge intimidatingly. "My situation. You mean you want to know how I became famous and successful?"

"More like how you ended up bitter and alone."

The words dropped into the alley like rocks into a pond. Strung tighter than a fiddle string, Devon still managed to deliver a credible smirk.

"Ah, but that's easy. The answer to both questions is the same."

Lilah shook her head. "I don't understand."

A hard light glinted in his blue eyes, turning them steely. "You're ready to blame Heather, aren't you? Sweet Lilah Jane. If I told you Tucker's mother blackmailed me into signing my rights away, you'd believe me. If I tearfully confessed how she keeps me locked out of my son's life, never lets me speak to him or see him, you'd cry for me. But as happy as I'd be to paint Heather as the evil bitch here, and God knows the woman has her issues, it's just too tired and hackneyed a script. I mean, come on," Devon warmed to his theme, voice dripping with cold disdain. "Poor, misunderstood guy wants nothing more than to be a great daddy to his son, but vindictive, alcoholic mom won't allow it."

Bewildered, Lilah said, "So that's not what happened? Heather didn't cut you out?"

Devon laughed, a cutting noise that scraped over Lilah's nerves. "Shit, no. I *opted* out. You think I could've built a media empire including a hit TV show, five restaurants, and my own line of cookware if I'd been running around changing diapers and watching Little League games?"

Lilah felt like someone had snatched the piece of pavement she was standing on out from under her. Devon gave up his paternal rights to further his career?

Standing stock-still, Lilah puzzled it through. "Why on earth are you saying this?"

"Because it's true." Devon shook his head in mock amazement. "It figures. For once, I'm being ruthlessly honest with a woman and she doesn't even believe me."

Lilah narrowed her eyes. "I believe you believe it. What I'm trying to figure is if you really are the kind of person who's so self-involved you couldn't go to a funeral without wanting to be the corpse—or if maybe, just maybe, you're every bit as confused when it comes to your own motivations as everyone else on this complicated planet."

"That's cute, honey, but I haven't made an uncalculated move since I was Tucker's age. Fair warning." Devon shrugged.

Lilah snorted indelicately. Shoot, she'd really been hanging around these uncouth chefs too much. "Right. That's why every time Tucker even comes up in conversation, much less enters a room you happen to be in, you either hem and haw or downright freeze like a raccoon facing down the barrel of a shotgun."

Devon ground his teeth audibly. The way his jaw tightened made the chiseled planes of his face stand out stark and dangerous. "Look. I'm trying, for once, to be a stand-up guy, and give you all the facts before you start building up dream castles in the sky where I'm the handsome prince under a curse and you're the only maiden pure and brave enough to break it."

Ouch. That one hit too close to home. Feeling blood heat her cheeks, Lilah shot back, "It's a little hard to take you at your word when you're telling me you don't care about your own child. I've seen the way you look at him, Devon. You might be fooling yourself, but you're not fooling me."

Devon smiled. It was a nasty one. "Wow. Never underestimate the blinders on a do-gooder who happens to be hot for you, I guess."

A haze clouded Lilah's vision for a second—long enough for her to make a fist, bring her arm back, and land Devon a good one right on his beautiful, mocking mouth.

He doubled over, probably more in shock than pain.

"I might should've prefaced that with 'Them's fightin' words,'" Lilah panted. "But I think you got the message anyhow."

Wringing her sore hand, she turned on her heel and left him in the alley.

What the fuck just happened?

Devon blinked, shaking his head to clear it, and hissed when the motion made pain flare all up through his cheek.

Why did he needle her like that? And that line about never making an uncalculated move. Jesus. Sometimes things flew out of his mouth like verbal projectile vomit, his brain limping along half a pace behind going, "Wait, no! Aw, crap."

The truth was, he hated that her opinion mattered to him. He'd made an entire career out of never caring for anyone's opinion but his own—and one single day after meeting her, Devon had looked into her earnest green eyes and realized his essential self-worth was somehow tied to Lilah Jane Tunkle's assessment.

Fuck that, he'd thought with a rush of dread-fueled fury. He was bound to disappoint her eventually. And suddenly, he wanted it over with, wanted her to stop looking at him like he might be someone she could care about, because it was all going to turn to shit anyway.

So he'd told her the ugly truth. He didn't deserve to call himself Tucker's father. He never had.

And when that wasn't enough to set Lilah straight, he'd deliberately provoked her.

Devon touched his tongue gingerly to the tender spot on his lip and tasted copper.

"Holy celebrity death match, Batman, what happened to you?"

The low, twangy drawl came from the alley entrance. Devon squinted against the light to see Christian Colby, the new bartender, walking toward him.

"What is this, Grand Central Station?" Devon asked irritably. "Doesn't anyone use the front entrance anymore?"

Christian's mouth twisted in a parody of a smile. "I thought I'd avoid the front of the house as long as possible, thanks. And way to sidestep the issue, boss! Is it a secret who popped you one, or are we using the old 'I tripped over a vegetable crate and smacked my face on a drainpipe' defense?"

"Doesn't matter. Suffice it to say I had it coming. You ready to work tonight? I need you at your fine dining best. Remember, we're not at your crappy little dive bar. This is a real restaurant."

Christian didn't bridle at Devon's characterization of

Chapel as a dive bar. That was one of the reasons the two men got along so well: Devon dished it, and Christian took it. With a minimum of fuss.

Besides, there was no arguing the point—Chapel was a total dive. That just so happened to be what made it great. Chapel was one of the few places Devon could go and still feel like himself.

"I hope I'll be able to tell the difference," Christian responded mildly. "As I recall, there's less stage diving in a restaurant, correct?"

"Very little," Devon agreed, amused. "Come on. Man up. It's only for a few weeks."

"Only you would call me in as a favor and then tell me to 'man up.'" Chris shook his head. "I had to promise Noelle double tips for the month if she'd open Chapel every night and work the bar until I can get there after dinner service."

"And I appreciate it."

Christian still looked conflicted. Much as he sucked at playing counselor, Devon put a hand on his arm and said, "Hey, I don't know what you did to piss Grant Holloway off, and I don't care. Work it out. Or don't. I'm pretty sure you could take him in a fight."

Christian laughed, but there were lines of tension around his eyes when he glanced at the back door to the restaurant.

Devon knew exactly how he felt. Behind that door were a variety of people who were none too keen on Devon right about now: one resentful sous chef, one panicking maitre d', one kid unlucky enough to have been born to a shit heel like Devon, and one spitting-mad Southern belle with a hell of a right hook.

Man up, Devon repeated silently. Still tasting blood at the corner of his mouth, he strode up the stairs and into the kitchen, his reluctant bartender trailing behind.

CHAPTER TWENTY

The first thing Devon zeroed in on when he pushed open the door was his kid standing on a stepladder beside Frankie, hanging over the sous chef's shoulder to peer with evident fascination at several piles of fresh herbs.

While Devon watched, Frankie used the point of his knife to gesture from pile to pile, presumably naming each herb for Tucker. Devon imagined himself in Frankie's place, how he'd describe the flavors, then have Tucker close his eyes and open his mouth, see if he could identify rosemary, sage, mint, or tarragon by taste alone.

Considering the kid clammed up and/or flinched any time Devon came within two feet of him, that wasn't likely to happen. Ignoring the herb tutorial, Devon gestured to Christian to follow him into the main dining room so they could go over the layout of the bar. Walking down the line, Chris slapped palms with the chefs, most of whom he knew from late nights at Chapel. Devon noticed that Frankie gave Chris a significant eyebrow wriggle, but if Christian read anything into the unspoken communication, he didn't choose to share it.

Devon sighed. The undercurrents of tension around here were enough to make any normal guy want to blow his brains out. Sex! Gossip! Intrigue! Backbiting! Who was sleeping with whose ex-girlfriend but hadn't told her best friend who had a crush on the guy who was flirting with the waitress who put out to all the chefs who nailed anything that moved . . . Devon shook his head. Leave it at home, guys.

Of course, that was before he came face-to-face with his own little slice of drama, perfectly and gorgeously embodied by the lovely Miss Lilah Jane, who was sitting at the bar, showing off her swollen knuckles to Grant. The manager leaned over her fingers with a commiserating "Poor baby," and Devon's blood pressure skyrocketed into *One-Night Stand* levels of aggression. Like, seriously, season-two levels, including that episode when the producers had set him up in the galley of a cruise ship and he'd puked for ten days straight.

Watching the good-looking blond manager coo over Lilah's hand—a hand she'd bruised on Devon's fucking cheekbone, no less!—tightened every muscle Devon was aware of into granite.

Shit. Grant really was after Lilah Jane. Worse, he had the advantage of a long, warm friendship with her, rather than a sexy but anonymous fling. And of course, Grant was a good man, while Devon was . . . not.

Which didn't mean Devon was ready to give up and just hand Lilah over to him.

Lilah glanced over and met Devon's gaze. She stilled, alerting Grant to the two men standing in the doorway. The maitre d' dropped Lilah's hand and stammered something about getting an ice pack, but Lilah didn't even move. Her fine, delicate features never tensed as she twisted on her barstool to stare at Devon.

As if aware that Devon's internal boiling point was closing in, Christian clapped him on the back and ducked behind the bar, saying, "Let me help you with that ice pack, Grant."

"Oh, that's all right, I don't need any help . . ."

"Grant," Devon cut in. "Take Christian down to the basement and show him where we keep the cases of liquor."

Thus outmaneuvered, Grant shot a glance at Lilah, as if to confirm she'd be okay left alone on the other side of the bar with the mean, mean man.

Devon wanted to snarl that she'd be fine, but he held his

tongue through sheer force of will. Lilah gave Grant a reassuring smile that had Devon catching a rumbling growl in his chest before it could vocalize, and walked over to him.

"Yes, Mr. Sparks?"

She was all chilly formality. So that's how they were going to play it? Fine, he could work with that.

Working not to snap, Devon said, "I hope your hand is okay. Wouldn't want you to have cracked a bone or anything."

That brought a slight, pretty pink to her cheeks, although her green eyes never flinched.

"Thank you for your concern, but it's not necessary. I assure you, I'm perfectly all right." She swallowed, the click of her throat audible to Devon, who was paying such avid attention he'd swear he could count the flecks of gray in her irises. "And yourself?"

Sweet Lilah Jane. Couldn't keep a good mad on for longer than a few minutes. Devon wanted to smile but he forced his expression to remain grave. "I'm very well, thank you."

Lilah seemed thrown, as if she'd expected this encounter to go very differently. Probably she'd envisioned it with more yelling and throwing of barware. He was sort of amazed she'd chosen to sit near anything breakable, given his reputation.

"Good. That's . . . good," she said. "Um. Is the restaurant open for lunch service today?"

"Sunday brunch," he told her. "Boring. Nothing but eggs Benedict and smoked salmon as far as the eye can see. Don't worry, though, I've got some plans to spice up the menu a bit."

Out of the corner of his eye, Devon thought he saw Grant wince, but he paid it no mind. The man wasn't a chef; what the hell did he know about setting a menu?

"I guess Tucker and I should be going soon. Is there anything you want us to get done today?"

Devon paused. "Like . . . what? Homework?"

Lilah gave him a look. "Yes. Other than shopping for new clothes and a toy or two, how would you prefer your son spends his time?"

Crap. "Whatever you think is best."

There, that ought to do it.

Lilah sighed.

Evidently not.

"Devon." At least she wasn't still calling him *Mr. Sparks*. "Boys Tucker's age need structure. They need to know what their boundaries are so they feel safe and secure enough to test them out."

"Sounds good," he said, a little desperately. "Let's go with that."

"With what? You haven't given me any . . . okay. You know what? Don't worry about it. I'll work something out for today. But Devon, you and me, we are going to have to talk about this. He's your son, I know you care about him, and you are by God going to show it by setting some ground rules for him while he lives with you."

Lilah's eyes were flashing, her rosebud of a mouth furled in bossy disapproval. Devon wanted to bend her over the nearest flat surface and kiss her senseless. What the hell was happening to him?

In an attempt to gain control of the runaway situation, Devon said, "You're on. Let's talk about it tonight after dinner service."

Lilah relaxed out of full-on Amazon mode. "Really? That would be fantastic, if you won't be too tired when you get home."

"Oh, not at home," Devon said. "The whole crew is going out after dinner service. To Chapel." He looked at Christian, willing him to go along with it. "To show our appreciation for Christian here, taking time away from his bar to help out at Market."

"Right," said Chris, expression bland. "Your hooligan brigade plus my tiny bar equals good, clean fun all around."

Grant bristled. "That dump of yours wouldn't know good, clean fun if it were full of roller-skating nuns," he shot back.

"Your idea of fun and mine are obviously a little different," Christian drawled.

Lilah gave them an uncertain glance. Leaning closer, Devon distracted her from the bickering men by dropping his voice and saying, "I have to be there tonight; I'm sort of the unofficial host of the party, you might say. I'd like it if you'd meet me there. Around midnight?"

"That late?" Lilah's voice was faint. Devon wet his lower lip slowly, testing the waters, and nearly grinned when her gaze followed the glide of his tongue. "I mean . . . what about Tucker?"

"I'll call my assistant. Daniel can come over and babysit while you're out."

"Has Tucker ever met your assistant?" Lilah fretted. She appeared to be trying to come up with reasons not to meet him at Chapel. "I wouldn't want him to be freaked out by having a stranger show up."

"At midnight? Surely he'll be long asleep." Sensing her wavering, Devon couldn't help but push. "I'm not asking you out on a date, Lilah. I'm asking you there as your employer, to discuss matters pertaining to your job. This is when it's convenient for me. I want you to be there."

As expected, his high-handedness raised flags of color in her rounded cheeks. Lilah tilted her chin up. "Of course, Mr. Sparks. I wouldn't dream of disobeying my employer."

With a regal nod to the guys by the bar, Lilah turned on her heel. Just as she got to the kitchen door, Devon called, "See you at midnight, Cinderella. Don't be late."

CHAPTER TWENTY‑ONE

Lilah had never seen so many people wearing so very little. The dark, smoky interior of Chapel was packed with sweaty, thrashing bodies in various states of undress.

Surely Devon didn't intend to try and have a serious discussion here. And yet she realized that some of the half-naked bodies around her were attached to vaguely familiar faces, people she knew from Market. They all looked extremely different without their trim, tidy chef's whites.

Wild music pounded from a tiny, elevated stage in one corner of the room where a woman with bright orange hair and a sparkly nose ring was wailing into a microphone. Her band was arrayed behind her, and Lilah was surprised to recognize Frankie hunched over a bass guitar and rocking out to the beat. A small but energetic mosh pit seethed around the stage.

Lilah spotted Jess Wake, the server whose station she'd abandoned halfway through her one and only dinner service, sitting at a round table with a dark-haired man she thought she remembered from the Market kitchen. They were talking animatedly, and she wondered how they could hear each other through the din. As she watched, Jess's gaze wandered from his friend to linger on the band.

Searching the crowd for Devon, Lilah found Grant instead.

He'd found a seat well away from the speakers and was glaring morosely into a martini glass half full of disconcertingly blue liquid.

Relieved, Lilah pushed her way through the throng to get to him. "This is quite a scene," she yelled above the cacophony.

"Lolly!" Grant looked as happy to see her as she was to see him. "Have a seat, sweetie."

"I can't, I've got to find Devon. He asked me to come so we could talk about Tucker."

"Right." Grant was skeptical. "He wants to have a nice little chat at a hundred decibels. I hope you know what you're getting into."

Lilah prayed it was too dark to show the uncertainty she knew must be written all over her face. She had no idea what she was getting into, or where it was going, but she'd discovered herself helpless to stop it. "I expected more of a party atmosphere here," she said, changing the subject gracelessly. "Even considering how loud and crazy it is, no one looks particularly jubilant."

"We usually come to Chapel to blow off steam after a good service," Grant said. "When the night goes well, you're wired, pumped up with energy and adrenaline, so far beyond exhausted that sleep becomes impossible."

Lilah studied the intense looks on the faces around her. "And if the night goes badly?"

"You get this." Grant looked like he wanted to make a sweeping arm gesture, but was too bushed to manage it. "All the rowdy, none of the fun. They're taking out their frustrations and mistakes on the dance floor, our eardrums, and massive amounts of alcohol."

"So service didn't go well."

"It was a fiasco. Starting with Devon's refusal to serve anything resembling brunch food at brunch and carrying all the way through to his perversion of the regulars' menu favorites with flavored foams and weird sauce reductions. I'm telling you, Lilah, every third plate was sent back to the kitchen. The line was in chaos, every chef on it was practically in tears. Devon got more and more grim as the night went on, but he never backed down and let the guys start doing what the customers have come to expect from Market—simple food, done superlatively well. I mean, mercy, I know it's only the second night. But I'm not sure the restaurant can survive much more of this. I'm not sure *I* can survive it."

"Sounds like y'all took a good licking tonight," Lilah said, her heart beating too hard and fast in her chest. The disloyalty of it made her throat ache, but as badly as she felt for poor Grant, all Lilah really wanted to do was find Devon and see how he was doing.

About ready to keel over, she was willing to bet. And covering it with arrogance and cold indifference.

"And what made it worse," Grant moaned, "was that *he* was there. Through the whole thing, being all . . ."

"Wait, who?" Lilah was confused. "Devon?"

"No, him!" Grant jerked his head toward the bar. "Christian Colby."

The way he spat the name, malevolently caressing each syllable, gave Lilah the shivers. "What on earth did that bartender do to make you hate him so much?"

"Look at him!" Grant exclaimed. "Standing there, pouring drinks, all sympathetic and quiet. Looks like the kinda guy you could tell anything to, doesn't he?"

Lilah tried to read between the lines. "Grant, sugar. Are you trying to tell me that bartender is blackmailing you?"

"No!" Grant looked genuinely horrified. "Oh, mercy, I hadn't even thought of that."

"But what could he possible have on you?" Lilah protested. "You're, like, the sweetest, nicest man who ever lived."

Grant squirmed in his chair. "Not that nice. Come on, Lolly, I mean, I'm human. I've done things I'm not proud of, like anyone else. I just . . . wish I didn't have to be reminded of them every single time I look at Chris Colby."

Mystified, Lilah swiveled in her chair, searching out Christian Colby with new interest. He was holding up a cocktail shaker as if offering the contents to one of his customers. Lilah cocked her head and tried to see what it was about the man that turned Grant into a whack-a-doo.

The bartender reminded Lilah of some of the guys her aunt hired in the summers to help work the farm. Handsome in a rough way, she decided, more cowboy than she'd ever expected to see in Manhattan.

Christian shook his head and reached behind the bar for a glass bottle. He uncapped it and poured a long stream into a short glass. He leaned on the bar and pushed the glass forward with a sympathetic smile, and for no reason she could articulate, Lilah's breath came faster. She craned her neck to see who took the drink, but there were too many people in the way.

"Do you see what I mean?" Grant asked. There was something perilously close to hysteria in his voice. "I can't work with him every day. I just can't."

It was Devon, she was sure of it. Like someone had flipped a switch that started an electrical current flowing between her body and Devon's, Lilah was suddenly absolutely certain she'd find him at the bar, tossing back whatever liquor it was that Christian had just served.

She got up and stood looking down at her best friend. "I love you to pieces, Grant, you know that, right? But sugar, you're not making a lick of sense."

Grant scowled down at the scarred tabletop rather than meeting Lilah's eyes. "Look. Colby knows something about me, okay? Something I never should've done, much less told anyone about, but it's over and done with now. No good can come of raking it all up. Can we just leave it at that?"

Lilah studied her best friend's face. He looked miserable. She hated to see him like that, but she wasn't sure what else to do or say. Unless . . . "Wait. Is this about . . . do you like him? Or does he have something against you because of . . . you know, that?" Wow, awkward much?

Color bloomed along Grant's cheekbones. "Geez, Lolly. No, it's not about that."

"Okay." Lilah was relieved. She'd always known her best friend preferred boys to girls; it was part of him, something she accepted without question. But, in true Southern fashion, they'd never explicitly spoken of it. She only knew she hated the idea of anyone looking down on Grant or disliking him for being gay.

"Look," he said. "I don't want to talk about it. There's no point."

Lilah stared at his stony face. He really wasn't going to confide in her. Stung, Lilah said, "Fine. I'm going to give you tonight to wallow, but tomorrow I want you back in top Grant form. Get a hold of yourself! Christian Colby won't be around forever; this is only temporary."

"Is that what you're telling yourself?" Grant glared at her. Lilah couldn't remember him ever looking at her like that before. "It's not forever, it's not even real, so you can have a fling with your boss and it'll all be okay because you know going into it that it's temporary."

The sounds of the bar faded like Lilah was suddenly plunged underwater. Her mouth opened but nothing came out. She didn't know what to say.

Grant gentled his tone. "A one-night stand is one thing. But you're living in the man's apartment now. Seeing him every day. Hon, leaving aside the fact that Devon Sparks is a complete and utter prick and I don't know what you see in him, you have to know that just because it's temporary doesn't mean your actions won't have consequences. And I'm not talking bun-in-oven consequences because you're smarter than that. But do you really think you're the kind of girl who can have an affair and not be devastated when it's over?"

If Grant had dashed his blue drink in her face, Lilah couldn't have been more shocked. She felt like he'd reached into her most deeply held secret wishes and dragged them into the harsh light of reality. Scraped raw, like the hulled-out inside of a sugar snap pea.

And then the empty hollow under her breastbone started to fill up with the cleansing fire of determination.

"I never have been before," she said, amazed at the steadiness of her voice. "But then, I've never been all that happy, either, have I? I came to New York to change, to build a new life as a new version of myself. It would be pretty pointless to have come all this way and then make all the same, safe choices I would've made back in Spotswood County. As King Lear would say, nothing comes from nothing. If I never risk anything, how can I expect anything wonderful to happen?"

That wasn't how Grant expected her to respond; Lilah could tell by the way he blinked like she'd whomped him upside the head.

"Wow. All righty, then. Have a good night and call me tomorrow."

Lilah had to laugh. "That's it? We're in the middle of our first fight ever and you just cave?"

"What do you want me to say?" He ran his fingers through the ring of condensation his glass had left on the table. "You're a big girl, Lolly, and you're going to do whatever you're going to do. I can't protect you, and maybe you're right, maybe I shouldn't even try."

Lilah relaxed, even though excitement continued to fizz through her veins. They were okay. "After all, it's better to take a chance and see what comes of it, right?"

Grant rested his head on one slender hand, his mouth curved in the saddest smile Lilah had ever seen. "If you say so. I hope you don't regret what you have to do to get your chance. Go on, at least one of us oughta get lucky tonight."

Back home, a comment like that might have made her blush, but here, tonight, Lilah felt a strangely exhilarating freedom. She laughed and bent her head to give Grant a smacking kiss on the mouth.

Framing his so-familiar, beloved face between her palms, she looked him in the eye and said, "Don't think you're getting away with holding out on me forever. Like I said, one night to wallow. Tomorrow, you and me? We're gonna work through this together."

Grant made a kissy face at her. "Oh, I think we'll stick to your secrets, Lolls. You'll have much more interesting things to share than I will, I'm sure."

"Let's hope so." She winked and ruffled his hair up, quick-stepping out of reach to avoid his outraged swipe.

Waving bye over her shoulder, Lilah ducked back into the crowd and started muscling her way to the bar.

Lilah Jane Tunkle was in the mood to make a bad decision.

The beat of the music pounded out of the drums, into the cheap, tacked-together floor of the makeshift stage, and up through the worn soles of Frankie's gray checked Vans. He felt the beat, breathed it, and matched it with his fingers flying up and down the neck of his bass guitar.

Squeezing his eyes shut against the stinging sweat that wanted to drip from his tangled black hair, Frankie fought to lose himself in the music.

It was good stuff Dreck was playing tonight, and the rest of the band was on top of their game, pouring energy and life into every bleeding note, but even though Frankie's fingers followed the beat automatically, pounding the frets and strumming the licks that kept everything moving and throbbing, he couldn't seem to let go.

Usually, playing bass was like drowning, everything muffled except for the rhythm and the interplay between the instruments. In practice sessions—not that Dreck practiced overmuch, no one in the band was too concerned with skill level—the drowning was almost peaceful, but in front of a live audience, Frankie loved to thrash against the waves that wanted to pull him under.

The eyes on him, the bodies throwing themselves around, flashing skin and heat and leather in what could only loosely be characterized as dancing—those things usually sent Frankie into ecstatic dervish mode, at once immersed in the music and in tune with the crowd.

Tonight the music eluded him. The crowd, rowdy as ever, didn't thrill him. Frankie's attention was well and truly snared. Snagged and caught on one little table a short distance from the stage, where Jess Wake sat, so very un-alone.

Frankie fumbled a chord. Noelle tossed a glare over her shoulder, toxic orange dreads swinging and banging into the microphone. Frankie acknowledged the singer with a two-fingered salute and a breakout bass riff that sent the crowd mad. Over at the Table of Doom, Jess whooped and shot out of his seat, leaving Wes fucking Murphy with his mouth hanging open in the middle of some no-doubt hilarious anecdote.

Right. That called for a bit of the old sex appeal. Frankie caught Jess's bright eyes and smoldered. Gave him a hint of the tongue between the teeth and a slow, subtle hip grind, too.

Might as well go all out.

The results were heartening: Jess swayed toward the stage like a mouse hypnotized by a snake, the man at his table forgotten. Frankie smirked. There was nothing quite like staking a claim in front of a bar full of sweaty mashers. Jess stared up at him, pretty blue eyes glazed over with want, and all of a sudden, Frankie was done with the gig.

He rushed the rest of the set, knowing he'd catch hell from Noelle and the others later, but just not giving a tinker's damn about it.

When it was finally, finally over, Frankie barely took the time to lift the strap of his bass over his head and lay the instrument down where he'd been standing before he bounded off the stage and over to Jess. Who'd sat down at some point, but leapt to his feet and tackled Frankie the minute he was close enough.

"You rocked tonight! I even liked the New York Dolls cover."

"Infidel," Frankie said. It was easy to be indulgent with his arms full of Jess. "*Personality Crisis* is a classic."

"It has a good bass line, anyway." Jess was determined not to like the Dolls, which Frankie couldn't understand. Luckily, the young squirt made up for it by loving the Ramones with a passion nearly as unnatural and fervent as Frankie's. Not to mention Patti Smith.

Thinking of the high priestess of punk made Frankie remember the night Jess had first talked to him, asking about the image of Patti tattooed on Frankie's arm. The idiot boy hadn't even known who she was, but he'd been drawn to her like he'd been drawn to Frankie—and Frankie had taken full advantage of that fatal attraction.

Eager to sample the delights of that attraction again, Frankie boa-constrictored Jess and whispered in his ear, "Let's head home, eh? Got some new pillows at the flea market; I'll let you toss 'em wherever you like."

The Garret was furnished with rugs, carpets, throws, pillows, and discarded sofa cushions. Frankie was on a perpetual hunt for pillows in exotic colors and fabrics.

Jess squirmed back far enough to see Frankie's face. "Ooh, new pillows. What are they like?"

"Lime green," Frankie told him. "Largish. Material's like nothing so much as shag carpeting." He arched a brow. "Appropriately enough."

Jess blushed—and God, how Frankie did love the fact that he could still make his boy blush—but pulled away.

"Soon," Jess said, a promise in his eyes. "But I can't leave Wes sitting here all by himself after I practically forced him to come out. Can we stay a little while?"

Bloody hell. Exactly what he'd hoped to avoid. Frankie could see the bloke over Jess's shoulder, young and beautiful in that confident, catalogue way Frankie could never manage in a million years.

Wes tipped his chair back and waved at Frankie, a smug expression on his supercilious face, as if he knew exactly what Frankie and Jess were talking about.

Probably wanted Frankie to throw a wobbly and insist on going home, so Wes could play on Jess's soft, squishy side and come out of it smelling like the good, supportive mate. Too bad for him that Frankie was smarter than that. He gritted his teeth and smiled.

"Right, then. Lead the way."

CHAPTER TWENTY-TWO

There were times in a man's life when he wanted a beer: kicking back, relaxing after a hard day, maybe with the game on in the background. And there were other times when he could enjoy a glass of wine over a fine meal, like the perfect pairing of Pinot noir with a seared duck breast. There were even times when a cocktail could be fun, and in Devon's experience, no one on earth mixed up a meaner drink than Christian Colby.

Despite Chris's presence behind the bar, however, Devon wasn't drinking cocktails. He wasn't having wine or beer, either. No. After the day he'd had?

Bourbon on the rocks. Nothing else would do.

Devon swirled the melting ice cubes in his third glass—or was it his fourth?—and lost himself in the rich, golden-brown color of the smoky-sweet liquid.

"Isn't that your girl?" Christian, idling at Devon's end of the bar with a ceaselessly wiping cloth and a sympathetic expression, nodded toward a new arrival.

Squinting through the gloom—and seriously, didn't off-duty cops come in here? Why they didn't write the place up for breaking the smoking laws, Devon would never understand—Devon could barely make out the curvy form of his own personal Mary Poppins framed hesitantly in the doorway.

"Lilah Jane," he said, feeling instantly better. She must be magic, he mused. Maybe it was a nanny thing. In books, they always seemed to have special powers of care and comfort. He watched her blearily for a moment, feeling comforted and cared for. Even the sartorial atrocity she called a shirt, overlarge and patterned with unlovely flowers, couldn't detract from the glow she brought to the dingy bar.

But then, just as he was about to stagger to his feet and wave her over, her face lit up and she began weaving her way to a table on the other side of the room.

Hooking one heel over the bottom rung of the barstool, Devon hoisted himself up high enough to confirm his suspicions. Yep, there she was, chattering away with Grant Holloway.

Devon settled on the stool and turned his back on them. "Hit me again, Chris."

"Come on, man, I think you've had enough."

Devon sneered. "I don't pay you to think."

"You don't pay me at all," Christian reminded him amiably. "Your accumulated tab would bankrupt Bloomberg."

Devon didn't dignify that with a response beyond tapping his empty glass imperiously on the bar. Christian sighed but poured another round, so Devon decided to forgive him. For the moment.

He couldn't really afford to alienate anyone else right now.

After the way both services today had gone, Devon was half-surprised he hadn't been lynched by an angry mob of drunken chefs yet. Maybe they were too tired from pulling a double shift. He'd have to watch out for tomorrow when they were rested up.

It was bad. Beyond bad, well into the realm of farce. If it were happening to someone else, it would've been funny.

Devon Sparks, self-proclaimed world's greatest chef and proprietor of five huge Michelin-starred restaurants across the country, couldn't manage to get cleanly through a single weekend of service at a 110-cover restaurant.

He'd lost the old magic, he thought mournfully. Hmm, maybe Lilah would rub off on him.

Hoo, down, boy, Devon thought, shifting a little on the stool. The image that danced gleefully into his brain was too delicious to dismiss entirely, even if fulfilling it was starting to look unlikely in the extreme.

Maybe he'd check on Lilah one more time. Righteous, somewhat inebriated, indignation coursed through him. She was supposed to be here meeting Devon, her boss! Not some high school sweetheart who was still panting after her.

Devon teetered a bit and elected not to try climbing his stool again. Instead, he planted both feet on the solid bar floor and stretched to see over the heads of the aggravating people who were in his way.

He got a good angle just in time to see Lilah take Grant's face in her hands and kiss him.

Devon sat back down with a bump.

She kissed him.

Lilah kissed Grant. On the mouth. On purpose.

He lurched to his feet intending to march over to that table and break up the lovebirds, but somehow he miscalculated the distance between his feet and the floor, and wound up leaning a bit further than he intended.

"Whoa, there!" A slender shoulder pushed up under Devon's arm, righting him. Glossy dark curls brushed his chin, and he breathed in the smell of lemon and thyme, clean and bracing after the squalor of the bar and the heady perfume of the bourbon.

"Lilah Jane," he said, her magic stealing over him again. What had he been so mad about a second ago?

"Are you okay?" Without waiting for Devon to formulate a reply, which, granted, was taking longer than it should've as his tongue kept wanting to curl into her ear instead of make words, Lilah appealed to Christian. "Is he okay? Oh, my stars and stripes, what did you give him to drink?"

"Bourbon," Devon said, smiling at the memory. "Hey, you want one?"

"No!"

"Suit yourself." He shrugged, and they were still pressed so tightly against one another, his body moved against hers in interesting ways.

"Hey," he remembered. "Weren't we going to talk?"

Lilah grinned, her dimple winking out at him. "I can't believe I was worried about how you'd deal with the rough service tonight," she said, gesturing at the empty shot glasses ranged on the bar. "Four shots of bourbon! What could be a healthier coping mechanism?"

"It was five," Christian put in.

Devon gave him the evil eye. "Your forgiveness is re-voked," Devon told him. "I don't care if you're my only ally, there are some lines that must never be crossed."

"I shouldn't have ratted you out," Christian agreed. "But I thought the paramedics might ask when Lilah has to call them later to pump your stomach."

Lilah gasped audibly, her pretty face going chalk white.

"Oh, my word, please tell me that's a joke."

"It is! Sorry, Lilah, I'm just ragging on him, Dev's fine," Christian soothed. "I shouldn't tease like that, but he so rarely shows his liquor, I couldn't resist."

"Too little, too late," Devon said darkly. "I break with thee, I break with thee, I break with thee."

Lilah and Christian exchanged a look they obviously thought Devon was too drunk to notice.

"All righty, then," Lilah said. "Let's get you home, boss man."

A thrill coursed through Devon when Lilah said "home" in that warm voice all rich with amusement.

It was comforting and intimate and somehow sexy as hell.

The goosebumps it raised, plus the feel of her curvy little body pressed against his side, brought the world into sharp focus.

He stared down into her sparkling mossy eyes and after three deep inhalations of the honeyed herbal scent of her, tonight's kitchen debacle faded into the background of Devon's mind.

Lilah shifted, pulling his arm more firmly across her shoulders, which also happened to push her soft, round breasts more firmly into his chest. Devon felt all the blood in his body drain south so fast it made his head spin. He hardened in a dizzying rush.

So. Turned out he wasn't that drunk after all.

"Some air would be good," Devon agreed, aware that his voice had gone raspy and deep. "Let's go home."

Frankie jiggled the ancient key in the rusted lock, long fingers twiddling the metal back and forth. He didn't bother swearing at the delay, even though he was aching to be upstairs in his Garret, alone with Jess for the first time in what felt like a donkey's age.

Sitting in Chapel, faffing about and making nice with Wonderful Wes was enough to make Frankie's hair stand on end. Even more than usual. Definitely the sort of evening that made Frankie long for the halcyon days of his misspent youth, when he'd spent every night off his tits and carefree as a lark.

Bloody rehab. Bloody recovery.

Jess, burdened down with Frankie's bass case, leaned wearily into him and said, "Need help?"

"I can do it," Frankie ground out. One last desperate jiggle and the tumblers cranked over. Thank Christ.

They climbed the private back staircase up to the Garret, Frankie brooding the whole time on the many ways Jess and Wes matched up.

Same age. Same drive to succeed, same need to prove themselves. Jess and Wes, he thought with a mental sneer. How sickeningly twee, even their bloody names rhymed.

Conversation, what little they'd managed in the din of the bar, had centered around Jess's photography club and Wes's plans for after he graduated from the ACA. No one inquired after Frankie's future plans, which was a damn good thing since he didn't have any.

Well, none that went beyond getting Jess inside and out of his clothes as quickly as humanly possible.

Bollocks to that, appeared to be Jess's feeling on the subject of speed nudity. Frankie watched, saddened but unsurprised, as Jess carefully arranged his precious cargo on the guitar stand in the corner before straightening and regarding Frankie with crossed arms and narrowed eyes.

Which was universal body language for "You'll not be getting into my knickers tonight," Frankie had always found.

With a sigh, Frankie kicked off his shoes and padded to the front hall closet. When he opened the door to sling them in, he remembered he'd stashed the new lime-green pillows in that closet. There they were, piled together on the floor, taunting him. They looked cheap and thin now, somehow, the cloth worn threadbare in spots.

"We need to talk," Jess said from behind him.

Frankie winced and shut the closet door.

"I saw that," Jess warned darkly. "And I know you hate RDTs, but we've put this one off long enough."

"RDT" was Jess–speak for "relationship-defining talk." "Aw, Bit, must we break our streak? We've gone so long without one, we ought to be well on our way to a world record."

Jess's mouth twisted in that way that meant he was trying not to smile. "I'm immune to your wheedling ways, Frankie. At least for the next hour or so."

"The next hour," Frankie repeated, aghast. "Don't say that, luv. Fifteen minutes, there's a lad."

"Frankie," Jess said, lips thin and eyes flashing. "We're having this talk whether you like it or not. Now nut up and take it like a man."

"Fuck me," Frankie said. "That's impressive, Bit. And more than a little sexy." He waggled his eyebrows suggestively, but even though he caught a flicker of heat in Jess's gaze, the boy remained firm.

Unfortunately, so did Frankie.

He cleared his throat. "Are there rules that say we have to

stand here all blokey and awkward? Or can we maybe make a nest and burrow in for the duration?"

"The bylaws clearly state that snuggling is acceptable." Jess kicked off his shoes, hesitated, then drew his T-shirt off over his head, too. Blue eyes dark and soft, he sank down into the closest mound of pillows, a lithe pale form amid the deep jewel-toned velvets and silks.

As ever, the sight brought the scratch of something hard and painful to Frankie's throat. "Come lie with me and be my love," he quoted softly and followed Jess down to the floor.

The slow-motion wrestle to find the perfect position curled around each other was familiar and comforting. Once they were settled, Frankie tensed up again, but despite his threats, Jess was silent for long minutes.

Long enough to lull Frankie into a nearly comatose state of contentment, reclined on the decadent, softness-strewn floor of his tiny, cramped pasha's tent of a home, with the world's warmest, funniest, most delightful man at his side. Jess's head was on Frankie's right shoulder, Frankie's right arm wound round Jess's naked back, their legs tangled inextricably.

Heaven.

When Jess spoke, his voice was so low and sweet it didn't break the spell but instead strengthened it. Frankie floated, finally achieving the peace his music hadn't afforded him earlier that night.

"I love you, Frankie Boyd. You know I do. You knew it from the first moment I set eyes on you in the kitchen at Market."

"Mmm," Frankie agreed, nuzzling the fragrant, silky hair so close to his face. "You were delicious, Bit, all nervy and shy."

"But I couldn't stay away, no matter how shy I was, or how many times I told myself you'd never be interested in someone like me."

Frankie made a protesting noise, and Jess amended, "Or at least, not interested for longer than a single night."

Buggering hell, was Jess ever turned around on that one. Frankie roused himself to say, "That's not entirely the way I remember it."

There was a pause. Then Jess's voice, cautious. "Frankie. Even after we got together that first time, you didn't let me spend the night here until my sister caught us making out and wigged over the whole gay thing."

Miranda had indeed wigged, although again, Frankie remembered the event a little differently: i.e., that Big Sis was less upset about the gay thing than she had been about Jess being with Frankie—older, wilder, nasty rep . . . in short, a bad, bad man.

"You were living with her," Frankie pointed out. "If you'd stayed over, you would've had to deal with being catapulted out of the closet that much sooner."

"True. But I don't think that's why you used to kiss me good night and send me back uptown."

Frankie fought not to stiffen, knowing that in their current position, Jess couldn't help but read and interpret every minute physical shift.

The conversation was skating disconcertingly close to one of the fault lines that ran jagged through Frankie's messed-up psyche. He had no interest in spelunking into the depths tonight.

Or ever, really.

"Is this actually what you wanted to talk about? Seems a bit like ancient history to me. After all, you're living here with me now, all snug and cozy, no late-night cab rides back to Big Sister's place."

"Maybe it's a tangent, maybe not," Jess said. Christ, Frankie hated it when he got cryptic. Bloody Americans, brought up on Yoda. "I wanted to talk about what happened after the show tonight, when we hung out with Wes."

Bugger. No power on earth was going to keep Frankie from tensing up in an obvious and easily detectable way at the mention of Wonder Wes. In the Garret, no less! In their nest!

Frankie did not like it.

Abruptly needing to be not quite so well cuddled, Frankie rolled away from Jess and got to his feet. He camouflaged the strategic retreat with a hunt for the pack of Dunhill's wedged into his back pocket.

Frankie lit up and took a deep, bracing drag before saying, "Yeah? What about it?"

Jess hadn't moved, apparently unfazed by Frankie's defection from the nest. "You were charming. You made us laugh. Wes thinks you're the king of awesome."

"So where's the bad?" He didn't mean to come over all truculent, but there it was.

Jess leveled him with a look. "You hated every second of it. What I want to know is why."

The Bit was going to keep pushing, Frankie could see that. "Wes is a wanker. Stuck-up little tosspot thinks he knows better than everyone in the kitchen." He paused, weighed his words, and decided *fuck it*. "An' I don't fancy the way he looks at you."

That brought Jess up onto his elbows, eyes flashing. "I thought it was going to be some load of crap like that."

"Crap?" Frankie was honestly offended. Here he was, sharing his innermost thoughts and feelings, and Jess called it shite? He stuffed down the voice that reminded him he was absolutely skimming over the real issue.

"Yes, crap," Jess retorted. "First of all, anyone who's seen the way I look at you knows I can't see anyone *but* you. And secondly, Wes is completely hung up on this chemistry professor of his back at the Academy. Who happens to be a woman, thank you very much. And anyway, jealousy over Wes is not what's got you so ticked."

Frankie pulled a mouthful of burning smoke into his lungs and held it there until his eyes watered. "Tell me, then, if you're so clever. What am I on about?"

Jess appeared to make an effort to collect himself. "I don't know. That's what this conversation is about." He smiled, but it was more of a grimacing twist of his lips. "You'll be happy to hear you're as much of an enigma to me as ever. Being in love with you hasn't suddenly rendered me capable of peering directly into your head to see what's going on."

That actually *was* quite comforting. "So you admit you can't tell for sure. Because I *am* jealous, Bit. Chartreuse with it. Fucking Wes."

"Oh, I believe you don't like Wes," Jess said. "I also believe there's more going on here than only that. Because I refuse to believe that after everything we've been through—everything I went through just to be with you—that you wouldn't trust me."

Direct hit. Game over, and Frankie knew it. When Jess's voice got small and quiet like that, Frankie's battleship was good and sunk because it meant he'd succeeded in actually hurting Jess.

Unacceptable.

Stubbing out the cig in the chipped china plate reserved for that purpose, Frankie tugged his shirt off and dove back into the nest on top of Jess. He wanted to be skin to skin, needed the connection like never before.

"I do trust you, Bit. It's him I don't trust."

It's me I don't trust.

Generous soul that he was, Jess immediately took Frankie's weight and melted warmly into him, arms and heart open in the way that made Frankie desperate to shield Jess from the harsh realities of the world.

But his Jess was no fragile flower in need of protection. "It's still crap," Jess said, crooned, really, into Frankie's ear. Frankie shivered, not sure if it was a reaction to Jess's heated breath on his temple or the fact that Jess knew him so well. "But it's okay. You're not ready to talk about it yet. I get it. But Frankie?"

"Yeah, luv?" Hoarse, damn it, he sounded like he'd smoked the whole blasted pack of cigs instead of half of one.

Jess got one hand on Frankie's chin and turned his face so they were forehead to forehead, close enough that Frankie could only focus on one bright blue orb without going cross-eyed.

"You should know. I'm not going to let you keep me at arms' length forever," Jess said.

The calm promise in his voice sent another shudder through Frankie, that old, familiar mixture of dizzy elation at how much Jess loved him—and terror at the thought of how much that love could cost them both.

CHAPTER TWENTY-THREE

Anticipation warred with amusement in Lilah's mind. Devon, it transpired, was a particularly affable drunk—cuddly without being handsy, chatty without babbling incessantly.

Although that might be because he wasn't nearly as intoxicated as Christian had made out. Either that or the drive uptown was sobering him up, because there were moments when Lilah could clearly see lucidity in Devon's hooded gaze.

Hence the anticipation. Because something was happening between them, building with every brush of hand on arm and every shared glance.

Lilah shifted on the smooth leather seat and caught Paolo's eye in the rearview mirror. She'd asked him to drop her at Chapel and go on home, intending to take a cab back to Devon's, but Paolo refused to hear of it. He'd told her in no uncertain terms that his standing orders were to drive her where she needed to go and wait for her, so wait he would. Lilah had to admit she was glad of it; when she and Devon had reeled out of the bar and up to the car, it had been nice to have help maneuvering Devon into the backseat without bashing him in the head or rolling him in the gutter.

Now, though, Paolo was a constant, silent presence in

the front of the car while Devon lolled indolently across the spacious backseat, taking up a considerable amount of room. Lilah couldn't quite pretend, even to herself, that she minded the way he listed against her, his hard, sculpted body a solid line of warm muscle sliding against her.

Devon tipped his head back to rest on the seat, his eyes closed. Lilah studied his profile in the light of the passing traffic. He looked peaceful, more serene than he ever seemed when his eyes were open and shooting bolts of energy and charisma every which way. And the lines of his face . . . sweet, fancy Moses.

One of the first things Lilah had done when she moved to Manhattan was to shell out for membership at the Metropolitan Museum of Art. The place was too big, too comprehensive, to ever be truly seen and appreciated in a single visit.

With that member card in her hot little hand, Lilah felt free to wander one hall at a time, spend half an hour gazing at Tiffany glass or medieval tapestries and leave the rest for another day.

Looking at Devon in repose now, all Lilah could think about were the marble statues in the Greek and Roman hallway. He embodied the classical ideal of male perfection in a way that was truly unfair, and more than a little intimidating.

Lilah traced with her eyes the broad, straight forehead, the sloping nose, the strong chin, the high cheekbones. He could almost be too handsome, verging on the beautiful androgyny favored by the Greek masters, but there was a sharpness to the lines of his face that rendered them indisputably masculine.

And then there was his mouth.

Hellfire and damnation, but Devon Sparks had a mouth shaped to tempt a woman to sin.

Lilah reached a stealthy hand to the rear-controlled air vents. Surely there was a higher setting they could be on.

In a display of the sort of awareness of his surroundings that made Lilah think Devon was sobering right up, he opened his eyes at the exact moment she started fumbling with the A/C.

"Feeling a tad overheated?" he said in a lazy, bourbon-soaked voice. His eyes, though, were intent and hot as a touch on her skin.

Lilah snatched her hand back from the vent. "I'm fine. How much longer till we get home?"

Devon's eyes darkened to molten silver, something like satisfaction flickering through his expression, but all he said was, "I think we're almost there. Right, Paolo?"

"Nearly, sir. The garage is a few blocks away."

"Excellent," Devon said. Lilah was in bone-deep agreement with the relief in his tone. "Drop us off, then go home and get some sleep, man. Sorry to keep you out so late."

"That's my job, sir. What time tomorrow?"

Devon slid Lilah a sideways glance that ignited a ball of fire in her belly. "Let's sleep in," he said, his eyes never leaving hers. "Call it ten." His lips curled. "It's not like it did me any good to get to the restaurant early, anyway."

To distract herself from the embarrassing liquid heat melting her insides, Lilah said, "What went wrong at the restaurant tonight?"

"What went right?" Devon parried. "My timing was off, my food was for shit, my sous chef resents the hell out of me, the bartender has my manager in a snit, and, oh, yeah, I'm suddenly a father." He pinched his forefinger and thumb together and squinted one eye at her. "I'm under just a smidge of pressure."

"You were always a father," Lilah couldn't help pointing out. "Your problem was you didn't have the chance to do much about it."

"Birthday presents. That was it. Well, Christmas, too." Dropping his hands to his lap, Devon picked at a dried splatter of something purple and sticky-looking. Without glancing away from his pants, he said, "So. What kinds of things did you two do today?"

Lilah knew better than to openly display her happiness at this chink in Devon's armor. "Oh, nothing much," she said

as casually as she could. "Tucker spent a few hours drawing—
he can be amazingly focused when he's trying to get his
rendition of a T-Rex just right."

The corner of Devon's mouth kicked up a little. "Yeah,
that backpack of his is full of colored pencils and stuff. I always bought him video games, remote-control cars, things
like that. Guess I was way off."

"It's hard to buy a gift for someone you don't know very
well." Lilah couldn't think of a more tactful way to put it, so
she just said it.

Instead of getting angry and defensive, as she'd half-
feared, Devon scrubbed his hands over his face and said,
"Yeah. I know. Fuck, I should've just let my assistant shop for
Tucker. Daniel would've had as good a shot as I did at picking the right presents."

But Devon hadn't farmed out that task—he'd done it himself. It wasn't much, Lilah knew. Certainly, it wasn't close to
everything he ought to have done. But the fact that Devon
guarded even that tenuous connection to Tucker gave her
hope.

"I was thinking," she said, putting a hand on his arm and
drawing her fingers in light circles over the slick material of
his button-up shirt. "Do you really have to be at the restaurant every day from lunch service all the way through dinner?
I bet if you gave yourself a break between shifts, you'd be so
much more energized and ready for the evening rush."

Devon looked from her face down to her doodling fingers
and back again. "You're going somewhere with this. And
much as I'd like to believe this suggestion is leading up to
spending the whole day together in bed, I have a feeling I'm
going to be disappointed."

Lilah felt blood rush to her face. Shoot, this coy thing
was harder to pull off than she'd expected. Giving up on the
arm petting, Lilah turned to face Devon head on.

"Not disappointed, I hope, but no, I'm not suggesting we
laze around in bed all afternoon. I'm more hoping I can convince you to spend that time with Tucker. Well, with Tucker
and me," she amended when she saw the panic take over his

expression. Despite herself, Lilah felt a pang of joy at knowing Devon needed her.

They both needed her, Devon and Tucker, and Ferdinand's words to Miranda in *The Tempest* floated across her consciousness; she could relate like never before to the image of her heart flying to the service of another.

"What would we do?"

The poor man sounded positively bewildered. Taking pity, Lilah said, "Any number of things! Like today. I mean, Tuck didn't spend all day on his art. We also went to the cutest little bookstore in the Village, Three Lives & Company. Have you ever been there? They had a great children's section that kept Tucker happy while I found a couple books on things to do with kids in the city. Don't you worry, I'm absolutely brimming over with activities for the three of us!"

Devon was silent for a moment. Lilah wondered if she'd blown the needle on the enthusiast-o-meter and scared him off. She took it as a good sign that he hadn't rejected the idea outright.

Finally he blew out a breath and squeezed his eyes shut. "Fine. I'll give it a shot."

Lilah felt the grin breaking over her cheeks before he'd even finished agreeing, but Devon held up a hand to forestall her exclamations. "If things get out of hand at the restaurant, I reserve the right to ditch out on the afternoon play date without being sent on a 'round-the-world guilt trip."

"Pinky swear," Lilah said, holding up her hand with all the fingers curled into a fist except the littlest one.

Devon groaned. "We can't spit in our palms and shake on it, like men?" But he was already holding out his pinky finger.

As they hooked fingers, Lilah said, "I'm not sure why exchanging bodily fluids should be considered a more binding form of promise. Also, I'm not a man."

"There are so many possible responses to that, I don't even know where to start. Maybe with the last part." He pulled her closer by her pinky, that tenuous point of contact enough to set Lilah's lungs on "pant."

"What? That I'm not a man?" Mercy, she sounded like her student actors at wrap parties after a play's successful run, when they sucked down helium balloons and laughed themselves sick at each other's breathy, high-pitched voices.

"Exactly," Devon purred. "I had, in fact, noticed that very thing about you."

He no longer seemed even slightly tipsy; his eyes were clear and focused. Desire had darkened them to the color of the Blue Ridge Mountains at dusk, and Lilah thought she'd never seen anything so alluring, not even the mountains themselves.

Even though she knew it was coming, was waiting and hoping and wishing for it, the first touch of his mouth on hers sent a shock through her system. Lilah squeaked, her eyes darting automatically to the rearview mirror.

Paolo was studiously avoiding checking his blind spots, Lilah saw. She sure hoped the Park Avenue traffic continued to be slow and steady.

And in the next instant, she ceased to care, because Devon's lips parted, nipping and sucking at hers until she gave in and opened her mouth with a moan. He slipped inside, quick and easy, and when his tongue stroked along the sensitive roof of her mouth, Lilah wouldn't have cared if they were suddenly transported to a crowd of tourists in the middle of Times Square. She probably wouldn't have noticed if the car swerved around a taxi and flipped end over end.

She forgot everything but Devon. She forgot her name. She forgot to *breathe*.

Luckily, the car's engine shut off in time to keep her from passing out. Lilah broke the kiss like she was breaking the surface of the lake after being held under by one of her rambunctious boy cousins. Gasping for breath and looking around for familiar landmarks, she saw that they were in the underground garage below Devon's apartment building.

Paolo got out of the car and came to stand by her door. Evidently trained in discretion, he didn't open the door immediately, but stood by, ready and waiting, his back ramrod straight and hands at his sides. Lilah was impressed.

And grateful. She needed a second to compose herself. Half a minute more, and she'd have been swooning in Devon's arms like a character out of *Gone with the Wind*. Melanie, not Scarlett, and what girl wanted to be Melanie? Not only insipid in her own right, but to have to end up with boring Ashley? Ugh.

Aware that she was hiding in literature to calm herself down, a tried-and-true Lolly technique, Lilah forced herself to meet Devon's eyes.

He looked amused, as if he'd been in on her mental book club discussion. Or maybe it was just his default expression.

"Everything okay over there?" Devon's tone was gentle, soft. Lilah had no idea if he was serious or if he was mocking her.

Assuming it was the latter, Lilah lifted her chin and stared him down.

"You probably think I'm going to freak out," she said, "but I'm not." *So there.*

"Thought never crossed my mind," Devon said, all chivalry. "Shall we?"

That twinkle in his eyes made him look like a cheerful sex demon. He had the seductive smile going, too. Lilah thought about shocking the heck out of him by pushing him back against the opposite door and ravishing his mouth, but that could so easily backfire. Chances were better than average that rather than reacting with shock, he'd ravish her right back and they'd end by steaming up the windows of his limo with the driver standing right outside.

They said good night to Paolo and made it to the elevator without mauling each other.

Lilah made sure to keep a foot of space between them in the elevator. She might be intent on busting out of her Lolly shell, but that didn't mean she was ready to put on a public show for any of Devon's neighbors who might have a yen to take the elevator, or for the doorman keeping watch over the security cameras.

Lilah wanted adventure and excitement; she did not want to star in anyone's homemade *Girls Gone Wild* video.

Not that she didn't feel a little on the wild side, she mused, casting a sideways glance at the Greek god to her left. The Greek god who, for some unfathomable reason, was interested in plain Lilah Jane from the middle of Hicksville. Lilah tried not to contemplate the eventual fate of most of the mortal women who'd tangled, however briefly and deliciously, with the gods of Greek mythology.

She was determined not to count the cost before she'd even had the joy. She'd lived her whole life like that, always doing the right thing, making the safe choice, trying to make her family proud and not be a burden—and what had it gotten her?

Not a fraction of the happiness she'd found in Devon's arms, that was for sure.

The elevator chimed—even the ding to let them know they were at Devon's private floor was elegant—and the door slid open.

"Good evening, Mr. Sparks." The quiet voice of Daniel Tan, Devon's assistant, broke Lilah out of her momentary fantasy of falling on Devon and taking him by storm the instant they were inside the apartment.

A flash of guilt assailed her. Right, the assistant. There to babysit Tucker. How could she have forgotten?

"I'm going to go check on Tucker," she said. "Is he in bed?"

"All tucked in and sound asleep, last time I poked my head in," the young Asian-American man assured her.

"Thanks, Daniel," Devon said. "I appreciate you doing this on short notice."

"Anything for you, Mr. S, you know that. Listen, a quick thing about tomorrow's calendar. Simon keeps calling, and I wasn't sure how you wanted me to handle him . . ."

Lilah left Devon negotiating his schedule and headed down the hall to Tucker's room. There she found Tucker sound asleep, looking tiny in the full-size bed. He slept on his stomach with one hand fisted by his face, the other buried under his pillow. His dark sable hair, so like Devon's, was a mass of tufts and spikes against the white cotton pillows.

A warm, solid presence at her back made Lilah smile.

"Is he asleep?" Devon's voice was hushed, almost awed, like a man talking during a hymn in church.

She murmured an assent and gave him a moment to take in the peaceful sight of his son slumbering away before she closed the door softly.

The living room appeared to be empty. Lilah glanced around and said, "That Daniel seems like a real nice boy. Did you send him on home?"

Devon nodded, his eyes kindling. "It's just you and me."

A shiver of delight raced through Lilah. She felt bold and fearless, but at the same time so full of nervy anticipation it was like her belly had been hollowed out to make room for a colony of junebugs.

"I want to make one thing clear before we do this," Lilah said, mouth dry. She turned to face him and forced herself to look him dead in the eye.

Devon cupped her cheek. His palm was rough in some places, soft in others, warm and strong all over. Lilah wanted to push into it like a cat, but she had a topic to discuss, dang it!

"What's that, Lilah Jane?"

Suppressing the shimmy of happiness her full name in his voice always caused, Lilah said, "I told you before. I'm not Jane Eyre—you're not Rochester."

"And thank God for that. Doesn't he get caught in a fire caused by his psycho wife and go blind?"

Lilah raised her brows. "Look at you, getting all literate. But that's not what I mean." She took a deep breath. "I meant I'm not going to fall madly in love with you if we h-have sex again."

Curses, how could she stumble over that last part? What a dweeb.

Devon didn't seem to mind, though, if the amusement brightening his eyes to sky blue was any indication.

"Very reassuring," he told her gravely. "Although if I were you, I wouldn't make any promises I might not be able to keep."

With that infuriating remark, Devon swooped his head

down and took her mouth, stealing the indignant retort right off her lips.

Her irritation at his cocksure manner burned to ash in the fire of that kiss. Their tongues danced and stroked, stoking the flames higher. Devon's hands were never still, sweeping down her sides and back up, knuckles grazing her jaw, her neck, fingers tightening in her hair.

Lilah gave it all up to him, throwing herself into the moment with the abandon she'd always dreamed of. It felt amazing, like flying, and suddenly greedy for more, she fisted her hands in his shirt and dragged him even closer. Their bodies aligned, Devon stooping and curving his body around hers to make the fit better, and then they were writhing against each other.

The friction of her own clothes was driving her crazier than Rochester's wife. Lilah panted into Devon's mouth, desperately wanting the clothes to just melt away like they did in books.

Her shirt stayed stubbornly in place, however, until she collected the presence of mind to let go of Devon in favor of wrestling with her own buttons. Tiny, fiddly little things, they didn't want to come undone, and Lilah tugged at them, nearly sobbing against Devon's kiss, frustrated beyond belief.

"This shirt is hideous anyway," Devon told her before gripping the collar and tearing it right down the middle.

Lilah gaped, shocked, but she didn't have time to dwell on Devon's fashion critique or his act of wardrobe violence because in the next instant his hands were on her skin, hot and sure against her soft belly. She shuddered under the stroke of his fingers, firm enough not to tickle—but the sensation was like that, so intense as to be almost unrecognizable as pleasure.

The rest of her body didn't seem to share Lilah's confusion. Her knees weakened, forcing her to lean into Devon; Lilah felt herself grow humid and hot between her thighs.

"Can we maybe take this someplace more private than

the living room?" she gasped out while she still had the brainpower.

"Your room is closer," Devon said, wasting no time in steering her down the hall.

CHAPTER TWENTY-FOUR

Lilah hustled, not because Devon was prodding her so much as because she had a sudden fear that she'd lose her nerve if they didn't get on with it.

Despite what she'd told Grant, and despite her body's clamoring desires, this was a big step for her. Bigger than her reckless decision to indulge in a one-night stand with a handsome stranger.

This was real. This meant something. She wasn't sure what yet, but . . .

"Having second thoughts?" Devon asked, pinpointing her mood with uncanny accuracy.

Lilah opened her bedroom door, doing a quick scan to make sure she hadn't left anything unmentionable lying around. But she'd only unpacked that afternoon, so things were relatively tidy. It was strange to see Devon standing there beside her bed; it was a sizable room, but his presence filled it from corner to corner.

She leaned back against the door. The heavy paneled wood was a welcome chill against the heated skin of her naked back.

"Why should I be? We've already done this once. It's old hat at this point." Just because she was a little nervous was no reason to suddenly start acting like a maiden aunt with an attack of the vapors.

"Old hat." Devon was laughing at her, the pig, but with his eyes only. His beautiful mouth was as solemn as ever.

"Not that I'm a tramp!" Lilah said. "I wouldn't want you to think that. Back home in Virginia, there weren't that many eligible men running around, and most of them tended to go for the debs and mini-Junior Leaguers, not high school English lit/drama teachers who still lived with their aunt and uncle. But I had one boyfriend, Preston Langford was his name, he worked at the high school, math teacher, and we went out for about a year. Mostly because neither one of us had much else to do, and it seemed like a suitable match on the surface."

Devon stalked closer while Lilah babbled. She watched him warily, but he didn't reach for her until she, mercifully, ran out of air and had to draw a breath.

"But underneath the surface," Devon cut in smoothly, lifting his hands to her hips and drawing her away from the door, "deep down, you wanted more than a 'suitable,' convenient man."

His fingers burned into her flesh even through the material of her khaki slacks.

"I did," she agreed breathlessly, her hands coming up of their own volition to grab Devon's wrists where he held her. From there, her greedy fingers inched their way up his arms to his powerful shoulders, gripping hard.

"So when we met that night at the bar and you kissed me before you even knew my name . . ."

Fire swept up Lilah's neck and into her cheeks. She was lucky the top of her head didn't go up in smoke. "Yes?" she squeaked.

"That was a test, wasn't it? Not of me—you weren't trying to see if I was the 'something more' you'd been looking for. You were testing yourself, to see if you had the guts to go after what you wanted."

His quiet perception knocked Lilah sideways. She

blinked. "The whole world's got you pegged wrong, and what's more, you actively encourage it. It's completely unfair and tricky of you to turn out *not* to be an arrogant bastard whose only concern is himself."

Something flickered through Devon's expression before his mouth curled up in a sneer. "Don't kid yourself, my little country mouse. I'm every bit as self-involved as they say. My only real concern in life is to get exactly what I want. And at this particular moment, what I want more than anything in the world is . . . well, you."

Against her will, Lilah's heart did an odd, fluttering dance in her chest.

Stop it, she scolded herself. *That body part is not supposed to be engaged in what's about to happen.*

"I want you, too," she said, determined to be bold. "So what happens now?"

Rather than answering her in words, Devon dipped his head to deliver more of those intoxicating kisses.

Lilah surrendered gladly, so happy to abandon the awkward, nervy whirl of her thoughts for the pure sensations coursing through her awakening body that she nearly missed it when Devon's hand reached around to deftly unhook her bra.

"Heavens, you're good at that," she gasped, feeling the cotton slip down her arms.

"You know what they say," he breathed against her neck. "Practice, practice."

The loathsome man kissed his way down to the hollow of her throat where her pulse kicked like a mule. He took a moment to suck a mark into her skin, drawing prickles of sensation up to the surface, before moving on to her collarbone, her chest, her soft, heavy breasts.

Lilah fought the urge to cross her arms over her chest. The overabundance of her curves was a source of embarrassment, and there was something about them in their naked state that accentuated their bounty.

Devon lifted a hand to cup her softly. He made a rough noise, deep in his throat, and Lilah stared down at herself, trying to see what Devon saw.

Creamy skin, round and full, capped with the tight, sensitive knots of her nipples, uptilted and embarrassingly eager.

The heat in Devon's gaze lit her up inside and consumed any possible embarrassment in a blaze of hunger. One look at Devon's eyes had Lilah shamelessly arching her back, lifting her breasts up as if in offering.

Devon groaned and took her wordless invitation. He bent his head to her skin and licked, delicate, restrained laps of his agile tongue—a shocking, teasing sensation when what Lilah wanted was to be devoured.

She protested the only way she knew how, by clutching her arms around his neck and hauling him in closer. A soft laugh vibrated against her flesh, sending shivers all through her.

"Stop laughing," she wanted to say, only she didn't have the breath, and anyway it was beside the point because at that moment, Devon opened his mouth over her and drew her aching nipple inside, sucking strongly. At the same time, his deft fingers dropped to her waistband and started fiddling with her pants button.

In Lilah's mind's eye, a bright, golden cord traveled from the point of her breast straight down the center of her body to the wet, tingling core of her, and with every suck of Devon's hot mouth, that cord plucked taut.

Vibrating with pleasure, Lilah speared her fingers into Devon's hair and held on for dear life.

Wait, a voice whispered in her head. *You're not just a passenger on this ride. Take the wheel, girl!*

Marshalling her scattered thoughts and intentions, Lilah committed a true act of will and tugged Devon's wonderful, devilish mouth away from her body.

He looked up at her questioningly and Lilah didn't even care that she was blushing like a virgin when she choked out, "Stand up. It's my turn."

Devon's blue eyes flared bright with laughter and desire, and Lilah found she didn't mind the former so long as she had the latter.

"Sweet Lilah Jane. As always, I'm yours to command. Where do you want me?"

"Bed," she said. Short, decisive words were better, she decided. Less likely to show the quaver in her voice.

"Naked or clothed?" he asked. He might've been inquiring whether she preferred coffee or tea.

"Naked," Lilah commanded, standing up straighter and narrowing her eyes. It was unacceptable that he could sound so calm and unconcerned.

Without taking her eyes off Devon as he backed toward the bed, Lilah let her hands drift to the front of her khakis. He'd managed to undo the top button, so she applied herself to the zipper. The sound it made as it pulled apart was loud in the silence of the apartment.

Devon was by the bed now, but he made no move to lie down. The laughter had faded from his face and now only the desire was left. Lilah watched in satisfaction as that desire turned darker, wilder, with every slow inch of skin revealed by the droop of her open pants. Hooking her thumbs in her white cotton panties, Lilah sucked in a deep breath and pushed them down along with the pants, kicking both to the side.

When she straightened up, fully naked, skin prickling in the chilled air of the bedroom, she saw that Devon was still frozen beside the bed, one hand fisted tightly in the coverlet.

There was nothing frozen about his eyes, though, and the air that had begun to feel too cool suddenly heated up under the warmth of his gaze.

"Now you," Lilah said. Her voice was husky and languid, a stranger's voice, as if a seductress spoke through Lilah's mouth. *Method acting,* she thought a little hysterically. *Feel sexy and you'll be sexy.*

And then all thoughts whirled away like dandelion fluff on the breeze, because Devon started pulling his clothes off.

His chest gleamed in the low light, the muscles clearly defined and sharp like something out of a magazine. He was golden tan all over, *all* over, and Lilah could just picture him on some exclusive private island, sunning himself in all his glory without a care in the world.

Her gaze fell to the thick, hard penis rearing straight up

against his flat, ridged stomach, and Lilah had to swallow hard.

This was nothing like the shower, where by the time Lilah knew what was happening, Devon was there and bare and making her head spin.

This was so deliberate. They were facing each other, eyes open and clear, stripping down to nothing in preparation for coming together in the most intimate way possible.

A frisson of fear skated up Lilah's spine. It was possible this was an even more dangerous decision than she'd first thought.

And then there was no time to worry about the consequences because she and Devon moved at the same time, arms out and reaching, and clashed together in the middle of the room with a desperate heat and speed.

His mouth was heavy over hers, teeth sharp and merciless, but Lilah was just as ravenous and out of control. For a wild moment, she wanted to bruise him, nip him hard enough to draw blood, to mark him as hers for the whole world to see in the light of day tomorrow.

Lord have mercy. Was she ever in trouble.

CHAPTER TWENTY-FIVE

Nothing in the world tasted better than Lilah Jane Tunkle's neck, Devon decided. He fastened his mouth there, on the left side of the slender column, and let the salty-sweet taste of her explode over his taste buds.

His hands mapped out her juiciest bits, the curves and hollows he remembered so well. She lifted into his arms, her spine bending and pushing her into him. Devon groaned as his cock slid against her belly. He rocked his hips indulgently, loving the silken glide of skin on skin.

Lilah wriggled, her thighs parting restlessly around one of Devon's, and he reached down to palm her delectable ass and drag her bodily into closer contact. The open heart of her pulsed wet and scorching against his leg, and the sound Lilah made as he pressed her down on him made Devon want to throw her to the ground and pump himself into her.

But she asked for the bed, so bed she would have. He picked her up and started to carry her over to it, but every step rubbed his thigh more firmly into the cradle of Lilah's hips, producing more husky little cries, and Devon got distracted.

Kneading his fingers into the softness of her plump cheeks, he took her mouth in a starving kiss. Lilah opened to him, panting into his mouth, and Devon's legs started shaking.

They weren't going to make it to the bed.

He dragged her down to the floor with him before they fell over, blessing his decorator for finishing this room with a lush, thick-piled rug of dusky blue and chocolate brown.

Devon went down on his back and pulled Lilah on top of him, reveling in the sight of her undulating torso rising over him as she straddled his thighs and sat up.

Her amazing hair spiraled out from her head and down her shoulders in an untamable mass of dark ringlets and corkscrew curls. A deep red flush suffused her cheeks and neck. Her eyes were nearly black with passion, all wide-blown pupil with a thin ring of jade.

"Now," she gasped. "Oh, please, now."

Devon's hips bucked involuntarily at that hoarse plea— and a sudden thought gripped his heart with terror.

"Oh, Christ," he said. "I didn't think . . . I don't have anything to protect you . . . Do you?"

"You don't keep condoms in the bedside table?" Lilah shrieked. "What kind of den of iniquity is this?"

"Sorry," Devon said. He didn't know it was possible to laugh when he was this hard. "If you give me a second, I can go get one."

Lilah gripped his waist with her thighs, though, and growled—honest to fuck *growled* at him—and that was it. Devon was done.

"Come here," he rasped, dragging her down to him. He pried open her jaw with one hand and sucked her tongue into his mouth. Their lower bodies writhed together, legs and hips working feverishly. Devon got a hand on the small of her back and pushed until he felt the tender head of his cock forge through the petal-soft folds of her sex.

She was open around him, mouth and legs and arms and sex, and Devon thrust up, letting his dick ride the slick seam of her body and scrape over the tiny nub of her clitoris.

Lilah shuddered and clamped down even harder over him, pushing the heat of herself over him from root to tip, trapping Devon's straining erection against his own stomach.

She moaned and shivered and moved on top of him, and he forced his eyes open to see her.

Lilah was a thing of beauty in the midst of mindless passion. Dark brows drawn tight in concentration, eyes buttoned shut. Her hips danced against his, the pressure maddening and perfect and everything Devon needed in this moment.

He wanted her exactly like this, transported and uninhibited, gloriously selfish in her pursuit of her own elusive pleasure.

His shaft still outside her body, yet sliding smoothly in her cleft, she ground down on him in a circular motion that made a series of husky groans spill from her throat and tremors shake her thighs. She hung there, suspended, and Devon encircled her back with his arms and pressed her down hard while thrusting up with all his strength.

One last pass of his painfully hard prick through the searing softness of her, and he exploded between them in jets of white.

Lilah was like warm cream against him, all limp and pliant in the aftermath. Devon's back started to hurt where his spine had been ground into the floor, and if they didn't get up soon they were going to end up glued together, but he couldn't seem to make himself care.

After long moments of doing nothing more than passing breath back and forth and tracking the slowing of their heartbeats, Lilah shifted and sat up.

Unsure of what he'd see on her expressive face, Devon folded his arms behind his head and schooled his expression to simple satisfaction.

She gazed down at him, the picture of heavy-lidded sensuality.

"Well. I certainly never did it *that* way before."

"What way? On the floor or without actual penetration?"

"Both," she clarified, without a trace of a blush. Devon smiled. He'd fucked the blush right out of her.

"Did you like it?"

"I did." She looked thoughtful. "I don't know what you've got against a bed, though. Too conventional for you?"

"Next time," he promised her.

"Oh-ho, so you think there's going to be a next time, do you?" Lilah said, grinning down at him. She appeared perfectly comfortable nude and smeared with the evidence of Devon's passion.

Devon admitted to himself that he could easily get addicted to the sight.

"There'll be a next time," he said. "I've got proximity and your sense of adventure on my side."

"Mmm," she purred, drooping against him. "I like that. Adventure. You know, you're probably the only person in the world who sees me like that. Or sees it as a good thing."

"Maybe I'm the only one who stands to benefit directly from it."

"Oooh, standing," she said, sounding delighted. "Let's try it that way next."

Devon groaned, but his cock lengthened and gave a twitch of interest. "Christ. I've created a monster."

Lilah leveled him with a pointed stare. It was very effective in the nude. "You created nothing. And don't swear."

"All right, all right. Geez. Bossy," Devon grumbled, but there was a warm glow of pleasure in his chest.

"That's my job," she said.

Devon tried not to tense, wondering if she'd remember her previous objections to her nanny job translating into sex with Devon.

He brazened it out. "So what do you think? Like this job any better than the last one? I imagine the perks are incomparable." It was surprisingly hard to dredge up a cocky, careless grin.

He relaxed when he felt her snort against his shoulder. "Bless your little heart. Your ego trip is a bumpy one, isn't it?"

"Not usually," Devon confessed. "Mostly it's a pretty smooth ride. Lately, though, with Market . . . And Tucker, too . . ."

Lilah clucked soothingly, like a mother hen. Devon wanted to mock her, but found himself unreasonably soothed by it, so he didn't.

For once uninterested in talking about himself, Devon said, "You want to take this to the bed? I think we can make it now."

"My knees are starting to get a little sore," Lilah agreed.

They hauled their weary, well-used bodies up off the floor and fell into Lilah's bed. Devon stretched like a cat against the bazillion-thread-count sheets and congratulated himself again on reaching a level of success where Egyptian cotton against his skin was a normal, everyday occurrence.

With gentle persistence, Lilah curled herself into his side and said, "Do you want to talk about Tucker? We never did manage to have that discussion about how he should be spending his time."

Devon froze. She wanted him to participate in the planning, take some responsibility. He understood that, but the idea of it terrified him. He was bound to fuck it up. "Not really. I agreed to hang out with you two. Can't we figure it out as we go?"

"Sure. That's good enough for me," Lilah said, although her tone indicated something more along the lines of "For now."

Devon decided to take what he could get. Seeking a change of subject that would be sufficiently distracting to get Lilah off his back about Tucker and other tricky topics, Devon said, "So tell me about this mythical Aunt Bertie you're always talking about."

"Aunt Bertie. What can I say about her? She and Uncle Roy took me in when I was a baby. My mother, her sister, got in trouble with the high school quarterback. He ran off before I was born, and my mother had me, dumped me with Bertie, who was already married and settled, and took off after him. For all I know, they're living happily ever after in Timbuktu."

"Jesus," Devon said, shocked despite himself. "Oh, come on, don't give me the eyes. That's definitely worth a little blasphemy. I'm sorry that happened to you, Lilah Jane."

"I'm not," she said stoutly. There was no hesitation in her voice or regret in her clear green eyes. "I was better off. Aunt Bertie and Uncle Roy raised me, along with a pack of cousins, on their farm. Everything I know about cooking, human nature, life in general, is due to my Aunt Bertie."

"You miss her," he said, a sinking feeling dragging at his guts. He didn't want to examine it.

"Of course I do," Lilah said. Then she sighed. "Well, I do and I don't. Aunt Bertie is a . . . fairly forceful personality. My uncle calls her Hurricane Bertie. She's one of those people who knows exactly the right thing to do in every situation—and always does it."

"Not very comfortable to live with."

"Not all the time, no. I got pretty good at it, though."

She fell silent and Devon rolled to his back and stared at the ceiling, contemplating this new information. Whatever Lilah wanted him to believe—hell, whatever she believed herself—he could read between the lines about that childhood in Virginia.

In a small town like that? Her mother's fall from grace would've been a scandal that dogged Lilah's footsteps everywhere she went. And life with Aunt Bertie and her brood . . . Devon felt a sudden, swift tug of kinship for the lonely little girl who didn't quite fit in, but wanted to, so badly that she ruthlessly suppressed her desire for excitement, passion, adventure, to live the safe, normal life her mother couldn't.

And he thought he understood a little better why Lilah was so quick to jump in when it looked like Devon was about to let Tucker go.

Lilah was falling asleep; her body rested more heavily against him with every passing moment. He urged her closer with an arm wrapped around her shoulders and didn't question his desire to stay awake, in spite of his exhaustion, and watch over her rest.

Just before she dropped off, she turned her face into his neck and muttered, "Tomorrow. Gonna catch fireflies."

Devon smiled. One more mystery to ponder before sleep took him.

CHAPTER TWENTY-SIX

Lilah was speaking quite literally when she said they'd catch fireflies.

It was on her list of Things to Do with Tucker to Make Devon Realize He'd Be a Great Dad. The list was long; she was proud of it.

On Monday, they went to the Metropolitan Museum of Art for an hour in the afternoon. Tucker was very interested in the paintings, although he pointed and snickered at the nude sculptures.

"Which painting do you like best in this room?" Lilah asked.

Cocking his head to one side, Tucker took the question seriously. "This one."

It was a gory scene, two men on horseback being attacked by tigers. Lilah wasn't terribly surprised by the subject matter he chose; what surprised her was the reason he gave: "The leopard, the dead one in the front, with the tongue going like this?" He demonstrated, unnecessarily. "I like how real it looks. Like you can see every hair in its tail."

"That's quite an observation," she said, impressed. She looked more closely. The painting was a Rubens. Tucker had good taste.

Devon cleared his throat. "You like art, huh? I've seen you drawing in that notebook."

Tucker shrugged. "Yeah, I like it. We started learning how to draw some cool stuff last year in art class."

A frisson of excitement raised the hairs on Lilah's arms. They were talking! They were having a moment!

Hoping to gently encourage it, she said, "What do you think you'll learn next year?"

Tucker shrugged again and turned away from the painting. "Nothing. We don't get to have art next year."

"Why not?" Devon asked.

Tucker scrunched up his face. "Ms. Donaldson, the art teacher? We had a big party for her at the end of the year because she had to go away. But there's not going to be a new teacher, they said. So we can't have class."

As they moved on to the next room, Lilah noticed Devon's drawn brows.

"Same story all over," Lilah said. "Public schools are losing funding for arts programs."

"That doesn't seem right," Devon said. "Where else are kids going to start figuring out what they like to do? I took home ec in high school to piss off my dad, but it turned out to be the best decision I ever made. I found cooking and knew I could be good enough at it to get out of Trenton. I can't imagine any other way I would've figured that out."

"Believe me, I know. I loved teaching drama—those bright, young faces all eager to explore the possibilities. For some of those county kids, practicing a scene in my class was the closest they'd ever come to seeing what else is out there in the wide world. But the school levy failed, cuts had to be made, and of course, the theater and art departments were the first things to go."

"And just like that, the job and the future you thought were so secure were ripped away," Devon said with one of his sudden bursts of insight.

"Not to be trite, but I do believe things happen for a reason. If I hadn't been let go by the school district, I wouldn't be here right now."

It was easy to be philosophical, Lilah found, when the handsomest man in the room was staring down at her with something perilously close to affection on his face.

"You'd still be Lolly, not my Lilah Jane." Devon smiled, the real smile he didn't wear on television or to get his way or to hide what he was truly feeling. It was small, a little lopsided quirk of the mouth, and it made Lilah want to drag him behind the nearest marble sculpture and kiss him breathless.

Instead, they followed Tucker around the rest of the European Paintings gallery before hitting the museum shop, where Devon spent a small fortune on art supplies for Tucker.

Lilah shook her head, but she recognized gift-giving was Devon's comfort zone with his son. She let it go and steered them both around the back of the building and into Central Park.

The late summer days were getting shorter, and just as Lilah had hoped, even at four o'clock in the afternoon, the Sheep Meadow flickered with elusive lightning bugs. Not many, and it was hard to see them before true dusk fell, but Devon had to get to the restaurant in half an hour.

Tucker gaped at the insects like he'd never seen fireflies before, then leaped after them like a young gazelle.

Devon and Lilah sat on the grass and watched for a while in contented silence before Devon headed off to work, and Lilah gathered up her sweaty, red-faced charge and dragged him back to the apartment for a bath.

When he was clean again, she stuffed Tucker's new art supplies in his backpack and got Paolo to drive them to Market.

Devon didn't look particularly surprised or pleased to see them, but he didn't throw them out, either, so Lilah counted it as a win. She let Tucker say hello to Frankie, to whom he'd taken a disconcerting liking. Then, since Violet was already done for the night, Lilah installed Tucker at the back pastry table with his notebook and colored pencils.

She sat with him awhile, chatted with Grant when he had a second, and just generally tried not to be in the way.

When Tucker started to frown and squint at the paper, running his hands through his hair the exact same way his dad did, Lilah packed up their things and carried him back to the apartment.

Devon took a moment to wave good-bye from his place up at the pass. Lilah's smile was so wide her cheeks hurt by the time they got home.

Hours later, when Devon walked in the door, he came straight to Lilah's room. She had waited up for him reading one of her New York City guidebooks—pretty soon she'd be able to give guided tours herself—and wearing the blue pajamas.

His eyes flared with heat when he saw her propped up in her bed, glasses on her nose. She'd toyed with the idea of waiting for him in something sexier (which she didn't really own) or maybe undies, or even naked, but now she was glad she'd decided not to put on airs. Or lingerie.

That look on his handsome face, and the way he touched her through the thin, soft cotton—Lilah threw her head back on a gasp, vowing to wash those PJs and wear them every single night.

Devon kissed her, and slid his hands down her body, and Lilah melted under the attention like ice cream left out in the sun. And when it was over, he stayed with her until she fell asleep.

That day set the pattern for the next few days. On Tuesday, they took Tucker up to the top of the Empire State Building. Wednesday and Thursday were reserved for the American Museum of Natural History, because it was too huge and too enticing for Tucker to rush through. The planetarium show was an especially big hit.

Every evening, Lilah and Tucker hopped into the big black chauffeured car and headed to Market for family meal with the restaurant crew.

At first, Devon mostly observed as his brigade took breaks to joke with Tucker (Frankie) or show off their knife skills (Milo, who could carve the most marvelous shapes out of vegetables) or let Tucker stir something on the stove

(Quentin, whose quiet, easy manner with the boy made Lilah smile).

But as time went on, Devon started jumping in. He'd throw a careless remark Tucker's way, or hold out his hand for a high-five as he passed by. Because Tucker tended to watch his father covertly and constantly, he always responded instantly, which had Devon grinning like a fool.

Sometimes Lilah had to bite her lip to keep from laughing—or maybe crying—at the tentative bob and weave of their father-son bonding ritual.

It was slow and a little painful to watch, but progress was being made.

Devon felt it, too, she could tell. Service hadn't improved much over the past week—customers were still unhappy and reservations had started dropping off as word spread—but Devon didn't descend into the black despair she'd seen in him that night at Chapel.

He wasn't thrilled, and obviously wanted desperately to do well at Market—but there was something else in his life now, something that was good and getting better, and Lilah could see the difference it made. Even if he wasn't aware of it yet.

And every night when he came to her bed and made her writhe and sob and act like a complete hussy, Lilah thought there might be more than Tucker making Devon happy these days.

By Friday, they were all getting tired of running around the city, so they made a quick trip to the magical wonderland of Dylan's Candy Bar before taking their treats back to the apartment and settling on the couch for a movie.

Lilah wasn't dumb enough to let Tucker or Devon pick; she had no interest in sitting through *Terminator 9* or something. The boys grumbled, united for once in their desire for explosions and car chases, but Lilah was implacable.

"*The Goonies* is a classic," she said, leveling a severe frown at the sofa. "It's disgraceful that Tucker hasn't seen it."

Devon's mouth twisted. "What would you say if I told you I haven't seen it, either?"

Lilah gave a theatrical gasp and fell backward, clutching her heart. She kept very still, eyes closed. Tucker squawked and jumped off the sofa to kneel by her head. It was hard not to smile or twitch when he poked her, but Lilah managed it.

"You killed her," he whispered to Devon.

"Good," said his father heartlessly. "That means we can watch whatever we want. Have you seen the *Evil Dead* movies?"

Tucker shouted with laughter as Lilah sat straight up, indignant. "Hey! A little respect, if you please. *Evil Dead* is hardly appropriate when your . . ." She stopped, suddenly uncertain what to call herself, how to relate herself to this unexpectedly warm family moment. ". . . *whatever* is dead."

She looked at Devon, who looked back at her. The moment stretched like taffy until Tucker, shockingly, broke it by saying, "Our Lolly. And you're not dead, so I guess we hafta watch the goons, huh?"

"*Goonies*, you little philistine," she said, but it came out all scratchy and tear-clogged.

Luckily, Tucker was too busy dealing with the high-tech gadgetry involved in putting on the movie to notice, but when Lilah ducked her head away from him she had to face the couch.

Devon's knowing gaze was heavy on her face. He laid his arm along the back of the couch in open invitation, and Lilah moved into it, shaky but happy and a little scared.

Dear Lord, she prayed silently. *Please don't let me want this too much.*

But when Tucker got the system working and scooted onto the couch on Lilah's other side, when she felt his warm little body curled into hers and Devon's hard side shifting against her ribs and hip, the heat of his arm behind her neck, she knew.

It was too late for prayers.

There was no help for it; not even divine intervention could stop her from falling for these two.

* * *

Another night, another awful dinner service. Devon dispirit-edly wiped a few droplets of the truffle foam he'd added to the rib-eye entree from the rim of the white plate.

He didn't even know why he couldn't seem to let the chefs go back to cooking the menu Adam had left in place. Pure assholic pig-headedness, probably. But it would feel too much like admitting defeat.

He sent the server off with a tray full of dinners that would probably come back half-eaten and looked over his shoulder to the one ray of light in the gloom-and-doom kitchen.

Lilah had Tucker next to her at a burner near the end of the line. They were out of the way of regular dinner-rush traffic, not that there was much of a rush tonight. Lilah was helping Tuck stir something in a cast-iron Dutch oven.

Curious, Devon called, "Frankie. Get up here and run the pass for a minute."

He ignored the look the sous chef shot him—seriously, what damn sous chef hated to call the shots at the hot plate? It was insane—and strode up the line to the last burner.

Lilah and Tucker were bent solicitously over something extremely noxious-looking. Devon recoiled a little.

"What the hell is that?"

"Language! Tuck, tell your father what we're making."

"It's green."

Devon snuck a peek. "Sort of. If you squint. It's more like the color of sewage. Sludge."

Tucker did the gagging noises he loved. "Sick!"

"Not green, sugar pop," Lilah explained with the exag-gerated patience of someone who'd made this explanation more than once. "Greens, with an 's.' Collard greens, to be exact. With bacon, apple cider vinegar, and caramelized red onions."

"And you intend to do what with this toxic mess?" Devon inquired in his politest tone.

Lilah narrowed her eyes at him. "This *delicious* and *nu-tritious* dish is for tomorrow's family meal. Billy has a late doctor's appointment, so we're filling in."

Evidently misinterpreting Devon's appalled look, Lilah

rushed to add, "Don't worry! I'll make a quick buttermilk cornbread to go with it. And the greens will actually be better tomorrow. Like with a stew or soup—the flavors develop and deepen overnight."

Devon shared an "ugh" face with Tucker. "Yeah, but why would you want to develop any flavor that smells like that?"

Lilah pointed her wooden spoon at Tucker, who stopped cackling immediately. "You. Don't knock it till you try it. Have I steered you wrong yet?"

By tacit agreement, Lilah had done all the cooking at the apartment after Devon's disastrous attempt at breakfast. He didn't care if it made him a coward; he hated the idea of scraping another plate of food he'd prepared into the garbage because his son couldn't choke it down. No plate sent back to the Market kitchen from an unsatisfied customer made Devon feel like half such a failure as the memory of that breakfast.

Still, he thought Tucker and he might be on the same page this time.

"Come on, Lilah Jane," Devon wheedled. "Don't inflict the Sludge of Death on us."

Shooting him an irritated look, Lilah went back to stirring. "What do you care, anyhow? It's not like you'll eat family meal with us."

Devon drew back, stung. Sure, he had too much to do most nights before service to sit down with everyone, but that's what it meant to be executive chef. Before he could defend himself, though, Lilah continued.

"And it's not like you'd taste it even if you did take a bite."

Devon blinked. "What do you mean by that?"

Lilah blew a damp curl out of her eyes with an aggravated huff. "You hardly eat. And when you do, it's so rushed you can't possibly taste anything! It's as if you don't even like food."

The floor shifted under Devon's feet.

He wanted to deny it, but with a shock that tightened his stomach, he realized he couldn't actually remember the last thing he'd eaten and enjoyed.

"That's ridiculous," he said, clearing his throat and attempting to steady himself. "I'm a chef. Liking food is in the job description."

Her hand slowed in its circular motion around the pot. Devon felt time slow down with it, as if his entire life, his whole future, hung on this conversation.

Lilah faced him fully. Her green eyes were wide and mossy, soft with something like compassion. Devon flinched under it like a blow.

"I watch you when you're up at the pass sending out plates to the customers," she said. "And I can tell you're not really tasting those sauces and foams and whatnot."

She spoke softly enough that the hustle of service kept the rest of the crew from being able to overhear, and yet Devon felt as if every word were being trumpeted through a bullhorn.

He made an instinctual gesture of denial, and Lilah put a hand on his arm to stop him from stepping away. "Oh, you put the spoon in your mouth, you go 'hmmm,'" she said. "But do you really *taste* it? I don't think so."

Shit. Cold sweat prickled along his hairline. Was she right? Had he lost his palate?

For a chef, a good palate was a must. The ability to discern individual flavors and the ways ingredients played off each other could make or break you in this business, and Devon wanted to shout and rage that he never could've become so successful, come so far from where he started, if he'd had a shitty palate—but he said nothing.

He stood there in his borrowed kitchen in dumbfounded, horrified silence.

The rumors, the vicious gossip—it was all true. Devon always knew the show was heavily edited, the situations carefully screened before he ever walked into them. This proved it. The show was a put-up job. Every "win," every episode where he beat the odds and pulled off a fabulous meal . . . that must all be a foregone conclusion before he ever stepped on set.

As for the continued success of his restaurants across the country, it had been years since Devon took credit for them, at least in his own mind. He'd hired great executive chefs to oversee each operation, then stepped back to reap the financial rewards. Sure, there were dishes he'd created on the menus at all of them, but they were all classic Sparks signature dishes. Nothing from the last five years.

The truth took Devon's breath away.

He wasn't a chef anymore. He was a fake.

More than the presence of his already demoralized temporary brigade stopped him from exploding. Even more than the innate reluctance to admit such a terrible weakness in front of the son whose good opinion Devon was just starting to earn, it was the look on Lilah's face that gave him pause.

Straight pity would've enraged him; condemnation or derision would've given him something to fight against. But there was no fighting the calm acceptance in her eyes.

"Uh, Chef?"

The stammered call came from the front of the kitchen, up by the pass. Devon tore his eyes off Lilah, still reeling, and snarled, "What?"

It was Grant. Great. Lilah's ex-boyfriend/high school sweetheart/best friend/whatever was not what he needed at this moment.

"Someone here to see you."

CHAPTER TWENTY⊰SEVEN

"Again? In the middle of dinner service?" Devon glanced from Grant to Frankie. "Does this happen when Adam's running the show? People feel free to waltz in, visit the kitchen brigade like the monkey house at the zoo?"

The picture of insolence, Frankie curled his lip. "Nah, must be you, mate. Ever so popular, you are."

Beside the pass, the door to the dining room swung open and Simon Woolf, Devon's ex-publicist, pushed past Grant and into the kitchen.

"Dev!" Simon hurried over, pausing for a disconcerted moment when he perceived Lilah and Tucker next to Devon. He squinted at Lilah as if he knew he ought to be able to place her, but couldn't.

A quick glance at Lilah's set lips revealed she had none of the same difficulty, but Simon didn't pause for introductions or reminiscences.

"There you are! Why haven't you been returning my calls?"

"In case you've forgotten, Simon, I fired you."

"That's not important right now." Simon waved a hand. "I know you didn't mean it. And even if you did, you must be ready to change your mind."

"I don't change my mind. You know that."

Except sometimes he did. Devon's gaze went to Tucker attempting to steady himself on Lilah's shoulder so he could stand on the stool. He glanced back to Simon to find the publicist's shrewd eyes on the woman and child by the stove.

Devon stiffened. "You're wasting your time, Si. Worse, you're wasting mine."

"Come on, Dev. I've got your best interests at heart. Don't I always?" he said as he sauntered over to the pair at the stove. "So who's your friend? Want to introduce me?"

Lilah gave the publicist a bland look. "I've already had the distinct pleasure of meeting you. I didn't catch your name, but I did get most of your drink. Down my blouse."

Carefully turning the heat to low and covering her pot of stewed weeds, she helped Tucker down from the stool and whispered something in his ear that had him bounding up the line to stand by Frankie at the pass. Devon watched him go, surprised to realize how many of the line cooks grinned at Tucker or high-fived him as he ran by.

Simon, with his usual studied poise, reflected none of the embarrassment he probably ought to feel from the reminder of that first encounter. He flashed his sparkling white smile, held out a hand and said, "Simon Woolf, PR to the stars. And you are?"

"Lilah Jane Tunkle. Charmed, I'm sure."

She gave him her hand, regal as any born-and-bred Southern princess.

Simon held on to her fingers a beat too long to please Devon, who growled, "Drop it, Fido. Time to get to the point. Why are you here?"

Unhurriedly letting Lilah go, the publicist gave Devon a wounded look. "I was worried. My biggest client falls off the grid—naturally, I wanted to make sure you were copasetic. And then, of course, when all the rumors started flying, I had to find you."

"Rumors?" Devon asked sharply. He cursed himself the moment the word flew out of his mouth and he caught the glint of triumph in Simon's eye, but it was too late. He was caught.

"I don't want to bother you if you're busy with Lilah," Simon said with a speaking glance.

Lilah, who apparently spoke fluent publicist, merely crossed her arms over her chest and planted her heels.

"It's fine," Devon said, impatient. "You can say whatever in front of her."

Simon didn't look startled, more satisfied—as if Devon had confirmed a suspicion. "All righty, then." He moved smoothly into his soothing-the-savage-celebrity voice. "I don't want you to get upset, because there's an easy fix, but you should know that rumors are circulating that Market has gone downhill since Adam Temple left you in charge." He paused for a grave moment. "I won't lie. Your reputation has taken a hit."

Okay. On some level, Devon knew this was coming. On the heels of Lilah's blunt assessment and his own realization of the staggering amount of self-delusion he'd been practicing, this new problem merely added to the defeated exhaustion dragging him down. "And you want me to do what about it? I'm weeded bad here, Simon. The rumors are right, we're in the shit every night. I'm messing this up like a first-year culinary school grad. Worse! We've got an ACA extern who's doing way better than me."

Devon heard Lilah's quiet intake of breath. She was probably in shock that he'd admitted it, but shit, what was the point of fooling himself? If he'd really lost his palate, he was done for. That was a career killer, right there.

"Not so loud," Simon hissed. "Have I taught you nothing about public perception? You project total confidence at all times, period. Nobody wants to see the man behind the curtain, Dev. You know that."

This time Lilah snorted, and it wasn't quiet.

Ignoring her, Simon went on, "Now, Dev, it's simple, really. All you have to do is hire me back. I'll arrange everything. You'll give a public statement with a credible reason for the downturn in Market's popularity—like alcoholism, for instance."

Devon winced, eyes zooming to Tucker, laughing at some damn face Frankie was pulling. "Shit. I don't have a drinking problem."

"Drugs, then," Simon said, waving the details away as inconsequential. "Doesn't matter. Oldest story in the world. You'll have to go away for a while, of course, for 'rehab'—it's a nice opportunity for a vacation, a break from everything, and really, I think it's the best thing for you. When you come back from vacay, I bet everything will look different."

It was nothing Devon hadn't heard before. In the four years since he'd hired Simon to handle public relations for the growing Sparks brand, Simon had engineered countless publicity opportunities for Devon. In the past, Devon had followed Simon's advice without a second thought—because he knew that he and Simon were driving hard toward the exact same goal.

Yet somehow, standing here with sweet Lilah Jane at his side, Devon wasn't so sure anymore.

Devon opened his mouth to tell his publicist where he could stick it, but Lilah stopped him with an imploring hand.

She undoubtedly meant to grab his elbow, but he shifted at the last second and her palm landed against his lower ribs. The touch jolted his system like a shock, the intimacy of it warm and welcome in the strange crossroads moment where Devon now found himself.

Lilah looked down at the hand on Devon's side as if surprised to find it attached to her wrist, but she left it there.

If she thought the weight of it would add to the strength of her imploring gaze, she was right. Lilah turned those big, baby-doll eyes on him and Devon was ready to do almost anything to keep her looking at him like that.

"Don't do that," she urged. "Oh, please, Devon, don't say you're going into rehab. You can't! What will happen to Tucker?"

A spike of annoyance shot through him. "Why do you

assume I would?" he demanded, ignoring the fact that up until a week ago, he wouldn't have hesitated for an instant.

"Oh. I just thought . . . I know how much your reputation means to you."

It was satisfying, the way her gaze slid down and to the side. Her hand dropped, too, though, which wasn't as good.

He backed away from both Simon and Lilah, tucking his hands under his arms and mustering up the biggest, cockiest smirk he could manage.

Reckless exhilaration swept through him. If Devon Sparks was going down, he was going down swinging.

"Damn straight," he said. "I worked too long and hard building this reputation to let it all go to shit over one misguided favor for a friend."

"So you'll do the press conference?" Simon put in, all eager beaver.

"Bet your ass I will," Devon said. He savored Simon's gloating face and Lilah's disappointment for five deliciously cruel seconds before finishing, "But I won't be announcing a stay at Betty Ford. I'll be inviting them all to cover my first annual charity fundraiser—to be held in one week, right here at Market."

Jaws dropped in tandem. It shouldn't have given him such a lowdown, delighted tickle, but it did.

If assholery were an Olympic event, I could go for the gold.

"Crank up the PR machine," he told Simon. "I want everybody who's been preemptively dancing on the grave of my career here next Saturday for the best dinner any of them have ever tasted."

Simon pressed his lips together so hard they were just a thin white line in his pink face, but he produced his beloved PDA from an inner jacket pocket and started tapping away at it furiously.

"We're going to fill the place up," Devon went on, "one hundred and ten spots, let's say eight courses, fifteen hundred dollars a plate. Proceeds to go to . . ."

He stopped. Thought for a second, then looked right into

Lilah's too-bright eyes, drinking in the tremulous smile on her rosebud mouth.

"All money raised at the event will go to support the Center for Arts Education of New York. Every kid in this city deserves to go to a school with programs like theater and fine arts."

"Devon Sparks," she breathed. "You dark horse, you."

Rocking back on his heels, Devon reveled in the moment. He intended to milk it for everything it was worth.

"Yeah, I've been reading up," he said smugly.

Lilah shook her head slowly, as if to clear it from a disorienting smack.

"Since when? How? Devon, this is so . . ."

"Do you know how many charity events I get asked to cook for? A celebrity chef bumps up the fundraising power of any nonprofit quite a bit. I have stacks of requests on my desk. After that day at the Met, I had Daniel flag any charities that had to do with the arts and public schools. I was just gonna donate money or something, but this will be so much better."

Satisfaction spread through Devon like the warmth from swallowing a shot of good bourbon. "We'll raise awareness for a good cause, redistribute the wealth of some people who can definitely afford it, and I'll have the chance to show all the two-bit critics and haters out there what I'm made of. It's perfect."

He ignored, for the moment, the question of his possibly corrupted palate, his uncooperative kitchen brigade, his apparently unappealing menu.

No one ever succeeded by focusing on the obstacles.

"I could kiss you right now," Lilah said in a low, intense voice.

"What's stopping you?" Devon asked, reckless with anticipation of the upcoming battle.

With a grin and an answering recklessness in her eyes, Lilah threw her arms around Devon's neck and gave a little hop, forcing him to catch her.

He got her laughing mouth under his and kissed her hard enough and long enough that by the time they were done, every cook in the kitchen was whistling and stomping, cat-calls filling the air like a standing ovation.

CHAPTER TWENTY-EIGHT

Lilah closed the door to Tucker's room and hurried back to the gleaming kitchen, where Devon was uncorking a bottle of wine.

He looked up at her with an easy smile. "He asleep?"

The chardonnay was pale gold and pretty in the fragile wine glass. "Before his head hit the pillow. Poor boy, we kept him out late tonight."

They'd stayed until service was over so Devon could talk to the cooks and servers about his amazing new plan, and now it felt good to be home.

Her heart was so full right now, Lilah was sure everything she felt must be spilling out of her eyes, her pores, the ends of her fingers and toes.

She was awash in love. And it was dangerously tempting to let the whole world know it.

Lilah took a sip of wine to keep her mouth occupied. She was afraid she'd start babbling her feelings any second.

"Hey, you didn't wait for the toast," Devon said, smiling.

Lilah swallowed quickly. "Sorry! Oh, hey, that stuff's really good. But sorry! What do you want to toast to?"

Looking amused, Devon held out his glass and said, "How about to the future?"

"To good food, good friends, and good weather," Lilah said. "That's my Uncle Roy's favorite."

"Then it's good enough for me," Devon replied, touching his glass to hers. The melodic chime that rang out made Lilah think their glasses, thin and delicate as they were, were actually crystal. She immediately shifted her fingers to hold the stem more gingerly.

The wine tasted even better now, probably because she wasn't gulping it down. It had a citrusy bite that shocked Lilah's tongue before it mellowed into a soft, peachy aftertaste.

Shoot. She might end up gulping the rest of it yet.

"I don't think the weather will be an issue," Devon mused. "At least, I don't think there's a chance it'll be anything other than muggy and scorching hot. August isn't New York's best month. But the other two parts of the toast—they could give me some trouble."

"Good food and good friends? I hope not."

There was a wry twist to Devon's mouth. "I haven't exactly been Mr. Popular with the Market staff."

"You've got me," she said, and her heart started pounding. "As a friend, I mean. Well, as more than a friend, but . . . well . . . you know what I mean."

Slow, lazy cat smile from Devon.

"And the food," Lilah babbled. "That's no problem, I mean, I'm sure you've got tons of dishes you're famous for at those restaurants of yours. Cherry-pick a few of those and you'll be ready before you know it!"

Devon sank down onto one of the bench seats in his breakfast nook. "No. I don't want to do something I've done a million times before. I want to prove—to myself," he emphasized, "that my palate's not gone. I can still come up with a great menu."

Best to be delicate about this. "How, exactly, do you mean to go about it?" she asked.

Devon gave her a look that said he knew she was trying to handle him.

"I think we'll start with a blind taste test." He set his glass on the table and cracked his knuckles like a man about to embark on a difficult task. His eyes, though, were shining with the challenge, which was such a beautiful change from the agonized loss that had filled his whole body earlier. Lilah was so caught up in enjoying the difference that she almost missed what he'd said.

"Wait. A blind taste test?"

"Oh, yeah. My brigade and I, back when I was first starting out in the restaurant business, we used to play this game all the time after service."

Devon hopped up from the table and started rooting around in one of the drawers until he pulled out a black linen napkin with a triumphant grin.

"We tie this on, like so." He mimed covering his eyes with the cloth. "And you put out a variety of different foods for me to taste. You time me, see how many I get right in one minute. I used to be able to do fifteen."

"That's it?"

"I valued accuracy over speed; it was always fifteen out of fifteen correct. And it's harder than you think. You don't realize how much you rely on your sight to give you information about what you're tasting until it's taken away. Then it's all about your palate. Nothing else."

Lilah licked her lips. It was probably stupid, but she was nervous for him. Devon was nothing if not mercurial; he was so energized and positive right now, she'd hate to see him fail and tumble back into the doldrums.

"Come on, Lilah Jane," he coaxed, as if sensing her reluctance. "I can do this, I know I can. I need to get back to basics. Help me wake my taste buds up."

"Can you see anything?"

Devon felt a shift in the air in front of his face, as if Lilah were waving her hand before his blindfolded eyes. He shook his head. "It's black as night under here."

"Okay. Boy, you've sure got some crazy stuff in this

kitchen. Even with both eyes open, I'm not sure what some of it is or how the heck you'd cook it."

Devon could hear her moving around the kitchen, gathering things from the fridge, the pantry. At least one item required chopping; another, mixing. She spent some time at the stove, made multiple trips back and forth across the kitchen. It was the auditory equivalent of spinning a kid in a circle before a game of pin-the-tail-on-the-donkey.

Except this wasn't child's play to Devon. As the knotted tension in his neck and the clammy palms of his hands could attest, this was deadly serious.

If he couldn't do this taste test anymore, if he couldn't recognize the flavors Lilah put in front of him, he might as well pack it in right now. He'd do the fundraiser with old, well-tested recipes, and that would be it. He'd retire.

Unwilling to confront the terrifying question of what he'd do *after* he retired, Devon shifted on the bench, making the leather creak loudly. He rubbed his hands dry on his pants and ran his tongue around the inside of his mouth.

He'd had plain crackers and a glass of water to bring his palate back to neutral after the wine. He was as ready as he'd ever be.

Lilah kept his jitters from escalating by placing something on the table in front of him with a quiet *clack*.

"Here we go," she said, and guided his hand to the rim of what Devon recognized as one of his glass nesting bowls.

He breathed out through his nose and dipped his fingers into the bowl. The roughly diced contents were slightly wet and cool to the touch. Vegetable, his mind immediately supplied.

Devon popped a couple pieces into his mouth and crunched down, releasing a sharp, almost licorice flavor.

With a burst of relief, Devon recognized it. "Raw fresh fennel root," he said.

"Right!" Lilah sounded so thrilled for him, Devon had to grin.

"Next," he reminded her. "Clock's ticking."

"Shoot, okay, sorry. Here you go."

This time his hand found the chill, matte edges of one of his small French stoneware plates. He knocked his fingers against a mound of tiny spheres that scattered and rolled when he touched them.

He captured a few and brought them to his lips. They were smooth and very fragrant, the scent herbal and lemony. The taste was the same as the smell, only sharper, the little balls dry and almost powdery against his tongue.

Devon dabbed up a few more and tasted again, frowning. Something about it reminded him of traveling through India. "Dried coriander seed?"

"Right again! This is fun. I can see why you and your cooks liked doing it. Okay, try this."

The next few items went quickly; he easily identified Hawaiian acacia honey, coconut milk, chopped hard-boiled egg, pomegranate juice, smoked Scottish salmon, tamarind paste, and minced chives. He wasted precious seconds on a spicy-sweet powder that smelled like Christmas—allspice? Ground cloves? Grated nutmeg?—and eventually got it right with ground mace.

"Sneaky," he told Lilah. "I'm impressed." He was—she'd managed to put together a great test with widely varied textures and flavor profiles. She hadn't taken it easy on him. Devon loved that about her.

"I can't believe you got that last one." She sounded faintly grumpy. "I thought I'd stumped you for sure."

"Mace is tough," Devon agreed. "It's actually the lacy shell covering the nutmeg seed, dried and finely ground. Extremely similar tastes, obviously—mace is a tiny bit more delicate."

Lilah made a "hmph" sound. "There's not a thing wrong with your taste buds, Devon. What have you been playing at over in that Market kitchen?"

Devon shrugged, the growing sense of frustration and confusion a nearly physical weight on his shoulders. "Hell if I know. My menu should be working; obviously my palate isn't dead."

It all boiled over in an instant, like scalded milk frothing out of a hot pan. The self-doubt, the humiliation, the knowledge he was letting his friend down—Devon banged his open hand down on the breakfast table, rattling the discarded tasting bowls.

"Damn it," he snarled. "What the hell is wrong with me?"

For a long moment, the only sound in the kitchen was Devon's harsh breathing. Lilah was so quiet, Devon wondered if he'd finally managed to scare her off, but then she said, "You've got about fifteen seconds left on the clock. You want another taste?"

Devon swallowed the bitter, acrid fear and cleared his throat. "Hit me."

The last item was warm; it must have been one of the things Lilah made a trip to the stove for. The smell tickled his brain, almost familiar, but he couldn't quite place it.

"Need a fork for this one," she said. "Open up."

He opened his mouth and let her feed him. The taste burst over his tongue, smoky, salty, mysterious—Devon chewed quickly and opened his mouth for seconds.

The second bite was even more delicious. It had a firm give when he bit into it, and there was enough liquid and enough of a leafy green texture to remind him of sautéed spinach, but it was nothing so simple as that.

He scowled; it was next to impossible to parse individual ingredients when they married together so well. But he thought he read bacon in the meatiness of the smoke flavor and he was almost sure he tasted the savory caramel of slow-cooked diced onion and the subtle heat of red pepper flakes. And then there was a bright tang of something acidic that brought the whole thing together.

"Oh, my God," he finally said, the last piece of the puzzle jigsawing into place. "I know what this is."

The timer dinged and Devon tore off the blindfold to stare down at the bowl of braised collard greens on the table in front of him.

"You tricky little witch," he said, admiration clear in his voice. "I didn't even know you brought that stuff home."

"When you go to the trouble of cooking up a mess of greens, you don't leave them sitting around a kitchen full of hungry cooks overnight. I wanted to have some left for family meal tomorrow!"

"I can understand your concern," Devon said, dipping the fork back into the dark green mound. "This stuff is addictive. Oh, my *God*."

"All right," Lilah laughed. "Enough with the commandment-breaking. You keep taking the Lord's name in vain, I'm going to have to stand across the room in case He decides to smite you."

"No," Devon said, going back to the bowl for more of the warm, comforting, complex braise. Every bite filled him with a kind of cozy happiness he couldn't recall ever experiencing before. Or at least, not in too many years to count. He felt dazed with contentment. Blinking down at the bowl, Devon was shocked to see how much of the greens he'd put away.

"I mean, it's not a curse or anything—I'm really . . . this is unbelievable. What did you put in this stuff?"

No doubt responding to the helpless bewilderment in his voice, Lilah raised both brows in indignant concern. "Nothing bad! It's my Aunt Bertie's recipe. Well, really, it's my grandmother's, or maybe her mother's. It's been passed down in my family for a long time. And I come from a very old Virginia family! Which might not be a big deal to you, but let me tell you, it's a big deal back home."

"Christ." He started laughing, rusty and hoarse enough to be just around the corner from tears.

Snatching up his bowl, Lilah said, "Hush that laughing. You're the most aggravating man, I swear. Why did you eat it all if you hated it so much?"

Devon sat back. He met her eyes, allowing all of the weird, vulnerable emotion to be visible on his face. "No. Lilah Jane. I loved it. I think it might be the best thing I've ever put in my mouth."

She gazed at him, then down at the empty bowl in her hand, then back again, her, strawberry pink mouth curving in a slow smile. "When I first moved up here, I saw signs for restaurants that served something called 'soul food.' Grant explained that what y'all call 'soul food' is what I always thought of as regular home-cooking: fried chicken, cornbread, barbecued ribs, pecan pie." She tilted the bowl a little. "Collard greens. I never heard it called 'soul food' down South; to me, it was just the way food always was. But up here, so far from where it originated, I think the name works pretty well."

Still feeling sleepy and dim from the aftereffects of a good food coma, Devon shook his head. "What do you mean?"

"Oh, sugar," Lilah said, setting down the bowl and sliding the table back so she could crawl into Devon's lap. She straddled his thighs and crossed her arms behind his neck, her pretty, round-cheeked face mere inches from his.

Devon moved by instinct to clasp her hips in his palms and hold her steady, a warm, exciting weight against him.

"Don't you get it?" Her voice was soft but intense with joy. "Your food hasn't been missing taste. It's been missing that something extra, that indefinable *oomph*, the secret ingredient that makes those collards so yummy. We didn't need to wake up your taste buds. We had to wake up your soul."

The truth of it resonated down to the marrow of Devon's bones. And when Lilah leaned forward and gave him her mouth, he felt the kiss like the sun coming out from behind the clouds, chasing away all the shadows.

CHAPTER TWENTY-NINE

Devon Sparks—the tosser so egregious that the rest of the tossers wouldn't have him at their New Year's Eve party—had gone potty. Screwy. Off his trolley. 'Round the twist.

Abso-bloody-lutely mad.

An eight-course meal for more than a hundred guests. In less than a week now.

Not nearly enough time to plan, and when it bombed, which it certainly would, Market's reputation would go down the drain along with Devon's. It was a disaster in the making, but Frankie couldn't get anyone else to see it.

He felt like that bird who was cursed to know the future but unable to get a single bloody person to listen to her. Cassandra something. Whatever became of her? Probably she was killed in some gruesome manner. Those ancients always seemed to be killing each other off in the most creatively nasty ways.

No use musing on Greek women who came to a sticky end, he told himself. *Things are going to be sticky around here, soon enough.*

Worse than the Tosser's mental breakdown was the fact that it seemed to be catching. When Devon first sprang the news on the crew two days ago, after Friday night's service,

Frankie felt himself blanch in horror—but the rest of the crew nodded like it was the best idea since lace-up leather pants.

Even Grant, who could usually be counted on to inject a dollop of gloom and doom into the proceedings, just shrugged his shoulders and gave a fatalistic "At least it's for a good cause."

Frankie snorted. "Right. Your Lolly got sacked by her school when they ran out of money for her drama program—you see no connection between that and Devon's choice of charities? He's only trying to get into her knickers!"

Grant shrugged. Infuriating.

"Come on, mate," Frankie complained. "Used to be you were always first in line to slag off the Tosser. Fuck me, you practically arm-wrestled Adam and me into leaving Appetite."

"I'm trying to give Devon the benefit of the doubt," Grant said, but he couldn't look Frankie in the eye. Something off, there.

Frankie didn't have time to puzzle out Grant's drama, though. Not when he was consumed by the need to suss out exactly what form of insanity Devon Sparks exhibited.

And speaking of exhibitionism, that kiss! In front of everyone, the kidlet included. Full-on, sweep-her-off-her-feet movie kiss, it was. No one could accuse the Tosser of subtlety.

Jess said Frankie was overreacting. Actually, Jess called him a paranoid, grudge-tastic cynic. Frankie grinned, thinking of it.

The grin faded, though, as his wayward thoughts moved on to the rest of that conversation, which consisted mainly of yet another attempt by Jess to bring up the subject of how things were going to change when he started NYU in a few weeks, followed by yet another artful dodge by Frankie.

He didn't want to think about the future he could feel breathing down the back of his neck like a bouncer at a posh club, just waiting for one false move to throw Frankie out on his arse.

Glowering down at his beloved grill, Frankie rubbed a thumb over the blackened edge of the seasoned cast-iron slats.

The future was coming, whether he liked it or not, he brooded. Did they have to talk it to death before it ever happened? Like living through it twice, that was.

He expected it would be bad enough just the once.

Loud footsteps banged up the back staircase. "No, the menu's not ready yet! Tell them it's a surprise. Spin it! That's your damned job!"

Frankie jerked around to see Devon stab viciously at the "off" button on his cell.

"I miss the good old days when you could crash the receiver into the cradle when you wanted to hang up on someone obnoxious," Frankie said.

It surprised a sharp bark of laughter out of Devon. Frankie didn't want to share a sense of humor with the prick, but the hell of it was, they weren't that different, Devon Sparks and Frankie Boyd.

Which, come to think of it, was probably exactly why Frankie couldn't stand him.

Determined to shore up the animosity that might've been damaged by the shared joke, Frankie leaned against the counter and said, "Menu trouble? Be glad to give you a hand if you're stuck."

There, that ought to brass him off.

Instead of getting irate, however, Devon rubbed his hands through his carefully tousled, artfully gelled hair and blew out a big sigh. "I might take you up on that. Christ, what have I gotten myself into? Fuck, fuck, fuckity fuck."

Frankie had to grin. "Taking advantage of Miss Lolly's absence, are we?"

"She and Tucker are on their way," Devon said absently, still engrossed in his menu. "We spent the afternoon at the Central Park Zoo and the kid managed to spill grape snow cone all down his front." He looked up, frowning. "Wait. What?"

Blimey, this was the longest Frankie and Devon had ever gone without insulting each other. Morbidly curious to see how long it would last, Frankie said, "The swearing, mate. Noticed she's pretty well trained you out of it when she's about."

Devon laughed. Frankie refused to soften, even if the man was showing some startling signs of being human. "I guess she has. God, how embarrassing. You never think it'll happen to you."

"What's that?"

"That you'll meet someone who changes you. Or makes you want to change. Be better, maybe. Come on, you know what I mean."

Frankie had to fight not to shuffle his feet like an errant schoolboy. How did this conversation get so out of hand?

"No, I don't," he said, not caring that he sounded sullen and childish.

Devon arched a brow, some of that old, familiar arrogance coming over his face and making Frankie feel more at home. "Bullshit. I've heard the stories. You took a bullet for that server kid you're seeing. Miranda's brother."

"Jess," Frankie muttered. "All right, so you may have a point there. The Bit can make me act like a prat. Oi!"

Frankie blinked, sifting through the natural defensiveness incurred by Devon's reference to Jess and finally putting together what Devon was actually saying.

Devon and Lilah were involved; after that kiss in the middle of the kitchen Friday night, the whole crew knew that much. But from the sounds of what Devon was saying now, there was more going on than just a bit of quick slap and tickle.

It sounded suspiciously like . . . well. Love.

"You jammy bastard," Frankie said admiringly. "Of all the buggers to get lucky with Lilah."

"I know," Devon said, looking justifiably surprised. "Sometimes I can't really believe it myself. She's gorgeous, makes me laugh, is better with my kid than I am, and as if that weren't enough, she's helping me with the menu for Saturday night."

Frankie's ears perked up. Maybe they'd manage to steer this steamship clear of the icebergs after all.

"You don't say! Good on you, mate." Fucking hell, the Pied Piper had nothing on Lilah if she could get a man as stubborn as Devon Sparks to dance to her tune.

Other cooks began to trickle in, the line filling up with the familiar sounds of Milo and Violet's bickering, Wes's quick, steady knife chopping shallots, Billy's quiet laugh.

Devon gave Frankie a genuine smile and moved off to confer with Quentin, something about braising techniques. Frankie tried not to let the smile make his head implode, but really, the entire conversation was a little much to take in all at once.

Love was a tricky bitch, in Frankie's experience. She could make a man over into a better version of himself, like as seemed to have happened to Devon, the poor sod, but the opposite was true, as well. Love could turn you mean, selfish, blind . . . self-destructive.

Frankie put it out of his mind and determinedly went about setting up his station, but he was aware of it always in the back of his head, like an itch he couldn't quite scratch, waiting for him to take it out and look at it again.

Waiting for him to do something about it.

"I declare, I don't know when I've been so run off my feet," Lilah said, wiping the back of her hand across her damp brow. Aunt Bertie's voice floated through her head: *Ladies don't sweat, Lolly. Horses sweat. Men perspire. Ladies glow.*

Lilah grinned. Aunt Bertie had obviously never spent an entire afternoon mixing, baking, and testing twenty different canapé recipes.

"We have a lot to do," Devon agreed. There was a bounce in his step that made Lilah's heart lift. "But it's all coming together, Lilah Jane, I can feel it."

"I like this one," Tucker announced around a mouthful of cheddar date roll.

"Really?" Lilah looked down at him, surprised. The date roll was essentially a buttery, crumbly biscuit flavored with extra-sharp cheddar and wrapped around a sweet date—not the most kid-friendly combination, she would've thought.

There was even a bit of cayenne in the dough to give it some gumption.

But Tucker nodded so vigorously that his brown hair flopped into his face. Lilah's fingers itched to smooth it back, but they were covered in dough. He needed a haircut in the worst way.

"S'good."

Devon reached for one of the date rolls and chewed it thoughtfully. "Who knew? It turns out that an excellent palate is genetic. Tucker's right, these are perfection—only I think I want them as part of the cheese course, not the hors d'oeuvres."

Lilah luxuriated in the thrill that coursed through her every time Devon tasted her food and loved it, wanted to share it with the guests at his big, fancy dinner. From the hectic red of Tucker's cheeks and the brightness of his blue eyes, he was feeling it, too.

There was something exhilarating about basking in the reflected glory of Devon's rediscovery of food.

"And I was thinking," Devon went on, blithely oblivious to the palpitations he was causing his kitchen helpers, "we're going to need a special menu listing all these amazing dishes we're coming up with. I want it to look cool, maybe some kind of design around the border."

Elaborately casual, he turned to Tucker and said, "Think that's something you could help me with?"

Lilah caught the minute shift of Devon's weight, the tightening at the corners of his eyes that betrayed nervousness. Maybe he wasn't as oblivious as she thought.

Tucker, ever his father's son, didn't shriek with the joy Lilah could feel coursing through his wiry little frame. Instead, he shrugged and said, "I guess. I mean, I could try to draw something. It probably won't be any good, though." His hands opened and closed as if were already reaching for his charcoal pencils.

"Nonsense," Lilah said firmly. "It will be wonderful! Why don't you run get started? I think your backpack's on the coffee table."

Tucker jumped on that suggestion quick enough to betray his excitement at having Devon ask for his help. In less than five seconds, he was racing from the kitchen to grab his art supplies.

Ignoring the flour all over her apron and the dough on her hands—she was in the middle of rolling out pie crust dough for the miniature savory pecan tartlets she and Devon were playing with—Lilah threw herself into the arms of the smartest, handsomest, most wonderful man she knew.

"You have the best ideas," she told him. "The menus will be gorgeous, absolutely unique. They'll be chock full of X-factor."

"X-factor" was their code for the elusive element that had been missing from Devon's cooking, which they were currently restoring through judicious applications of Lilah's family recipes. Lilah would've been happy to keep calling it soul, but for whatever reason, that word made him roll his eyes in embarrassment every time, so . . . X-factor.

"He's part of it," Devon said. "A big part of why I'm hosting this dinner. There has to be some tangible evidence of Tucker at that meal. And not for nothing, but the kid can draw. Did you see those sketches he did after we got home from the Met?"

Lilah quietly adored the paternal pride in Devon's voice. "I hope you're prepared for the possibility that your fundraiser dinner menus will feature man-eating tigers."

"The sick part is, I'm sure I'll think they're the most wonderful man-eating tigers in the history of illustrated feline violence," Devon said, somewhat helplessly. "I guess I'm starting to get the hang of this fatherhood thing."

"You are," Lilah told him, heart in her throat. "You really, really are."

"It's bizarre." Devon went back to chopping pecans. Lilah had noticed that whenever conversation skirted close to X-factor issues like his feelings for Tucker, Devon talked them through better if his hands were busy.

"What's that?" she asked, keeping her voice light while making swift, sure passes of the rolling pin over the dough.

"I didn't think it would be so easy to care of Tucker. I thought . . . being a good dad must be hard, like there was a trick to it I'd never be able to work out. But it's not hard at all, really. Maybe it's Tucker. He makes it easy."

Lilah hummed in agreement, aware that they were very close now to one of the darkest, tenderest spots in Devon's X-factor.

From the little bits of information she'd been able to piece together, she knew that somewhere along the way, something went badly wrong in Devon's relationship with his father. Something that had caused lasting damage and colored Devon's entire perception of his own potential as a parent.

It was about time for Operation Fatherhood, Phase Two to go into effect, she mused. If she could just get Phil Sparks to acknowledge Devon's success in some way, to show his support . . .

Lilah pondered and rolled out pastry until her hands were numb. It was worth it, though, because by the time the tartlets came out of the oven, she had the inklings of a plan.

CHAPTER THIRTY

Frankie was right. It would be so much more satisfying to be able to slam down his phone instead of having to hunt and peck the "off" button.

Devon debated compensating by chucking his cell across the office, but decided against it. He didn't have time to go pick out a new one.

Still, Devon wished he'd stuck to his policy of avoiding his publicist's calls.

They'd waited to post the ticket availability until the last minute; Simon had some idea about building anticipation by keeping people on the edge of their seats and not letting them secure their spots right away. A twinge of remorse for the way he'd jerked Simon around lately had Devon agreeing to the scheme.

See? Devon wanted to say. *I can be a nice guy. I can be a team player.*

Which was all fine and dandy except for the way Simon's plan sent Devon's already sky-high stress levels into full-on orbit.

Devon had waited for days to find out if he'd have any guests at all tonight. He'd all but resigned himself to the idea of serving a pack of comped reporters and food bloggers, and picking up the tab for the rest of the dinner himself.

Finding out not an hour before the doors were set to open that, according to Simon, the fundraiser had sold out within fifteen minutes of the ticket availability being posted on the Center for Arts Education's website threatened to unhinge Devon completely.

That's what we want, Devon told himself. *It means you haven't irreparably damaged your reputation by fucking everything up the last two weeks. You can still pull it out. You can save it.*

The added pressure of knowing he had a full house tonight, though? *That* he could've lived without.

Devon hated to admit how nervous it made him to be staking his entire reputation, his entire professional future, on this one dinner.

It had to be the meal of his life.

He'd cooked his heart out getting ready for it, tasting new dishes, discovering new flavor combinations with Lilah, and working with the Market cooks to perfect the recipes.

He was more than a little stunned at how the mood in the kitchen had lifted over the last few days. He'd let the cooks go back to the old menu for regular dinner service, and he could taste the difference in the quality of food they were putting out. Adam's menu was pretty frigging delightful without all those flashy, expensive additions, Devon was forced to admit.

Not that he'd ever say that out loud. This X-factor stuff only went so far.

Almost better than the rising quality of food, however, was the rising tide of fun in the kitchen. As the line cooks relaxed, they started joking and messing with each other, and the energy of the place started to hum like a generator. They never got out of hand, Devon didn't let things slip so far as that, but the difference from the previous week's funereal atmosphere was palpable.

The food experiments he and Lilah were conducting opened up so many memories in Devon's mind, tossing him right back to his first restaurant job, a tiny chowder hut on Long Island, where he'd first realized that a kitchen crew was a tightly knit group of compatriots, brothers-in-arms, a family. Love them or hate them, they were there in the trenches with you every step of the way. It was a bond as strong as any Devon had ever encountered.

He put aside the cold, bitter, swearing character he'd believed himself to be and thought about those long-ago nights. He remembered the older, more experienced cooks he'd learned from, had once modeled himself after, and let himself become part of the flow at Market.

Like loving Tucker, it proved startlingly easy.

The unspoken truce he achieved with Frankie was the start of it. Once the icy conditions between Devon and the sous chef began to thaw, the rest of the cooks warmed to him.

A lushly curved body pressed into him from behind, plump, strong arms sliding around his waist.

Devon smiled. His relationship with his brigade wasn't the only thing heating up.

"I didn't hear you come in," he said, turning in the circle of those arms to stare down into the beautiful, wide eyes. He felt immediately soothed on some deep, untouchable level.

"You had your shoulders set in your manly aura of hyperfocus way," Lilah laughed. "I bet I could've shaved half your head before you knew I was in the office."

"Not a chance. No matter what I'm focused on, the minute you touch me everything else goes away."

She hummed, delighted. "I like that."

"Mm. That's why I can't have you in the kitchen tonight. Too dangerous. But hey, you being out in the dining room means you had to dress up, huh? Let me get a look."

Lilah did a self-conscious twirl for him, and Devon's mouth watered a little at the scrumptious spill of her breasts over the purple bodice of her dress.

"Like it? It's new. Grant helped me pick it out."

He'd watched her go off with Grant for a day of shopping, and he hadn't even felt a twinge of jealousy. Maybe Grant wanted her, maybe he didn't—but either way, Devon knew who made Lilah's eyes sparkle, who made her laugh that husky chuckle, who made her sigh and moan and scream with pleasure. He stared at the dress, and he knew exactly who she was wearing it for.

Devon was the luckiest son of a bitch in the city.

"Yeah, I like it," he managed to choke out, his eyes glued to the neckline. Was that what a sweetheart silhouette was? For all he'd educated himself on men's fashions since getting the hell out of Trenton, he didn't know much about women's clothes other than how to get them unfastened and tossed aside.

Whatever this neckline was called, Devon decided, it was now his favorite way for any dress to be put together.

"You look very handsome," Lilah said. "I like you in your chef whites." Her cheeks were dark red.

"You always do that," he said, stepping close and palming her jaw. "What?"

"Whenever anyone gives you a compliment, you brush it off like you don't believe it."

Lilah fussed with the bodice of her dress. "It's hard, you know? I'm not used to it. Not like my family back home called me names or told me I was ugly, or anything, but when there are that many kids in one house, all fighting and scrapping for attention, it's easy to fade into the background. I guess I'm still more comfortable there."

Devon started down at her porcelain brow, long, sweeping lashes and perfectly tiny mouth curving just a bit down at the corners. "Then I've got bad news for you, Lilah Jane, because everyone who sees you in this dress is going to notice how exquisitely beautiful you are."

"Stop it," she said, laughing and pushing at him a little, but her mouth was curving up now, so Devon didn't stop.

"It's true," he declared. "In fact, I almost want to forbid you from wearing this thing in public—I kind of hate the idea of the whole world catching on to what I see every time I look at you."

Fluttering her lashes coquettishly, Lilah grinned up at him, the hottest pink blush still staining her cheeks. "And what is that, exactly?"

He framed her face in his hands and let his voice show how serious he was. "No matter what you're wearing, even if it's one of those hideous, oversized flowered shirts, I just see you. My sweet Lilah Jane. And I couldn't ask for anything more."

She arched up and pressed a swift kiss to his mouth. When she spoke, her voice was hoarse with emotion.

"I swear, Devon Sparks, you could charm the birds from the trees."

"Is Tuck upstairs?" Devon wanted to show him the final menus, all printed up with the eight delicious courses. They looked awesome.

"Frankie spirited him away the minute we came in the door. Something about teaching him a neat new trick. I shudder to think."

Devon smoothed her sable curls back from her pretty, heart-shaped face. Smiled when they sprang instantly back into place. "Ah, Frankie's okay. Not saying I'd hire him as a male nanny—what would that be, a manny?—but he's all right."

Lilah gave him one of those laser looks that seemed to sear right through him. "And how are *you*?"

"Freaking out." He didn't really hide things from Lilah anymore. Didn't see the point.

"Oh, sugar." Lilah attempted a sympathetic look, but couldn't quite pull it off given her own obvious excitement. She'd been almost jittering ever since she came in.

"Looks like you're thrilled enough for the both of us," he noted.

"I might be," she said with an air of exaggerated mystery. "I might, just possibly, have a surprise for you later. But only if you're very good."

"I am loving the sound of this," Devon purred.

"Not that kind of surprise!" She hit him on the arm. "Okay, well, maybe that, too. Would it make you less nervous to be thinking about . . . *that* instead of concentrating on all the people out in the dining room?"

He loved that after all the things they'd done together, the ways they'd learned to please each other, she still fumbled over what to call it.

"Absolutely," Devon told her. "In all fairness, I think you should give me a teaser now, just to be sure my head's in the right place." He trailed a hand down her front, fingers nimbly slipping into her bodice to find warm skin.

"That's what would be fair, huh?" Her eyelids had slid to half-mast, her breath starting to come faster. Christ, they were good together.

"Oh, sure," he breathed, bending down to mouth the words into the pale column of her neck. "Common decency is dictating the whole thing."

The couch was close, but the desk was closer.

A few—embarrassingly few—hot, sweaty minutes later, and Devon was feeling quite a bit looser. Lilah twisted her flyaway hair into a knot on top of her head and gave him a smug smile. Perfectly permissible, under the circumstances. Devon eyed the red mark his mouth had left on her throat and felt more than a little smug himself.

"Feeling better?" she asked solicitously.

"I think it gets better every time, actually."

She pinked up enough to match the hickey, but her expression was pleased. "There's that silver tongue again. I can't imagine how I ever thought I'd be able to live in your house, see you every day, and not succumb."

"I'm pretty wonderful, it's true," Devon said. He frowned. "Let's just hope the diners and critics tonight agree."

"They will," Lilah promised. "Everyone who eats your food tonight—they're going to be able to tell how much of yourself you poured into it. And take it from someone who found out the hard way."

She wrapped her arms around him and leaned up for one last, soft kiss.

"When you give yourself over to something, Devon Sparks, it's beyond the scope of mortal man or woman to resist."

*　*　*

Lilah fairly danced back upstairs and out to the front of the house. She collected Tucker along the way and hustled him into the booth Grant had reserved for them.

Everything looked perfect! Grant had truly outdone himself with the décor. He'd lined the back of every booth with beautiful, dainty rectangular planters growing velvety green grass. The visual effect was simple and elegant, with a playful edge that was perfect for the event.

He'd taken down the regular art from the walls, stowing the copper vine sconces in the pantry, and replaced them with the framed final projects from Tucker's now-defunct art class.

That had been Lilah's idea, and as she gazed around the walls at the amazing, colorful pieces created by a handful of fourth-graders, she knew she'd made the right call.

No one could look at these drawings, the talent and potential hanging all around them, and not be moved.

Hopefully, they'd be moved in the direction of their pocketbooks.

The dining room was filling up with eager guests, so many you couldn't stir them with a stick, all dressed in what would've been, back home, their Sunday best. Here in New York, Grant said it was called "smart/casual." Lilah was glad he'd talked her into buying this racy, purple number she was wearing. It was more fitted, and definitely lower-cut in the front, than anything she'd ever owned before, but the way Devon had reacted when he saw it made Lilah sit up straight in her seat, the angle of her head high and confident.

Even if she felt like it was only being held up and over her chest with a lick and a promise, so long as this dress made Devon Sparks, womanizer extraordinaire, fall on her like a starving man on a dish of apple pie, Lilah could hold her own in any smart, casual crowd.

Her chest constricted as she remembered what he'd said about the way he saw her. Even more than his words, the memory of his open expression and the honesty in his eyes made her heart feel too big for her ribcage.

Or maybe that was the dress. It was a scoche tight across the bust.

The waiters circulated with trays of canapés while the arriving guests milled around the bar, ordering drinks and chatting. Some people found their tables and sat down while others mingled, but everywhere she looked, anticipation colored the air.

The moans and sighs of appreciation for the hors d'oeuvres probably helped twist that knot a little tighter, she mused with a grin.

Tucker, who'd been momentarily struck dumb by the glittering crowd of adults, suddenly found his voice as he gazed down at the amber glass charger in the center of his place setting.

"Hey," he said. "There's my drawing!"

The menus he'd designed were printed on lovely, heavy card stock about the size of a paperback book. Lilah and Devon had collaborated on the wording of the tasting menu, but the border was Tucker's province. Lilah had to choke back a happy sob the first time she saw it.

Tucker's inspiration was clearly their evening catching fireflies in Central Park. He'd done an ink sketch of intertwined leaves coiling around the outside of the menu card. Lightning bugs peeped out from the curlicued vines, some mere specks with wings and lines of light radiating from them, others large enough to have funny, sweet little faces partially obscured by the greenery.

No two faces were alike, and the longer Lilah studied the drawing, the more she noticed resemblances between Tucker's fireflies and the Market crew. One had a thatch of black hair, for instance, while another sported Violet's signature blonde. The details were tiny but unmistakable to anyone acquainted with the cast of characters in the kitchen.

The bottom left corner was Lilah's favorite—it featured three lightning bugs in close formation: one with ringlets corkscrewing out from its head, one with a perfect wave of dark hair and even a suggestion of cheekbones, and a smaller bug hovering between them.

Looking at it now, Lilah felt her throat thicken with tears. Every place setting had one, centered beneath the see-through charger plate. It was beautiful.

"Your dad wanted to show them to you, but he had to get in the kitchen and start things rolling," she explained, getting her feelings under control. "Do you like how they turned out?"

Tucker picked up his charger and stared at the table, then turned his wide eyes—younger, more unguarded than she'd ever seen them—on Lilah. "Wait. Lolly—is everyone gonna see it? When they sit down, oh, man, they're all gonna see it."

Suddenly worried, she put a hand on his arm. "Is that okay, sugar bean?"

"Okay?" A huge grin broke across his face. "It's completely awesome! I'm going to be famous!"

Oh, yes. He was his daddy's boy, all right.

The thought made Lilah's heart pound, because it reminded her of the other big reason for her excitement tonight. She almost rolled her eyes at herself. As if contributing to a menu at a fancy restaurant where the man she loved was about to make his big comeback to the culinary world wasn't enough!

And yet, there was more. Because Lilah had figured out the perfect way to cap off the triumph of what would be, she was certain, a perfect evening.

She'd done some digging through Devon's home office—for such a good cause, her conscience barely even whimpered—and found the contact information for someone named Connor Sparks.

One slightly awkward phone call later, she knew Devon had a younger brother who missed him, and she had a New Jersey number where Connor said their parents could be reached.

Fingers crossed so hard for luck that they were nearly too numb to dial, Lilah had punched in the number and held her breath until she got an answering machine. A weird combination of relief and disappointment had her leaving a longer, more rambling message than she meant to, but the upshot of it was that Devon's parents were invited to the fundraiser dinner.

It was exactly like directing a play. Everything was in place. She'd made her choices, put the actors in place, set the scene. Now all she could do was sit back and watch as it played out onstage.

So when Jess approached their table with a twinkle in his eyes and a tray full of pecan tartlets, Lilah grinned at him and held out her hand.

The miniature tart was still warm, the all-butter crust flaky and perfect. Lilah closed her eyes and chewed happily, making a mental note to compliment Violet on her pastry-dough skills. The crust was almost as good as Aunt Bertie's!

Anyone looking at the tartlet would be expecting the familiar dessert, a burst of gooey brown-sugar sweetness. But Devon had played with that expectation by taking Lilah's recipe for pecan pie and turning it into a salty little surprise using smoked pecans and a touch of kitchen wizardry.

The earthiness of the pecans was accented by a base of duxelles, a lovely thing Devon had introduced Lilah to, involving finely diced mushrooms, onions, shallots, and herbs sautéed in butter and reduced to a rich, savory paste.

The shiny, sticky sherry glaze over the pecans imparted a hint of sour to cut all the richness, and Lilah fought back her own indecent moan of satisfaction. A tug on her sleeve brought her out of the haze. She looked down to see Tucker making big, starving-orphan eyes up at her.

"More?" he said hopefully.

Jess, who'd been smart enough not to move away yet, laughed and held the tray where Tucker could get to it. "I thought you might want seconds, and these are going fast. People are snarfing 'em up faster than I can hustle back to the kitchen for more."

"That's a good sign, right?" *Oh, please,* Lilah prayed. *Let this evening go well.*

Jess winked. "The best."

God must've been in the mood to heed the prayers of

shameless hussies, because people sat down and were poured
wine, and the first course, a variation on Billy Perez's cold
corn salad served on crisp, bitter endive leaves, was sampled.
Lilah took in the big smiles and transported expressions on
the diners' faces. The night seemed to be going about as perfectly as possible.

The only fly in the soup was that no matter how she scru-
tinized her fellow guests, none of them looked the way she'd
imagined Phil and Angela Sparks would look. Not that there
were any pictures to go by in Devon's apartment, but surely
she'd be able to see a family resemblance.

She looked at Tucker, kicking the table leg and drawing
on the back of his menu, already improving on his design.
He couldn't be more obviously related to Devon if he were a
clone.

Genes that strong had to come from somewhere. Lilah
was betting either Phil or Angela had those trademark ice-
blue eyes, but no one in the dining room seemed to. She was
about to get up and find Grant at the host stand, quiz him
about any empty tables, but someone pinged a fork against a
wine glass, and the whole room quieted.

Devon emerged from the kitchen, resplendent in his pristine white chef's jacket with the sleeves rolled up to the elbow. Clearly at ease in front of a crowd, he gave a charming
smile and launched into a short introduction followed by a
rundown of the Center for Arts Education's mission.

He concluded with an impassioned call for support of a
well-rounded education in New York City schools that had
Lilah reaching for her napkin to dab surreptitiously at her
eyes.

She was such a sentimental fool.

Lilah distracted herself by leaning down to explain to
Tucker that his dad was trying to get people to chip in enough
to keep art classes going at schools like his. He rolled his
eyes, said, "Duh," and went back to his drawing.

All righty, then.

A swell of applause signaled the end of Devon's speech.
A representative from the Center for Arts Education stood

up and took over, thanking Devon for hosting the event, while Devon smiled graciously and hoped that everyone enjoyed the meal.

He stopped by Lilah and Tucker's table on his way back to the kitchen.

"How do you think it's going?"

"Excellently," Lilah said, forcing a brightness she couldn't quite feel with the disappointment in Devon's no-show father weighing her down. "The food is wonderful. You're all outdoing yourselves back there."

"Jess said he almost ran out of pecan pies," Tucker informed him. "Are you going to run out of the date rolls? Because I want three. No, four. I want four!"

"Tucker! Don't be a pig," Lilah said.

Devon just laughed, a big, happy sound that made the four tables closest to them look around and smile.

"Don't worry, Tuck," he said easily. "I'll save a couple extras for you. As payment for doing such an awesome job with the menus."

"I'm going to be famous," Tucker replied in all seriousness. "I'ma have my own TV show and everything."

"Trust me, kiddo, it's not all it's cracked up to be."

Tucker shrugged and went back to his drawing and diligent kicking of the table leg.

Lilah shared an amused look with Devon, who twisted his mouth up and said, "I've got to get back. It seems to be going smoothly, which of course means any second it's all going to fall apart like a soufflé collapsing in a hot oven."

CHAPTER THIRTY-ONE

But through the next six courses, nothing went wrong that Lilah could see. The kitchen banged out fried chicken livers with a chipotle maple dipping sauce, crunchy on the outside and smooth and rich on the inside; a terrine of smoked salmon, bread crumbs, capers, red onion, and crème fraîche, which was Devon's take on the traditional New York bagel with lox; pan-fried quail with a fresh white grape juice reduction; soy honey-glazed short ribs; and Delmonico pudding for dessert. Lilah had argued against serving that pudding, since it was strictly a holiday treat in her family, but once Devon tasted the almond macaroons soaked in custard and meringue, he couldn't be dissuaded from putting it on the menu. He substituted chopped crystallized ginger for the more traditional candied red-and-green pineapple topping and said, "There. Not just for Christmas anymore!"

Lilah had to admit as she licked her spoon clean that Delmonico pudding made an excellent summer dessert. It was served chilled, rich and delicious with the fragrant sweet almond cookies dissolving in creamy vanilla custard. The macaroons retained some of their trademark sticky consistency; the custard layered into and over them provided the perfect smooth counterpoint. The topping was the only change Devon would allow to this particular recipe, since, in his words, they didn't have time to waste trying to improve on perfection.

Not for the first time during this meal, Lilah wished her Aunt Bertie could be here. If anyone would appreciate the lengths Devon had gone to preserve what made her recipes precious while reinvigorating tradition with a boost of fresh flavor and innovative technique, it was her aunt.

No, Lilah told herself. *You left that safe life behind. It's time you make it on your own.*

As Lilah pushed her spoon through the last of her pudding, she acknowledged the high hopes she'd pinned on Phil and Angela Sparks. If Aunt Bertie couldn't be here to share this moment with Lilah, at least Devon's parents, who only lived an hour away by easy train ride, ought to be here for him.

She was horrendously grateful now that she'd decided to keep it a surprise for Devon. Lord, what if she'd built it all up and he'd gotten invested in the idea and then they hadn't showed? Or even worse, what if they *had* shown and Devon got upset with her for meddling?

She had trouble understanding why anyone—especially someone with as much heart as Devon—wouldn't want their family with them on such an important night. But for the first time since she came up with her grand master plan, she wondered if "family" meant something different to Devon's parents than it did to her.

After all, if they couldn't be bothered to buy a train ticket to come help celebrate their son's success, they were clearly a different species than she was.

And a different species from Lilah's aunt and uncle, too. There may have been times, growing up, when Lilah felt the lack of a mother and father of her own—but looking back, she knew she'd never truly lacked for love. If tonight were her triumphant night? Aunt Bertie and Uncle Roy would be here with bells on.

Lilah pushed her disappointment in Devon's family aside and put on a cheerful face. As so often happened, once she started acting cheerful she found she really *felt* more cheerful, so when she and Tucker went backstage to do the post-performance round of praise, she was able to greet the cooks with true exuberance.

"Lolly," shouted Frankie. He would *not* be scolded out of using that stupid nickname. "Are we or are we not entirely badass?"

"It was staggering," she said, putting the back of her wrist against her forehead and making a swoony face. "I was overcome, simply overcome with the amount of sheer genius put forth by this kitchen."

Tucker pulled impatiently on her hand, for once unwilling to stop and chat with the sous chef, so Lilah let him tow her to the walk-in kitchen where they found Devon reaching down a couple of bottles of champagne from the highest wire shelf.

"Perfect timing! Can you give me a hand with these?"

Tucker ran forward to help, receiving two chilled dark green bottles with pride. "I ate *six* date rolls," he told Devon. "Lolly gave me hers."

"They're your favorite, huh?"

"Well," Tucker said, cocking his head. "I liked the little chickens. But the rolls are the best thing."

"That's my man," Devon said, face flushed and arms full of booze. "I love quail, too."

"Give me some of those to carry," Lilah said, leaning up to peck a soft kiss on Devon's warm, stubbled cheek. Close enough to his ear for a whisper, so she breathed "You were phenomenal. Prepare to be surprised until you can't stand up once we get home."

"Yowza," Devon said, gaze going liquid silver. "You're making me wish I hadn't promised the crew we'd celebrate tonight."

"Uh, guys?" Tucker's impatient voice dissipated the cloud of lust threatening to choke Lilah's good sense. "These bottles are cold. And we're standing in a big fridge. Can we get out of here?"

"You bet, sugar bear." Lilah took a hurried step away from Devon's too-tempting body and juggled her own chilly bottles. "Go on and head back out, we'll be right behind you."

Tucker went, rolling his eyes and making gagging noises the whole way.

Devon's smile was naughty enough to make Lucifer blush. "I get the feeling he knows we stayed in here for a reason."

"Enough banter," Lilah said. "If you're going to kiss me, make it snappy. I can see my breath. And blue is not a great color on your *mmph . . .*"

Devon cut her off with a long, hot kiss that opened her up and delved right into the heart of her. Every stroke of his tongue seemed to core her out and leave her breathless, without will or volition or the sense to pull away, even when the condensation from pressing cold glass bottles between their warm bodies dampened the front of her dress and turned her nipples to ice picks.

When he finally lifted his head, Lilah blinked. "Why are you stopping?"

"I thought you were cold," he teased.

"Not anymore. But I suppose we'd better get out there before Tucker sends a search party in after us."

They made it out of the walk-in cooler before Frankie and the other chefs started beating on the door, but only just, if the smirks and smiles on the faces around her were anything to go by.

She looked at Devon, who grinned at her, completely unrepentant and unashamed, and Lilah decided, why be embarrassed? So she jumped him in the freezer! There were legions of women out there who watched Devon's show and would agree that he was eminently jumpable.

The champagne bottles clanged as she set them down on one of the stainless-steel counters. It was the same counter she'd tumbled off of and into Devon's arms that day after their first night together.

A one-night stand that turned into so much more, she thought, shivering a little at how far they'd come since then.

"Listen up, chefs," Devon said. "I've got to go out front

and glad-hand the potential donors a little; I promised the Center for Arts Education lady I would. But before I go, I wanted to pop some wine open and raise a toast."

With one deft twist, he ripped the foil cap off the bottle in his hand and eased the cork from the neck. He didn't shake it up or make it spew everywhere; Lilah knew it was a combination of personal fastidiousness in not wanting to be covered in sticky, drying wine, and a reluctance to waste what looked to be a very nice vintage Veuve Clicquot. The fact that she knew that about Devon made her feel kind of squishy inside, as bubbly as the champagne he poured into a water glass.

Raising the glass, Devon looked around the kitchen to include everyone in his toast. "It was a fantastic night," he said. "You pulled together and rocked it like Springsteen at Madison Square Garden."

"Nah, like the Ramones," Frankie shouted, red-faced and sweaty from standing over the grill.

"The Pixies," Violet, the pastry chef, countered.

"No, no. Sinatra," Milo argued. Then he licked his lips and said, "I'm talking Nancy Sinatra. Those go-go boots. Rowr!"

Everybody laughed, including Devon. "Okay, okay, simmer down," he said. "Just let me get through this before the champagne goes flat and I swear I'll be out of your hair for good."

He cleared his throat. "You've probably all seen my show. The part after the credits where I say . . ."

"Anything you can do, I can do better," the cooks all chorused.

"Right." Devon sighed. "Well, tonight, I couldn't have done any of it without you. Anything I accomplished with this meal, this fundraiser, it was only possible because of all of you. So thank you, from the bottom of my heart. I'm sure you'll be happy to see the back of me. But honestly? I'm going to miss you—this—when Adam comes home tomorrow."

There was a long silence, punctuated by a sniffle or two,

until Frankie finally said, "Fuck that, Chef. You'll come back and visit, and then when Miranda finally agrees to get hitched we'll shove them off to a proper honeymoon and have you back at the helm!"

A shouted cheer swelled all up and down the line. Lilah was thrilled to hear it, almost as much as it thrilled her to be standing close enough to hear Devon's quiet words to Frankie as he poured the sous chef a glass of wine.

"Don't sell yourself short, Boyd. You could run this kitchen in a heartbeat. The next time Adam needs a day off, let him leave you in charge. I'm serious, man. Thanks for all your help."

Lilah saw Frankie struggle with the seriousness of the man-to-man moment for a full five seconds before he finally blew out a breath and shook his head. "That kind of responsibility—it's not for me, mate. So it's a damn good thing you were here to step in."

As if unable to take another instant of real emotion, Frankie rocked back on his heels and downed the champagne in a single, impressive gulp. "Whoo!" He shook his head like a horse bothered by flies and made his wild black hair stand up all over. "Let's get this party started!"

He grabbed the open bottle of champagne and shoved it into Lilah's hands. She started pouring it out for the cooks while Frankie worked on opening another bottle.

"You're gonna go talk to the money guys, right?" Tucker asked Devon.

"I don't want to," Devon made a face, "but yeah, I guess I am."

"Can I come? I want to show them my newest drawing. Maybe if they see it, they'll want to pay for the art classes more."

Lilah hid a smile as Devon blinked down at his son.

"Tucker. You . . . How did I spawn such a marketing wiz? That's a great idea. Come on, let's go talk some rich people out of their spare cash."

Lilah watched them go, her heart full to the brim with

something that felt every bit as sparkly and effervescent as the wine she was pouring.

Operation Fatherhood was a roaring success!

Everyone in the dining room wanted to talk to Devon. Or maybe they just wanted to coo over Tucker and his drawing.

Devon grinned as yet another bejeweled Upper East Side matron clasped her heavily ringed hands and called Tucker "a little Picasso." Pablo Jr. didn't seem to enjoy the attention as much as he'd expected, if the scrunched-up nose was any indication.

Knowing that a good father would rescue his son from such obvious torture, Devon started making their excuses to the fawning lady. "Oh, too bad, so nice to see you, thanks for coming, there's someone over there I absolutely must go and speak to . . ."

He gestured across the dining room in a vague sort of way, hoping the lady wouldn't ask who it was he had to talk to, and suddenly locked eyes with a blue stare identical to the one he saw in the mirror every morning.

Dad.

Devon stilled, the polite words freezing in his mouth like ice cubes. All the blood in his body rushed to his brain, which felt like it shifted immediately into hyper-drive.

What was he doing here? Was Mom with him? Did he come for dinner? What did he think? What the *fuck* was he doing here?

The woman he'd been speaking to gave a shrill, embarrassed laugh and pinched Tucker's cheek. Tucker shied away from her, backing into Devon's hip and stumbling.

Devon looked down at his son, and back up at his father, standing motionless by the exit like he was already thinking about making a break for it. Dad never liked fancy restaurants much, Devon remembered, always seemed ill at ease when the family went anywhere nicer than a diner or a pizza parlor.

"Sorry." He ripped his attention away from Phil Sparks and back to the woman whose name he'd forgotten. "You were saying?"

"Oh, nothing, nothing, just how wonderful the meal was, and how unlike anything I've had in the city recently. So fresh and original! However did you come up with the menu?"

"He had help," drawled a slow, honeyed voice as Lilah came up behind him. "Thank you for coming, won't you excuse us?"

The guest nodded, looking more relieved than anything else to get away from the sudden odd turn their conversation had taken. But Devon couldn't seem to get a handle on his emotions, couldn't seem to force himself to look back across the room and see if his father was still there.

And then suddenly Phil was right in front of him, looking older than Devon would ever have believed possible, weathered and lined and gray.

I shouldn't have stayed away so long, was all Devon could think. *But maybe it doesn't matter. He came here, to see me.* A cautious hope flickered to life in his chest, warming him from the inside out.

"Dad," he croaked out. Christ, how humiliating. He sounded like he had laryngitis.

A swift, indrawn breath reminded him of Lilah, who had moved to Tucker's other side, her hand on the kid's shoulder. Eyes shining like she'd just gotten the best birthday present ever, Lilah said, "Oh, Devon, is this your father? Mr. Sparks, I'm so very, very pleased to meet you. Thank you so much for coming to the dinner!"

"I skipped the dinner," Phil said gruffly. "Ate at home; good, plain, simple food. Anything too rich doesn't agree with me."

"Ah," Lilah said, clearly disconcerted. "Well. It was still nice of you to come all this way. Devon, are you going to introduce us?"

Oh, God. Devon squeezed his eyes shut for a heartbeat, then opened them. There was no way to avoid how much this was going to hurt—but he hadn't thought it would matter! He never thought his father would show up here, reenter his life in any way. Devon's head swam, and had to bear down hard to remember how to speak.

"Lilah, this is my father, Phil Sparks. Dad, this is Lilah. My . . . my friend," he concluded in a strangled tone.

Lilah turned beet red, but her Aunt Bertie would be proud; she didn't miss a beat in offering her hand.

Phil shook with Lilah, then turned his attention to the silent boy at Devon's side.

"And who is this?" Phil demanded. "Out pretty late, aren't you, for a—how old are you, boy?"

Tucker shrank into Devon's side but spoke up. "I'm ten. And three-quarters."

Phil stared down at the kid, and Devon could see the moment when realization dawned over his father's hard face.

Numb with the inevitability of it all, Devon waited, braced himself.

"God Almighty," Phil breathed. "I have a grandson."

CHAPTER THIRTY-TWO

Lilah gasped. Devon squeezed his eyes shut.

Yeah, she read that little dialogue correctly. Devon had never told his family about Tucker.

He didn't see the point, was all. They hadn't spoken in years! And it wasn't like Devon was part of Tucker's life.

But that was changing, he reminded himself. God, everything was changing, so fast he could barely keep up.

He looked at his father, the familiar bone structure reflected in Devon's mirror every morning, and in the small, round face starting up at them. The fierce surge of pride in his son nearly brought Devon to his knees.

Please let this go smoothly, he found himself praying.

"Yeah. This is Tucker, my son. Tuck? Meet your grand-dad."

When Tucker retreated into the stony silence he favored whenever life threw too many curve balls, Devon realized he should've expected it. The kid stared up at Phil Sparks without a flicker of expression.

Phil sent a wry smile in Devon's direction. "Takes after you, huh?"

Devon wasn't sure what to make of that. "Um. How's Mom? Did she come . . . ?" He craned his neck to search the room, but didn't truly expect to see his shy, quiet homebody of a mother.

"No," Phil confirmed. "It's vestry week at St. Ignatius. You know how hard she works, putting together the charity auction and whatnot."

Devon knew. And he also knew his dad would never let Angela Sparks miss a vestry committee meeting for something as trivial as their son's big night. Heavens, no! People might talk.

Forcing down the bitter voice whispering that nothing had changed, Devon looked at his father, whose presence at Market was proof that there'd been at least a tiny shift in the murky waters of his family.

"So. How's Connor? He's back stateside, I hear."

A familiar gleam of pride entered Phil's eyes. "Your brother's doing good, real good. He got out of the service about a year ago. Now he's a cop."

Devon had to laugh, even as fear for his brother clutched at his guts. Devon knew about the stint in Afghanistan—he'd actually bought body armor for Con's whole unit, because the thought of his happy-go-lucky kid brother out there with nothing between him and death was unacceptable. The anonymous donation helped Devon sleep at night.

He and Connor had emailed occasionally once he'd finished his tour. It had been a while, though, and last Devon heard, Connor was just trying to settle back into civilian life. Figured that rather than taking a well-deserved break from risking his all for God and country, he'd go for one of the highest-risk jobs he could find.

First the army, then the Trenton PD? Little danger junkie. "One of the boys in blue, huh? Who would've guessed."

Phil went stony. "Me, for one. I always knew he'd end up doing something important. He won't ever be famous, but we're damn proud of him."

Here we go.

"I'm proud of him, too," Devon said, gritting his teeth against the frustration simmering in his throat. "I get it. What

I don't get is how being proud of him means there's nothing left over for anyone else. Like there's a finite amount of pride in our family, and Connor gets all of it."

"You saying you think what you're doing here is more important than your brother, out there protecting us all . . ."

"No, Dad, that's not what I'm saying at all," Devon interrupted before Phil burst that blood vessel in his forehead.

"My goodness," Lilah said loudly, catching their attention—and the attention of everyone in a ten-foot radius. "What a shame the whole family couldn't be here! But I'm sure Tucker will get to meet his grandma and uncle sometime soon. In the meantime, Tuck, do you wanna go in the kitchen with me? Say good night to the chefs?"

She held out her hand and Tucker took it gratefully. Devon sent her a look that was every bit as grateful. This. This ugliness, this resentment was exactly why he never told Phil about Tucker. Hell, it was why he'd never tried to be a dad himself. Devon hated who he became when he was around his family.

What kind of person begrudged his war hero brother the honest admiration he deserved? It wasn't like Devon had any illusions about himself. He'd never make the choice to join the armed forces; he'd never want to face what Connor had faced overseas.

The hell of it was, Devon admired his little brother every bit as much as their father did. So why did it sting so badly to be compared to him, and come up short?

Lilah beamed a big, fake smile and pulled Tucker to her side, but Phil wasn't about to let them out of his sight.

Eyes sharp, he said, "My son's 'friend,' eh? I take that to mean you're not the mother."

"No, but . . ."

"So where is she?"

"Oh! She's . . . well." Lilah bit her lip.

Devon became aware of heads turning in their direction, whispers circulating around the still-crowded room. "Can we move this out of the public dining room to someplace more private?"

Christ, this was going to be all over the place before he even managed to get his father back on the train to Trenton.

"That's a joke—you worrying about what people think. You never cared when it was your mother and me who couldn't hold our heads up on a Sunday morning when anyone at the church with the money for a *Post* could read about what you got up to on Saturday night." Phil shook his head.

Devon's jaw was clenched hard enough to make his neck hurt. "Well, if you don't want to make *Page Six* yourself, come down to the restaurant office with me and we can finish having this out."

Without another word, he turned and strode for the kitchen door. He didn't check to see if Phil was following—with Devon's luck, there was no way his dad would just give up and leave.

He banged through the kitchen door and headed straight for the relative privacy of the stairs down to the basement level.

The chefs, who were in the middle of clearing down their stations, froze in mid-clean. Impatient to be away from so many watchful eyes, he barked, "What are you all still doing here? Get finished cleaning and head to Chapel. Tell Christian the drinks are on me—and I'll actually pay the tab this time."

"You got it, Chef," Frankie said, taking a break from scraping up the charred bits of meat from the wood-fired grill. "We'll see you there later to celebrate, yeah?"

Devon had never felt less like celebrating in his life, but he dragged up his empty Hollywood smile and said, "Sure. Just got one thing to take care of first. Dad?"

Every head in the kitchen swiveled to Phil, who tightened his jaw and sent Devon an unreadable look. Probably he didn't appreciate being categorized as a chore, but Devon couldn't make himself care. He just wanted this to be over.

Jerking his head toward the staircase, he said, "You coming?"

Phil took the hint and disappeared down the stairs. Lilah stopped Devon from following with a hand on his arm.

"Are you going to be okay? Do you want me to come with you?"

Devon struggled for a moment, torn between humiliation at being coddled in front of his cooks and gratitude that she wanted to help him. "Sweet Lilah Jane," he said. It came out sounding sarcastic, and she flinched back. Devon didn't know how to smooth it over when he felt so jagged. He was all rough, raw edges tearing into everything around him, and he wasn't sure how to stop it.

He looked down at Tucker, small fingers still clutched in Lilah's hand, and took in the carefully blank look on his face.

He had to get them both away from him, before this ball of anger expanding in his chest exploded all over them.

"I'll be fine on my own," he told her. "I always am."

Unsure if he was trying to convince her or himself, Devon ignored the stricken look in her pretty green eyes and headed for the stairs where his father waited.

They made it all the way down the narrow, dark stairs and into the office in a tense silence. But the moment the office door closed, Phil exploded.

"A child, Devon? Out of wedlock? And then to not even have the common decency to tell your mother and me that we were grandparents. We didn't raise you like that."

"You didn't raise me at all," Devon fired back. "When you weren't punishing me for being different from you, you were ignoring me. Yeah, you were a model father."

"Oh, and you're doing so much better with your kid, huh?"

The memory of Tucker's withdrawn expression ripped into Devon. It was that same overly adult, emotionless façade he'd almost lost in the last two weeks. Devon knew what brought it back—all this loud, pointless shouting and angry talk.

Tucker was afraid of him again.

Shit, Devon thought, stomach clenching hard. *Dad's right. I'm completely screwing this up.*

There wasn't enough air in the cool, musty-smelling

basement. Devon couldn't get a good breath. If he could just breathe in, he could defend himself—except, no, there was nothing he could say.

He remembered that first night at Market—God, was it only two weeks ago?—when the police officer offered him a choice between taking custody of Tucker, and letting his son go into foster care.

And Devon had *hesitated*. What kind of man, what kind of *father* did that? So what if he'd been scared he might turn out to be like his old man.

There was that word again. Scared.

Devon had chosen his career over his family; it was the choice he'd been making every day since he graduated from high school.

Since the last day Phil told him he wasn't good enough, would never be good enough. Since the last time his mother listened to him say it, her silence a tacit agreement despite the mute suffering on her face.

Devon had heard everything Phil was saying before. There was no reason it should cut so deeply now. All he knew was that it did.

"Don't worry about Tucker," Devon forced himself to say. "I don't have much time to inflict the Sparks family brand of parenting on him. His mother, my ex, she's . . . away on a trip, but she'll be back in a couple of weeks. He's only with me until she comes home."

It was nothing but the truth—well, the truth with a little editing—but the words slashed at Devon's heart as unerringly as anything his father had said.

In another two weeks, this would all be over. Tucker would go back to Heather. Lilah wouldn't have any reason to stay.

How the hell had he allowed himself to forget and start playing house? He thought he'd laid the happy family fantasy to rest long ago. The humiliating moment of hope when he first caught sight of Phil tonight told Devon he hadn't buried those ludicrous feelings as deeply as he thought.

"And let me guess. You won't have time in the next few

weeks to bring the kid out to the neighborhood to visit your mother."

"Good guess," Devon said. "Come on, Dad. Look what happens when we're around each other for five minutes. Part of the reason I never told you about Tucker before was that I didn't want him exposed to our particular family dynamic. I mean, shit. Just because we're completely fucked up is no reason he has to be."

Phil's mouth tightened ominously. "I know you're a big shot now, lots of money, fancy apartment, fast car—and I know you look down on the life your mother and I live, but we did our best for you and your brother."

"Your best. Right." Bitterness boiled up in Devon's throat, sour and hot. "What whitewashed version of my childhood are you remembering? Never mind. This conversation is going in circles. Just . . . tell Mom I hope the St. Iggy's charity thing goes okay. If she wants me to donate something to be auctioned off, she knows how to reach me."

"She won't," Phil growled, ramming his arms into the sleeves of his worn navy jacket. "We don't need your piles of cash, Devon. And don't think you can buy yourself a clean conscience, either."

"Hey, my conscience is fresh as a daisy," Devon lied. "How's yours?"

Phil wrenched open the office door. "Don't bother walking me out; I'm not sure I can stand the sight of you right now."

Devon shoved away his stupid hurt feelings and covered them with a sneer. "Give them my best down at the union hall."

Phil paused in the doorway. Devon tried not to notice how old and tired he looked, with his stooped shoulders and ruthlessly combed gray hair.

"I can only thank God your mother didn't come here with me tonight; the shock of all this would've been too much for her. I wish I could say I can't believe you'd keep our flesh and blood a secret from us, but unfortunately, that's exactly the kind of selfish behavior I expect from you."

The dig sliced into Devon like a knife, filleting the flesh from his bones. He stared at his father, a little amazed that the old man's mouth wasn't filling up with blood, cut to ribbons by the sharp words.

And the worst of it was, Phil didn't even stick around after his parting shot to watch Devon bleed out, messy emotion and stupid, pointless hopes all over the floor.

CHAPTER THIRTY-THREE

Pacing really wasn't a very effective tool for managing stress. On her seventeenth pass by the basement stairs, Lilah realized she wasn't actually going to be able to force Phil Sparks to leave the restaurant using the power of her will alone.

"I'm going down there," she announced.

"No, you're not," Grant countered, the way he had the first five times she'd tried to leave. "I know it goes against your nature, but stay out of it, Lolly."

Lilah wondered if he might be right. It wasn't like her meddling had gone very well recently.

Which reminded her that this entire Phil Sparks calamity was her fault. "It's my mess, I should help clean it up," she argued.

Grant was inflexible. "Leave it alone."

Lilah fretted. Glancing over at the grill, where Frankie was attempting to get Tucker interested in how to clean and season the cast-iron slats, she had to wonder how much of her frustration was due to the fact that while she wasn't helping Devon with his father, she was equally useless here in the kitchen.

Tucker had withdrawn into himself again. Nothing she said appeared to make a dent in his stony façade. Even his favorite restaurant person, Frankie, hadn't succeeded in getting so much as a grin out of him.

It was just like that first night, only worse, because now Lilah knew what Tuck's face looked like all lit up with laughter. She could recall in perfect detail the way his blue eyes got shifty when he was up to some mischief. This robotic child who, even as she watched, pulled away from Frankie's attempt to ruffle his hair, was a stranger.

Without a word, Tucker retrieved his ever-present backpack from the pastry table and wedged himself into the back corner of the kitchen, near the alley door. Lilah watched him root through his pack and decided to go sit with him.

Even if he gave her the cold shoulder, at least she'd be doing something. *Besides,* she told herself, *he's only a little boy. He might not want company right now, but he doesn't know what he needs.*

Ignoring the fact that it was exactly that sentiment that landed them in this situation, Lilah moved toward Tucker only to be distracted by the bang of footsteps on the basement stairs.

Her heart jumped and lodged somewhere near her breastbone.

A moment later, Phil Sparks appeared. Alone. He strode through the kitchen looking neither right nor left; cooks jumped out of his way like the Red Sea parting before Moses.

Lilah held her breath as he neared the pastry station at the back of the kitchen, where Tucker had spread out his art supplies. Would he stop and talk to his grandson?

Phil slowed when he caught site of Tucker, who glanced up from his drawing and froze. The standoff lasted for only a heartbeat before Tucker hunched back down over his paper and colored pencils, a ferocious scowl twisting his face. In spite of everything, Lilah couldn't help feeling a pang of sympathy for Phil as he straightened his shoulders and continued out the back door without another word.

Tension streamed out of the kitchen in his wake like air let off from a hot-air balloon. The cooks went to work with a will, wiping down counters and lugging stacks of dirty pans to the dishwashing station.

Grant headed back out to the front of the house to supervise the exit of the last straggling guests, and Lilah took the opportunity to slip down the back staircase and find Devon.

Not that she needed Grant's permission or anything. But she found herself feeling very unsure, second-guessing everything. It was a familiar state of being, one she'd hoped she'd left behind in Virginia. The reemergence of the old Lolly, here and now, was completely unwelcome.

At least now she knew that overwhelming feelings of guilt and regret were a trigger.

She'd give anything to be able to go back in time and stop her idiotically Pollyanna-ish self from making that phone call to New Jersey, Lilah mused as she knocked tentatively on the office door.

"Can I come in?" she asked.

"It's safe," Devon called. "My father is on his way back to Trenton."

She found him leaning on the desk, arms crossed and long legs stretched out in front of him. His eyes were like ice chips, sending shivers down her spine. But not in the good way. The contrast between the chill in the air now and the sauna-like ambiance the office had held before the party, when she came down to wish him good luck, made Lilah's heart hurt.

"Yes, I saw him go," she said carefully, approaching Devon like she would any wounded animal.

"And good fucking riddance."

Lilah swallowed her instinctive reaction to the cuss word. Something in Devon's expression told her he was itching for a fight.

"No matter what your father said, you did a wonderful thing here tonight. I'm proud of you."

He stared at her for a long, taut moment, then his face softened. "God, Lilah Jane. It was so . . . I hadn't seen him in a long time. I guess it was bound to be difficult."

Lilah wanted to squirm. "I know. I'm sorry."

With a rough sound of frustration, Devon slumped and rubbed his hands through his hair. "It's been ten years. What the hell made him come here tonight?"

"Oh." Lilah twisted her hands together until her knuckles throbbed. "Well. I can actually answer that."

"What?" Astonishment rolled off him in waves.

Here goes nothing.

She squared her shoulders. "I invited him."

"You. You did what?"

Devon couldn't believe what he was hearing—or, no. He didn't *want* to believe it. The truth was, it was all too easy to swallow.

After all, Lilah Jane Tunkle never met a problem she didn't want to solve.

Even when it was none of her fucking business.

"I know! I'm sorry! But I didn't think it would turn out like this."

He almost wanted to laugh, except he wasn't sure he'd be able to stop once he started. "What the hell did you think was going to happen? That we'd take one look at each other and all the wonderful, warm, fuzzy family memories would come rushing back?"

"Of course not," she said, although the blush rising up her neck messed with the credibility of her denial. "It's pointless to dwell on the past. But the present! I wanted your parents to have a chance to see how much you've accomplished. I thought they'd be proud of you."

"My father has never been proud of me, and he never will be." It was one of the concrete, bedrock truths of Devon's life. He might've forgotten it for a second earlier tonight, but he never would again.

"That can't be true." She looked so unhappy at the very idea, Devon experienced a strange urge to comfort her.

"Sorry to disappoint you, honey. But despite the front my parents put on for the neighbors, I grew up knowing exactly how little Dad thought of me."

"But you're so successful . . ."

"Not to hear my dad tell it." Devon hated the echo of disaffected teenager in his own voice, but couldn't quite stamp it out. "He disapproves of my playboy lifestyle and thinks I use my big piles of money to assuage my guilt over living in filthy sin."

"Well, I can't say I entirely approve of your playboy lifestyle, either. But that's not all there is to you."

The laugh grated Devon's throat on the way out. "Don't bet on it. I told you, Lilah Jane, what you see is what you get with me."

It was definitely safer that way. This way? Blew goats.

Lilah got that stubborn set to her mouth. "Baloney. I know who you are, Devon Sparks. You can hide all you want, but I see you."

"This isn't a fucking game of hide-and-seek," Devon shouted. Her refusal to understand, to acknowledge that sometimes life was shitty and people sucked, made him want to throw something. "And it's not my fault if you're incapable of distinguishing between reality and your fairytale version of what you wish life would be like. Oh, I know, it's such a great story—poor little country mouse comes to the big city, meets a rich guy with a cute kid, gets a makeover, strengthens father/son bonds all over the place, and lives happily ever after."

She sucked in a breath, and crossed her arms defensively over her chest. Her mouth was still a firm little line, though, and Devon knew she wasn't getting it.

"I don't expect life to be a fairy tale," she said.

"Oh, yeah, you do. And that's sad, it's a fucking heartbreaker, because in two more weeks, the dream is over. We stop playing house, Tucker goes back to his mother, and reality sets up shop again. Because this? Our happy little family? Is an illusion, like every other so-called 'happy family' in the world. And no amount of wishful thinking or manipulation or *meddling* is going to change that."

Lilah didn't look stubborn anymore. She looked stricken.

Her eyes were wide and wet, her mouth an unhappy curve. "I said I was sorry about calling your folks. There's no call to talk like this."

"Why not? It's the truth," Devon said, holding to what he knew because to allow himself to hope for anything more was to open himself up for the worst kind of pain. "Just because you don't want to hear it doesn't make it any less true."

She watched him for a long moment, her eyes fathomless. And even though he waited with his breath caught in his lungs, the tears that trembled in her lower lashes didn't fall.

When she finally spoke, he caught himself flinching at the soft sound. "Maybe I was building castles in the clouds, dreaming on you and me and Tucker all living happily ever after. But if that's truly how you see your life, how you see yourself? I'm sorry for you. Sorrier still for that boy of yours, who deserves better. But as sorry as I am, I won't stick around to watch you burn my dream castle to the ground."

He let her walk to the door, the same door his father had used to leave him. Devon's arms and legs felt heavy, immovable.

"If you're so determined to be miserable, Devon, I can't stop you," Lilah said, meeting his gaze dead-on. The tears she'd held back for so long finally spilled over, and she brushed at her cheeks with stiff, impatient hands. "I can't stop you, but I will be damned if I let you make me miserable, too."

Then she was gone. And Devon was alone.

The way he was always meant to be.

CHAPTER THIRTY-FOUR

Lilah shivered in the chill air of the Park Avenue apartment and thought about asking to turn down the air conditioning, but didn't.

She wouldn't be here long enough for the temperature to matter.

As cold as she felt outside, Lilah was a hundred times more chilled at the bone.

The ride back to Devon's apartment had felt like a hundred dismal lifetimes jammed into twenty minutes. Devon sat up front with his driver, while Lilah sat in the backseat watching Tucker stare out the window. The minute they got into the apartment, Tucker disappeared into his bedroom and slammed the door behind him.

Lilah sighed, heartsore and unsure if she was doing the right thing.

"Thank you for driving me back to pack up my things," she said. It was easier than she would've thought to keep her voice polite. All that early training with Aunt Bertie had some use after all; Lilah found that in the midst of the worst disappointment of her life, she could take refuge in manners and at least pretend to a calm she certainly didn't feel.

"Paolo drove," Devon said, as distant as if they'd never stood in this exact same spot, this light, airy living room full of modern Italian furniture, and kissed until Lilah's lips were swollen and hot.

"I know. I just meant . . . I could've called a cab."

Devon shrugged and cast himself onto the lounge chair covered in black and white cowhide. Lilah had laughed at it once, and Devon had gotten all sniffy and offended, informing her that it was one of the most famous design pieces of the twentieth century.

She sure didn't feel like giggling now.

"Go ahead and say it." It was a clear challenge, issued in an almost bored undertone.

"I have nothing more to say to you," Lilah informed him.

"Fuck that," he said, his deliberate crudeness stiffening her spine like nothing else. "When have you ever held back on what you really think? You're ditching out, anyway."

Hurt and resentment ate away at her resolve. "You made it impossible for me to stay."

"So you might as well tell me what you think of me on your way out the door."

Lilah licked her lips, the temptation to lay into him and straighten him out, once and for all, overpowering and impossible. There was no straightening this one out. As Aunt Bertie would say, he was too twisted for color TV.

"I don't see the point in lowering myself," Lilah said, with withering formality.

Something blazed in Devon's eyes, but was banked at once. "Aw, Lilah Jane," he said softly, the sound of her name in that voice like a twist of the knife, "you've always seemed to like getting down and dirty with me."

Anger flashed over to nuclear. Lilah had to squint to see him through the red mist. "You arrogant, unfeeling . . . absolute monster of a man. I can't believe I ever saw anything good in you, can't believe I fell for your poor-little-rich-guy act—and I can't believe I told you all that stuff about my parents, and how my mother gave me up without a second thought, only to have you turn around and do the same exact thing to your own child. He needs his father in his life, Devon, for longer than one stupid month."

The something in Devon's eyes flared in satisfaction when she started to read him the riot act, as if he wanted her insults and anger, but by the end, as Lilah's voice hitched and caught, Devon's reaction changed, too. He leaned forward on the chaise, his fingers white-knuckled against his knees, and for a second, Lilah thought she might have gotten through to him.

"Christ, Lilah," he said in a strangled voice. "I didn't think about that. I'm sorry."

That made her madder than almost anything else.

"You know what?" Lilah panted for a moment. "*Screw* your sorry. Tucker probably *is* better away from a self-absorbed egomaniac like you."

The moment she said it, Lilah wanted to take it back. The look that crossed Devon's face—she hoped she never saw that particular combination of acceptance and self-hatred again.

"You'd be better off, too," he said after a second of staring at one another. "You want to pack your things? I can have Daniel do it and send them to you. I assume you'll go to Grant's."

"I . . . hadn't really thought about it," Lilah said, her knees suddenly feeling wobbly. She practically collapsed onto the sofa. "I guess I will. Go to Grant's."

"Okay." Devon looked calm, that smooth, unfeeling mask back in place, but Lilah thought she could see the brittleness of it now. He was just waiting for her to leave, trying to push her out the door before it shattered like a glass thrown at a wall.

"Devon," she said. "What the heck is going on here?"

"I'm not in the mood for trick questions. Get your stuff and get out."

"Not until I say good-bye to Tucker," she retorted.

"Whatever."

Lilah sat there in the pristine coolness of Devon's bachelor pad and watched him grab a magazine at random and start flipping through it. His pose was a study in casual chic, but the rigid line of his shoulders gave him away.

"One day," Lilah said into the stilted silence. "One day, maybe not too very far off, you're going to wake up and realize you're tired of being alone. And it's going to be too late, Devon. You will have pushed away everyone who ever tried to love you. And you'll be alone forever."

"Cheery," he said, eyes flickering. "Anything else?"

Lilah forced herself to stand, not sure her legs would take her weight when it felt like her entire body was made of straw. "I just want you to understand what's happening here."

His throat worked. "What's that?"

She met his defiant blue gaze. "You're throwing away your best chance at happiness. Like it's garbage. And Devon? Take it from someone who's been lucky enough to get one— second chances are few and far between."

Devon didn't move from the couch when she went to say her good-byes to Tucker, and he didn't move when she came back, suspiciously red-eyed and blotchy, and let herself out the front door without a backward glance.

He felt the quiet *click* of the door closing behind her as viscerally as if she'd slammed it hard enough to shake the walls.

Devon sat in his quiet living room thinking about the fact that Adam and Miranda were flying home tomorrow. Back when he first agreed to helm the Market kitchen, Devon had offered to work that last Sunday-night service to give his travel-wrecked, jetlagged friends a chance to recover.

So he'd work one more dinner at Market, get a new nanny for Tucker, and in a couple of weeks, he'd be able to get back to his regularly scheduled life.

Huh. That should've felt more like a relief than a prison sentence.

Trying to ignore the knowledge that once Tucker left, too, his apartment would always be exactly this quiet and depressing, Devon took a stroll past his son's closed bedroom door.

When a soft knock produced no answer, he cracked the

door open and peered in, squinting to see in the darkened room.

There was no movement other than the steady rise and fall of the lump curled up beneath Tucker's colorful dinosaur-print bedspread.

Devon stood there watching his son breathe and trying to remember how it felt to be able to just fall asleep at night, no tossing and turning, no second-guessing or regretting.

Lying in his huge, soft bed later, Devon stared at the ceiling for so long that he was surprised to wake up and see sunlight streaming in his windows.

His entire body ached like he'd run a marathon. Groaning, Devon sat up and wondered what fresh hell today would bring.

Ten minutes later, when he went to Tucker's room to roust the kid out for breakfast, Devon got his answer.

The room was empty, the bed covers rumpled and twisted. His eyes went straight to the bedside table where Tucker's beloved backpack lived.

No sign of it.

"Tuck?" Devon called, heart pounding. "Tucker?"

He repeated the name over and over, every iteration more desperate than the last as he raced from room to room. But he knew from the way his shattered voice echoed back at him that it was no use.

Tucker was gone.

CHAPTER THIRTY-FIVE

Daniel Tan had a potential second career as a professional clothes packer if he ever got tired of being Devon's assistant. Lilah was impressed with the state of her wardrobe after it made the trip from Devon's Upper East Side penthouse down to Grant's place in Chelsea.

She closed her suitcase again, not ready to deal with putting things away. Maybe she shouldn't bother; maybe she should zip up that suitcase and hail a cab to the airport, get on a plane back to Virginia.

Or maybe she should put on her big-girl panties and march right back uptown to that penthouse.

After a restless night of playing and replaying that last, horrible conversation with Devon and the look on Tucker's face when she went to his room to say good-bye, Lilah was pretty sure she'd made a huge mistake.

Yes, Devon had said and done some awful things—but it wasn't as if Lilah hadn't made any mistakes. She cringed to think of her own strident, self-important belief that she had the right to butt into Devon's complicated relationship with his father. She couldn't really blame Devon for being angry, and she could only guess at the pain his father had inflicted down in that office.

Devon wasn't the kind of man who turned the other cheek. He was more of the Old Testament persuasion, an eye for an eye, giving back pain for pain. So he'd lashed out. Fine. She could decide whether or not to forgive him for that.

What she maybe couldn't forgive was the fact that she'd so completely betrayed her own newfound courage. The moment the road went from smooth pavement to pitted gravel, she'd turned tail and run off, leaving Devon to deal with his anger and hurt—and worse, leaving Tucker.

Lilah went to the mirror to pull her hair back and wound up staring at the circles under her eyes, drowning in indecision and fear.

But it was really very simple, she realized.

She had to go back.

No matter what happened with Devon, Tucker needed her. Even if it was temporary. Even if after two more weeks of caring for him, it would be like ripping her heart right out of her own chest to leave him.

That didn't matter. What mattered was that Tucker be made to understand how much she loved him, and wanted to be with him.

Lilah felt like she used to when she and her cousins would jump off the high rocks into the swimming hole near the farmhouse. That plunge into the mountain stream so icy it stopped her legs from kicking and made her forget to wave her arms, and then after long seconds of scary sinking, she'd finally manage to hit the bottom hard enough to push off and shoot up and up through the breath-stealing cold of the water until she broke the surface with a big, satisfying splash.

Dragging in what felt like her first deep breath in hours, Lilah grinned at her reflection and whirled to grab her still-packed bags.

Her phone rang as she was struggling to heft the stupid suitcase. Lilah bobbled both and dropped the phone, losing it for a second in the cushions of Grant's deep, smooshy couch. Excavating it out, she got it to her ear in time to bark out a hurried, "Hello? Are you there?"

"Lolly," Grant said. He sounded weird. "Is there anything you want to tell me?"

"Um. No? I mean, aren't you at work? I know I said I'd spill about what happened with Devon, all the gory details, but maybe it could wait until later."

A pause. Then, "I think you should come up to the restaurant."

"I can think of few things I'd be less inclined to do," she said, her heart squeezing at the thought. "I don't want to see him yet, Grant. I don't think I can handle it. Besides, I need to find Tucker. Did Devon bring him to the restaurant? Because that's the only thing that could get me over there right now."

There was a strange noise, kind of a choking sound, quickly covered, then Grant's careful voice. "Hon. Trust me on this. You want to be at Market right now."

Her heart fluttered like a hummingbird in her chest, battering at the cage of her ribs. "You're scaring me. What's going on?"

"Nothing I'm going to tell you about over the phone. So get here. Now."

He hung up. Lilah stared at the phone, open-mouthed and faint.

For Grant to call and summon her, when he knew how hard she was taking all this stuff with Devon, something terrible must have happened. Terror squeezed her heart and gave Lilah a speed she never thought she'd possess. She was practically pushing people out of the way to get to the subway, flying down the street until she realized it might be faster to take a cab. So she waded out into traffic and threw her arm into the air with authority, the way she'd seen New Yorkers do, and sure enough, a cab swerved out of the flow of cars and stopped for her.

They made it up Tenth Avenue in record time with Lilah pressuring the poor cabbie every block of the way to go faster, find a better route, bypass the traffic snarls. He heaved a sigh of relief when they pulled up in front of Market.

Lilah shoved a couple of twenties at him and scrambled

from the cab, her heart in her throat. She took the steps up to the door in one flying leap and pushed her way inside, afraid of what she'd find.

Brain unspooling image after image of Devon having cut off a finger, collapsed at the stove, the whole kitchen held hostage like the awful night Grant had described a few months before, Lilah stopped short just inside the door.

Everything looked normal. It took a moment to process what she was seeing, but so far, it looked like just a normal night of dinner service at Market. Maybe a little more full of customers than she was used to, and maybe they all looked happier, smilier, but that was it. No panic, no alarm, no cops or ambulance people milling around.

Lilah walked as sedately as she could toward the back of the dining room, looking around for Grant the whole time.

He wasn't on the floor, but she caught the bartender's eye, that handsome, country-looking Christian, and he tipped his head toward the kitchen.

Lilah nodded and quickened her pace.

As she got closer, she could see a slice of the kitchen through the open pass, and from the front of the house, it looked like things were moving smoothly, if quietly. When she got to the door and peeked inside, Devon was nowhere to be seen. Frankie was expediting orders with a grim, purposeful manner that made Lilah's heart seize again.

Oh, dear Lord.

Closing the kitchen door firmly behind her, Lilah demanded in a voice shrill with fear, "What on earth is happening? Where's Grant? Where's *Devon*?"

Frankie wiped the rim of a plate with swift, economical movements and said, "Downstairs, Lilah. In the office. Table nine, away!"

Lilah wasted no time in pounding down the stairs. The fact that no one seemed to want to tell her what the heck was going on made her lightheaded with dread.

The scene in Adam's office did nothing to alleviate that fear. Devon was slumped over the ancient, scarred metal desk, hanging onto a phone and scrubbing his hand over his face.

Grant was pacing, his cell phone out, too, and both of them were talking at once, although they paused when she came in.

It hurt to look at Devon, beyond a quick once-over to ascertain that, yes, he was still in possession of all his fingers, so she looked at Grant. Who looked at Devon. Who stood and said, "I'll tell her."

His voice sounded awful, like he'd shouted his throat raw.

"Somebody better tell me something quick, before I start having a hissy!"

Devon moved as if he wanted to come around the desk to her, but Lilah took an involuntary step back. He stopped, holding himself still with visible effort.

"Tucker is missing. Grant called because we thought, you know, he's run off before. Maybe he would come to you." Hope blazed in his eyes, turning them electric blue, but his voice stayed monotone and grating. "He didn't, did he?"

"Sweet baby Jesus," Lilah said, the bottom dropping out of her stomach. "No, I haven't heard from him. Oh, Devon. Oh, my *God*."

The cracked leather of the old office chair squeaked under his weight as he dropped back into it. He put the phone back to his ear. "No. I just talked to her, she says she hasn't seen him. I don't know anything else to tell you. Come on, Connor, I need you. What else can I try?"

Lilah swayed on her feet and Grant was there, putting his arm around her and tugging her over to the sofa in the corner. "Sit, hon. Breathe. It's going to be okay, we'll find him. I'm sure he just needed a little break. Like that time he hid from you in the restaurant, remember?"

"How long has he been missing?" Lilah choked out.

"He was gone when Devon woke up this morning around eight. He's on the phone with his brother now, I guess he's a cop in Jersey. The NYPD is already on the case; with a missing child, you don't have to wait twenty-four hours to file the report, so that's really good, Lolly."

"How can anything about this be good?" she cried. Tears

were slipping down her cheeks, but she hardly noticed beyond the sudden stuffiness of her nose and head. "Tucker could be out there, for who knows how long, all alone and scared. Oh . . ." She gasped as a new thought occurred to her. "What if someone took him?"

The office chair screeched across the floor. Devon's face was bloodless and stark with the purest terror she'd ever seen. Lilah's heart stopped.

He lifted the phone back to his ear and said in an unnaturally even voice, "Con? There's one more lead to follow. Tucker's mother is in a rehab facility upstate, I can't remember the name. An Officer Santiago here in the city would know. Have her check and make sure Heather Sorensen is where she's supposed to be."

Replacing the phone gently on the receiver, Devon looked over at Lilah. His eyes were like holes burnt in a sheet, stark pools of fear in his white face. "I have to go home. I only came here because I thought there was a chance he might show up at the restaurant. But the cops say I should wait at the apartment, in case he comes back there."

"Well, I'm coming with you," Lilah said, pushing to her feet. "No arguments, mister. You might think you don't need other people, but you are *not* going through this alone. Not if I can help it.

A little color swept Devon's high cheekbones. Gratitude was a better look on him than sheer panic. "Let's go, then. Grant?"

"I'll hold down the fort," Grant said.

They trooped upstairs and Devon went immediately to Frankie's side. "I need your help. I've got to leave. Now. Can you take charge of the kitchen?"

Frankie passed a hand over his brow, his mouth firm and, for once, serious. He pressed his lips together, and Lilah caught the glimmer of nerves in the way his fingers tightened briefly, but all he said was, "You can count on me, Chef. Do what you have to do. Bring Tucker home, yeah?"

"Yeah," Devon said. "I will." He stood up straighter and when he turned back to her, there was a new layer of strength hardening into a tight lid over the roiling emotions beneath the surface.

Any doubts that had resurfaced in Lilah's mind about Devon's ability to love his son died in that moment.

"Lilah Jane? Are you with me?"

She swallowed around the lump in her throat.

"I am."

It was the longest drive of Devon's life. Paolo couldn't seem to maneuver the town car through the traffic quickly enough.

When they finally pulled up in front of the apartment building, Devon had the doors open and one foot out of the car before Paolo could get out to perform his duties.

"I'm sorry, Mr. Sparks," the chauffeur panted. His dark eyes were liquid with regret. "He's a good boy. If there's anything I can do, please let me know."

Devon could barely force a nod, but Lilah pressed a hand to Paolo's arm and said, "Thanks. It's going to be okay, Paolo. We'll find him."

Even in the midst of the worst day of his life, Devon heard that. "We," united. The two of them against the world, neither one alone anymore.

It actually accomplished the impossible; it made the unbearable ache of the last few hours slightly more tolerable.

CHAPTER THIRTY‑SIX

"If we were down South, where I grew up, we'd be swimming in casseroles right about now."

They'd finally gotten the terrifying news that Heather Sorensen was, indeed, missing from the Sunny Valley Drug and Alcohol Rehabilitation Center. It took about an hour of concerted effort, but Lilah had at last gotten Devon to stop pacing, stop calling his brother every few minutes, and stretch out on the leather couch with his head in her lap.

She tried to soothe the lines of tension from his face, but no amount of petting was going to relax him. She knew that. Nothing but the sight of Tucker all in one piece was going to make either of them feel better. And as much as Devon burned to be out there scouring the city for any trace of his ex, Connor was very clear about the fact that the best thing they could do would be to sit tight.

So Lilah talked. To distract him, and herself, from the grinding misery of waiting for news.

"That's the Southerner's answer to any calamity," she continued. "Casserole. Preferably the kind that freezes beautifully and can be reheated later when the afflicted family gets around to it."

"Yeah. That doesn't really happen in New York."

"Have you even met your neighbors?"

"Only passed them in the elevator, the mail room. You know."

Lilah didn't know; it sounded insane to her, not knowing your neighbors' names, or where their kids went to school, or anything. But she made a noncommittal sound and kept stroking Devon's hair.

They were silent for long moments where, Lilah was sure, Devon's thoughts drifted to Tucker just as inevitably as hers did.

He proved it a minute later by saying, "I'm so fucking scared right now, Lilah Jane."

"I know. Me, too." She swallowed hard. "You know, I was coming back. I was halfway out the door when Grant called. For Tucker, because I didn't want him to think I didn't care enough about him to stick it out."

Devon closed his eyes. "I didn't know it was possible to care this much about another person."

"Then why weren't you prepared to fight to keep him with you? How could you even contemplate letting him walk out of your life when this is what it feels like?" She wanted so badly to understand.

"I do want him here," Devon said, his voice fierce with longing. "Not just so I know he's safe and not off somewhere getting in a car with his drunk-ass mother—" he choked and stopped talking for a second.

Lilah tangled her fingers in his hair and held on tight, working to regulate her breathing.

When he found his voice again, it was halting and rough, as if every word were difficult to form. "But before—God, was it only yesterday?—before, when we had that fight, I thought . . . I don't know. That letting you both go would be the right thing. Because Tucker deserves better than me. You both do. There's something wrong with me, Lilah. I mean, my parents were wonderful with Connor; they just didn't know what to do with me. I'm not like them. Never was."

"What are you like, then?" Lilah kept her voice soft, kept her hands moving. They were approaching the heart of Devon's swirling pool of strange self-hatred. What would she find there?

"I'm . . . driven, I guess. To succeed. You know, I didn't get into the restaurant business because I was so great at it—I chose it because I was good enough at it that I knew I could make money, enough to get out of New Jersey. That's all I wanted."

Such an innocent, childish wish, to be rich and famous. Was it still all he wanted?

"And once you made it to New York, once you landed four stars from *The New York Times* and your own TV show, what was supposed to happen then?"

"I don't know. I never really planned that far ahead."

The phone rang, startling them both. Devon lunged for it.

His face as he listened to whoever was on the other end gave Lilah heart palpitations.

"Uh-huh. Uh-huh. Okay, send them up, please."

He set the phone down carefully.

"What is it?" Lilah cried.

"There's somebody down in the lobby to see me."

"Huh. Maybe there's a New York casserole tradition you don't know about."

Devon was shaking slightly; Lilah could see it as he got up from the couch and moved to open the front door. He didn't wait for a knock or a ring at the doorbell, he just opened the door wide and stood staring out into the hall, waiting for the elevator doors to open.

Afraid to hope, Lilah joined him.

When the chime sounded to announce the arrival of the elevator, Devon braced himself against the doorjamb. The doors shushed open, and Lilah heard a high voice shout, "Dad!"

Then a short, dark-haired form streaked across the hall and barreled into Devon.

Tucker.

Lilah's knees almost buckled at the wave of relief.

There was a sound from down the hall, and she looked up

to see a thin, blonde woman step slowly from the elevator. The woman's face was lined with strain, almost haggard, and the look in her eyes when they fell on Devon and Tucker was full of enough regret to make Lilah's heart go out to her.

Lilah walked forward, hand out, face expressionless. "Heather Sorensen, right?"

The woman started. "Yes. I'm sorry. You must be Lolly. Tucker told me all about you."

"Has he been with you the whole time?" Lilah asked.

"Yeah. I mean, he called the rehab facility and asked me to come get him from a diner in Times Square where they let him use the phone . . . so I did. But as soon as I had him, all he did was talk about Devon. He wanted to come back almost as soon as he left, I think, but he got lost. So here we are."

Dull pain throbbed through Heather's voice during her brief recital of the facts, but Lilah wasn't quite ready to pull out her hankie and dab the woman's tears away.

"How did you get out of rehab?" she demanded. "I thought it was court-ordered, not the kind of thing you could check yourself out of."

"It wasn't easy," Heather said. "But Tucker called. His voice on the phone . . . he wasn't happy." She shrugged. "What could I do? I'm not perfect, I know that. I've done stupid things, taken stupid chances—I probably don't deserve to call myself his mom. But if I'd gotten that call and refused to listen to my son—I couldn't do that."

You could've called to let us know he was okay, Lilah wanted to say. But somehow, despite the frantic panic of the past few hours, Lilah couldn't bring herself to beat up on this sad, struggling woman. Heather was like a cornfield after a storm, beaten and bent almost to the ground, but not quite broken.

"You're not as bad a mother as you seem to think," Lilah said gently. "Tucker loves you very much."

Heather looked past her to where her son was still clinging to his father. Devon had lifted him up against his chest and lowered his head to Tucker's ear. Lilah couldn't hear them, but she could imagine the words Devon was saying. Her heart swelled. Devon's arms were strong around Tucker's back, their dark heads close together.

She glanced at Heather in time to see the woman lower her eyes. "I love him, too," she said, her voice thready. "But he needs to be with his dad right now. He's smart enough to know that. And so am I."

When Devon could breathe through the crushing weight of joy he'd pulled up to his chest along with his son's slight, squirming form, he gasped out, "Don't ever do that to me again. I'm serious. This dad stuff is new to me, but I'm telling you now, I can't take it."

Tucker had called him "Dad" when he ran out of the elevator, Devon thought. It was the first time he'd ever done that.

"You said it was only temporary," Tucker said, plaintive, but with an edge of stubbornness. "I heard when you were talking to Lolly, down the stairs. You said it wasn't real, we weren't a real family, and we couldn't be happy."

Ah, God. "You heard all that, huh?" Devon said around the crack in his heart. "And that's why you left."

Tucker became very interested in the collar of Devon's shirt, his thin, artist's fingers coming up to twist and pull at the seam. "I thought maybe . . . it was because of me. And maybe if I left, Lolly would come back and you could be happy. If I wasn't there."

God, please don't let me start sobbing like a baby right now.

"Look at me." It took a second, but the kid raised wary blue eyes to meet Devon's. "I was wrong to say those things. Not just because they made Lilah very unhappy—I was the one who made her leave, Tuck, not you—but because they weren't true. They were the opposite of true."

Devon took a deep breath and threw himself off the cliff.

"The truth is, Tuck, I can't be happy if you're not here."

Tucker ducked his head again, but this time it was to hide a goofy grin. "Really? 'Cuz I wished I didn't leave. I walked for a long time, and then when I wanted to come back, none of the streets sounded right and I didn't know where I was and I didn't know your phone number. So I called Mom at the place where the cop lady said she'd be, and she came and got me."

Devon finally became aware of the world beyond his son. Christ, there was Heather, right there. She looked tired and sad, and older then he remembered. Well, of course she was. It had been years since he'd seen her—and evidently, they'd been hard years.

He didn't know what he'd thought he'd feel when confronted with the person who brought Tucker back to him. It was complicated, too, by the fact that in some ways, Heather was the person who'd taken Tucker away . . . except Devon couldn't fool himself about that. He'd started this whole nightmare in motion himself by letting his son think he wasn't wanted.

Still, he'd imagined some anger, some uncontrollable need to lash out at the cause of the worst few hours of his life. But when he looked at Heather, all he felt was gratitude.

Their eyes connected. He wondered if she was thinking about the same thing he was, the heady whirlwind of their relationship. For all the screaming matches and fights and bad feelings and broken promises, something good had come out of it.

"Thank you," Devon said. He hardly recognized his own voice, it sounded so sincere. "For bringing Tucker here today. For giving me temporary custody in the first place. I swear, I'll do a better job of taking care of him from now on."

He heard the click of her throat as she swallowed. "Yeah, you will," she said, breath hitching. "Because I can't right now. In fact, I need to get back."

"No!" Tucker wiggled hard enough that Devon nearly dropped him. Which seemed to be what the kid was after, actually, because he pushed on Devon's shoulder and kicked his legs until his feet touched the ground. Reluctant as his arms were to open up and let Tucker go, Devon found himself unable to begrudge Heather the bittersweet joy of her good-bye hug from Tucker.

Who was not happy at this new turn of events. "Why?" he yelled. "Why can't we all just stay together? There's plenty of room here, you could stay, Mom. Dad and Lolly don't mind, right?"

Devon's mind went blank, but luckily Lilah was there, jumping in with, "Oh, sugar pop, of course your daddy doesn't mind. But your momma has somewhere she needs to be. Just for a little while, yet."

"I'm sorry," Heather said, burying her face in Tucker's hair. "I'm so sorry, kiddo. But I'll work hard, I promise, so I can come back to you soon. And when I do," she glanced up at Devon, "your dad and I will have a long talk about the best way to go forward. So you can have us both, and we can share our time with you. Because you deserve two parents who love you very much."

Her words unlocked something inside Devon.

Love. That's what Tucker deserved. And Devon could absolutely give him that. Was helpless to do anything else, really, as terrifying as that thought was now that he'd had proof of just how painful love could be.

Love was the ultimate act of courage, he understood now. Because you had to go into it knowing it could be snatched away by forces beyond your control. And if that happened, you'd be a shell of a person, a shadow of yourself, and nothing would ever be any good again.

But it didn't have to be that way. Sometimes love could last. And in the meantime, it was worth it.

Tucker cried and clung to his mother a little, which made Devon want to hit something, but he managed to thank Heather again before she left, and promised to testify if anyone questioned her temporary defection from rehab.

Then Heather thanked Devon, and it was looking like it might turn into a whole endless round of mutual indebtedness and appreciation until Lilah stopped the cycle by gently pointing out how late it was and suggesting it might be time to put Tucker to bed.

Which was easier said than done. The kid was extremely wound up, despite his obvious exhaustion, and he was already missing his mom.

Thank God for Lilah, was all Devon could think. There was something soothing about her, a calming effect like sunlight through trees or the sound of waves, and eventually it settled Tucker down enough that he nodded off with Lilah on one side, and Devon on the other.

Devon sat on the edge of his son's bed, reflecting on how utterly satisfying it was, on a very primal level, to have both Tucker and Lilah with him, under his roof—sort of, communal apartment roof, really, but still—and safe.

That was the main thing. Everyone he loved was in one room, safe and sound.

Wait.

What?

Lilah smoothed the hair back from Tucker's pink, sleeping face and smiled across his still body, curled under the covers. Devon couldn't even smile back, he was so shocked.

Christ. He'd known Lilah was important to him, but love? He'd just gotten used to the idea of loving his son. Just gotten over the near-hysteria-inducing idea that his happiness depended on the well-being of another person.

That wasn't the most natural of ideas for Devon to wrap his brain around. It certainly wasn't the way he'd lived his life up till now.

But then, how happy had he been, really? All the parties, the women, the money, the fame, the magazine articles and interviews and reviews and the TV show—above all, that damn TV show—what had any of it done for him? He'd spent most of his free time downtown at Chapel, drowning his loneliness, his sheer boredom, in bourbon and meaningless fucks.

Now—he wanted to believe he had a chance to be happy, for real, finally, but he didn't want to fool himself. Despite how content he'd be to let the world stop turning and trap them all in this moment, everything was still up in the air.

He must've sighed loudly or something, because Lilah

put her finger to her lips and tilted her head in invitation before tiptoeing from the room.

Devon waited until she was gone, then leaned over and pressed a very light, definitely-too-light-to-wake-him-up kiss to Tucker's forehead. Standing up and staring down at the sleeping boy, Devon loved him so much it felt like his heart had been scraped raw and dunked in salted water.

Painful, but true.

He sighed again, more softly this time, and followed Lilah from the room. *Time for another painful round of truth,* he mused.

Lilah waited for him in the living room, sitting all prim and straight-backed on the edge of one of his black leather Barcelona chairs.

He wanted to attach some significance to the fact that she was there at all, clearly ready to talk, but the knowledge that she probably just wanted to clarify exactly what a gutless, soulless monster he was made Devon a little glum going into this conversation.

Still, he had things to say to her, and if she was willing to listen, he could only be thankful.

"You were amazing tonight," he said, throwing himself down on the couch and stretching out his legs. He was tense enough that he would've preferred to stand, but every muscle in his body ached from having been clenched tight for the past five hours. He needed to sit.

Lilah's face went a little pink. "I didn't do anything," she denied.

"You held it together. Held me together." Devon looked down at his feet propped on the glass coffee table. "I wouldn't have made it through today without you."

"Nonsense," she said briskly. "You didn't need me any more than you ever have."

Devon's stomach plummeted. He knew what that meant. She wasn't sticking around.

"Come on," he said, trying for a charming smile. "I need you. I always needed you, Lilah Jane. Even when I didn't know it."

"I thought so when I first met you," she said, her eyes soft and thoughtful. "I thought you needed shaking up, needed to be taught a lesson about how to treat people, needed to learn what it was like to love and be loved." She paused, his pretty Lilah Jane, and Devon felt his breathing speed up like he was running a marathon. "But now I think you didn't need me at all. You're a natural at it, Devon."

Well, that was unexpected.

He blinked. "Lilah—"

She held up a hand, and Devon stopped talking gladly; his voice was on the verge of breaking like a spotty teenager's.

"I should never have implied that you were incapable of loving your son," Lilah said, standing. "Anyone seeing you today, while Tucker was missing, would know just how much you care about that boy."

Was she leaving? Devon managed a shrug, his eyes riveted to her nervous, stiff form. "Tucker makes it easy. And I appreciate all your help with him, I truly do. But if you think he's the only reason I need you, you're nuts."

She had a look on her face, like she was afraid to ask what he meant, and it was so similar to the sensation pushing at Devon's chest that he started to feel a whole lot more hopeful about the outcome of this conversation.

"You see," he said, feigning casual confidence by lacing his fingers together behind his head, "and you should write this down, because you're one of very few people in the world who've ever heard this from me: You were right. About the dream castles, about the happy family. About everything."

Lilah sat back down again, hard enough to bounce on the firm leather seat. "What?"

"Think I'm going to say it twice?" he scoffed, heart beating hard. "I may be head over heels for you, but I'm not an idiot."

"You're . . . oh, my stars and stripes, what did you just say?"

"Come on, Lilah Jane, I've never known you to be at a loss for words before. Or . . . ." he stopped, forced himself to keep his eyes level on hers. "Maybe Tucker is the whole reason you're here. I wouldn't blame you, you know. If you loved him, but not me."

Christ, this hurts. No wonder I never wanted to do it before.

She stared at him, her eyes huge and filled with some indefinable emotion. Until suddenly, they lit up like emeralds in a jewelry case at Cartier, and she launched herself across the coffee table and landed in his lap.

Framing his face in both hands, she had to raise her voice to be heard over Devon's delighted laughter. "Don't get too big for your britches, Devon Sparks. You most certainly *are* an idiot if you don't know how much I love you."

Her palms were warm against his cheeks, her green eyes even warmer as she gazed down at him.

Warmest of all, though, were her lips when he tugged her closer and attempted to imprint the wild, surging emotion coursing through him onto her mouth.

This love stuff isn't easy, Devon reflected as Lilah made a soft mewl and kissed him back, *but it has infinite potential.* And like everything Devon had ever decided to succeed at, he'd work tirelessly until he got it right.

CHAPTER THIRTY-SEVEN

Everyone had gone home. Paying customers, servers, line cooks, a bartender, even a restaurant manager. Market was as close to quiet as it ever got when Frankie was around.

Drained dry, Frankie stretched his neck and reached to crank the volume on the small CD player. *Halfway to Sanity* was already in, and the first track, *I Wanna Live*, captured his mood perfectly. Johnny Ramone's guitar screamed out of the tinny speakers, half jubilation, half desolation.

And as Joey started singing about lovers exposing the truth and being a damn fool, Frankie shivered. Then footsteps on the stairs up from the employee locker room. He wasn't alone. Yet.

When Jess stepped into the kitchen, all slicked down and freshly scrubbed in jeans and a blue striped Oxford with the sleeves rolled past his elbows, Frankie was ready with a grin and a lazy hip bump.

"Oi, changed into your muftis already, eh?"

Jess arched a brow as he dumped his messenger bag on the counter. "Watch it, you know that Brit-speak gets me hot."

Frankie gave him a flash of tongue. "What makes you think I mind?"

Blue eyes alight, Jess leaned up for a kiss, but Frankie jittered out of his reach and around the kitchen island.

Oh, bugger, oh, damn, oh fuckfuckfuckityfuck.

No, he told himself as sternly as a first-form teacher. *You mustn't. No teasing, no tempting, and absolutely no seducing.*

It's time to grow up, Peter Pan, and start thinking about what's good for someone other than yourself, for a change.

Chance would be a fine thing. Frankie could almost hear his father's rough, sneering voice saying the words.

But Frankie knew better. He knew how to love.

He knew how to do it so well, no one would ever suspect the depths of it. And what he knew, above all, was that it was impossible to love someone and allow him to sacrifice his future for you.

"It was mad tonight, yeah?" Frankie rushed to say, hoping to cover the momentary awkwardness of being unable to resist baiting Jess into coming closer while simultaneously vowing not to touch him. Tricky, that.

"Yeah, it was," Jess replied slowly, not fooled for a minute. "I was proud of you."

Frankie adored that quick mind, but he could wish it weren't quite so speedy just at the moment.

"Frankie, what's going on?"

Busted, as Adam would say. Frankie hid a wince. He was looking forward to getting his best mate back and available for war council. The recent relationship pow-wows with Devon, while enlightening and no doubt salutary, had left Frankie more gutted than uplifted.

And with a clear fucking sense of what he needed to be getting on with. So Frankie got on with it.

"Nothing, Bit. Just been thinking." Mother of God, why was this happening in the kitchen instead of in the alley where he could have a smoke?

Because you and Jess talked, really talked, for the first time in that alley behind the restaurant. And you can't handle doing this there, with the ghost of that all around you.

Frankie scowled. Damned perspicacious of the voice in his head. He didn't like it.

"What about?"

Jess looked wary, his perfectly curved mouth pulling into a flat, worried line. Frankie's heart stuttered. "About your sister. She and Adam are probably back now."

"They are!" Jess lit up all over again, his eyes shining. "Miranda texted me when they landed. Something about how they're going to Adam's place to crash and will probably sleep for about eighteen hours straight. After which, she wants to see me." He laughed.

Frankie arched a brow. Perfect segue. "Bet I know what she wants to talk about."

"Oh, come on. She's just been to Europe for two weeks! Surely she's got more on her mind than my housing applications."

"The way she was after you to turn them in before she left? Doubtful, Bit." Needing to hide his face for this next part, Frankie ducked his head and started unbuttoning his chef's jacket. He'd worn it tonight out of respect (grudging, unwilling, shocked as hell respect) for Devon, since it was the man's last service. And a damn good thing, too, since Devon had shown up wild-eyed and doing his nut because Tucker'd gone missing.

Frankie might not ever be best mates with Devon Sparks, but he wouldn't wish that kind of pain on his worst enemy.

And, wonder of wonders, Frankie didn't bollocks it up too badly when he had to take over expediting while Devon dealt with the nabbed kid. Or not nabbed, with his druggie mum, and Grant said it was all fine now, which was a relief.

Frankie didn't kid himself that he could run the kitchen every night. The very thought made his fingers twitch for a calming cigarette. There'd been far too much excitement around the place lately. Frankie wanted things back to normal. With Adam calling the shots, Grant organizing the troops, and himself . . . pissing around and buggering off and generally being Frankie. An unrepentant fuck-up.

Or unrepentant until recently, anyway.

But just because he was suddenly aware of and embarrassed over his own shortcomings didn't mean Frankie could suddenly grow a whole new personality, like growing out his hair after a bad bleach job.

It sucked, but there it was. He'd never be different. Never be better. Never be good enough for Jess.

"She knows why I don't want to live in crappy student housing," Jess groused. Sly, happy mischief twisted the annoyance on his handsome face into something almost elfin. "I'd rather live in crappy housing with you."

This was why Frankie had to end it. Jess was forever trying to give up bits and pieces of his life as a student, as a young man with a future, to hang out with Frankie at Frankie's grotty attic flat. It had to stop.

Instead of defending the Garret, as was Frankie's vociferous habit whenever anyone slighted his much-loved domicile, he said, "I think your sister might be right."

All movement stopped.

Frankie froze like he'd been cornered by the police and Jess had the unnatural stillness of someone who'd been dealt a killing blow.

When Jess's voice came, it was careful. Quiet. "If you want me to move out, that's all you have to say."

He waited and Frankie could almost taste his desperate hope that the response would be anything other than what it had to be. "Yeah. You should move out. You should turn in those forms, get yourself a nice roommate."

"I thought I had one," Jess whispered, then squeezed his eyes closed. "Fuck. Forget I said that."

Frankie was sure he'd never forget it; memory wasn't usually kind enough to allow him to remember only the lovely bits of life. Still, he waved it away.

"No worries, Bit." The nickname almost made him flinch as it came out of his mouth here in this kitchen, where he'd thought it upon seeing Jess for the first time: a bit of all right.

Frankie didn't let it show, though. He gave Jess a grin and said, "All settled, then? It's been fun and all, but it's time to move on. For both of us."

And the band said Frankie didn't have the onstage persona to be front man. Frankie deserved a fucking Tony for this performance.

As expected, Jess read between the lines and cast the worst—or best, depending on if what you were trying to accomplish was to rip his sweet heart out—possible interpretation on Frankie's words.

"Bored with me, are you?" Jess shook his head, anger finally spilling in to displace the lost misery clouding his blue eyes. "Looking back, I guess I'm only surprised it took this long. I mean, what could someone like you want with a pathetic, inexperienced little twat like me?"

Frankie couldn't help flinching, and of course, Jess caught it. Eyes narrowed, color up, he looked magnificent, like an avenging angel out for blood. "And that's all bullshit, isn't it?" Jess breathed. "Whatever's behind this, boredom isn't it. I know you, Frankie, better than anyone. I *see* you."

"What do you see?" Frankie asked, voice destroyed like he'd shrieked along with the chorus to *God Save the Queen*. The Sex Pistols version.

Jess stalked him like a lithe young tiger, all slink and slide. Pinned by that hot blue gaze, Frankie let him get closer. Closer.

Until Jess was a breath away.

"I see somebody who's scared. Scared of responsibility, of commitment, and most of all, scared of what he feels. For me."

Frankie's mouth felt dry and cracked like the morning after a bender. Something in his face must have communicated his sudden, intense panic because Jess pulled back, a grim set to those pretty lips.

"Don't worry," Jess said. "I'm not going to fight you on this. If you can't be bothered to fight for us, why should I?"

Fair point.

"I want you to know," Jess went on, relentless. "I want it out on the table, so we *both* know, this isn't about what's best for me and my future, or whatever piece-of-shit excuse you're giving yourself. It's about you. And your fear. And the fact that even though I know—I *know*, Frankie—that you love me . . ."

For the first time since Frankie dropped his bomb, Jess wavered. His breath hitched in a way that made Frankie want to kill whoever was responsible, as quickly as possible, which in this case meant hari–kari with a fish knife.

"Bit," he murmured helplessly.

"No," Jess said, his voice ragged. "Don't call me that. I was going to say that even though I know you love me, apparently that's not enough. And I can't live like that. I have to be enough, Frankie. Just me. So I'll go without a fuss, like you wanted. I've still got the keys to Miranda's old place; I'll stay there tonight and get the rest of my shit from the Garret tomorrow."

Frankie took a shuddering breath.

"Okay?" Jess prompted, eyes hard on his face.

This was the moment where he could make or break them, Frankie knew. It was still salvageable, like a separated sauce that just need a few seconds more whisking and a little more oil to be perfect again.

But despite the accuracy of some of Jess's arrows, Frankie still believed this was the right thing. For Jess. Who deserved more than Frankie could give him.

He clung to that like a drowning man and said, "Right. Tomorrow. I might be out."

The light in Jess's eyes died, leaving them a dull, flat blue-gray, like wet newspaper.

"Fine," he said. "I'll leave the key under the mat."

Frankie nodded, drinking in what felt like his last view of Jess. After this, everything would change. He could only hope the change would be for the better.

If lucky happenings and life-altering flukes were doled out according to what hurt the most, Frankie and Jess ought to be due for a major haul.

CHAPTER THIRTY-EIGHT

One month later ...

"Do we really have to go see him?" Lilah asked, putting on her best pout. She was improving her feminine wiles through trial and error.

The amused look Devon sent her way said he was aware of the wiles and appreciated them, but wasn't planning on falling for them this time. "I know he didn't make the best first impression on you, Lilah Jane, but I promise he can help us."

It was impossible to hang onto her ineffectual pout when thinking about what she and Devon were trying to do; the prospect made her too giddy for anything but a big, silly smile.

She worried, sometimes, that this much happiness must be imaginary. Maybe she was still dreaming, fantasizing her wonderful new life with her very own wickedly charming prince, living in a penthouse in the clouds.

"Are you sure about this?" she asked.

Devon looked down at her, and, in full view of the entire bustling lobby of this very shmancy office high-rise, grabbed Lilah around the waist and dipped her back for a breathtaking upside-down kiss.

"Very sure," he whispered against her laughing mouth, and kissed her again, the bold strokes of his tongue making heat roar to life in Lilah's belly.

A pair of expensive loafers clicked across the marble floor toward them. "Such a spectacle. Did I not teach you anything, Dev?"

The mocking tenor sent a different kind of heat spreading up Lilah's chest and neck. She pushed at Devon's shoulders until he pulled her back to vertical and let her go with one last nipping bite.

Turning unhurriedly to face Simon Woolf, publicist to the stars, Devon said, "Thanks for meeting with us on such short notice."

Simon's eyes gleamed. "Hey, there's always room in my schedule for my biggest client, you know that. And for you, too, Ms. Tunkle, of course. Shall we go up to my office?"

"Let's take a walk instead," Devon suggested. They'd discussed it ahead of time; Lilah thought Simon was more likely to cave to their request—and less likely to fuss over the bad news they were breaking—if they got him off his familiar turf. "It's nearly lunchtime; I saw a halal cart on the far corner that has a line around the block."

"Yeah, that guy's awesome," Simon said. "Sure, I could go for some shwarma."

Lilah slipped her hand into Devon's as they headed back out into the crisp fall air. While Devon and Simon caught up on inconsequential chitchat, Lilah let the hustle and bustle of Sixth Avenue swirl around her in a kaleidoscope of business-men with briefcases, grand dames in furs, and perky Upper East Side nannies in aggressively matching track suits.

Recalling her own nanny days made her smile. Maybe she should buy one of those pink hoodie sweatshirts and a pair of pants with something inappropriate written across the seat. Devon would probably get a kick out of that.

She grinned and tuned back into the conversation when they hit the end of the line for the Middle Eastern food vendor.

Devon was saying, "I don't think I ever thanked you for your help with the Center for Arts Education fundraiser. And not just the dinner itself, but the surprise floor show afterward."

"That's my job," Simon said, puffing out his chest. "The only thanks I need is my hourly retainer. Ha ha!"

Jackass, thought Lilah.

Still, she felt sorry for him, since she knew what was coming next.

"Well, I'm about to give you a whole new way to earn that hefty retainer, Si," Devon said. Lilah squeezed his hand and he met her gaze calmly, his eyes deep, still pools of blue.

Lilah got the dreamy weightless feeling of happiness again. "Go for it," she said.

"Go for what? Dev?" Simon sounded nervous.

Devon grinned and turned back to the publicist. "I'm quitting *One-Night Stand*."

"What?" Simon's squawk startled a nearby flock of pigeons pecking around for scraps of pita into flight. The people ahead of them in line, however, didn't even turn to see what the commotion was. Lord, Lilah loved New York.

"You can't mean it. Dev, think about what you're saying. That show made you famous!"

"That show made him miserable," Lilah said. "He's not really into being miserable anymore."

"I'm making some changes in my life," Devon agreed. "Starting with the show. Breathe, Si. It's going to be okay."

"Yes, don't worry. Your retainer is secure." Snide, maybe, but Lilah couldn't quite feel guilty about it.

"I need to sit down," Simon moaned.

"Buck up," Lilah told him. "There's more."

"More?" He gulped.

"Lilah and I are starting a new project, and we need your help. No one creates buzz like you, Si."

Shooting Devon a raised eyebrow that communicated exactly what she thought of his blatant flattery, Lilah said, "Yes. We need buzz. And you don't want to lose your star client. Everybody wins!"

"Wait a minute." Simon's expression sharpened. "What, exactly, is this new project? It's not illegal, right? Because that costs extra."

Devon lit up like he always did when he talked about their brainchild, and Lilah lost her heart all over again.

"It's not illegal, you scumbag. We're founding the Sparks Culinary Classroom," he said. "A cooking school for kids. We want to work with the New York City public schools, offer courses for free to their students to help fill the gaps in extracurriculars caused by lack of funding."

"Kids, huh?" Simon wasn't impressed. "That sounds . . . nice, I guess. Not very sexy. Might be tough to rebrand you as an upright, concerned citizen, if you know what I mean."

"That's why we're here," Lilah said. She got a grip on her gag reflex and continued, "We needed the best, so of course we came to you."

Devon rubbed between her shoulder blades consolingly. He knew what that cost her. She was only able to spit it out because it was true—they needed public perception of Devon Sparks to switch from foul-mouthed celebrity hothead to patient teacher and caring father, or no school would take a chance on partnering with their fledgling program.

As Tucker and Devon worked on strengthening the bond Lilah liked to think she'd helped foster, they naturally gravitated to the kitchen. Maybe it was genetic, maybe it was his innate artistic ability, or maybe it was the simple desire to do well at something his father loved, but Tucker got a genuine thrill out of cooking.

Even more interestingly, Devon loved teaching him. Lilah, who found she missed the atmosphere of the classroom more than she would've believed, finally asked Devon what was stopping them from setting up their own little culinary academy.

It was perfect. Devon had plenty of time and reason to play in the kitchen exploring his newfound soulful cooking style. And Lilah got to use her education experience designing a curriculum and reaching out to local schools.

"It'll be a challenge," Simon mused. "Your brand isn't exactly the most kid-friendly. And there's the backlash from dropping *One-Night Stand* to consider, although maybe I can work that . . . Okay, I'll do it."

"I never doubted you for a second," Devon said.

Lilah never doubted Simon's ability to spot a golden opportunity when he saw one, but she kept her mouth shut.

"Listen, I need to run back to the office and start making calls," Simon said. "Rain check on the shwarma? You're gorgeous, both of you, this is going to be great."

And he was gone in a swirl of heavy-handed cologne, pulling his PDA out of his pocket as he walked.

"That went well," Devon said. "You want to go home? We can make our own falafel."

"Sounds great," Lilah said without having the faintest idea what falafel might consist of. She was pretty certain between the two of them, they'd make it delicious.

Paolo rounded the rear bumper of the town car in time to open Lilah's door for her. She wasn't sure she'd ever get used to having a chauffeur, but she was sure as heck going to try.

"How are you feeling?" she asked as they settled back into the plush leather seats. "Now that it's all official, I mean."

Devon took a moment to think it over. "Fantastic," he decided. "Like the future is a big, empty pot just waiting for me to fill it up with all the things I love best."

"Hmm," Lilah said, relief making her bounce a little. "You mean like collards and bacon?"

"I meant more like you and Tucker," Devon said. "Maybe a stock pot wasn't the best metaphor."

"I don't know. Nothing says 'love' like cannibalism."

Devon laughed. "Hey, speaking of food, Connor's coming over tomorrow night. Tucker promised to cook him the famous cheddar date rolls. Is that okay with you?"

"Of course it's okay," Lilah said, her heart full. "I always like having Connor over—he's great with Tucker, and he helps with the dishes. He's the perfect dinner guest."

"I'm glad we started talking again," Devon said. "I mean, it sucks that it took me thinking my kid was in mortal peril to make me call him, but hey. That's my family."

His mouth twisted, and Lilah knew he was thinking about his parents. He hadn't spoken to his father since that awful night, although he'd talked to his mom a couple of times. She wanted to meet Tucker, and Lilah was doing her best to subtly nudge Devon in that direction. She had faith that Angela Sparks would be making an unprecedented trip into the city alone sometime soon. A woman would brave a lot to get to meet her only grandson.

Heck, if they hadn't already promised to bring Tucker down to the farm for Thanksgiving, Lilah knew her aunt would already be camped out in the penthouse.

They planned to follow the regular school year with the Sparks Culinary Classroom, offering classes after school and on weekends, and shutting down during the summers. That was at Tucker's request—after hearing countless stories about the pretty Virginia valley where Lilah grew up, he wanted to see it. They planned to spend most of the summer down South; Lilah couldn't wait to toss her little city boy in the swimming hole and see him riding a tractor with her Uncle Roy and gathering eggs from the henhouse with Aunt Bertie.

Lilah even harbored a secret hope that she could convince Heather to come down to Spotswood County with them. Heather was doing well with her recovery and all, but still, the country air and simple living would do her a world of good.

"Uh-oh," Devon said. "I know that face."

Lilah widened her eyes. "What face?"

"That's your Making Plans face," Devon said accusingly. "You are at this very moment concocting a scheme to interfere in some poor, unsuspecting bastard's life. Who's getting the Lilah Jane treatment this time?"

Rats. He knew her too well. "Heather," she admitted. "I want her to come down to Virginia next summer. Think how happy Tucker would be to have us all together!"

"You're unbelievable," Devon said.

Lilah peered at him. She didn't think he was complaining; there wasn't usually any doubt about it when Devon threw a hissy.

"I'm not unbelievable, I'm practical," Lilah said. "And I happen to have excellent instincts about how to improve the lives of those around me."

"What you have," Devon said, voice soft, "is an unparalleled capacity for love. I'm awed by your ability to give it, show it . . ."

"Make it," Lilah interjected, pleased and embarrassed at the same time.

"Mmm. That, too."

Devon leaned his head back against the seat, his gaze steady and open on her face.

"I love you so damn much," he said, his voice low and full of feeling. "Will you marry me?"

They both froze.

Lilah's lungs stopped working, like her brain was diverting all power to figuring out what she should say. *What would the old Lolly do*, she wondered frantically. Obviously, Lolly would jump on it—in the back of her mind, she'd been worrying about the two of them showing up on Aunt Bertie's doorstep at Thanksgiving *not* engaged. But on the other hand, wasn't it much more of a new Lilah-type adventure to agree to marry a man she'd only known for six weeks?

"I'm sorry. Shit! I didn't mean to blurt it out like that," Devon said, sitting up straight. "I don't even have the ring with me! Crap, what kind of proposal was that? I suck at this."

The distress on Devon's handsome face somehow, paradoxically, drained all the distress right out of Lilah. The thought crystallized in her mind as if it had always been there: she didn't have to choose between Lolly and Lilah— they were both a part of her. She could just be herself and stop worrying about it.

And in this case, the response to Devon's question was unanimous, anyway.

"Yes," she said, too softly.

Devon paused while running his hands through his hair, leaving it sticking straight up. "What?"

"I said yes, I'll marry you," Lilah said more strongly. "I don't care about the ring, or the fantasy proposal of you down on one knee, or whatever you're thinking you should've done. I just . . . I don't care about that stuff. All I care about is you, and the life we can have together."

His face actually crumpled a little, his chest heaving with strong emotion, and Lilah pushed through her own surging feelings to give him a tremulous smile.

"You know," she told him, "you're not half bad at showing the people you love how you feel."

"No?" His voice cracked a bit, and love overflowed her heart.

"No! You're improving by leaps and bounds," she said encouragingly. "You're really starting to move past that grumpy, bitter, emotionally stunted half-man you were when I met you."

Devon shouted a laugh and made a grab for her. Out of the corner of her eye, Lilah caught Paolo's smile in the rear-view mirror as he hit the button to make the tinted privacy shield slide into place.

Lilah let him catch her and pull her onto his lap so she could lean back in his arms, secure in the knowledge that he'd never let her go.

"Oh, Lilah Jane. I think you'd better come here and let me practice."

His warm, aroused voice was like a full-body hug. The naked kind.

"Practice what?" she asked, breathless.

"Showing you how I feel," he said, his mouth finding hers in a quick clash of teeth and tongues and laughter and so much joy, she was afraid her heart might actually burst.

Well, she thought hazily as he coiled her curls around his fingers and nuzzled into her neck. *Practice makes perfect.*

AUTHOR'S NOTE

The charity Devon chooses for his fundraiser benefit is the Center for Arts Education of New York, and that organization actually exists. Committed to restoring and sustaining quality arts education to all grade levels of New York City's public schools, the CAE has a fantastic and very informative website at www.cae-nyc.org/. Check it out! Every child deserves a well-rounded education. Find out what you can do to make a difference.

And a quick note on the recipes included in this book: the corn salad is completely new, dreamed up by me and rigorously taste-tested and kibitzed by my husband and best friend, Meg Blocker, but the other two are extremely old family recipes from my mother's side. They're so old, I had to update the Cheese Date Rolls to use butter and shortening rather than oleo! And the Delmonico Pudding is technically a blancmange, a style of dish that actually originated in the Middle Ages. My family's modern version probably dates from the mid 1800s when the Manhattan restaurant of the same name was at the height of its popularity. As Lilah says, it's traditionally a holiday treat, at least in my family, but with the substitution of candied ginger and pine nuts for the festively green and red candied pineapple, Delmonico Pudding works year-round! I hope you enjoy all the recipes as much as I enjoyed developing them.

MEXICAN STREET CORN SALAD

4 ears corn, shucked
¼ cup mayonnaise
2 tablespoons lime juice
¼ teaspoon chili powder, or to taste
3 green onions
1 medium red bell pepper
1 teaspoon salt
pepper to taste
½ teaspoon chili powder
1 cup freshly grated Parmesan cheese
chopped fresh cilantro
1 lime, quartered

Cook the corn in a large pot of boiling, salted water for no more than two minutes. You want it to stay crunchy. Drain and allow to cool while you prep the other ingredients.

Mix the mayonnaise with the lime juice and cayenne. Thinly slice the green onions, both the whites and part of the green. Seed and dice the red pepper—you want about half a cup. Cut the corn kernels off the cooled cobs and add to the green onions, the diced bell pepper, and the mayonnaise. Stir in salt and pepper to taste.

Divide the salad between four plates. Top each with chili powder, freshly grated cheese, and a little chopped cilantro. Serve with lime wedges.

CHEESE DATE ROLLS

> 1 pound of the sharpest cheddar cheese you can
> find (white is fine, but orange gives the rolls bet-
> ter color), shredded
> 10 tablespoons unsalted butter, cut into small
> pieces and chilled
> 6 tablespoons shortening
> 3 cups sifted all-purpose flour
> ½ teaspoon cayenne pepper
> ½ teaspoon salt
> 1 16-ounce package of pitted dates (the biggest,
> plumpest dates available will really take these
> over the top)
> Whole pecans, about two cups

Put the flour, cayenne, and salt in a food processor and pulse
once to mix. Add the cold butter and shortening, then pulse
five or six times until incorporated. Stir in the shredded cheese
and let the dough rest at least two hours in the refrigerator.
(The recipe can be made ahead up to this point; dough will last
for several days refrigerated in an airtight container.) Remove
the dough from the fridge about half an hour before you want
to bake the rolls.

Preheat the oven to 350 degrees.

While oven is heating, stuff fifty dates with one whole pecan
each. Pinch off a walnut-sized lump of dough and flatten it
between your palms, then mold it around one stuffed date,
making sure to smooth out any cracks or holes. Repeat until
dough is gone. Place the rolls on a cookie sheet covered with
wax paper or a silicone baking mat. Bake for 20–25 minutes,
until the rolls have a nice golden color. Remove to a rack
to cool.

DELMONICO PUDDING

2 packages unflavored gelatin
2 cups whole milk
5 eggs
1¼ cups granulated sugar, divided salt
1 teaspoon vanilla extract
1 pint heavy whipping cream
3 dozen small almond macaroons (make sure they're almond, not the more common coconut kind!)
5 tablespoons pine nuts
2 tablespoons crystallized ginger

Dissolve the gelatin in one cup cold milk.

Separate five eggs. (Refrigerate whites while making custard.) Beat yolks, gradually adding ¾ cup sugar. Slowly beat in the remaining cup milk and a pinch of salt. Cook over low heat until mixture begins to thicken into custard. (Be patient! Eventually, it will coat the spoon.) Cool slightly and add vanilla. Stir in the gelatin/milk mixture and refrigerate for about one and one-half to two hours.

When the custard begins to set, beat egg whites into a stiff meringue. Gradually add ½ cup of sugar.

Beat the whipping cream until it forms stiff peaks. Fold the whipped cream into the meringue mixture and divide into two equal parts. Fold one part into the custard. Reserve the other part for a topping.

Line a 9 × 12 inch pan with a layer of almond macaroons. Pour the custard mixture over the top. (If the cookies rise to the surface, push them back down to the bottom of the pan with the back of a spoon.)

Carefully spread the reserved cream and meringue mixture over the top of the custard. Refrigerate for at least 24 hours and preferably longer.

When ready to serve, toast pine nuts in a skillet over low heat, stirring constantly for about two minutes until they are slightly brown. Chop the ginger as fine as you can. Arrange individual portions of pudding in serving dishes or martini glasses. Sprinkle the top of each serving with pine nuts and a little ginger.

Keep reading for a sneak peek at Louisa Edwards' next novel

JUST ONE TASTE

Coming in September 2010 from St. Martin's Paperbacks

The classroom door opened, admitting a young woman Wes didn't recognize. He frowned. Most of the students in his section had been in overlapping rotations together, through the thicks and thins of the grueling culinary arts program, for the past eight months. They'd wrestled with pasta dough together, learned basic hygiene and kitchen safety together, broken down flocks of chicken, fabricated countless fish and brewed up gallons of stock together. He knew most of their secrets, their histories and their hopes, and even if none of them knew Wes's, this group was still about as close as he'd ever found to a family.

But this woman? Was so brand-new she practically squeaked.

Or wait. That was her shoes.

Wes stared at her feet, realizing all at once what was so strange and different about her.

She was out of uniform.

The Academy of Culinary Arts had a strict dress code. The place was famously well-run and hyper-regulated; there were severe consequences for breaking any of the myriad rules and regulations set forth by the Academy's president. Some of the worst penalties came from code-of-dress infractions.

Everyone at the Academy wore black pants, a white chef's jacket, and regulation black-leather kitchen clogs. Every single person, from the chef instructors to the students, on up to President Cornell. No exceptions.

Except, apparently, New Girl.

Who was clad in what looked like regulation geek-wear. Baggy khakis that made her appear even shorter than she was, topped with a beige T-shirt featuring . . . Wes's feet slipped off the rung of his chair. *Whoa*. Was that a freaking Wookie?

And on her feet, squeaking against the sterile tile floor with a noise like she was wearing Styrofoam panties, were black Converse sneakers.

Wes stared in silence. In fact, the whole classroom went dead quiet, as one by one, the sleepy culinary students registered the stranger in their midst.

New Girl didn't appear to notice, at first. Clutching a stack of notepads and papers to her chest, she shuffled quickly, head down and shoulders hunched, up to the front of the classroom. But instead of taking a seat at one of the student tables, she kept going.

Wes watched, fascinated by this tiny stick-figure of a person, all jerky movements and shiny blonde hair twisted into two messy braids down her back.

Until she reached the podium next to the chalkboard, where she paused, appeared to take a deep breath in, and turned to face the class.

And Wes got his first good look at her face.

Wide-set blue-gray eyes, her bottom lip was plumper than the top, giving her a permanent pout. And her nose . . . damn it. Wes had to swallow hard. Her nose was interesting rather than perfect, and it was enough to take her face from merely pretty to knockout striking.

Crap. She was adorable. She looked like the beautiful starlet they cast to play the smart girl, who transforms by the end into the gorgeous woman she always was, with the help of contact lenses and pants that fit.

And obviously, she was the newest addition to the teaching staff.

Crap. Crap. Crap.

Wes really didn't need this kind of distraction.

"Oh," she said, her wide eyes going even wider at the sight of the class sitting there, silently watching. It was as if she was surprised to see them. "Um. Hello. My name is Dr. Rosemary Wilkins."

She paused, glanced at the chalkboard.

Wes knit his brows. Surely she wouldn't . . . okay, maybe she would.

Dr. Rosemary Wilkins stepped to the board, grabbed a piece of chalk, and wrote her name in careful, looping script.

Dusting off her hands, she turned back to the class and continued. "I have a bachelor's degree in Organic Chemistry from Yale, a PhD in Physical and Analytical Chemistry from Johns Hopkins, and a PhD in Biological Chemistry from Bryn Mawr. I'm here at the Academy to study food. By which I mean, of course, the chemical processes and interactions between ingredients under controlled conditions. The ACA has unparalleled facilities for the kind of research I'm interested in conducting, but apparently, in return for the use of those facilities, I have to step in and take over Professor Prentiss's class when he can't be bothered to keep his penis in his pants. So. Here I am. What do you want to know?"

Wes looked around the room. He could practically hear the crickets chirping.

Dr. Wilkins arched a brow. She didn't appear even slightly surprised. "No? Nothing? I told President Cornell this would be a waste of time. You all want to make good food, but none of you wants to know the reasons behind what works and what doesn't." She shook her head as if baffled. "You probably all think of cooking as a creative endeavor, as 'art'."

Who the hell was this woman?

She looked about Wes's age, certainly no older than twenty-five. Which meant she must've been in her teens when she got that first degree.

Dude. Prodigy alert.

One of the students, Bess, a plump blonde who was categorically not a prodigy, said haltingly, "Are you really our teacher?"

Wes winced. Well, at least she hadn't asked if Wilkins was a real doctor.

"No." Dr. Wilkins looked affronted at the very idea. "I'm a scientist. Teaching is a waste of my prodigious mental acuity and valuable research time. As I already told President Cornell. He, however, seems to think there's something to be gained by forcing a woefully overqualified genius to teach a basic-level chemistry course any monkey could run. I can only be grateful that the semester is almost over. More than three weeks of this nonsense would put me severely behind in my research."

"Wow." Wes heard Sloane's awed whisper. "I kind of love her."

"That's because you're a sociopath," Nate told her. "This woman is like your soul sister or something."

"I'm surprised you don't dig her, Nate," Wes said out of the side of his mouth. "You usually love being told you're a moron eight different ways before breakfast."

All eyes followed their new instructor as she shrugged and moved to the podium. Dr. Wilkins shuffled her papers until she had the one she wanted on top, then proceeded to sit down on the floor at the front of the room and read. Silently.

Slowly, like the hiss of steam spouting from a boiling kettle, a buzz of whispered conversation streamed up and out of the students. Immersed in her reading, Dr. Wilkins appeared unaware.

Wes studied her while the others huffed and speculated. He noted the curve of her pale cheek, the relaxed spread of her denim-clad legs as she became absorbed in whatever that paper was. She was short, he decided, but perfectly proportioned. Her skin was like the porcelain tableware they used at La Culinaire, the Academy's student-staffed restaurant, creamy white and so fine it was almost translucent.

And he could tell it wasn't faked, that total lack of interest in the physical world around her. For all intents and purposes, she wasn't in this classroom anymore. The realization got under Wes's skin like the juice of just-diced Serrano peppers.

He'd never been able to stand being overlooked, and he especially hated being called stupid. It was pride, nothing but pride. He knew that. And pride, which had gotten him in big, bad trouble on more than one occasion, should've been kicked out of him years ago. Only somehow, it hadn't been. It was a given now. He knew himself, knew his own hair-triggers, and accepted them.

The question was, what would he do about it in the case of the incredibly insulting and dismissive Dr. Rosemary Wilkins?

Smart answer: absolutely nothing. She was his instructor, she held his grade in the palm of her little hand.

But then, no one had ever accused Wes of jumping to do the smart thing.

Slowly, deliberately, Wes raised his hand.